Awakened by a Kiss

Awakened by a Kiss

Lila DiPasqua

BERKLEY SENSATION, NEW YORK

THE BERKLEY PUBLISHING GROUP
Published by the Penguin Group
Penguin Group (USA) Inc.
375 Hudson Street, New York, New York 10014, USA
Penguin Group (Canada), 90 Eglinton Avenue East, Suite 700, Toronto, Ontario M4P 2Y3, Canada
(a division of Pearson Penguin Canada Inc.)
Penguin Books Ltd., 80 Strand, London WC2R 0RL, England
Penguin Group Ireland, 25 St. Stephen's Green, Dublin 2, Ireland (a division of Penguin Books Ltd.)
Penguin Group (Australia), 250 Camberwell Road, Camberwell, Victoria 3124, Australia
(a division of Pearson Australia Group Pty. Ltd.)
Penguin Books India Pvt. Ltd., 11 Community Centre, Panchsheel Park, New Delhi—110 017, India
Penguin Group (NZ), 67 Apollo Drive, Rosedale, North Shore 0632, New Zealand
(a division of Pearson New Zealand Ltd.)
Penguin Books (South Africa) (Pty.) Ltd., 24 Sturdee Avenue, Rosebank, Johannesburg 2196,
South Africa

Penguin Books Ltd., Registered Offices: 80 Strand, London WC2R 0RL, England

This book is an original publication of The Berkley Publishing Group.

This is a work of fiction. Names, characters, places, and incidents either are the product of the author's imagination or are used fictitiously, and any resemblance to actual persons, living or dead, business establishments, events, or locales is entirely coincidental. The publisher does not have any control over and does not assume any responsibility for author or third-party websites or their content.

PRINTING HISTORY
Berkley Sensation trade paperback edition / August 2010

Library of Congress Cataloging-in-Publication Data

DiPasqua, Lila.
    Awakened by a kiss / Lila DiPasqua.—Berkley Sensation trade pbk. ed.
        p.   cm.
    ISBN 978-0-425-23556-0
    1. Fairy tales—Adaptations.   I. Title.
    PS3604.I625A97 2010
    813'.6—dc22

                                                            2010013217

PRINTED IN THE UNITED STATES OF AMERICA

10   9   8   7   6   5   4   3   2   1

Acknowledgments

This book wouldn't have been possible without a number of special people. With gratitude and affection, I wish to dedicate this book to them.

To my amazing editor, Kate Seaver, and my fabulous agent, Caren Johnson Estesen, who both believed in me, my writing, and these stories from the moment they first read them. Thank you for your enthusiasm for my work, your invaluable suggestions, your wisdom and your patience in answering all of my many nervous newbie questions. It's absolutely wonderful and an incredible privilege to work with you.

To my critique partners, Carolyn Williams, Donna Jeffery, Franca Pelaccia, Vickie Marise, and last but certainly not least, Mary Barone. We've critiqued together for several years and worked on many manuscripts together. I can't begin to express how blessed I feel not only to have you as critique partners, but also as dear friends.

To my dear friend Rose Tanel, who is always there for me. Thanks for the laughs, for the talks, for reading my first drafts. And thank you for all the times you offered to babysit—taking my three children home to your three—watching six kids, just so I could write. Dearest friend, you are the best!

To my Dad and Mom and uber-talented brother who have run out of friends and family to tell about this book and have moved on to random strangers in grocery stores. These three are easy to spot. They're the ones walking around, beaming with pride.

To my three rascally but beautiful children who have been my biggest—and loudest—cheerleaders through all this. I love you, my sweets.

Finally, to my gorgeous husband, Carm. Thank you for your unwavering faith in me and my writing. For enthusiastically reading all of my work and offering your male point of view. I couldn't have done this without you. I love you madly.

A Historical Tidbit

Writer Charles Perrault lived in seventeenth-century France during the reign of the Sun King, Louis XIV. Louis was a lusty king. His glittering court was as salacious as it was elegant.

During this most wicked time period, Charles wrote stories that have delighted people for centuries: *Sleeping Beauty*, *Little Red Riding Hood*, *Puss in Boots*, *Bluebeard*, and the ever-popular *Cinderella*, to name a few.

The following are loosely based on three of his famous tales. Step into the world when fairy tales were born . . .

Happy Reading!

Lila

Contents

Sleeping Beau
1

Little Red Writing
119

Bewitching in Boots
247

Glossary
339

Sleeping Beau

Moral of the Story of *Sleeping Beauty*

To wait so long,
To want a man refined and strong,
Is not at all uncommon.
But: rare it is a hundred years to wait.
Indeed there is no woman
Today so patient for a mate.
Our tale was meant to show
That when marriage is deferred,
It is no less blissful than those of which you've heard.
Nothing's lost after a century or so.
And yet, for lovers whose ardor
Cannot be controlled and marry out of passion,
I don't have the heart their act to deplore
Or to preach a moral lesson.

CHARLES PERRAULT
(1628–1703)

1

France, 1685

"Will you do it, Adrien? Say yes. You simply must. I'm your *sister.*" Charlotte's whine taxed Adrien's already thin patience.

Adrien Christophe d'Aspe de Bourbon, Marquis de Beaulain, stared out the window at the gardens below. Lords and ladies milled about, clustering near the fountains and along the pathways bordered by flowerbeds. His mood was foul. His audience with his father, the root cause. It hadn't gone well. It never went well. Days after the fact, he was still irritable. He'd only just arrived at the Comtesse de Lamotte's château and already Charlotte had him wanting to leave. Her unexpected presence and the absurd scheme she'd devised had effectively soured his plans: a few days at Suzanne's abode, indulging in drink and debauchery to lift him out of his ill humor.

"You're my half-sister, Charlotte. We have *different* fathers," he replied bitterly. Raised in Paris at the Hôtel d'Aspe by his three uncles, Adrien had had all the male influence he'd needed.

Or wanted. Except for the occasional horrid visit, his father had been absent from his life—that is, until a year ago when Adrien's mother had died. Since then Louis had injected himself into Adrien's world. Though Adrien wanted nothing to do with the man, his father was not someone he or anyone could simply ignore.

Charlotte rose from the settee and stopped beside him. "You needn't remind me of that. Your father is the King. At least he has legitimized you, given you title and lands—"

"He legitimized all his illegitimate children. Not just me. And it is a wonder there's any land left in the realm, given the multitude he sired. I doubt even he knows how many mistresses he's had." Their mother among the masses.

"Well, the Baron de Chambly still won't recognize me as his. He's never given me a moment's thought, much less wealth."

"Charlotte, nothing comes without a price." His tone dripped with disdain.

"Come now, Adrien. Enough of this. We are family. *I need you.*" Her bottom lip was out in a full pout. "What I ask of you is not so strenuous. You and I both know you'll bed some of the women here before the week is up. All I ask is that you bed Catherine de Villecourt as well. Charm her. Convince her that marriage is not what she wants. Lure her away from my Philbert. You're my only hope, Adrien. He's set to wed her in two weeks." Tears glistened in her hazel eyes. "I don't want to lose him. He's been so distant lately. I fear if he weds, I'll never get him back. She's younger than I. Fifteen years his junior." Two tears spilled down her cheeks. "He'll focus on his new bride and forget all about me."

Exasperated, Adrien let out a sharp breath. Charlotte and their mother were so alike. She, too, had harbored the illusion that she could accomplish the impossible: maintain her lover's interest indefinitely and remain his favorite for good.

"Charlotte, find yourself a new lover. You don't need Philbert de Baillet."

"Yes I do," she protested. "I love him! I don't want to live without him."

How many times had he heard those very words from his mother's mouth about his father? Love. It was highly overrated. He'd no idea why anyone would pursue it. Love caused suffering. Lust was much easier to deal with. And far more pleasurable.

Adrien was about to rebut when she added, "Look down there. There she is now. With our hostess."

Mildly curious about Charlotte's rival, he glanced down at the manicured grounds and spotted their hostess, Suzanne de Lamotte. She was with a woman whose rich auburn hair looked a tad too familiar. He stared harder. From this distance, he couldn't make out enough details to be certain . . . but . . . The hair on the back of his neck stood on end. *Dieu*, it looked like *her*.

Could it possibly be . . . ?

Visions of the redhead naked in his bed materialized in his mind. He still remembered her face. Her scent—jasmine. And the sultry sounds she made each time she came. Their carnal encounter was like none he'd ever known. Perfect spine-melting passion. Her delectable mouth, her lush form, and her hot, creamy sex clasped snugly around his thrusting cock had him on fire the entire night.

In the morning, he was shocked to discover that she'd spiked his burgundy with an aphrodisiac. And she was gone. He'd been confused, a bit disoriented, and uncertain if the whole thing hadn't been a dream. But the scent of jasmine lingered on his skin.

And on the sheets, glaring back at him, was the stunning proof that he'd taken a *virgin*.

Furious that he'd been played, tricked, he'd questioned his friend Daniel, Marquis de Gallay, the host of the masquerade. Made discreet inquiries everywhere. No one knew who the auburn-haired seductress was. For the longest time he'd been unsure whether he'd be hauled to the altar or called out. But the lady's family never stepped forward.

She'd left him with a sizzling memory and unanswered questions. Worse and even more maddening, after all these years she still made appearances in every one of his erotic dreams.

Was it possible that after five years he'd found the mysterious beauty who had sneaked into his chambers and awakened him with a searing kiss?

He stalked to the door and snatched it open.

"Well? Will you do it?" Charlotte called out. "Adrien? Where are you going?"

Adrien crossed the threshold with purposeful strides.

* * *

Moving through the gardens, Catherine walked arm in arm with Suzanne—her friend and former sister-in-law and the only good thing to come out of her brief, scandal-ridden marriage. If Suzanne's guests were privy to gossip about Catherine's late husband, the Comte de Villecourt, they gave no indication of it.

Strains of music from the violins sweetened the summer air and blended with the trickling sounds of the fountains.

Her tension easing, Catherine was starting to enjoy herself. She'd remained in mourning two years—longer than her marriage had lasted—and had thereafter kept to herself at Château

Villecourt, away from the gossipmongers who'd gleefully spread the sensational details leading to her late husband's fatal duel.

It was Suzanne who had convinced her to visit last year. It was Suzanne who'd introduced her to her present betrothed, Philbert, Comte de Baillet. And it was Suzanne who'd persuaded her to take this sojourn before her impending nuptials.

"You aren't really going to marry Baillet, that old bore, are you?" Suzanne asked, her hostess's smile affixed to her face as they moved past the guests.

Catherine's smile was genuine. "I am. I shall proudly be the Comtesse de Old Bore." Her laugh moved Suzanne to one as well.

Sobering, her friend remarked, "I know my brother made you suffer, Catherine. I only want your happiness."

Catherine arrested her steps. "I am happy. Philbert and I will get along fine." Philbert was not the most exciting of men, but she'd endured enough *excitement* to last a lifetime while married to Villecourt. Philbert was the right choice. She'd have a quiet existence, financial security, and that was enough to satisfy her. Shoving aside the twinge of regret, she silenced the small voice inside her heart that opposed the notion. It made no difference that he didn't love her. Or that she didn't love him. Such marriages were virtually unheard of. At least Philbert had enough regard for her to treat her with respect and to be discreet about any paramours he'd maintain.

Suzanne sighed. "I suppose . . . but . . . beneath that very proper exterior lies a vivacious woman. One desperate to get out. I fear the sheer dullness of the man will kill her."

"Suzanne—" Catherine's retort was interrupted.

"Madame de Lamotte!" a woman called out behind her.

Turning, Catherine saw two women about her age briskly approaching.

"Ah, *Dieu* . . ." Suzanne murmured softly.

The two dark-haired females stopped before them, cheeks pink and slightly breathless.

"Is he here, madame? Has *le Beau* arrived?" blurted out Madame de Noisette the moment Suzanne had finished with the introductions.

"Yes, do tell," her friend Madame de Bussy prompted.

"He is here." Suzanne's statement was weighty with a certain amount of smug pleasure.

Excitement bubbled out of the two women, the sound much like that of a gaggle of geese.

Catherine hid her amusement over their reactions. "Who is *le Beau*?" she inquired, her curiosity piqued.

Madame de Noisette's brown eyes widened. "You don't know *le Beau*?"

"I'm afraid I've never heard of him."

"Why, he's only the most handsome man in the realm," she explained. "He's one of the King's own bastard sons—Adrien, Marquis de Beaulain."

"And I hear he's between conquests," Madame de Bussy added. "His reputation as a master swordsman and"—she blushed—"in the boudoir is renowned. In fact, they say he's had more women than his father."

"Oh?" Catherine remarked, unimpressed.

Madame de Noisette tittered. "He's living up to the curse."

That grabbed Catherine's interest. "Curse?"

"Why, yes." Madame de Bussy looked around then stepped a little closer and continued sotto voce. "His mother was, for a time, the King's favorite. It is said that at le Beau's christening, one of the King's former favorites was overcome with jealousy, burst into the chapel, and cursed the child the moment the holy oil was placed upon his forehead."

Madame de Noisette shook her head. "Can you imagine such a thing?" Knowing how superstitious the King and his court were, Catherine understood the horror in the woman's tone. Uttering ill-intended words toward the babe was bad enough, but to hurl them at the anointing of the child was far worse. "Tell her what she said. Go on," Madame de Noisette urged her friend.

"Yes, of course . . . She said the babe would grow up to be exceptionally beautiful, charming, break women's hearts, as his father did, yet be *nothing but grief* to Louis. The King became instantly incensed at the woman. One of le Beau's godfathers, for his mother had three brothers and couldn't choose between them for such an honor, tried to mollify the King. As the story goes, he placed a hand upon the infant's crown and said that the child's looks and charm would indeed be great and that all would marvel at him. That he would fill His Majesty with pride, for a son so fine could only belong to the ruler himself."

Catherine glanced at Suzanne and caught her rolling her eyes.

"Really, madame, that tale has been retold too many times with too many variations to be believed," Suzanne said.

"It is true!" Madame de Bussy insisted, then turned to Catherine. "It's all come to pass. He most definitely has looks and charm, and at the age of majority, barely fifteen, he pricked his first woman."

Her friend laughed. "My dear, I believe you mean *he used his prick* for the first time to tumble a woman."

Madame de Bussy's face turned crimson. "Ah, yes, yes, that is exactly what I mean. And he has been using that particular part of his anatomy to delight many fortunate females ever since." By the sparkle in her eyes, Catherine could tell she was anxious to be his next conquest. Since most men preferred to live at their hôtels in Paris while their wives were banished to their country châteaus, the ladies before her could easily take a lover without anyone being the wiser.

"And, my dear, let us not forget how often His Majesty has had to look the other way each time *le Beau* has broken his own father's law—" Madame de Noisette's words froze on her tongue, her mouth remaining agape as she stared beyond Catherine.

"It's him!" Madame de Bussy exclaimed.

Catherine was just about to turn around when Madame de Noisette squeezed her arm. "Don't. Don't turn around. He is looking this way and it will seem as though we are speaking about him."

"We are speaking about him, madame," Suzanne said blandly.

"Oh, my." Madame de Noisette removed her hand from Catherine's arm and pressed it to her bosom. "He is coming this way."

Suzanne was now facing her approaching guest with a welcoming smile.

Unable to resist a peek at the roué, Catherine peered over her shoulder. Her stomach dropped the moment her gaze locked on to a set of arresting green eyes. Sinfully seductive, intimately familiar light green eyes. Her limbs went cold and her knees felt suddenly weak.

"Dear God, it's him . . ."

"Hmmm? What did you say?" Suzanne asked, still focused on the ever-nearing *le Beau.*

"No, nothing." *Oh God. Oh God. Oh God. He's the bastard*

son of the King! She'd tainted his wine with an aphrodisiac. He could have her arrested for that. For her rash—idiotic—act. Every fiber in her body screamed, *"Flee!"*

"Suzanne," she croaked out, her heart hammering.

Her friend dragged her gaze back to her, her smile instantly dissolving. "Catherine, are you all right? You're flushed."

"I've suddenly developed a terrible headache. I'm going to lie down. Excuse me." She fisted her skirts and made her way across the gardens, forcing herself to keep to a swift walk and not a full-out run. She maneuvered around the guests, never making eye contact, never turning around, using the bushes to shield her from le Beau's view whenever possible. Around the side of the château she'd find the servants' entrance.

Ten more feet and she'd be out of sight.

Her breaths were ragged.

Eight feet. *Hurry!*

How could Odette have been so mistaken? Her maid had told her that the beautiful stranger she'd spotted at the masquerade five years ago was a foreigner. From Vienna.

She rounded the side of the château. *At last . . .*

Tossing a quick glance over her shoulder, Catherine bolted for the wooden door, all but falling against it when she reached it. Briefly fumbling with the latch, she opened it, ducked inside, and raced through the kitchens, negotiating around each busy servant who got in her way, ignoring their curious looks. Smoke and the heavy scent of roasting meats assailed her nostrils and scorched her throat. *Move! Move! Get to your rooms!*

She rushed up the servants' darkened stairs and stopped at the door that led to the upstairs hallway. Cautiously, she opened it and peered out. Empty!

Only twenty feet remained between her and her chamber door.

Wasting no time, she stepped into the long corridor and made her way to safety, her legs wobbly with each rapid step she took.

"Madame?" A male voice arrested her steps.

And her breathing.

She heard footsteps approaching.

Don't panic. It could be anyone. *Let it be anyone other than—* she turned. Her knees almost buckled.

Le Beau.

2

Where had he come from? The shadows? Likely the grand stairwell.

Two final strides and he was before her. Tall. Muscled. With hair the color of a moonless night sky. Her fingers began to tingle. Catherine clasped her hands tightly together. She could still feel its cool silky texture between her fingers, as if it were only yesterday that she'd caressed his dark shoulder-length hair. She'd forgotten just how large a man he was—his broad shoulders, his magnificently sculpted form. She felt small, very feminine near his powerfully built body.

Give nothing away. He doesn't remember you. He can't. Then why did he leave the gardens so quickly? Why is he here?

Schooling her features, she expelled the air from her lungs and met his gaze unwavering. "Yes?" she said, amazed at the coolness in her tone when she was on the brink of discomposure.

Those unforgettable light green eyes scrutinized her face. She fought not to fidget. His presence and proximity were disquieting on so many levels. Her insides quaked.

"I believe we've met, madame."

Her heart lurched. She managed a small smile. "I'm afraid you have mistaken me for someone else. Now, if you'll excuse me." She turned.

He caught her arm. A jolt of sensations shot through her.

"Unhand me," she said, shaken, a dizzying combination of excitement and dread inundating her.

He released her, the corner of his sensual mouth lifting, stopping short of a smile. Without a word, he slowly walked around her, his bold assessing gaze moving over her body. She could feel his tactile regard right through her clothing, making her hot from the inside out.

"Sir, your conduct is outrageous." Did she sound as breathless as she felt? "You are being extremely rude."

He stopped, his towering form now a formidable obstacle between her and the door to her rooms.

"It's you," he said.

She swallowed and lifted her chin a notch. *"Pardon?"*

"You're the woman who sneaked into my chamber that night five years ago."

Stirring memories filled her mind. She shoved them aside as she'd done many times throughout the years.

"You are mad. I told you—I don't know you."

He tilted his head to one side, a smug look in his eyes, much like the cat that had cornered the mouse. "Madame, you do know me—in the biblical sense. Though there was nothing but sinful delights in what we shared."

Heat crept down her face and neck to her chest. "Tell me," she responded with as much calm as she could muster. "Is this a habit of yours? Skulking around hallways? Making lurid—unfounded—accusations?" she asked. "Or perhaps this is your twisted way of enticing women? By telling them of your sexual exploits. Are there women who actually fall for this ploy?"

He stepped closer. Awareness rippled through her. Yet she refused to step back, knowing he was trying to intimidate her. His mouth was oh so close to her own . . . Images of that skillful mouth on her body, grazing over her skin, drawing on her breasts made her sex clench and moisten.

"Perhaps you and I have a different definition of *twisted*," he said. "I'd like to know what twisted motives you had when you decided to taint my wine and surrender your innocence to me."

"It sounds like you had quite an evening," she said without flinching. "Though I can't comprehend why—after five years, did you say?—it would be so vivid in your mind. How can you be certain that it was I? Surely, you managed to find a woman or two since then willing to overlook your barbaric manners. You are"—she shrugged—"mildly attractive."

His brows shot up, surprised at first, then his lips twitched as he fought back a smile.

"Have I amused you?" How she wished he'd step back. His closeness was making it difficult to breathe. Or think. She had to get away from him. From the château.

Preempt her vacation.

"You have. I'm not accustomed to receiving a setdown from a woman." He slipped his fingers beneath her chin and caressed his thumb along her cheek. Pleasure streaked from his touch down to the tips of her breasts, causing her nipples to harden.

She took a quick step back and bumped into the wall. He braced his palms on either side of her shoulders, trapping her.

"I am also not accustomed to having a woman dupe and drug me." He stared at her pointedly.

Catherine glanced at her chamber door. It was so close, yet it might as well have been on the other side of the country. She couldn't simply race to it and bolt the door behind her. That would only make matters worse.

You've got to convince him he's mistaken. Fail and he could have the King draw up orders. They'd arrest her and leave her to languish in prison—until her trial and certain execution. Other women had suffered this fate. Because of the recent poisonings at court, administering *anything*, even something as harmless as a love potion, without the other person's knowledge was punishable under the law.

Adrien scrutinized the woman before him with the discerning eye of a libertine. Her skin was flushed and her breasts rose and fell with her quickened breaths in the most mesmerizing, mouthwatering way. *Jésus-Christ*, that auburn hair, delectable form, and those brandy-colored eyes . . . She was just as alluring as he remembered.

He was *not* mistaken.

She was indeed his midnight temptress.

She knew it. He knew it. And so did his unruly cock. She hadn't done anything more heated than to glare at him, yet she had him stiff as a spike, his hard prick straining against his breeches. The way her small pink tongue unconsciously licked her lips was driving him to distraction.

Her haughty airs and indignation were an act. She was trying to conceal not only the truth, but her arousal as well. Her nipples were hard and her frequent glances at his mouth were telling. Thoughts of taking her to her chamber, stripping her naked, and sinking his length into that tight juicy core of hers—of purging her from his system for good—were running rampant in his mind. *Merde*, there was no short supply of willing women. The last female he should want was one who'd schemed and stooped to such trickery. Unfortunately, his cock didn't agree with his head.

No woman had ever occupied his thoughts or dreams the way she had. And he resented it.

He resented that the best fuck of his life had been drug-induced.

She'd left him to imagine every possible scenario that had motivated her actions. With no way of confirming any of them. Now that he'd found her and knew her name, he wasn't going to relent. No matter how lovely she was, how enticing, how physically pleasurable that night had been, she *was* going to admit what she'd done and tell him why. He was going to have answers to the questions that had plagued him for years.

She owed him as much.

"Perhaps you are reluctant to discuss the matter because of who I am—or better yet—who my father is. But I assure you I want answers, not revenge," he said. It had to be a barrier for her. One he wanted out of the way to clear a path for the truth.

"I've nothing more to say to you. This conversation is over. Please step back." She had an obstinate look in her eyes, one that said she wouldn't confess. That she'd never confess. It steeled his resolve. If she wanted to engage in a round of wits and wills, he'd play along. She'd started this game. He'd finish it. And win. It was time to chisel away at her façade.

Since it was clear she wasn't immune to him, he chose his course of action.

Adrien dipped his head. The light scent of jasmine inundated his senses with a heady rush. "Catherine . . ." he said softly in her ear, her edible little earlobe so temptingly close to his hungry mouth. "I've thought of that night many times." She placed her hands against his chest as if to stave him off but didn't push him away. Encouraged, he continued. "I remember the sweet taste of your mouth . . . your pink nipples . . . details of your beautiful body . . . You remember our night together. Having me inside you . . . as you came, again . . . and again . . ." She shivered with excitement. It reverberated inside him. His cock began to pulse. "*Ma belle*, admit it was you." He brushed his mouth over the sensitive spot under her ear. She made a strangled sound and turned her face away, inadvertently giving him better access to the slender column of her neck. Or perhaps it wasn't so inadvertent.

But stubbornly, she remained silent.

Urgency thundered through him. Her soft skin beckoned. He drew her warm skin between his lips and gently sucked. She fisted his shirt and gasped. Her pulse beneath his mouth was as wild as his own. She tasted of jasmine. And slightly salty. Sweet womanly sweat from her nervous excitement. "Tell me what I wish to know," he murmured. "And I just might give you what your body is begging for."

He moved to her earlobe and lightly bit it. This time she moaned, the delicious sound making his sac tighten and his heart hammer harder. She was too damned desirable. The crest of his cock was moist with pre-come, his body clamoring for him to take her right here against the wall.

He'd been with enough experienced women to know that she was not. In the last five years, she hadn't gained any significant experience. He couldn't believe this sexual novice had him this undone. Just as undone as he'd been five years ago when—in his ravenous state—he'd overlooked the signs of her innocence.

Pulling back slightly, he gazed at her face. She was panting, his breathing no less affected. She stared back at him. Her cheeks were pink and her lips were parted, begging to be kissed. Hers was no ordinary mouth. It was extraordinary—made to drive men wild.

Grappling with self-control, Adrien could barely moderate himself. "There is a way to put this to rest, you know. To prove once and for all whether or not you are the woman I seek."

Something flickered in her amber depths. Confusion? Curiosity?

"You see," he continued, "the woman who came to my bed that night had lovely breasts, much like yours . . . and on her left breast, right here"—he stroked his fingers along the outside curve of the soft mound, and she gave a delightful gasp—"she had three small freckles. A pretty constellation that, if connected, would make a perfect tiny triangle."

He thought he saw her flinch, though it was so slight, he wasn't certain he'd seen it at all. The sexual haze in her eyes dissolved, replaced by a fire of a different sort.

She shoved his hand away. "Are you suggesting I show you my *breast*?" she said, clearly incredulous.

He pressed his palms against the wall once more, and tilted his head to one side, his mouth mere inches from hers. "It would prove whether or not you're my mystery lady. Come with me to my chambers or invite me to yours—someplace where we'll be more comfortable. I promise, you'll enjoy every moment." Her gaze once again dropped to his mouth. His greedy cock jerked in response. Adrien leaned in a little closer, their lips all but touching. "Which is your room, Catherine?" he whispered against her tempting lips. He was dying to possess them. He was dying to possess her.

"Adrien!" a male voice called out.

She squeaked, ducked down, and slipped out from under his arm so quickly, he almost kissed the wall.

"Merde," he growled, shoving himself away from the wall. His head snapped around in the direction of the intruder, with every intention of venting his full fury over the interruption.

Merde. Merde. Merde! His three godfathers stalked toward him. What the bloody hell were they doing here?

Was everyone he was related to going to show up?

He looked at Catherine. She'd paled and was using him as a shield from his approaching uncles. Her intoxicating eyes were large, beseeching, as if she thought he'd make the situation worse. They both knew that she'd been caught in a compromising situation with a man who had a shameless reputation.

He stepped in front of her to better conceal her from the ever-nearing trio. "Go," he said over his shoulder.

Dainty footsteps quickly retreated down the hall behind him and then a door closed just as his godfathers stopped before him.

Adrien clenched his teeth, his muscles taut, his body rioting for release. He was in sexual agony, *unnecessary* sexual agony, for given a few moments more and he'd have had the auburn-haired enchantress behind closed doors . . . "Before I ask you what you are doing here, I wish to tell you that your timing couldn't be worse."

"Or better—depending how you look at it," said Charles, the eldest of his three uncles.

"I don't know if I agree with that." Paul looked past Adrien. "I got a glimpse of her. I think I'd be rather distressed to miss out on a tumble with that mademoiselle." He grinned, and Robert laughed.

Charles simply scowled.

Though Charles had always been less of a skirt chaser than his two younger brothers, he was no saint. In short, Adrien had been raised by no fewer than three rakes. Not to mention, his father was the greatest womanizer by far. In truth, Adrien came by his womanizing ways honestly.

"I, my brother, got better than a glimpse," Robert said. "Wasn't that Madame de Villecourt?"

A novel emotion clenched in Adrien's gut as he wondered how his libertine uncle knew Catherine. The emotion took him completely by surprise. He was not the possessive type. His dalliances were always brief, recreational, without any sort of emotional involvement whatsoever.

Charles's salt and pepper brows arched. "Madame de Villecourt? Are you certain?"

Robert gave a wolfish grin. "Indeed I am. Though I haven't seen her in years, I never forget a beauty like that." He looked pointedly at Charles. "She's just as beautiful as her late aunt was."

Charles scowled anew.

"So, Adrien, is the lady as fiery in bed as her hair would suggest?" Paul needled.

Adrien turned and marched down the hall, aggravated, frustrated, with a raging erection and his blasted godfathers on his heels. He wasn't about to relay any juicy details about Catherine, nor did he care to hear about Charles's likely conquest of Catherine's departed aunt.

Upon entering his rooms, he went straight to the brandy decanter on the ebony side table and poured himself a liberal amount. He tossed it back and downed a second goblet before he was ready to engage with the three men before him.

Paul walked up to him and took the decanter out of his hand to fill his own goblet.

"My father sent you," Adrien stated.

Charles folded his arms. "He wants you at Versailles, Adrien."

"I've already told him no."

"Yes, and that answer isn't satisfactory to the King." Charles accepted a goblet of brandy from Paul.

Adrien held back the expletives thundering in his head, striving for calm. How was he to keep his distance from the man who'd wreaked such havoc in his life? Especially when he mixed parental authority with royal command.

He wanted nothing to do with Louis and his court. Every time his father reentered Adrien's world, he caused him anguish and suffering.

He'd done enough damage during Adrien's childhood.

His beloved mother had been born into nobility and widowed at a young age. Using her beauty, wit, and charm, she chose her lovers wisely, until she eventually caught the roving eye of Louis XIV. For a time, she held the coveted position of the King's favorite mistress. But his mother made one grievous error: she'd allowed herself to fall in love with her lover. Enamored as she was, she never shared Adrien's jaundiced opinion of his father. Even when she'd been replaced by another woman and sent to live with her brothers, she still clung to the hope of rekindling Louis's interest.

She'd anxiously awaited each infrequent visit.

Adrien had dreaded them.

Louis would stay long enough to pat him on the head and bed his mother. Then he'd be gone, leaving her bereft each and every time. Heartbroken, she eventually abandoned Adrien and Charlotte to their uncles and entered a convent.

Robert sat down near the hearth, accepting a goblet of the amber liquid from Paul. "Louis feels that living at Versailles will curb your wayward ways."

Adrien finally exploded into a string of oaths. "What wayward ways?"

"Asks the man who was just caught with a most alluring widow." Smiling, Paul sat down beside Robert on the settee.

Adrien tightened his jaw. He was in no mood for Paul's ribbing.

"Duels are against the law," Charles began.

Adrien raked his hand through his hair. "Not this again."

Charles pressed on. "The King has looked the other way each time. Your hand is too quick to the scabbard."

"I've not fought a duel for over a year. Does that not satisfy him? Perhaps he disagrees with my paramours? Too few? Too many? Maybe he wishes me to join the Order of Malta? Does His Majesty want me to take the required vow of celibacy?"

"A vow of celibacy." Paul shuddered in horror. "Is there anything worse? Or more unnatural?"

"Adrien," said Robert, always the peacemaker, using his be-reasonable tone. "We know how you feel about your father—and with good reason—but he is the King. He has treated his children well—if not his mistresses."

"He has?" Adrien snorted. "I must have missed that day. When was that? It certainly didn't occur during my boyhood. Ah, yes, perhaps it was last year—just after my mother died. Fully aware of her passing, her body not yet cold in her grave, he demanded I attend the festivities at Versailles. Was that the day, Uncle? He'd shown her little regard during her life and couldn't even muster any for her—*or me*—after her death. *'The King abhors any talk of the dead. He doesn't tolerate any expression of grief,'* I was forewarned as I arrived. I spent two excruciating weeks, forced to smile and make merry, attend picnics and hunts, forbidden to mention my mother's name for *'it would sadden the King and His Majesty doesn't like to be melancholy.'* Was that one of the benevolent examples you're referring to?"

Charles hung his head. Robert rose from his seat, walked over to him, and placed a hand on his shoulder. "She was our sister. We feel your pain."

Did they really? Did they know the extent of his devastation as he watched his mother withdraw from him and Charlotte? All love and warmth slipping from her heart and demeanor until all that was left was a shell of her former self? He was eight when she'd informed him—cold and detached—that she was leaving. He'd wept. He'd begged her not to go. To no avail. At the convent, he'd thrown himself on the front steps, a pathetic, childish attempt to stop her, his heartbreak evident in his anguished wails. He could still see her expressionless face as she clutched her skirts, stepped over him, and climbed the final steps to disappear behind the large wooden doors of the Convent of the Sacred Heart. Vanishing from his life.

Paul rose and approached. "He has removed the blemish of being illegitimate, elevating all of his children in society by providing each of you with lands and a title—"

Adrien slammed his goblet down on the side table and walked away from his uncles, feeling suddenly suffocated. Stopping before the window, he braced his hands on the wooden frame, silencing the agony welling inside him. He'd mastered the pain long ago. He never let it overwhelm him anymore. It was why he preferred to maintain a comfortable level of detachment in all relationships. Especially with women. Being in control both in and out of the boudoir was paramount. He limited the time he'd spend with each female and didn't allow feelings to be fostered—for either party. His encounters with women were about sex. Mutual pleasure in the moment. The women—utterly forgettable.

Except his midnight temptress.

The pretty little conniver, thanks to her potion, had robbed him of his control and branded him with a memory so heated, he couldn't vanquish it.

"I care nothing about the lands or title. I care not if he takes it all away."

"He knows that about you," Robert said.

"I won't live at Versailles. I'd sooner have him place me in the Bastille. I prefer that prison over the gilded one he has planned for me."

Robert sighed. "He knows that about you, too. That is why he sent us to reason with you. He doesn't wish to take such measures against his son."

Adrien turned. "*Jésus-Christ*, he has many 'sons.' And daughters, too. Why is he so focused on me?"

"Perhaps it is because you remind him of himself," Charles responded. "Everyone knows what little regard he has for his heir. The Grand Dauphin doesn't have the mental and emotional fortitude to take the throne. And though he will succeed him nonetheless, Louis has no respect for him. But you . . . you he respects."

Paul nodded. "Probably because you resist him, at times defy him, when others wouldn't dare."

He wasn't trying to be defiant. He was simply trying to encourage a parting of ways.

"At least consider joining him at court, Adrien," said Charles. "There are plenty of women there to entertain you. Please him, and he'll likely let you select your own bride, and offer a high-ranking position where you will—"

"Enough of that, Charles." Robert walked up to Adrien. "Adrien has already made it clear that none of that entices him." Robert turned to Adrien. "Stay here. A week. A month. Whatever you need. But do consider the matter carefully."

There was nothing to consider. He wasn't going to change his mind, and he was angry that his uncles were even asking this of him.

"Robert is right," Charles said. "Stay. Drink. Enjoy yourself— just don't do so with Madame de Villecourt."

"And why the hell not?" Paul asked for him.

Charles crossed his arms. "Because I heard, while at Versailles, that she is to marry Philbert, Comte de Baillet."

"So?" Adrien saw that as no hindrance.

"The Comte de Baillet is a man Louis holds in high esteem."

Paul waved a dismissive hand. "That makes no difference. Everyone poaches."

"If Adrien chooses to deny his King—a colossal mistake, I might add," Charles said, "then I should think he wouldn't want to give Louis more reasons to be annoyed with him—that is, if he wants to walk away unscathed."

His Majesty ruled by intimidation. If there was a way to force Adrien to comply, Louis would have done it. He wouldn't have sent his uncles to "reason" with him. Adrien *was* going to walk away unscathed. Louis wasn't going to strip him of his lands and title or have him arrested or do anything whatsoever to raise the curiosity of his courtiers. To risk having anyone learn that his son had denied his request and hadn't cowered before the mighty Sun King would, in Louis's mind, make him look weak. And that he would never do.

However, his father wasn't going to simply relent. He was going to quietly, incessantly try to break Adrien and get him to acquiesce.

No, if he wanted his father to be out of his life—free himself from his clutches—he'd have to press the matter further.

Philbert de Baillet was going to assist in that regard.

The man was an ass. He had no backbone to speak of. He'd never call Adrien out no matter what he did with Catherine. More important, Philbert had the ear of Louis's most pious wife, Madame de Maintenon. He'd run straight to her and lament—as he had in the past when someone fell out of favor with him. Louis was absolute ruler on matters of state, but when it came to religious observation and devotion, he looked to Madame de Maintenon, his second wife. She'd greatly influenced a vice-ridden King and his court, curbing their ways.

Madame de Maintenon didn't think much of hedonists like Adrien.

She'd been cordial to Adrien. Respectful of him the entire time he'd spent at Versailles, keeping her opinion of him to herself. But a dalliance with the future wife of someone she considered a dear friend would loosen the woman's tongue. It would likely convince her that Adrien was corrupt by nature, and therefore unredeemable. And she'd express to the King her vehement displeasure at having Adrien permanently at Versailles.

Madame de Maintenon and Philbert de Baillet were about to aid in his cause and become Adrien's unwittingly allies. As would the lovely Catherine.

He felt a smile tug at the corners of his mouth, pleased for the first time since this conversation began.

Charles's brow furrowed. "Why are you smiling?"

"Why, Uncle, you just made Catherine de Villecourt even more appealing."

3

"Odette, we're leaving!" Catherine announced the moment she located her maid in her rooms, her insides still quivering.

Odette was holding two of Catherine's gowns, one over each arm. Her brown eyes widened. "But, madame, you've only just arrived. I was unpacking—" Catherine's belongings were spread across the bed.

"Gather everything. We must leave right now." She'd leave the country. Where could she go? She had virtually no money. Perhaps Suzanne could advance her some funds. *Dear God, he knows your name* . . . Her hands shaky, she snatched up one of her gowns off the mattress and tossed it back in her trunk, then turned and grabbed another and tossed it in, too.

Perplexed, the older woman watched her haphazard packing. "What has happened? What is amiss?"

Catherine pulled the gowns from Odette's arms and tossed

them into the trunk as well. "I'll tell you what is amiss. The gentleman whose wine you spiked five years ago is *here*."

Odette's mouth fell agape. She clamped it shut and swallowed. *"He—He is?"*

"Yes, and that's not all. He isn't from Vienna. He's French."

Ashen, Odette sank into a nearby chair, looking suddenly older than her forty-nine years. *"He—He is?"*

"He is! And will you stop repeating that."

"Has he . . . seen you?"

"Oh, yes. He has seen me. And recognized me as being the woman who tainted his wine then gave herself to him."

Odette blinked. *"Pour l'amour de Dieu . . ."*

"Oh, and it gets better," Catherine continued. "Would you like to know who his father is?"

Odette wound her apron around her finger. "Well . . . to be quite honest, madame . . . *not really*."

Catherine crossed her arms. "I shall tell you anyway."

"I feared as much," she mumbled to her lap.

"His father is well-known. A rather important man. Perhaps you've heard of him? The. *King*."

Nervous, Odette smoothed her hand over her hair and mustered the semblance of a smile. "Oh? And which King might that be? Some small nation somewhere far—"

"Of France."

"Oh. That King."

Catherine threw up her hands. "Odette, you told me he was from Vienna."

Odette rose. "It's what I heard," she defended, then stopped and thought for a moment. "Or was it Venice? No. No. No. It *was* Vienna. I'm certain." She scratched her head. "Well, someone at that masquerade was from Vienna."

Catherine placed her hands on her maid's shoulders. "Odette, please focus. The man we tricked that night was the Marquis de Beaulain. He's the King's son. And he's demanding answers. For tainting his burgundy, he could have me arrested. In light of the recent poisonings at court, I could be tossed in prison . . . You remember what they did to Madame de Brinvilliers and the others . . ." As Catherine spoke, Odette was staring at her neck in the most peculiar way, her brows knitted together. Catherine continued because most of what Odette did was peculiar. Over the years, she'd learned to ignore most things. "I've told him that he's mistaken, but he doesn't believe—" Catherine stopped when Odette began tilting her head to one side, then her body at the waist, her gaze still fixed on the side of Catherine's neck.

"Odette, what are you staring at?" Catherine released her maid's shoulders.

Odette righted herself and peered closely, then pulled back, a slow, steady grin spreading across her mouth. "It would seem that Monsieur le Marquis was not altogether cross with you." She walked over to the table and picked up a hand mirror. "Your Marquis has been perhaps whispering sweet words in your ear— among other things?" She handed the mirror to Catherine.

Catherine brought it up to her neck and saw the glaring, undeniable marking of a love bite just under her ear. It was her turn to sink into a chair, which she did with a groan.

Her forehead fell into her palm. "Can this day get any worse?" she bemoaned.

The heavens responded with a thunderclap, followed by a sudden heavy rain, torrents striking the windowpane.

Her head snapped up. "Oh, no . . ." She rose and moved to the window. Sheets of rain were pouring from the sky.

"It doesn't look as though we can leave," Odette said behind her. "The roads will soon be useless."

Was this penance for her misdeeds? For conspiring to drug an innocent man and relinquishing her virtue? She thought she'd already paid for her sins during the course of her marriage.

"By the love mark on your neck, madame, I don't think you have anything to fear from him. Clearly, his interest in you hasn't anything to do with having you arrested."

Catherine closed her eyes briefly. A fresh rush of warmth flooded her already heated body.

Oh, to feel his mouth on her again had been sublime.

It left her starved senses famished for more.

The bulge in his breeches practically undid her. His magnificent erection was impossible to ignore. She'd aroused him. No aphrodisiac needed. It was a dizzying notion.

The man was not only impressively endowed—she recalled every glorious inch—but *le Beau* knew how to use that part of his male anatomy with mastery.

She couldn't believe he'd remembered so much about her. At first she thought he was lying. That it was impossible for a man as beautiful as he, with as many females as he'd bedded, to have such a clear memory of her.

But he had.

He'd even remembered her freckles.

It was amazing. Inflaming. It made her ache. The bud between her legs throbbed for his attention. She hadn't felt desire in so very long. Not since one incredible night in the arms of a beautiful stranger after a masquerade ball. She didn't regret their night of rapture. She'd no idea sexual pleasure could be so keen.

"Madame, if I may suggest, why not simply enjoy him—until your betrothed arrives at the end of the week?"

She turned to face Odette. "Have you not heard what I've said? What could happen to me should he decide to have orders drawn up against me?"

The older woman shrugged. "From what I see, the Marquis de Beaulain would likely keep his mouth shut about the tainting of his wine if he had some other way to occupy it." She smiled.

Catherine frowned. "And what about Philbert?"

"What about him? It isn't a first marriage for either of you. And he already has an heir. Neither of you is in love. Most husbands expect discretion, not loyalty."

Catherine walked over to the hearth and stared at the flickering flames. Her life had finally fallen into place. She'd help raise Philbert's children and perhaps even have a child of her very own. She'd given up on romantic notions of love a long time ago. Security and a peaceful existence were all she hoped for. Was she going to lose everything because of something she'd done five years ago? Because of a chance meeting with the man who had the ability to collapse the foundations of her world.

What if she went to *le Beau*? What if she explained why she'd done what she'd done? Would he understand?

What if you offered yourself to him and enjoyed him as Odette suggested?

Catherine tamped down the fluttering that erupted in her stomach. Too risky. She'd already attempted something daring five years ago and look how disastrously that had turned out. This was a matter of life and death. Hers. She had no reason to trust *le Beau* and confide in him.

She'd have to maintain her innocence against his claim, put on a believable performance that would convince him he was wrong about her, and then leave Suzanne's château as quickly as she could. Staying in her rooms the entire time and feigning an illness was out of the question. He'd know she was hiding from him. It would only confirm in his mind that he was right about her. *God only knows what he'd do then.*

No, she had to carry on until her betrothed arrived at the end of the week. She'd show *le Beau* that he didn't rattle her in any way.

Easier said than done, Catherine. Look at your shocking behavior in the hallway.

Another thunderclap resonated in the angry skies.

Trapped at the château with the most sinfully seductive man of the realm. How, by all that's holy, will you resist his over-whelming allure?

*   *   *

Arresting his steps in the corridor, Adrien crossed his arms with a sigh the moment he heard Charlotte call out his name behind him.

He was in a hurry. There was an auburn-haired beauty he had every intention of intercepting before she made it to supper. He'd barely had time to bathe and change his clothing after his uncles had left his rooms.

Charlotte stopped before him. "You've had a good look at Catherine. Can I count on your help, Adrien? She's reasonably attractive, although I am prettier." Though her last remark was a statement, it was said with self-doubt.

How he wished Charlotte wasn't so much like their mother.

"*Ma chérie*, forget Philbert de Baillet. If you have to work this hard to hold on to him, then he isn't worthy of you. You are very pretty. You can easily have someone else." He wasn't about to tell Charlotte of his plans for Catherine and have her enthusiastic over a lost cause. Catherine had little to do with Baillet's indifference. Baillet had lost interest in Charlotte. Plain and simple. There was nothing she could do to recapture it. It was best Charlotte ended the affair before he did. She'd save face. Her pride. Moreover, her heart. His godfathers were in agreement with Adrien.

Baillet would only bring Charlotte heartbreak.

Charlotte's eyes filled with tears and her bottom lip began to tremble. "*Pleeeease*, Adrien." Tears slipped down her face. "You'll do it, won't you?"

How he hated it when she cried. He despised it as much as he'd despised his mother's tears. He shouldn't be softened by them. But instead of being firm, "I'll see" tumbled from his mouth.

Her face lit up. "You'll do it!" She threw her arms around him and kissed his cheek.

He frowned, pulling her arms from around his neck. "That's not what I said."

She still beamed. "You love me, Adrien, though I know it's difficult for you to say. I know you'll do this for me." She squealed in jubilation and clapped her small hands. "No woman can resist *le Beau*. You must hurry. Supper will begin soon. Catherine de Villecourt will be there." With that, she rushed away.

"Charlotte, wait." But she didn't stop or turn around. "I'm not promising anything." She'd disappeared around the corner before he'd finished his sentence.

Adrien gnashed his teeth and walked away, clearing his mind of everything, except the captivating Catherine. Ironic that she'd be his pawn when he'd once been hers. But first, she was going to admit to her misdeeds.

The next left turn in the corridor brought him to the door he sought.

Catherine's door.

He stopped across from it and waited. Anticipation mounted by the moment. Adrien took a deep breath and let it out. He actually felt . . . nervous. He'd never been nervous around women. He hadn't even been nervous with his first woman. The reactions she elicited from him were astonishing.

The door opened. Catherine stepped out. *A vision in a royal blue gown.* His heart lost a beat.

Adrien stood transfixed, his cock thickening. Her breasts, exquisitely defined, were an inciting sight to behold. His eyes feasted on the creamy skin above her décolletage, her delicate bare shoulders and her elegant neck adorned by several strands of pearls. A slight purplish mark just under her ear grabbed his attention. A love bite.

His mark on her.

The sight inflamed him further.

The moment she saw him, her body went rigid. The servant with her gasped.

Catherine dragged her gaze from him, turned and walked down the hall, regal as a queen, dismissing him as if he were a common hand. As vexing as she was, he had to admit she was refreshingly different from any female he'd ever known. Hers was not the sort of greeting he was accustomed to receiving from women. The fact that she was going to be a challenge spiked his interest tenfold.

"Catherine . . ." He raced to her side, falling in step with her quickened pace. "I'd like a word with you."

"I have nothing to say to you except, go away." She kept her gaze straight ahead. "And stop addressing me in such a familiar manner," she added curtly. The older woman with her scurried along beside her, casting him the occasional timid look, seemingly distressed if the way she chewed her bottom lip were any indication.

"I thought since we were well acquainted, you wouldn't mind," he said.

"We are not well acquainted. I don't know how many times I have to tell you—I've never met you before. We haven't even been introduced."

"Ah, well, I agree with your last statement. If it's an introduction you require, allow me to introduce myself—"

"Please don't bother."

"I'm Adrien d'Aspe, bastard son of Louis XIV, and yes, most of the rumors you've heard about me are true. But, of course, you know a good deal about me. You've made inquiries."

She shot him a sharp look without breaking her stride. "I most assuredly have *not* made inquiries. You have the women here atwitter. They openly speak of you. I don't care who you are . . . or, in fact, to know anything about you."

"Come now, Catherine, don't be difficult. Dismiss your servant. Allow me a private moment. I promise you'll not be late for supper."

She surprised him when she stopped abruptly. "Sir, you are deranged. I have no interest in anything you have to say. If you don't leave me alone, I'll be forced to tell our hostess about your deplorable comportment." She turned and stalked away.

Despite himself, he felt a smile tugging at the corner of his mouth. When she was all afire like that, her eyes took on the most seductive glow.

He caught up to her and her servant again and stepped in front of Catherine so quickly that she walked into him and would have fallen back had he not caught her arms.

A mixture of frustration and outrage erupted from her throat.

She opened her mouth, likely to toss out a few hot words at him, but he placed his finger over her lips, silencing her.

"Whatever your relationship to Suzanne may be, I can assure you she'll not ask me to leave. She's been begging me to fuck her for months."

Her eyes widened, obviously caught off guard by his blunt answer. He removed his finger from her mouth. How many times had he thought about those ruby lips? Fantasized about them? Of sliding his cock between them into the wet warmth of her mouth. In five years, he hadn't been able to forget those lips or the delicious kiss that awoke him that night.

Taking advantage of her unbalanced state, he clasped her hand in his and stalked toward her rooms with her in tow.

"Madame! Madame . . . wh-what should I do?" the servant called out.

"If you don't let go of me, I'll scream," Catherine threatened.

"Go ahead." He reached her door, wrenched it open, and pulled her inside.

"*Madame . . . ?*"

"It's all right, Odette. I'll take care of this," she said, just before he shut the door. He'd called her on her bluff. She wasn't about to scream. Or make a scene. If she wasn't scheming, she was lying to him.

She was always playing games.

Well, he had a game for her. One that would overwhelm her senses, break down her resistance. Only, he wasn't going to resort to drugging her—as she had him. But he *was* going to take control—a control she'd snatched from him that night.

His game was one he'd mastered a long time ago—seduction.

She narrowed her eyes. "What do you want?"

He stepped closer. She stepped back into the door. A crack in her façade.

"I want you to scream," he reiterated, his tone matter-of-fact. "I'm going to make you come, and I want to hear you scream out your pleasure."

4

"Pardon?" The word rushed out on a breath, Catherine's bravado vanishing. In its place was stunned disbelief, and—Adrien was certain—a quiver of excitement.

He was wrong. There *was* something honest about her. Sexual arousal. She was naturally sensuous. Made for passion.

She craved it—beneath the veneer of propriety.

So why was her experience so limited? She'd been married, and as beautiful as she was, she could easily have her choice of lovers. Then there was Philbert de Baillet. Hadn't he sampled any premarital delights? Marriage was the last thing on Adrien's mind, but if he were betrothed to a woman like Catherine, he would have bedded her long before the exchanging of the vows.

Adrien snaked his arm around Catherine's waist and pulled her to him tightly. Ignoring her gasp, he threaded his fingers in her soft hair, resting his palm on the nape of her neck. His fever for her spiked the moment their bodies touched. His cock pressing against her belly was already pulsing painfully. What was it about this woman? She scintillated his senses with no effort at all.

"You asked what I wanted, Catherine. I want to have another go at you, without any aphrodisiacs involved. But first and foremost, I want your mouth."

He swooped in for a kiss, her jasmine-scented skin inebriating him. She fisted the material of his knee-length coat against his back but, thank God, didn't push him away. Instead, she made tiny sounds at the back of her throat each time he locked and relocked their mouths.

Her breathing was already erratic, inciting his own. Yet by the slight stiffness in her body, he knew she warred with her desire, wanting to stop him as much as she wanted him to continue. He forced himself to slow down. To concentrate on her responses, keeping her enthralled so that she didn't pull away from him.

Adrien brushed his tongue against her lips, coaxing them apart, sliding his tongue inside her mouth, penetrating it, possessing it the moment she complied with his sensual demand. He celebrated in her surrender. She tasted delicious. Even better than he remembered.

Her soft form melted against his body, dragging a groan up his throat. *Dieu*, he wanted her.

The moment he felt her hands relax and flatten against his back, he cupped her breast and grazed his thumb over the hardened nipple. She rewarded him with a sultry moan. Pinching the pebbled tip through her clothing, he had her writhing and arching hard against him.

Catherine's hands shot up his back and tangled in his hair, her kisses now frantic. She gave his tongue a long, sensuous suck that practically buckled his knees.

His heart pounding against his ribs, he plucked at the ribbon between her breasts, loosening the front of her gown. Just as he started to spread open the bodice, she grabbed his hand and mewed, "No . . ." in protest ever so faintly against his mouth. She'd guessed his intent—that he had more than just sexual interest in seeing her exposed breasts. There were three small freckles on the outer curve of her left breast that he wanted revealed.

She didn't.

Cursing his eagerness, he stilled his hand, fearful of shattering her sexual abandon altogether. "Shhh, I won't, *ma belle*." This was novel. He always had carte blanche in the boudoir. No one ever said no to anything he wanted. "We'll only do that which we both want," he quickly assured her and reclaimed her mouth, starved for more. Gripping her pert derrière, he pressed his thigh between her legs and against her sex with enough pressure over her clit to draw a gasp from her, bringing her focus back to the pleasure at hand, away from his blunder.

"I know what you want." Adrien rubbed her clit with his thigh. She jumped. He broke the kiss and looked into her eyes. Her cheeks were flush, and she had that fiery glow in her eyes that had nothing to do with anger and everything to do with hot, fierce desire. "This is what you want, isn't it? It's what we both want, Catherine. You're going to come for me—so hard—"

She grabbed his face and thrust her tongue inside his mouth, cutting off his words, her lower body rocking erotically against his thigh. Sounds of her sharp, short breaths, as her tongue tangled with his, stoked his lust. Decimated his control.

He pushed her up against the door and removed his thigh from between her legs. Lifting her voluminous skirts with urgent yanks, he at last reached her drawers and cupped her through the cloth of the *caleçons*, already damp with her juices.

He caressed her lightly. "You're wet for me, Catherine."

"Oh . . . God . . ." Her voice was shaky. She pressed against his palm, more seductive sounds emanating from her. Urging him further. He needed no encouragement. He was so hard, he felt dizzy, the ferocity of his need stunning.

"Open your legs wider." His voice was gruff. Using his foot, he widened her stance. "Stay like that." Adrien slid his fingers in the slit of the garment, through her moistened curls, grazing over her slick flesh. She was hot, dripping with desire, and moaning louder.

Slowly, he pushed a finger inside her, feeding her a knuckle at a time until he buried it completely. The silky wet heat clasped around his finger was mind-numbingly tight. His prick twitched with anticipation. He couldn't wait to sink his cock into her.

He eased his finger out and slid two back in. She whimpered, her head falling back against the door.

"You're soaking my hand. Your body is begging for more." Massaging her clit with his thumb, he pushed and pulled his fingers with a deep and steady rhythm. She squeezed her eyes shut, dug her fingers into his shoulders, and bit her lip, trying to muffle her sounds of pleasure, her lovely breasts rising and falling rapidly. She looked gloriously wanton.

"You like this, don't you? It feels good, doesn't it?" he asked. She gave him a shaky nod.

"Does it feel as good as it did five years ago?"

Maddeningly stubborn, she wouldn't answer.

"You know I know how to make it feel even better." He curled his buried fingers and rubbed the sweet spot inside her vaginal wall. She cried out and bucked her hips at him, her soaked sex pouring more juices onto his hand.

"Should I stop?" he rasped. Without relenting on the

ultrasensitive spot, he lightened the pressure and was no longer teasing her clit, deliberately keeping her on the edge.

She rolled her head against the door, her eyes still closed. "No!"

"You want to come badly, don't you?"

She swallowed hard. "Yes . . ." The sound of her breathless voice tightened his groin.

"Look at me."

She opened her eyes.

"Tell me you want my cock inside you." He had to have her. He couldn't stand it a moment longer.

"I want . . . I need—"

"What do you want and need?"

She licked her lips. "You . . ."

"Adrien, I need your cock," he amended, barely able to speak. "Say it."

"I need your . . . cock . . . Adrien."

Though he'd heard those words before, hearing them out of her lush mouth shot a bolt of lust through him that rocked him to the core. He pulled out his fingers. She shuddered in his arms. Clutching her skirts in one hand, he loosened her *caleçons* with the other and watched them slip down her thighs. The sight of the wet, downy curls between her legs made his mouth water.

Yanking open his breeches, he freed his stiff prick, gaining little relief as it sprang from its confines. Glancing at Catherine, he noticed her gazing hungrily at his engorged cock. If he hadn't been so aroused, he would have smiled. Here was the real Catherine: a highly sensual woman naturally drawn to decadent delights.

Grabbing her hips, he captured her mouth in a fierce kiss and slid his shaft between the folds of her sex, coating it with her essence, making it slick for easy penetration. He was so far gone, he knew he wasn't going to be gentle. "This is what you need." He wedged the crest of his cock at her opening.

"*Yes . . .*" She panted. "*Hurry!*"

He drove his prick into her, possessing her with a single thrust. She cried out.

Adrien closed his eyes and rested his forehead against the door, his chest heaving. Her hot, creamy sheath was stretched so tightly around him it made his cock throb, the pleasure rippling down his length momentarily rendering him speechless.

Pinned against the door, impaled on his shaft, she trembled. He felt her tighten her arms around him, her warm, fast breaths tickling his neck.

"I need your cock," she whispered near his ear.

That undid him.

He reared and thrust again. And again. And again. The friction felt so good. She felt so good. She had the sweetest sex. It was to die for. Vaguely, he heard her gasps and moans over the blood roaring in his ears.

She shoved her hips forward, taking fully each solid thrust he gave her. "Don't stop . . . Don't stop . . ." she pleaded each time he slammed into her.

As if he could? As if he had the will? "Tell me you're my midnight enchantress." His voice was so rough, it didn't even sound like his own. "Tell me . . . what I want to hear, Catherine . . . Tell me . . . you're the woman who came to my bed that night and I'll let you com—"

She screamed, her body jerking sharply as her orgasm crashed over her, taking them both by surprise, her inner muscles squeezing and releasing around his thick cock, milking his thrusting shaft with each powerful spasm.

Digging his fingers into her soft bottom, Adrien clenched his teeth and growled her name. Exquisite contractions running along his prick went on, and—*ah, Dieu*—on. He drove into her repeatedly, fiercely, fighting back his orgasm to bask in her incredible cunt as long as he could.

How many times had he dreamed of this? Of having this woman again. Of sampling more of the scalding desire they'd shared. She was rapture incarnate. No aphrodisiac was necessary between them, and somehow he'd known it all along.

Her sex clamped down around him a final time, snapping his flimsy control, his climax suddenly rushing over him. He jerked his prick out of her at the last moment, snatched her from against the door and crushed her in his arms just as his explosive release rocked him, his semen shooting out of him in hot torrents. His mouth against her shoulder, he let out a long, fierce groan, his body shuddering with each spurt of come until he'd emptied his cock.

His legs felt weak. His body, lax. Ecstasy hummed in his veins. Memories of their last encounter, years ago, materialized in his mind. It had been exactly the same—soul-satisfying sex.

The night when you unwittingly took a virgin.

The sexual fog dissipating little by little, he became aware of his harsh breathing, the light scent of jasmine that hung in the air, and her soft breasts crushed against his chest.

Adrien eased his hold on her. She slumped against the door. Her eyes were closed, her lips slightly swollen and parted. She had the prettiest blush to her cheeks. He brushed back a lock of her hair from her delicate brow. She looked like a woman who'd been well fucked and thoroughly sated.

A smile lifted the corner of his mouth. He took a small step back and glanced on the floor. His come was on her fallen drawers. Adrien kicked them out of the way, and wiping his glistening cock with his shirttails, he readjusted his clothing. Unlike his father, he took care not to make bastards.

Catherine opened her eyes. At first she looked away, seemingly embarrassed, but then she straightened her spine and met his gaze.

Lightly, he caressed her cheek with his knuckles. How he loved the feel of her skin.

Adrien felt mellow. He felt oddly content. He felt good.

No, he felt great.

"I've made a mess of your *caleçons*," he said. Not to mention he'd mussed her lovely hair and horribly wrinkled her gown.

"It doesn't matter." Her voice was soft.

His smile grew, pleased that she wasn't put off.

She cleared her throat. "Thank you for the . . . tumble." She slid out from between him and the door and stepped away, her gown falling into place. "Please see yourself out."

Adrien felt as though cold water just splashed him in the face. *Jésus-Christ*, she'd dismissed him. As though he were a stud for hire.

She didn't get more than two steps away from him when he caught her arm. Her head snapped around. "We're not through." His ire mounted.

Her fury flashed in her eyes. "You got what you wanted. Let go."

Stepping closer, he captured her chin and her undivided attention. She'd erected a wall between them again, and donned a false mask to conceal herself from him. He wanted it torn down. Stripped away. Wanted her naked both literally and figuratively. He wanted the truth.

Moreover, and most irritating, he wanted to know everything about her. And he had no idea why he should be interested.

"Catherine de Villecourt, you haven't come close to giving me what I want. But you will. We have only just begun."

Thunder rumbled in the sky.

5

Hundreds of candles shone tiny stars of light in the *Salle de Buffet*. Wall sconces and the silver candelabras on the long table illuminated the room with a warm orange glow.

Ladies' gowns and gentlemen's justacorps of rich blues and greens, of deep gold and reds, lent to the opulence of the surroundings.

Catherine tried to concentrate on her conversation with the Comte de Champagnier. Seated to her right, the man had the most unfortunate monotone voice. It didn't help that his take on the Latin classics was uninspiring. Though reasonably attractive and only a few years older than she, he was incredibly dull. An avid reader, Catherine would have enjoyed a lively debate. Welcomed the much-needed distraction. Instead, the Comte's comments often blended into the din of the room. Catherine smiled politely and made the occasional brief remark—brief because it was clear

Champagnier was more interested in voicing his opinions than in hearing hers.

She didn't have anyone more interesting to talk to on her left. The ancient Madame de Jauloux was already chin-down, softly snoring before the meal was even served.

Catherine was stuck with Champagnier.

Her heart pounded away the time, knowing Adrien would arrive for supper at any moment. The room was full. Every seat was taken except the chair at the head of the table, which naturally Suzanne would occupy, and the one to its right. Suzanne had likely arranged for Adrien to sit there, a spot that was across from Catherine and over two.

In short, uncomfortably close.

Shaken by their torrid encounter, she'd stopped trembling only minutes before entering the room. After what his kisses and touch had done to her, after her heated surrender in his arms, how would she get through the meal with him sitting so near? Her actions still had her reeling.

A few squeaks of delight and a rush of whispers rippled in the room, grabbing Catherine's attention.

Her heart lurched at the sight of Adrien standing in the doorway, Suzanne on his arm. He, too, had changed his attire. Now, he was dressed in a silver-green justacorps with matching breeches. He looked regal, princely, the knee-length fitted coat accentuating his broad shoulders and muscled physique perfectly.

He scanned the room. Those light green eyes—the downfall of many women—were a devastating contrast to his dark hair, wisps of which teased his lashes.

No man should be that beautiful.

She felt mortifying moisture pool between her legs. The

very sight of him quickened her heart and ignited her senses—inspiring ardent thoughts and shameless urges no other man ever had.

Adrien escorted Suzanne to the table. Her dark hair was adorned with tiny ribbons that matched the row of green satin bows down the front of her bodice. Her gown, the height of fashion, was embellished with gold embroidery over alternate green and gold bands of satin. When her husband was alive, Suzanne didn't own such finery. Nor did the château look as it did now. Over the years since Comte de Lamotte's death, her wise selection of lovers had filled the once modest coffers. Hopelessly riveted, Catherine watched as Adrien whispered in Suzanne's ear. She glanced at Catherine as he spoke, her smile slightly slipping.

Catherine pulled her gaze away from the elegant couple. "Monsieur de Champagnier," she said, returning her attention to the Comte. He, too, watched Adrien and Suzanne—as did much of the room. "Tell me, what do you think of Spanish literature? Have you any favorites?" That should have the man talking again, and give her something else—albeit ever so arduous—to focus on.

Champagnier began his prattle immediately, his flow of words arrested when a strong masculine hand gripped his shoulder.

Catherine glanced up. Her breath lodged in her throat. The hand belonged to Adrien.

"Good evening, Monsieur de Champagnier." Adrien's tone was genial, his manner polished.

Champagnier twisted around. "Good evening to you, Monsieur de Beaulain."

"There's a small problem, monsieur. It seems you're in my seat."

Catherine's stomach flip-flopped.

Champagnier's brow furrowed slightly. "Monsieur, I'm afraid you're mistaken. The seats were assigned and—"

"Yours is over there." Adrien gave a nod to the empty chair near the head of the table, his tone firmer, though still pleasant. He lowered his head and his voice. "Do be a good man and take your place across the table without further ado. Unless, of course, you wish to make an issue of the matter?" A threat.

A few shades paler, Champagnier excused himself, murmured his apologies, and vacated his chair. Being outranked hadn't motivated Champagnier to move, but the possibility of facing Adrien in a duel clearly had.

Catherine's gaze darted down the table. Her heart plummeted. Every eye in the room was on them.

"*Cher,*" Suzanne said, placing a hand on Adrien's arm. Dear God, she hadn't even noticed Suzanne standing there. "Allow me to introduce my darling friend, Catherine de Sanvais, Comtesse de Villecourt. Catherine, this is Adrien d'Aspe de Bourbon, Marquis de Beaulain."

Adrien took her hand and pressed a kiss to her knuckle. "*Enchanté.*"

The ludicrousness of the moment struck her. She was being introduced to the man who'd deflowered her and, not an hour ago, debauched her. Catherine might have laughed if she wasn't so horrified.

"Madame de Villecourt was married to my late brother," Suzanne offered. "He passed away three years ago."

"Really?" Adrien's green eyes turned to Catherine, his expression unreadable, his vexation with her outwardly concealed. "My condolences, madame." He bowed at the waist.

Her heart pounding, she mustered a murmur of thanks.

"Enjoy," Suzanne said, looking at Catherine, before she swept to her seat.

Adrien sat down next to her.

Catherine cast another glance down the table. It wasn't difficult to note the looks. The whispers. They were talking about Adrien. About her. About them. Adrien was the closest thing to royalty in the room. Not to mention a source of interest to the nobility at large. Everything he did was noted and analyzed. Curiosity had gripped Suzanne's guests as they likely speculated at Catherine's involvement with the King's roué son.

Outwardly, she gave nothing away. Beneath the table, she clenched her hands together. During her excruciating eighteen-month marriage, she'd been the subject of gossip. The object of scandal.

The last thing she wanted was more of the same.

Platters with steaming meats were brought out by a parade of servants. Adrien's thigh brushed hers as he exchanged pleasantries with the Baron de Neveux on his right. She flinched and tried her best to ignore him and the tingling in her leg where their bodies had touched. Catherine turned to Madame de Jauloux, who was now awake and watching the arrival of the food eagerly.

"Why, madame, that's a lovely necklace," Catherine said.

"Don't bother." Adrien picked up his goblet. "The woman is stone-deaf. Aren't you, Madame de Jauloux?" he added a little louder.

She didn't appear to hear Adrien at all.

"You see?" he said. His eyes briefly dipped to Catherine's décolletage as he brought the goblet to his lips. Her nipples hardened. "You look lovely, Catherine."

Catherine squeezed her fingers a little tighter. "Please don't speak to me." *Or look at me like that.*

Adrien took a drink and placed his goblet back down. "Why not? We've been properly introduced." Despite the desire in his eyes, she sensed his underlying ire.

"You know exactly why not. Thanks to your spectacle, you have everyone wondering whether or not—"

"I'm fucking you?"

Nervous, she glanced about, her cheeks feeling hot. Immersed in conversation, thankfully no one seemed to have heard him. Madame de Jauloux was happily engrossed in her poached egg soup.

Catherine clenched her teeth. Oh, she was definitely paying for her misdeeds this night. All of them. Including what she'd done with the devilishly handsome *le Beau* a short time ago. How much worse was this evening going to get?

Before she could offer a retort, a bowl of soup was set before her, her stomach instantly balking at the thought of food.

Adrien leaned in to her slightly. Too close for her sanity. In fact, being in the same room with him was proving to be too much. "Why do you care what they think? Why should any of these people matter enough to you to waste a moment's thought on them?"

Catherine noticed Madame de Bussy and Madame de Noisette—the ladies she'd met in the gardens—openly observing her. Cordially, she nodded at them. "You are a man," she said with a frozen smile for the sake of outward appearances. "You are judged differently than a woman."

He shrugged. "I don't allow anyone's judgment—of any kind—to affect how I live my life and neither should you."

"Not everyone can afford to be as blasé."

Warm fingers closed over her cold hands beneath the table linen. She jerked.

"Easy." He lightly squeezed, his thumb grazing the back of her hand. A quick look told her no one noticed that his hand was on her lap. She couldn't pull away. He had her trapped, for any sudden movements would likely garner unwanted attention. His hand was so close to her sex, she could feel herself getting wetter.

Clearly, he was going to torment her on many levels. Her ire spiked.

"You are playing with me. All of this is a game to you," she shot back, sotto voce, furious with herself over the situation she found herself in. Frustrated with his effect on her.

"On the contrary, it is a game you play. You could be honest and tell me the truth. In truth, your desire is the only thing that's honest about you. It's the only thing that's honest between us." He brought her hand to the bulge in his breeches. She gasped. He ran her hand down his length then back up. "It's what you do to me . . . just sitting near you."

The bud between her legs began to throb. She fought back the urge to tighten her grip on his glorious cock.

Adrien held up his goblet with his free hand. A server was there in an instant to fill it up with wine.

Did the servant not see? Catherine scanned the guests again. Didn't anyone notice what was happening under the table linen?

"I'll not denounce you," he said when the servant stepped away. "Whatever your reasons were for doing what you did five years ago, I'll not report it."

"Let go," she demanded quietly. Their eyes locked and held. For a moment she thought he was going to refuse, but then he loosened his hold, still keeping his palm lightly pressed against her hand.

She slipped her hand out of its tantalizing spot, sliding it away from his erection.

Taking in a fortifying breath, she let it out slowly, and chose her next words carefully. "Why, if a woman is faced with trial and possible execution, should she believe you? There would be a lot at stake for her in bestowing that trust."

He gave a nod. "True. But it's a matter that would be brought to the attention of the King, and I prefer to limit my dealings with His Majesty," he said. "Ask anyone. I have a strained relationship with my sire."

The "curse" Madame de Bussy had mentioned earlier flitted through Catherine's mind. Had the silly thing actually come true? It certainly sounded as though father and son were at odds.

Adrien leaned in again, his incredible green eyes disarming. "No one knows about that night except me and the host of the masquerade. He's a good friend. Most discreet. If you were I, would you not have the same questions I have? Would you not feel you deserved answers to them?"

That hit its mark. She lowered her head, feeling contrite. How could she argue with that? He did deserve answers. He had every right to them. He had every right to be angry with her, too, and yet he never once hurled vicious words as her husband used to whenever he was irked, which was more often than not. And then there was Adrien's touch. Whenever he touched her, it was always with genuine passion. It was beguiling. It made her feel feminine. Desirable.

An idea came to her. There *was* a way out of this after all—a way where everyone would benefit and no one would suffer. She decided she'd take a different approach to the matter. Hope welled inside her.

Catherine spied three men at the end of the table watching her. Two were smiling, almost grinning, while the third frowned.

"Do you know those men at the end of the table?" she asked.

Adrien's gaze moved down the row of seated guests. Then he frowned. "Ignore them."

"Who are they?"

Reaching for his goblet, he drained it. "My uncles. They are harmless."

"I don't want any scandal, Adrien. I've had more than my share."

He studied her silently. "Oh?"

She arched her brows. "Surely, you've asked about me? Didn't someone tell you about my late husband?"

"No. I made no inquiries. I don't care for gossip. Nor do I want to learn about you from someone else. I want to learn about you, from you."

Catherine was speechless. She didn't know anyone who didn't partake in gossip—men or women. Some more viciously than others. It was refreshing to find someone else who shared her disdain for it.

Music started up in the Grand Salon, the harpsichord and violins playing a *menuet*. Catherine tore her gaze from Adrien's handsome face and noticed that already guests were moving to the next room. Adrien's uncles were also leaving, a pretty dark-haired woman exiting with them. Briefly, the woman met Catherine's gaze. A venomous look flashed in her hazel eyes so quickly, she wasn't certain if she'd imagined it.

A banquet of roasted duck, partridge, and quails, fruits, salads, and pastries was spread out before her. Though most everyone had had their fill, none held any appeal for Catherine. Least of all her cold soup that she'd neglected to wave away.

She returned her attention to Adrien. He was watching her.

All that masculine beauty focused solely on her. Her insides danced.

"I don't wish to speak here," she said. "I'll come to your room tonight."

"No. Wait out a few dances then retire to your rooms. I'll come to you."

"Very well. As long as you promise not to do anything to cause tongues to wag here."

"Agreed. And you'll agree to provide answers."

She nodded. "I'll have answers for you." And a bargain to sweeten the deal and ensure his silence.

* * *

"Adrien," Paul said as he approached with a smile. "You'll soon bore holes in the Marquis de Verdier's back with the look you're giving him. Could it be it's because he's dancing with your lady?"

Adrien tightened his jaw. The moment Catherine entered the Grand Salon, she was besieged with offers to dance. This was her third dance already. Her radiant smile was telling. She was clearly enjoying the allemande, bewitching every one of her dance partners as they left looking smitten.

"She's not my lady," Adrien said, surprised by the twinge of regret.

"Why are you not dancing with her yourself?"

Why indeed? Why on earth had he agreed to keep his distance and not make their involvement more evident? *You know why.* It was something he'd seen in her eyes. A sorrow that stirred his compassion.

Instinct cautioned him against such sentiment, warning him not to be drawn in. Something told him that perhaps he should back off—that it might be best if he didn't learn the reasons behind her actions five years ago after all.

But as he watched her turn and curtsy, the final notes fading away to end the dance, he silenced the niggling doubts.

He knew nothing could keep him from her room tonight.

6

Pacing in her rooms, Catherine stopped dead in her tracks when she heard the expected knock at the door.

Adrien.

The moment of truth had arrived.

She'd promised him answers. The question was: what would he think of her answers?

Nervously she smoothed her skirts and opened the door. Adrien was leaning against the doorframe with his forearm. As usual, his presence sent a thrill through her.

She stepped aside, allowing him to enter.

"Please sit." She indicated the settee near the hearth in the antechamber.

He moved across the room, all muscle and masculine grace, and sat down, his rapt attention on her. Grappling with how to begin, Catherine clasped her hands, then released them and smoothed her skirts again. She'd practiced the words. But they were stuck on her tongue.

Adrien rose and approached her, his brow furrowed. Her nerves jangled; she braced herself, unsure what he was about to do or say.

He cupped her cheek. "Are you all right?" he asked.

It unbalanced her. She wasn't expecting him to be concerned about her emotional state. Her father and husband never were. She'd learned to stand strong on her own long ago. To lean on no one.

Feeling vulnerable was unsettling in the extreme.

"You can trust me," he told her.

Did she have a choice? She'd failed miserably to convince him he was mistaken. He could have her arrested at any time. The freckles on her breast would ultimately condemn her.

She'd have to find the courage to open herself up to him and pray for the best.

Adrien saw fear in her eyes. She was clearly skittish. If he didn't proceed slowly, she'd likely bolt for the door.

He didn't want her to be afraid. Oddly, he found himself longing for her trust as strongly as he longed for the truth.

Something in the corner of the room caught his eye. An artist's easel and paintings propped against the wall. He moved toward them. On the easel was a lovely depiction of a valley at sunrise. It was serene. Lush. Beautiful.

"Did you do this?" he asked, marveling at the piece.

She moved to his side and blushed. "It isn't finished. It isn't very good . . ." she replied, quickly dismissing her work.

He leaned in closer to the painting and silently scrutinized it. "I think it's wonderful."

The initial look of surprise on her face was precious, as was the joy his praise gave her. It delighted him to see it more than he'd admit.

He motioned to the paintings on the floor leaning against the wall. "May I?"

She bit her lip, and after a moment's hesitation, gave a nod.

He picked up the paintings one by one and studied them, genuinely impressed. Paintings of gardens, of children, and one of water nymphs were among the works.

"You're very talented, Catherine," he said with all sincerity.

She looked embarrassed by his compliment. "Thank you. That's very kind of you to say, but . . . I'm rather an amateur . . ."

Her modesty was endearing. "Do you do portraits?" This was a first for him. He was alone with a beautiful, passionate female, his cock fully alert to her presence, and yet he was not acting on the powerful urgings she inspired.

"I've . . . never really tried . . . My late father and husband both thought painting was a frivolous expenditure of time, especially for a woman."

"But you don't. You love it," he stated. "It's evident in these paintings. In the painstaking details. Each stroke of your paintbrush brought you joy, no?"

A smile returned to her lovely visage. "Yes. I do love it," she admitted softly. *Dieu*, this softer side of her was oh so appealing. The woman was beyond beguiling.

"Excellent. Then you'll paint my portrait and one for each of my uncles," he said, ignoring the warning in his head against lengthening his involvement with her.

Her eyes widened.

"I'll, of course, pay for supplies," he continued, enjoying the astonishment on her face, "and for your—"

"I can't."

"Oh? Why not?"

She turned and walked over to the settee. Her back to him, he saw the stiffness in her delicate shoulders. "I'm to be married soon to the Comte de Baillet." She faced him. "He'll be here by the end of the week." Her statement added to the distance she'd just placed between them.

Adrien's dislike for Baillet grew each time he heard the man's name.

"I'm certain you think I'm rather shameless . . ." she said, her words trailing off.

She was still skirting around the issue, discussing matters other than the events that occurred five years ago.

Adrien closed the space between them and took her hand. "I don't think that." Lightly, he caressed her wrist with his thumb, relishing in the satiny feel of her jasmine-scented skin.

She didn't pull her hand away and it pleased him. Her expression was open. Unguarded. And that pleased him as well.

"What happened today . . . between us . . . I never intended something like that to happen," she said.

He didn't want her voicing any regrets. "We're attracted to each other, *ma belle*. Intensely so. There's no shame in that."

A small smile graced her lips. "You can be quite irresistible, but I'm certain you've heard that enough times."

"I've also heard I'm mildly attractive," he teased, pleased she didn't seem to be remorseful.

She laughed, a soft, sweet sound. "If no one tries to keep you in check, dear Marquis de Beaulain, you'll become unbearably conceited."

"Well then." He bowed over her hand. "Madame, I thank you for your efforts. I'd hate to become intolerable." He kept the mood light though a new all-too-insistent question was now plaguing him, gnawing away at his brain.

Smiling, she shook her head. "You're incorrigible. But definitely charming."

"Then all hope for me is not lost." He brought her hand up to his lips and kissed the sensitive spot on the inside of her wrist.

Her smile faded, and she pulled her hand away. Adrien fought back the urge to take it again.

"Do you love him?" He was stunned at himself. The question eating at him just tumbled out of his mouth. He hadn't intended to ask. It shouldn't matter a whit if she did.

"My betrothed?"

"Yes." The last thing he wanted to hear from her were the same ill-placed words of adoration for Baillet his sister had.

To his relief, she shook her head. "No. Nor is he in love with me."

"Why are you marrying him?"

"After my father's death, Villecourt gained control of my inheritance."

"And squandered it," he surmised.

She looked down. "Yes. He had . . . extravagant ways. I find myself in dire straits. The château is in a state of ill repair. I've had to let most of the servants go."

There was more about her marriage she wasn't saying. She'd mentioned something about a scandal. But none of that was any of his concern. He wouldn't inject himself into her troubles. It wasn't why he was here.

Adrien slipped his arm around her waist and drew her to him, her soft form molding against him ever so delectably. Lust licked up his spine.

"Catherine, tell me what happened five years ago."

Suddenly unable to look him in the eye, she dropped her gaze to his chest. She was vacillating. Concerned she'd renege on her promise, he pressed on, untying the ribbon between her breasts, making quick work of the fastenings on her bodice with his practiced fingers before panic flared in her eyes and her hand shot up, stilling his with a firm squeeze.

He leaned in, the scent of jasmine dazzling his senses. "It's all right," he said softly in her ear. "Trust me. Let's put an end to the denials and lies. I only want the truth." He pulled back to gaze at her face.

She wouldn't look at him, her body rigid in his arms. Her hand still clutched his tightly.

"Let me," he urged gently. "On my word, it will be all right."

Keeping her gaze averted, she released her hold of his hand slowly.

Adrien opened her bodice and eased down her chemise, uncovering her skin an inch at a time until at last he located the three tiny freckles on the outside curve of her breast. There they were—those pretty freckles that had tantalized and tormented him in so many dreams. He caressed them with a finger.

Seeing them again triggered a rush of memories that weren't only heated. There was something else about that night that made her unforgettable, the experience unique. More than the intensity of it. More than the discoveries he'd made the next morning.

It was the tenderness.

Somehow she'd infused a certain softness into their carnal encounter.

Interwoven with the salaciousness, there was tenderness in her touch. In her kisses. She'd taken what was supposed to be an anonymous copulation and made it far more intimate. Strikingly different. And most disconcerting—simply by how deeply satisfying it all was.

Taking several steps back, she readjusted her chemise, then covered her breasts with her arms.

She could pull away from him, but she couldn't backtrack now that he'd seen the freckles. "No more denials," he repeated. "It's time for explanations, Catherine. Why don't you start by telling me how you gained admittance into the masquerade? The guest list was rather exclusive. Daniel de Gallay swore to me that he didn't invite anyone fitting your description."

She paused. "The invitation was delivered to our town house in error. It was meant for our neighbor, the Comte de Quantin."

"You know Quantin? You lived on Place Royale in Paris?" It was relatively new, an elegant stretch of homes for the privileged.

"Yes. Once. The town house is long gone now." There was sadness in her tone.

"Thanks to your late husband?"

She nodded. "He lost it in a game of *Basset*."

"You used Quantin's invitation, then."

"No. I made an exact copy before I had one of the servants deliver it to the Comte."

"Why the strong desire to attend?"

Tears shone in her eyes, but she didn't shed them. "I was desperate. Why else would I go to the trouble of forging an invitation and sneaking out of my home?" She rubbed her arms, as though she were cold. "My family had made its fortune collecting taxes for the Crown. Father was determined to elevate our family into nobility through marriage. I was the sacrificial lamb. To that end, he chose the Comte de Villecourt as my husband." A rueful smile formed on her lips. "I wish I could have mustered some affection for him. I wanted to like him. Perhaps it sounds hopelessly romantic, but I truly wanted to fall in love with him. I held out hope, until I met him."

"What was he like?" he asked quietly.

She swallowed hard. Clearly, she was battling her emotions, trying to maintain her composure. He'd never known any female to hold back her tears. It was yet another reason why she stood out from the masses.

"He was . . . angry," she said.

Adrien's stomach tightened. "Did he ever . . . hurt you?"

"He never struck me, if that is what you mean. He tried to hurt me with words, but over time, I became numb to them. It was then he found different ways to torment me."

"Why would he wish to?"

She clutched her bodice to her bosom. "Villecourt was very much against marrying me to begin with. A bourgeois was far beneath him—a fact he never let me forget. He hated it that he'd had to accept me as a wife simply to replenish his family's coffers. We saw each other three times during our betrothal. He made no attempt to hide his disdain. He told me that if he had to suffer me as a wife, he'd make sure I was equally miserable. I begged Father to cancel the marriage contract. To reconsider and look for another. He refused. I knew I would live in sheer misery if I married Villecourt. It all felt so hopeless . . . and then the invitation arrived. I took it as a sign. A chance to escape my horrible fate."

The pain in her golden eyes wrapped itself around Adrien's heart even when he didn't want it to. "So, you decided to attend the masquerade to—"

"Purposely render myself unmarriageable. I'm sorry, Adrien, for what I did to you. I'm sorry for whatever distress I caused you. If it's any consolation, my plan failed horribly and caused me further suffering in the end. It didn't break my betrothal, as I'd hoped. A larger dowry than originally promised mollified Ville-court's debt-ridden family's objections to my sullied state. As for Villecourt, it only fueled his resentment and made him more spiteful toward me."

Adrien was amazed. He had considered this scenario a possibility, and dismissed it. A maidenhead was a commodity. Of great value to a woman's future. Though there had been females who'd surrendered their innocence outside of marriage for a multitude of reasons, he'd never known a woman to go to such lengths to purposely discard it.

"Foolishly, I thought it was the perfect plan," she continued. "No one knew of my presence at the masquerade, and with a mask, I maintained my anonymity."

"Except I removed your mask in bed," he reminded her.

"It didn't matter. You didn't know me. You never asked my name. And I purposely didn't ask for yours, so that it couldn't be coerced from me by my father later on. I didn't want to involve you in my situation any more than I had to."

Adrien arched a brow. "You didn't know who I was? You didn't know anything about me when you stole into my room?"

She gave a mirthless laugh. "Only that you were from Vienna."

"*Vienna?*"

She shook her head. "It's what my maid told me—obviously in error. A foreigner was the perfect choice. I wasn't supposed to ever see you again. Clearly, with my many mistakes, it was a plan doomed to fail. My greatest error was in believing that in the end Father would open his eyes and ultimately choose his daughter's happiness over his own wants."

Her words stabbed into Adrien, her remarks resonating inside him.

A single tear slipped down her cheek. Impatiently, she swiped it away. "I was wrong about the depth of my father's affection. I guess I'd hoped he actually cared."

Adrien felt as though he'd stumbled upon a kindred spirit. And that was the last thing he thought he'd discover about her.

He turned away and raked a hand through his hair, tamping down the soft sentiment welling up inside him. "Why the aphrodisiac?" he asked, staring at the shadows and light on the wall above the torchère.

"How did you know it had been added to the wine?"

Adrien turned back around. "I found a powdery substance at the bottom of my goblet the next morning. Given the heated intensity of our lascivious exchange, it wasn't difficult to guess what the powder was." He crossed his arms. "You still haven't answered my question: why the aphrodisiac?"

"I have no idea how to seduce a man. The aphrodisiac ensured success. I couldn't very well approach you and say, 'Excuse me, would you care to bed me?' What if you had refused?"

Dieu. Could she really have no idea how desirable she was? "Catherine, had you made that proposition to every man in that room, you'd have had unanimous acceptance of your offer. No man would have refused you."

A pretty blush colored her cheeks, obviously unaccustomed to compliments about her appeal.

"Didn't your husband ever tell you how beautiful you are?" From the sounds of it, Villecourt had been a colossal ass, but surely in the throes of passion he'd stated the obvious, no? The vision she made naked in Adrien's bed still haunted him to this day.

"No. Never. He indicated . . . quite the opposite, in fact." She lifted her chin a notch. "He had no desire for me, in or out of the boudoir." Those statements were weighted with hurt and suffering and Adrien couldn't help but admire her bravado. No doubt Villecourt had had a favorite mistress—thus the reason for his disinterest.

"You said he'd found different ways to torment you. Do those ways relate to the scandal you've mentioned?"

Reluctantly, she nodded.

"What did he do, Catherine?" He had no idea why the hell he was asking questions about her marriage. Why did any of it matter?

"He"—she clasped and unclasped her hands—"gleefully made us the talk of every salon in Paris. It was not easy to live in the city as he carried on with his . . . lovers. After the first few months of our marriage, he made no attempt to hide them at all."

This was puzzling. "Who was he bedding? What made them so noteworthy?"

She let out a sharp, exasperated breath, her expression a mixture of agony and anger. "If you must know every sordid detail of my marriage, I shall tell you from beginning to end, although I don't understand why Villecourt should interest you. My late husband only came to my bed twice and under duress because of pressure from his family to procure an heir. Each distasteful time he told me he found me repulsive. It wasn't until I walked in on him having sex with one of the servants that I learned the true reason for his disgust. My husband didn't desire me because I wasn't . . ."

"What?"

"A . . . man."

Now there was an answer Adrien hadn't expected, though he

should have. What other reason could there be for a man to find this ravishing woman undesirable?

She approached him. "You asked who he was bedding. He was bedding most of our male staff as well as men of higher rank. His favorite was the Baron de Nogaret. He became quite open about his sexual preferences and even tried to blame me for them. His involvement in a lovers' triangle—Nogaret the object of interest for Villecourt and the Comte de Ragon—led to his demise. He died in a duel over his favorite male paramour." She opened her arms. "There. Now you know the horrid truth. All of it. Because of him, I've endured pitying looks, mortifying whispers." She held up a dainty finger an inch from the end of his nose. "I want you to know he didn't break me. He tried. But I remained strong, despite his vicious tongue, the humiliating gossip, the financial ruin. I don't want anyone's pity—"

Adrien pressed his fingers to her lips, silencing her. He'd lost all desire to use her as a pawn. He didn't have the stomach to put her through more scandal. He'd find another way, another opportunity to drive his point home to his sire. "I think you are strong and brave." He removed his hand from her soft lips. Those were words he'd never uttered to a woman before.

"Oh." Catherine's eyes softened. "Thank you . . . I truly meant it when I said I was sorry. I regret the trickery. But not our night." He didn't know why but her statement pleased him immensely. "If I had it to do again, I would proposition you instead of . . . doing what I did to your wine. If you will permit me, I have a proposition to make to you now."

"Oh?"

She bit her delectable bottom lip, something he was dying to do. "For your silence about the event that occurred five years ago, I will . . . I would be . . . your mistress for the next five days."

His semihard cock turned stone stiff at the inflaming offer. "For five days?"

"Yes, that's when Philbert will arrive." She glanced down and noticed the blatant bulge of his erection. When she looked up, she was smiling, clearly feeling confident of his answer. "What say you?"

Adrien tilted his head to the side. "For my silence you're willing to do this?"

"Yes. I am yours for five days." She clasped her hands behind her back—a purposeful pose that caused her bodice to gape open, giving him a better view of her tempting tits.

"Interesting . . . a day for every year since the masquerade." A day for every year he'd fantasized about her. Days and nights to indulge in each and every fantasy.

"Yes." She was still smiling.

He stepped closer, their bodies all but touching, and slipped his fingers under her chin. "Your proposition is difficult to refuse."

She maintained his regard, her golden eyes darkening with desire. "Is it now?"

He brushed his lips against her warm mouth. "Hmmm . . . it is."

"And"—she swallowed—"what is your answer . . . ?"

He trailed his mouth along her jaw to her ear. "My answer is . . ." he murmured and nipped at her earlobe, making her gasp. "No."

7

Catherine's mouth fell agape. She clamped it shut the moment she realized Adrien was stalking toward the door.

"Wait!" she called out.

To her relief, he stopped abruptly and turned around.

Flustered and suddenly afraid, she marched up to him. "Why not?" She gestured toward the bulge in his breeches. "You are clearly interested."

"I don't want a woman who is intent on playing a martyr in bed. I told you, I have no intention of telling the King or anyone about what happened between us. I came here for answers. You supplied them. The matter is done. Laid to rest. So, if you want sex, Catherine, say so. If you'd like to indulge in carnal pleasures with me for the next few days, be honest about it. I'll not entertain any more deceptions or denials from you. Speak to me of desire and I am interested. Speak to me of this ridiculous martyrdom, and I will direct my 'interest' elsewhere."

"All right! Yes, I desire you," she blurted out.

He crossed his arms. "Go on."

He wasn't going to make this easy, was he? "I have always desired you. From the moment I saw you across the Grand Salon at the masquerade that night, I . . . craved you. You stirred a hunger in me. I am famished for more. I've yearned for you countless nights. I want you to be my lover. I want to revel in all the carnal delights you can bestow. I want to know what I missed in my marriage bed and what I will miss in the next. Is that honest enough for you?"

His sinfully tempting mouth lifted in a smile. "It is an excellent start." He removed his justacorps and tossed the knee-length coat carelessly to the floor. "Here are the conditions for our interlude of bliss—"

"Conditions?"

He tilted her chin up with his strong, warm fingers. "My conditions are as follows: You will give me carte blanche in bed. You will let me have you as often as I want, any way I choose, without reservation or inhibitions getting in the way. Agreed?"

A thrill rippled down her spine. "Agreed."

Smiling, he pulled her up against his large sculpted body. "Good. This is a perfect time to begin, wouldn't you say?"

She flattened her palms on his chest. "Wait."

"Wait?"

"I haven't given you *my* conditions."

"*Your* conditions?" He asked the question as though no one had ever given him any.

"Yes. They are as follows: You will give me carte blanche in bed. You will let me have you as often as I want, any way I choose, without reservation or inhibitions getting in the way."

He burst into laughter. "Ah, Catherine, you are a delight. I am very much looking forward to the next few days, my spirited lady. It seems we are in accord." He lowered his head for a kiss.

She pressed her fingers against his lips, arresting his descent. "I'm not through. In addition, you will be all mine. For five days, there will be no other woman. Just me."

The astounded look on his handsome face was darling. Clearly, no one had ever made that request of him.

Catherine stepped back. "Well? What say you to that?"

The corner of his mouth jerked as he fought back his amusement. "I say you're about to obtain an unprecedented promise from me. I agree to your wish of exclusivity." He pulled her back into his arms. His delicious erection, so solid and thick, pressed enticingly against her belly. "Anything else? Or can we begin?"

"One last thing."

His head fell back with a groan. "What is it, *ma belle*? Be quick so that we can move on to more pleasurable pursuits."

"I wish the utmost discretion. No one is to know about our arrangement. The last thing I want is to give gossipmongers more to talk about. Or to cause Philbert the sort of pain and embarrassment Villecourt caused me."

Adrien's jaw tightened, his expression difficult to discern. Then he brushed his knuckles along her cheek. "No one will know," he softly pledged. Taking her hand, he pressed his hot mouth to her palm. Sensations tingled up her arm. "Come." His voice, low and husky, reverberated down to her sex.

He led her out of the antechamber into the bedchamber. Thinking about what he would do to her, what she wanted him to do to her, raced her pulse. She'd given him carte blanche. She couldn't explain it, this wanton she became around him. But she didn't dwell on it. Not when she was on fire for him.

Adrien was all hers for the next five days. She was going to relish every moment of it.

Stopping at the foot of the bed, he released her hand. His gaze perused her body. With her bodice open, she felt cool air against her heated skin, but it did nothing to diminish the fever he inspired. Anticipation made her tremble. The ache between her legs was fierce. If he didn't touch her soon, she'd die.

Impatient, Catherine pulled off the pearl necklace she'd borrowed from Suzanne and dropped it on the bed. Grabbing his shirt, she crushed her lips against his and thrust her tongue into his mouth. His taste was intoxicating. Her kiss was ravenous, stroking and sucking his tongue. Delirious with need, she couldn't get enough.

Cradling her face between his palms, he slanted his mouth over hers and gave her a slower, more languorous kiss.

Her frustration squeaked out her throat. Determined to quicken the pace, she reached down and grabbed hold of the ties on his breeches, desperate to free him of his clothing, to touch his skin once more, but her hands shook and her fingers fumbled.

He stilled her frantic hands. "I like your enthusiasm," he murmured against her mouth. "But there's no need to rush. We're going to savor every sensation. Slow down. I promise, it will be just as good."

Slow down? Was he mad? She was about to expire on the spot with lust. "I'd like to 'savor every sensation' quickly."

He let out a chuckle and shook his head. "Be patient."

His answer was exasperating, but at least he was untying his breeches. Riveted on his deft fingers, she doubted she'd notice if the room caught on fire.

At last, he freed his shirt from his breeches and removed it, tossing it to the floor.

Her eyes feasted on his strong shoulders. His chiseled chest. And—her gaze moved down his body—the impressive cock straining out of his breeches, the sight weakening her knees, making the nub between her legs throb.

The corner of his mouth rose as he clasped her wrist and brought her hand to his shaft. Catherine eagerly curled her fingers around him. His skin was warm, velvety, yet he was thick and solid. "Is this what you need, Catherine?"

Oh, God. "Yes."

"How long has it been since a man made you come the way I made you come today?"

He wanted to talk? *Now?*

"Tell me . . ." he urged softly. With his hold on her wrist, Adrien was keeping her from stroking him the way she yearned to.

She licked her dry lips. "Five years . . . two months . . . one week. The night of the masquerade . . . with you."

His green eyes darkened. *"Jésus-Christ.* Everything you do, everything you say makes me want to fuck you."

Joy and excitement fluttered in her belly. "Then take me."

He dipped his head and kissed the sensitive spot below her ear. "I will. I'll ride you all night long. You'd like that, wouldn't you?" He stroked her hand down the length of his erection and then back up. Her sex tightened and released hungrily. "Answer me, Catherine. Tell me you want my cock inside you all night long." Adrien trailed his mouth along her neck and released her hand, leaving her free to stroke him on her own.

"Yes. I want your . . . cock inside me. I want you to take me again and again until we're sated." She'd never spoken like this in her life. Never uttered such brazen statements. Never voiced her wants. Not for many years now. They'd always been ignored. Except by him. He'd been the only one who'd ever given her what she wanted.

"As you wish," he whispered in her ear; she heard the smile in his voice. Slipping his hand inside her opened bodice, he rolled her hardened nipple between his fingers, his delicious torment sending wave after wave of sharp pleasure streaking from the tip of her breast down to her heated core. Her sex ached to be filled. Enveloped by salacious sensations, she closed her eyes. Suddenly, her clothing was too hot, her skin too warm. The urges too powerful, thundering in her blood.

"Now . . . Adrien." She panted. "I need . . ."

"I know what you need, beautiful Catherine . . ." He stripped away her clothing, discarding each article onto the floor. She didn't care what he did with her clothes, though she had precious few good things left. She wanted her garments off. His garments off. His skin against her skin. She wanted him inside her and the divine friction their bodies created.

Catherine tried to help with the removal of her clothing, but ceased when she realized she was only impeding his progress. Instead, she used the moments to gaze at his beautiful face, desire and determination etched thereon.

As soon as her *caleçons* and chemise hit the floor, he tossed her onto the bed. She landed on the mattress with a surprised gasp and a small bounce. She rose onto her elbows, quivering from the inside out. Standing at the foot of the bed, Adrien discarded the remainder of his clothing.

"Open your legs for me," he growled in all his naked glory.

Her heart missed a beat. A heady rush of excitement swamped her. Slowly, she parted her thighs, her face feeling red-hot. One at a time, he sank his knees into the mattress between her legs.

"Bend your knees, Catherine. Let me look at all of you." He ran his warm palms over her trembling thighs.

Biting her lip, her heart wildly pounding, she obliged, leaving herself completely open to his view. His features softened, and he stroked his fingers along her slick flesh. A moan slipped past her lips. His touch was light and so deliciously decadent.

"You're very beautiful. Everywhere."

His words swirled around her heart, when she knew she shouldn't let them.

"I haven't forgotten a single detail about you," he said, amazement in his tone.

Neither had she, though not from lack of trying. No amount of wishing had made her unlearn what she'd discovered in his arms.

"You're wet. Ripe for the taking," he said with a wicked smile on his face. He lowered himself on top of her. His mouth was only inches from hers, their breaths, ragged and rapid, mingling together. The press of his body was sublime. Despite the urgency coursing through her veins, she tenderly brushed his dark hair from his brow and gently cradled his cheeks between her palms.

He grasped her wrists and lowered them to the bed. "Catherine, this is about sex. Mutual pleasure. Nothing more."

She wasn't going to allow herself to forget that. "I know." She thought she heard something in his voice, or perhaps it was the way in which he spoke his words, as though he was trying to convince not only her, but himself as well. She instantly dismissed the notion as absurd.

"This is definitely about sex," she said with a saucy smile. She played with fire. A novice at recreational fornication, she could be burned, but what woman could resist the allure of Adrien d'Aspe? He could have anyone, and yet, "You want me."

He arched a brow. "You want my cock," he countered.

"You want to give it to me."

A chuckle rumbled in his chest. "On that point I'll cede." He stroked his length along the slick folds of her sex, grazing the head of his shaft over her clitoris and back down, muffling her whimper with a hard kiss.

He released her wrists. She had her arms around him in an instant, returning his kiss with equal fervor.

He tore his mouth from hers. "To hell with this prolongation. It will be as you want—fast and hard." Rolling off, he flipped her onto her stomach.

Startled by the suddenness of his actions, she looked over her shoulder at him. "Adrien . . ."

His face contorted by desire, he snaked an arm under her hips and lifted her derrière in the air. Her fever spiked. "I'm going to give you what you want. What I want. What we're here for."

Her warm cheek against the cool sheets, she quaked with anticipation, her legs wobbly and weak, desperate for his possession.

He dug his fingers into her hips and wedged the head of his sex at her entrance. She choked back a sob. Instead of driving into her as she longed, he slowly slid his broad shaft inside her, stretching and filling her an inch at a time, working his way deeper and deeper.

He groaned. "You have the tightest, sweetest cunt."

She shut her eyes and gripped the sheets, unable to find her voice, to protest against his unhurried penetration. When he hit the door to her womb, her legs gave out. She collapsed to the bed, his body following hers down.

He reared then and used his strength and weight to drive his cock back into her, hard and deep. She cried out, enraptured. Trapped beneath him, his large form pressing her into the mattress, she took each powerful thrust, unable to move, the friction inflaming her further.

"This is how you want it, isn't it, Catherine?" he said near her ear between harsh breaths.

"Yes!" Her body was awash with sensations, her every nerve ending vibrating with life. She clenched her inner muscles. He let out a sharp groan. Realizing there was a way to affect him in this position after all, she clutched and released around his thick thrusting shaft. He grunted with each plunge as she milked him toward his climax.

Without breaking his rhythm, he shoved his hand under her hips and found the pulsing bud between her legs. He fingered her with devastating finesse. She whimpered, the beginnings of her orgasm rushing over her.

"Adrien . . . I'm . . . going to . . ."

"Come for me . . . Do it!" He pinched her clit.

Catherine screamed into the mattress, her release shaking her to the core. On her next breath she choked out a long, ragged sob. Of ecstasy. Of gratitude. And thankfulness. He was the greatest joy she'd ever known.

8

Catherine awoke to the sound of a steady heartbeat beneath her ear and two strong arms around her. Her cheek resting on a very masculine, solid chest, she peeked up to see Adrien fast asleep. Carefully, she rose onto her elbow and allowed herself the simple pleasure of gazing at him. His cheekbones, straight nose, jaw, and kissable mouth were etched forever in her mind. It was incredible, really. She'd envisioned this very visage for years and here he was. In the flesh. In her arms. Not just a fantasy come to life, but a dream come true.

Lightly, she caressed his cheek. He stirred in his sleep.

She couldn't hold back her smile.

The slight tenderness between her legs was a pleasing reminder of their glorious night. Unaccustomed to sexual excess, she should have been exhausted, but she wasn't. Not in the least. Last eve had been a night of incomparable bliss—so similar to their interlude five years ago when she'd awoken with the same rare sense of happiness that had nothing to do with the success of her ill-fated plan. And everything to do with him.

She didn't have to sneak away this time.

This time they'd enjoyed a compatibility that was not just physical. Between rapturous diversions, they'd laughed. Teased. Talked. Though she understood the boundaries of their relationship, she yearned to know more about this man. She sensed a profound unrest in him that resonated in her.

Catherine was about to snuggle back down beneath the bedding when a thought occurred to her.

Odette.

She glanced at the window. The sun shone brightly. It was well past dawn. Her loyal maid would arrive at any moment. Though she loved the woman dearly, eccentric in her ways, one never could predict Odette's behavior. It was best to avoid embarrassment all around and not have poor Odette stumble upon Adrien in her bed.

Reluctantly, Catherine eased herself from Adrien's arms.

Scooping up her chemise, she threw it on, quietly dashed from the bedchamber, softly closing the door behind her. She got three steps into the antechamber when she heard a woman's scream.

Catherine closed her eyes. *Too late.*

Wrenching open the door, she ran back into the other room.

Odette stood beside the bed with her hands covering her eyes. Adrien was sitting up, a murderous look directed at her maid, clearly irked by her presence and the way she'd startled him awake.

Why couldn't the woman have used the door in the antechamber, as was her practice, rather than the bedchamber door?

"Odette," Catherine said.

Upon hearing her name, her maid dropped her hands. Her

gaze shot to Catherine. "I—I'm sorry, madame. I—I had no idea you had . . . company." She glanced at Adrien, let out a squeak, and slapped her palms over her eyes once again.

Adrien rolled his eyes and reclined into the pillows.

From Catherine's vantage point, he was a sight to behold. His dark hair was mussed, his sculpted chest was bare, and the bedding lay tantalizingly across his waist—the outline of his shaft visible to her hungry eyes.

This was a first. She, Catherine de Villecourt, had never had a man with such potent appeal in her bed.

Stop ogling. Collect yourself. Say something.

She formed a smile. "Good morning, Adrien."

The wicked gleam in his eyes made her knees weak. "Good morning, Catherine." Oh, the way he said her name. She felt a quickening in her belly.

"If you will excuse me, I'll return momentarily." She grasped Odette's arm. The older woman's hands were still affixed to her face.

He slipped his hands under his head. "Hurry back." A slight smile tilted the corner of his mouth. Those two seemingly innocuous words held such sinful promise.

"I will." She dragged Odette toward the door to the antechamber. Tossing a glance at the older woman, she noticed her maid's head was slightly turned toward the bed and her fingers were separated, giving her left eye a clear view of Adrien.

"Odette," Catherine scolded in a firm whisper.

Odette's fingers immediately closed and her head snapped forward.

The moment they were behind closed doors, Odette removed her hands from her eyes and slapped them over her mouth just as a fit of giggles seized her.

Catherine placed her hands on her hips, ready to chastise her, but with her heart so light, she found herself fighting back a giant smile.

"Oh, madame, I'm sorry." Odette tried to sober up. "But it's just a delightful surprise . . ." Another giggle bubbled out of her. "Your handsome Marquis looks even better abed."

Catherine dropped her arms to her sides with a wistful sigh. "He does look very good, doesn't he?"

"Most definitely!" Odette's eyes widened. "And he is so big."

"Yes, he is a tall man."

"No, no, madame, I mean he is *large*." She held out her hands several inches apart and wiggled her brows.

Catherine blushed. "Odette, really now . . ."

"There is plenty there to delight a lady." Joviality erupted from her again. She covered her mouth once more to muffle it.

The last thing Catherine wanted to do was encourage Odette, but a full smile tugged hard at the corners of Catherine's lips, despite herself. "There is much about him that would delight any woman," she responded. There was much about Adrien d'Aspe that delighted *her*. Sinful skills, looks, and charm aside, to her surprise, he was an avid reader. He enjoyed books. He enjoyed all of the same Latin and Spanish classics as she did. Moreover, he had compassion. The understanding he'd demonstrated when she'd confided the circumstances surrounding the masquerade moved her. The kindness and interest he'd shown in her paintings touched her.

Catherine knew she was on dangerous ground. These tender emotions she felt would only bring heartache if she didn't somehow quash them.

"I take it you've worked things out with Monsieur le Marquis, then?"

"Yes, we are in accord. In fact, for the next few days I need you to—"

"Say no more, madame. What happened just now will not be repeated. I'll be most discreet and circumspect. Now, go on. Enjoy your handsome Marquis." Odette rushed to the door leading to the hallway, then stopped and turned with a smile. "Madame, if I may say one last thing before I go?"

"Of course. What is it, Odette?"

"I'm so very happy to see you like this. If you could only see your face . . . It is aglow. And your eyes sparkle as they never have before."

Three days later.

The scent of jasmine lingered on his skin as Adrien strolled back to his rooms with a smile. Memories of the last few hours making love to Catherine ran through his mind. He'd awoken her that morning by gently sucking her clit; the friction of his tongue and the pull of his mouth as he alternated licking and suckling her sweet bud had sent her straight into a strong orgasm.

Each afternoon they'd sneaked back to her chambers. Each morning he left her rooms later than the day before.

The fact that he stayed the night—every night—was novel in itself. He found himself anxiously awaiting their next private moment. The next stirring kiss from her luscious mouth.

He couldn't remember a time when he'd enjoyed a woman's company more. Deliciously sensual, intelligent, beautiful, and brave, she was a breath of fresh air in his stifling world.

Catherine was different from other women. Everything with her was different. He *wanted* to know more about her and about her interests. Seeing the happy glow in her amber-colored eyes as she spoke of her painting and her favorite books pleased him more than he could ever admit. This level of intimacy was new to him, and he didn't know why or how she'd inspired it.

He refused to dwell on his unprecedented actions or try to decipher the meaning behind them. They had two days and nights left. He wanted to revel in every moment with her. Stay in the present and not consider the future when she left.

Thinking about Catherine back in his arms in a few short hours quickened his heart. His smile grew. He had a plan for this afternoon he knew would delight her.

Reaching the door to his chambers, he opened the latch and entered his rooms. Charlotte was seated near the window. She rose as he closed the door.

"What are you doing here, Charlotte? You have your own private apartments."

A smile formed on her face. "Your bed hasn't been slept in."

"So?"

"So, you've been entertaining Catherine de Villecourt."

He sighed, resentful that his genial mood was about to be threatened. "Charlotte . . ." he began and tossed his justacorps onto a nearby chair.

"You're doing admirably! The plan is working beautifully."

Adrien took in a deep breath and let it out slowly, grasping for patience. "I am not doing 'admirably.' There is no plan. I'm not going to be part of your scheme, Charlotte."

"Ah, but you are." She walked up to him and placed her hand on his arm. "I've seen the way she looks at you in the gardens, at each meal, when she thinks no one is observing her. She's quite smitten."

"Catherine is not the problem. Whether she marries Baillet or not, it won't change your situation."

"It will! Philbert wouldn't be so distracted . . . Things between us will be as they were before." Her eyes glistened with tears. "I already lost Jean-Paul. His death almost killed me. I cannot lose Philbert, too."

"Charlotte, you are looking for someone to blame for Baillet's disinterest, but the reality is—"

"Stop!" She pressed a trembling hand against his chest. "I don't want to hear any more. Philbert still loves me. He does! You'll not convince me otherwise. You don't know him as I do."

"Charlotte, if he loved you, no woman could distract him, *ma chère*. Don't you see that?"

"Wh-Why are you being so cruel?" Tears spilled down her cheeks. "Why do you want to hurt me? Just because you're not happy, you don't want me to be happy." She ran to the door, audibly sobbing.

"Charlotte, wait! That's not it. I want your happiness."

Grabbing the door latch, she threw him a vicious glare. "I hate you, Adrien," she cried. "*I hate you.*" She ran from the room as if he were Lucifer himself.

Adrien remained frozen, the air around him suddenly heavy and cold.

Sinking into a chair, he rested his elbows on his thighs and shook his head. *Merde*, how had things come full circle? How many times had he heard one of his uncles have the very same conversation with his mother? How many times had his mother reacted just as Charlotte had? There was no point chasing after Charlotte. She'd be inconsolable for hours yet.

Tossing his head back, he closed his eyes and took in a fortifying breath. This was what happened when one blurred the lines between sex and love. A mistake he'd never make. The soft sentiments he was feeling for Catherine had to be reined in. Kept in check.

She was his *temporary* mistress.

In two days she'd be gone. In two days he would have satiated himself. He had two more days in which to purge her from his blood and mind. He couldn't, wouldn't, crave her or think of her after that.

With renewed determination, he stalked out of his rooms intent on making afternoon arrangements with his lovely midnight temptress.

In his experience the only thing that cooled a carnal fever was sexual excess.

9

"A few steps farther," Adrien said behind Catherine, his warm hands covering her eyes.

Trusting him implicitly, she moved forward, letting him guide her blindly.

"Perfect." He arrested her steps and pulled his hands away.

She opened her eyes and grinned, ridiculously happy over the sight before her.

In a clearing, beneath a large tree, in the forest that bordered Suzanne's grounds, a blanket had been spread, encircled by flower petals of white, yellow, and lavender. A basket of food had been placed nearby.

A picnic.

It was lovely!

Catherine turned and wrapped her arms around his neck.

The gray skies overhead let out a grumble.

She ignored the distant thunder. This moment was too perfect. Keeping their encounters secret hadn't been easy. He'd gone to such touching lengths to make these preparations.

"You planned all this for me." It was a statement. She was incredulous.

"Of course." He was smiling. "You're pleased?"

She gazed at his beloved face. "I am. Thank you. No one has ever done anything like this for me before."

He pulled her tightly against him, his erection pressing against her. Arousal flared low in her belly. "Well, then, I'm honored to be the first."

Oh, he was her first in so many ways. Her first lover. The only man to inspire her affections. She'd tried to fight her feelings with all she possessed, telling herself the joys he brought her were only physical. That she wasn't in love with him.

All unconvincing lies.

In truth, he'd slipped inside her heart—years ago. The times she'd spent with him were the happiest she'd ever known. But time was running out.

Glancing up at the sky, she was dismayed by the threat of rain in the darkened clouds. The day had started out sunny, but the sky became angrier as the hours passed.

"Forget the weather," he said. "We'll not allow anything to ruin our picnic." He gently brushed an errant tress from her cheek. "Now, where were we . . . Ah, yes, you were voicing words of appreciation for my efforts." He gave her one of his disarming smiles. "I am open to any and all expressions of gratitude, you know."

She laughed. "Are you now?" The cheeky devil oozed charm.

"I am," he assured. "However, I am happy to provide nourishment first." He nodded toward the picnic basket.

"That's excellent. I'm starved . . . *for you.*" She caressed the side of his face.

Hunger flickered in his eyes. He leaned in for a kiss, sliding his tongue past her lips. Waves of pleasure flooded her body at his possession. His kiss was heated, yet unhurried and tender, resonating inside her heart.

Raindrops hit her shoulders, despite the leafy canopy overhead. She didn't care, refusing to break contact with his mouth. She wanted more. Of him. How was she going to live without him again? He made her long for the things she used to dream about. Romantic notions of loving and being loved.

The sky rumbled. More raindrops struck her heated skin.

Adrien broke the kiss and swore at the inclement weather brewing in the clouds, its quick turn for the worse dampening their plans.

She reached for the ties on his breeches. "We'll not allow anything to ruin our picnic." She repeated his words.

He frowned. "It's raining, *ma belle.*"

"It doesn't matter." She pulled his shirt out from his opened breeches. "Take this off."

He gave her one of his heart-fluttering smiles and removed his shirt, tossing it onto the blanket. His thick, hard cock strained out of his breeches.

A steady drizzle now fell from the sky. She watched with heated fascination as water droplets hit his chest and rolled down his skin, dripped off his stiff sex.

Desire swamped her senses. She had to touch him. Curling her fingers around his shaft, she stroked him, moving her hand languidly up and down his length.

He groaned. His mouth was on hers in an instant, his skilled fingers pulling and loosening and opening the front of her gown, exposing her to her waist.

Cool rain against her warm breasts was startling. Exhilarating. His hot mouth latched on to her breast. He sucked greedily. Each tantalizing pull dragged a moan up her throat and made her sex wetter. She arched to him, her fingers tangling in his damp hair. He turned to her other breast and feasted on it with equal finesse. Suckling. Laving. Gently biting. Her legs almost gave way.

The moment his mouth returned to hers, she kissed him voraciously, trailing her mouth along his jaw, down his neck, his chest. His wet skin was delicious. But it wasn't enough. After a night of oral pleasures—not to mention the morning, too—she had to taste him again, hungry to have him in her mouth. Only two days left to create memories she'd cherish for a lifetime. Then he'd be gone for good. She pushed back the sadness and regret and lowered herself to her knees.

His eyes narrowed, knowing exactly what she was about. She looked up at him, rain on her face. His dark hair wet, he fixed his green eyes on her. Holding his gaze, she gripped the base of his erection and brushed her lips across the sensitive tip. His breath hitched. Reveling in his heated response, she swirled her tongue around the head of his penis.

"Catherine," he rasped, his fingers gripping her head.

Impatient, she plunged him deep into her mouth. A throaty growl erupted out of him, his hips jerking slightly.

"*Dieu* . . ." Adrien had to close his eyes, his head falling back. If the feel of her sucking his cock weren't enough, the sight of her submissively on her knees pleasuring him was too much. "I love your mouth," he groaned. It took everything he had not to grab her hair and thrust like a madman. Instead, he let her dictate the pace.

His ragged breaths mingled with the sounds of rain. The cool raindrops teeming over his bare chest and arms were a magnificent contrast to the heat of her mouth. She drew him in and dragged him out, tender, yet ravenous—so uniquely Catherine. She had him on fire, as always.

Every fiber of his being was acutely aware not only of the sensations inundating him, but of the very woman inspiring them. He was going to come. Hard. Soon. But not this way. Not this time.

Opening his eyes, their gazes locked. She slid him out of her mouth and licked off the dab of pre-come that dripped from his tip. Strands of her auburn hair were plastered to her shoulders and wet creamy breasts. Gently removing her hand from his cock, Adrien lowered himself to his knees, the blanket wet, and cupped her face.

She furrowed her delicate brow. "Have I done something incorrectly?"

"No, you were perfect." She was, in every way that mattered. Everything a man could want and more.

And he wanted her—too much.

Threading his fingers through her wet hair, he ran his tongue along her bottom lip before giving her a long, languorous kiss. A shiver of delight quivered through her.

"I want to make love to you." He sat down on the blanket, not caring that it was soaked. "Come here." His voice was rough with need.

The sweetest smile graced her lips.

A few easy movements and his auburn beauty was straddling him. She slipped her arms around him. Her breaths were sharp and shallow, much like his own. A surge of emotions he couldn't quell crested over him.

Jésus-Christ, he simply had to break this infatuation. What if he couldn't? What if years from now he still felt this constricting ache in his chest?

Adrien shoved away the doubts, and her gown, bunching the material around her waist. He then gripped her hips, intent on refocusing on the carnal pleasures at hand.

"I am all yours," she said softly, placing her hands on his wet shoulders.

Her words unbalanced him.

She was *not* all his, he quickly reminded himself. Even if he wished it at the moment. In time the feeling would pass. He wasn't going to do anything to hold on to her or deviate from old patterns and familiar ways.

She rose up and brought her slick opening down onto the head of his cock, the enticing heat beckoning and beguiling. Her pink nipples, at mouth level, dripped with raindrops.

Adrien leaned in and licked the water droplets off each sensitive tip.

She moaned and then suddenly bore down onto his erection. Clutching her hips, he halted her descent. "Too fast. Take it slowly." Adrien eased her onto his cock, her moist heat engulfed him an inch at a time.

She squirmed, frustrated by his slow progress.

"Don't fight me. Just enjoy it." He was going to squeeze out every ounce of pleasure he could from the encounters they had left, hoping it would be enough to silence the maddening turmoil whirling inside him.

The head of his shaft butted against her womb. He gasped. She whimpered.

Buried to the hilt, his cock throbbed inside her snug sheath. She encircled him with her legs. Adrien closed his eyes and held her still. Enveloped by her, he basked in the moment.

Endearingly impatient, it wasn't long before she was rocking her hips, fanning the fire, making his heart pound. She clenched her inner muscles around his cock. A groan shot up his throat.

Kissing his face, mouth, neck, she told him how much she wanted him, needed him, needed what he could give her. Adrien's control snapped. In an instant, he had her on her back, giving her deep, steady strokes, using his body to shield her from the rain. Holding her gaze, he increased the tempo and force of his thrusts with each downward plunge.

Desire shone in her golden eyes. Yearning was etched on her lovely face.

"You're so very beautiful," he murmured.

Her hands moved tenderly down his back, despite her fervent state. "So are you."

Her artlessness during sex was adorable.

The tension coiling tighter and tighter, they were racing toward a shattering release. Shaking with effort, he held his back, the need to let go and discharge his aching cock immense.

She sucked in a sharp breath, squeezed her eyes shut, and arched hard against him. "Adrien," she cried. He braced himself. Her orgasm shuddered through her, tearing a scream from her throat.

Fisting the blanket on either side of her head, Adrien thrust fiercely, glorious spasms rippling along his length. His climax triggered, his release shot down his cock with such volatile force, he barely pulled out in time. Collapsing on top of her, he pressed his forehead to hers and groaned long and hard as he drained his prick onto the blanket with mind-melting intensity.

Spent, trembling, they held each other, the rain drizzling onto his back, their breathing slowly calming.

This was bliss. How fortunate was he to be given this taste of Heaven.

Another roll of thunder sounded in the sky.

* * *

Catherine and Adrien stopped outside the servants' entrance to the château. Catherine sighed as he gave her a deep, stirring kiss. They were drenched, their clothing ruined, and neither of them cared. They'd walked back in the heavy rain, hand in hand, occasionally stopping for kisses and caresses.

"I'm sorry our picnic was spoiled," he murmured. "The food was ruined."

"I don't think the picnic was spoiled at all. I enjoyed every moment."

A smile formed on his lips. "So did I."

She cocked her head to one side. "I'm sure the rain has nothing to do with the fact that you're cursed," she teased.

His brows shot up. "Don't tell me you've heard about that. What version of that foolish tale was recounted? The one with magical fairies at my christening?"

She laughed. "I missed that version."

"There is no curse," he assured. "I don't get along with my father. Plain and simple. He doesn't approve of the way I live my life. He thinks me too reckless."

"And are you?"

He brushed his mouth against hers. "I'm just reckless enough."

He kissed her again, a slow, inflaming kiss that warmed her blood, heating her from the inside out.

Thunder boomed. She jumped.

Adrien looked up at the sky, rain drizzling on his face. "We'd best get inside." He took her hand. "There will be more of the same on your dry bed," he wickedly promised.

The moment they stepped into the kitchens, Odette swooped in on them. "Madame!" Concern etched on her face, she wrung her hands.

Catherine tensed. "What is it, Odette?"

The older woman looked around to ensure none of the servants in the kitchen were listening.

"It's the Comte de Baillet," she whispered. "He's here."

Her words hit Catherine like a blow to the belly.

"He's arrived? *Early?*" Adrien asked the questions she couldn't force up her throat.

"Yes, monsieur. Early." Odette looked at Catherine. "He's asking for you. He's eager to see you."

Adrien tightened his hold of Catherine's hand. "It's too soon. He's not supposed to be here now," he growled.

Tears burned in her eyes. Catherine turned to him, overcome by a sense of cold grief and sadness. "I know," she managed to say without collapsing into complete discomposure. Their time together was over. She'd have to leave. Every fiber in her being screamed "no!"

"Madame, we must get you upstairs, bathed, and changed into some dry clothes. I told Monsieur le Comte that you were taking a nap. He'll expect you up soon."

Catherine gazed at Adrien's cherished face, a lump welling in her throat.

He cupped her cheek. "I'll see you later," he stated firmly and kissed her trembling mouth.

"Come, madame." Odette pulled at her hand. "You must hurry."

Her chest tight, her heart constricted, she let Odette lead her away.

Time was up. There'd be no later.

10

In the *Salle de Buffet*, flanked by his uncles, Adrien held his goblet in a white-knuckle grip. He hadn't touched any of his meal. At the opposite end of the long table Catherine sat with Baillet and Suzanne. The dimwitted Madame de Noisette and Madame de Bussy were nearby, enraptured by Baillet's tales of his recent visit to Versailles.

Adrien was drowning in emotions he'd forbidden himself to feel. Choking on his own misery.

Catherine was leaving.

Too damned soon.

Damn Baillet and his early arrival. Adrien felt cheated and furious at the situation. And at himself, for allowing feelings to foster.

"Perhaps we should check on Charlotte?" Paul suggested. "She was quite overwrought after her visit with Baillet this afternoon."

Charles shook his head. "Leave her be. She sleeps, the seasoned wine thankfully aiding in that regard."

Wine seasoned with the juice from unripe poppies. A concoction Adrien's mother had often consumed, especially after visits from his father. Today Baillet advised Charlotte that he wasn't interested in her company any longer—of course, only *after* a final fuck.

Charlotte was devastated.

News of his sister's distress only added fuel to Adrien's ire.

Eyes narrowed, Adrien drained his goblet as he watched Baillet dip his head toward Catherine in conversation, blocking her from his view. Seeing his proximity to her was torture. The thought of Baillet claiming his conjugal rights was all consuming.

"I should call him out," Adrien snarled. A murderous rage burbled in his blood.

"For what?" Robert asked. "For dismissing his mistress? Does a man not have the right to end an affair when he wants, Adrien? Let it alone. Dueling Baillet over something like this would definitely set off the King."

His father could go to hell, for all he cared.

"Your contempt for Baillet isn't simply over Charlotte," Paul said. "The lovely Catherine de Villecourt plays a part, no?"

Baillet sat back and covered Catherine's hand with his.

The possessive gesture was a stinging sight.

Adrien looked away. "I need to speak to her." He rose, his chair dragging across the wooden floor.

Charles's eyes widened. "Now?"

"Yes. Now. This minute." *Merde*, the anguish was unbearable. "Have Suzanne escort her to the library—alone. Keep Baillet busy in the meantime. Perhaps expressing some dismay over his treatment of Charlotte, regardless of his 'rights,' would not only be warranted, but will also keep him occupied."

*   *   *

Adrien paced in the library, his heart beating in hard, rapid thumps. He was on unfamiliar ground. For the first time in his adult life, a woman had slipped past his defenses. The fact that an affair was dwindling down was not new—only the reactions he was having.

The door opened.

He stopped dead in his tracks as Catherine stepped inside and Suzanne quietly left, closing the door without a word.

His eyes devoured the sight of her. His midnight temptress. An angel. In but a simple yellow gown, her hair up with long auburn ringlets teasing her shoulders, she was ravishing.

Unshed tears glistened in her eyes, her sorrowful expression stabbing into him.

The next thing he knew, he'd crossed the distance between them and was holding her in his arms. "Catherine . . ." he breathed, pressing his cheek against her soft hair.

She trembled. So did he.

Adrien looked down at her upturned face and swooped in for a hungry kiss, needing her mouth with shocking desperation.

She broke the kiss sooner than he wanted. "Adrien . . . I'm leaving tomorrow."

His stomach clenched. "Why so soon? You are not getting married for another two weeks."

"He wishes to return to Baillet. I must go with him."

Don't go. Stay with me. Adrien swallowed down the words just in time. He hadn't uttered those words in years. Not since a life-altering day. He wouldn't beg. Or plead. Or lay himself emotionally bare that way. He'd never utter those words to anyone again.

"One last time." He caressed her cheek. "I need you one last time." He prayed for a miracle. For it to be enough to sate his need for her at last. Somehow, someway, he had to silence what he was feeling. Her leaving was tearing him apart. "I'll come to your rooms—"

She shook her head and pulled free of his embrace. "I can't. Now that he is here—"

"He'll be in your bed tonight?" The question tumbled from Adrien's lips, uncensored.

"No. He'll not come to my bed until we're wedded. He has said as much. But . . ." A tear slipped down her cheek. She swiped it away. "Getting in that carriage tomorrow and leaving here, leaving . . . you . . . will be difficult enough as it is. If I spend the night in your arms . . . then tomorrow . . . the departure . . . will be unendurable torture."

Adrien turned away the moment he felt the mortifying sting of tears in his eyes. He was horrified by them. He was heartsick. The pain was so keen, like a blade slicing through him by slow, excruciating degrees. This pain he knew. This was the pain he'd spent much of his life avoiding.

He spotted the brandy decanter on the ebony side table and stalked to it. Snatching up a goblet, he filled it with the amber liquid, his hands shaking. *Merde, collect yourself!*

By strength of will he'd master his emotions. He'd done so before. There was no reason to believe he couldn't do it again.

Adrien downed the fiery fluid, desperate for it to numb his insides. He heard her approach.

Catherine stopped beside him. He could see her from the corner of his eye, but couldn't bring himself to look at her. Instead, he stared at the goblet in his trembling hand as he fought to calm his sharp breaths.

She pulled the goblet from his grasp and placed it on the side table. "Adrien."

Against his better judgment, he met her gaze. Her lovely golden eyes were still filled with tears.

"I know this was supposed to be nothing more than an interlude of bliss," she said. "I understand the nature of our arrangement. I tried to hold to it, but couldn't separate heart and body. Sex and . . . love."

A lump welled in his throat. He wanted to tell her to stop, to say no more, but couldn't summon his voice.

"I love you, Adrien. What you have given me are memories I will treasure for the rest of my days."

He flinched. Women had uttered those words to him before. Why, when she spoke them, did he feel his soul tear? From her lips they had a stunning impact.

She cradled his face between her warm palms. Rising up onto the balls of her feet, she kissed him, her tears on her sweet lips.

The kiss was soft, poignant. It made him ache, heart, body, and soul. His eyes closed of their own volition and he returned her kiss, unable to resist. Yet somehow, someway, though he yearned to touch her with every fiber of his being, he managed to keep his hands to himself, fearing that if he put his arms around her now, he'd never let go.

She broke the kiss. "Forgive me, but I wanted you to know how I felt. How much you mean to me. Thank you for what you've given me. I will think of you every day. And every night. You will be in my fondest dreams and most cherished thoughts." She stepped back.

He knew she was about to leave the room and walk out of his life.

Say something. Don't let her go. The voice rose from the empty chambers in his heart. But as Adrien stared back at her, he felt familiar walls rising up, steeling his resolve.

He cleared his throat before he croaked out, "I . . . wish you . . . much happiness."

With a woeful smile and a soft "thank you," she spun on her heel and walked out of the library, closing the door softly. With finality.

The silence roared in his ears.

In muted misery, Adrien stood alone for countless minutes, his chest heaving from the sheer exertion it took not to run to her.

Finally, he drew in a ragged breath and let it out slowly. He left the room on shaky limbs, forcing each foot forward, the decanter of brandy clutched firmly in one hand.

* * *

Cold water splashed him in the face. Adrien sat bolt upright, startled out of slumber. A sharp pain ripped through his head.

Clutching his throbbing skull, he shot a string of expletives out of his mouth.

"Ah, good, you're awake," Charles said, holding an empty pitcher in his hand.

Adrien turned a dry raw eye to him. "*Merde*, what are you trying to do? Drown me?"

"I thought that is what you were doing to yourself—with brandy."

He was in no mood for this. He'd spent the night and into the early morning hours imbibing, trying to obliterate visions of Catherine in Baillet's arms.

In Baillet's bed.

"Go away," Adrien snarled. Thanks to his uncle's antics, he and his bed were drenched.

"We need to talk. About women."

Adrien closed his eyes, willing the pounding in his brandy-soaked brain to stop. "You explained 'the mysteries of a woman's body' to me years ago, Uncle. I know everything I need to know about sex."

"Don't be so damned sarcastic. What I have to say to you is important. It involves your very happiness and future."

At the moment, the words "happiness" and "future" didn't seem to fit together.

The only thing greater than his headache was his longing for Catherine. Looking into the future, he had no idea when this torment would end, though he had every intention of ending it, by any means necessary.

Charles stalked to the windows and threw open the curtains. Adrien squeezed his eyes shut against the blinding sunlight and cursed softly.

He heard his uncle pull a chair up beside his bed.

"I was much like you at your age," Charles said.

Jésus-Christ, he was serious about his desire to talk.

"Only I was better looking," Charles added.

Adrien pried open an eye and cast him a sidelong glance.

Seated, Charles chuckled and crossed his arms. "I see I have your attention. Good, then I'll continue. Like you, I too had my share of women. Still do, by the way."

"Uncle." Adrien opened both eyes as far as a squint, the light still too bright to tolerate. "I am well aware of your impressive sexual prowess. We are in accord on that point. What say you to ending this conversation?" All he wanted to do was sleep. Not think. Not talk. Or feel. Just sleep. Judging by the amount of sunlight in the room, the day had begun hours ago. He'd had very little repose.

"I say no. I also say you're a fool. I know fools. I am one, too. Like you, I fell in love once."

Adrien was about to rebut when Charles held up a hand. "Say nothing. I saw your face last night when you looked at Catherine de Villecourt. You are in love with her. As in love as I was, *am still*, with her aunt, Elise—even these many years after her passing. I was about your age when I met her. She, like her niece, was beautiful." Charles's smile was woeful. "I used to think that love was as repugnant as an affliction. I'd seen it turn the brightest men into dimwits, while others writhed in agony when it slipped from their grasp. In short, love held no appeal for me." Charles unfolded his arms and briefly looked down at his hands. When he raised his gaze, Adrien saw his own anguish mirrored in his uncle's eyes. "I let her go, Adrien. I was madly, deeply in love and I let Elise go. I could have married her. We would have had joy-filled years together, perhaps even a child. Instead, I've had years of empty encounters and meaningless moments."

Adrien was speechless. This was a side of Charles he'd never known.

"Don't be as imbecilic as I, Adrien. Don't let Baillet have her. He doesn't deserve her. It isn't too late. She left a few hours ago. They'll be stopping at the town of Maillard for the night. Go to her. Tell her you love her."

The door burst open.

Robert and Paul entered, anxious expressions on their faces.

"Charlotte is gone." Paul held up a letter.

"What do you mean, gone?" Adrien rose from the bed, ignoring the stabbing pain that hit him between the eyes. His empty stomach roiled.

Robert snatched the letter from Paul's hand and brought it to Adrien. "When we went to check on her, we found this. She says she's going after Baillet. She refuses to let him go. She blames Catherine for everything. She's intent on *'removing the obstacle'* from her path. "

Adrien forced his eyes to focus on the parchment in his hands, scanning its contents. Charlotte's venom astounded him, his heart quickening with each incensed, irrational word she wrote. Her final phrase knocked the breath from his lungs.

. . . and I have the means to do it.

Jésus-Christ! Terror slammed into him. Adrien snagged his baldric and ran from the room in the direction of the stables, his uncles on his heels.

* * *

Pushing the horses to their limit, Adrien and his uncles raced toward Maillard, only to be halted abruptly upon entering the town.

Adrien's heart plummeted.

Shops on the main floors, homes directly above, the roads and abodes were filled with activity; the streets chaotic and clogged. Its calamity spiked his frustration and anxiety as Adrien and his uncles maneuvered their way through the mass, unable to race the final stretch of the two-and-a-half-hour journey.

Two-and-a-half torturous, fear-laden hours.

The sun burned down upon him. Wiping the sweat from his

brow with a sweep of his sleeve, Adrien desperately searched for the inn. Shouts from the windows above, haggling merchants and customers, squeals and laughter of dashing children, and the nickering of horses clashed together, and yet it was all a distant din. Adrien's heart was pounding so fiercely, it resonated in his ears, muffling the noise.

"You there!" he called out to a pauper who caught his eye in the throng. "Where is the inn?"

"To the left." He pointed up the street. "The first street to the left, my lord."

Adrien's gaze darted in the direction. It wasn't far, but with the congestion before him, it was going to take a while. He tossed the pauper a coin and began shouting to those blocking his path. It moved people along. Too slowly. It was all too damned slow!

Every horrible scenario of what Charlotte might do tormented his mind and twisted his entrails. He prayed, he prayed, he prayed he was in time.

From her note, Charlotte wasn't going to stop until Catherine was dead. Even more terrifying was the fact that Catherine was completely unaware Charlotte had been Baillet's mistress. His sister could easily fabricate an explanation as to why she was at the inn.

Catherine wouldn't have any reason to mistrust her.

Would Baillet notice Charlotte? Would he somehow foil her plans? Adrien desperately hoped so.

Finally turning the corner, Adrien spotted the inn at the end of the cobblestone road that was lined by three-story half-timbered buildings. He was almost there. His heart hammered harder. The inn was ever nearing. But not fast enough. *Merde.* Too many carts, horses, and people were in the way. Every minute mattered. Ready to jump out of his very skin, Adrien could wait no longer.

He leaped off his horse in the middle of the street, leaving it for his uncles to attend to, pushing and shoving his way through the afternoon crowds. His destination—the front doors of the inn.

The moment he tore across its threshold, he stopped dead in his tracks, giving his eyes a moment to adjust to the darker interior. He heard weeping. A woman's tears.

Scanning the few occupants in the room, some standing, some seated at the tables before him, he spotted Catherine's maid and Baillet in the far corner.

Odette pleaded. She wept.

His blood froze. Seeing how distraught she was, he knew he was too late. Dear God, something had happened to Catherine.

The maid met his gaze. "Monsieur!" She rushed to him.

Adrien gripped her shoulders. "What has happened?"

Tossing a quick glance about, Odette lowered her shaky voice, "Your sister . . . she has . . . poisoned my madame. My sweet, kind madame." Her chin dropped. She wept harder, her shoulders shaking.

Adrien's knees almost gave way.

"Y-Your sister has locked herself in one of the rooms upstairs, and won't come out," she bemoaned. "Sh-She has the antidote. She won't hand it over. I don't know if it's too late. I don't know what poison she gave her." Tears welled from her eyes. "She's in a terrible way. . . and Monsieur de Baillet refuses to help. He-He's leaving."

Baillet approached then, his expression bland. "That's correct. I am leaving." He looked pointedly at Adrien. "I hope you enjoyed fucking my betrothed. It seems you did such a thorough job of it, she's no longer interested in marrying me. None of this"—he gestured toward Odette—"is any of my concern."

"You would actually leave her to *die*?" Adrien asked, stunned.

"As I said, this isn't my problem. I do, however, intend to speak to His Majesty about your sister. I feel it is my duty to rid society of this madwoman. She tainted the broth and then admitted to it. For God's sake, she could have killed me."

Adrien snapped. Grabbing Baillet by the lapels of his justacorps, he slammed him backward onto a nearby table.

"You are to blame for all of this!" Adrien bellowed.

Baillet stared up at him, his eyes wide with fear. "Un-Unhand me!" His hands flew to Adrien's wrists, but he couldn't pry himself loose.

"You toyed with Charlotte's affections! You used her. You misled her into thinking you cared. *You* brought this on!" He pulled Baillet up then slammed him back down, so that his head struck the table with brute force. Baillet yelped. "You'll not speak a word of this to the King, Madame de Maintenon, or anyone, for if you do, I'll call you out and end your worthless life."

"Your—your sister poisoned a lady. That is against the law!" Baillet was foolish enough to protest.

"It will be Catherine's word against yours, since she is the one lying on a bed right now. Not you."

Adrien released Baillet.

Baillet sat up and smoothed his jacket. "If she lives."

Rage exploded inside him. Adrien smashed his fist into Baillet's jaw, knocking him off the table and onto the stone floor.

"Adrien!" Paul rushed in and grabbed his arm, Robert and Charles following directly behind. "Leave him to us. Go help your lady."

Charles and Robert were already yanking a disoriented Baillet to his feet none too gently.

Adrien turned and ran up the stairs, two at a time. Odette was quickly on his heels, calling out which room. Upon bursting into Catherine's room, the air shot out of his lungs, the sight before him hitting him like a physical blow. Leaving him cold and breathless.

Her auburn hair was fanned out on the pillow. A delicate hand clutched her stomach as she softly moaned and writhed, eyes shut. Horrified, he moved closer.

She was pale, so pale. Her complexion was almost gray.

Odette sobbed anew. "The pain gets worse at times. She had the tainted broth over an hour ago . . ."

Adrien sank down on the edge of the bed, taking Catherine's hand in his. Her skin was cold. Clammy.

She opened her eyes. "Adrien," she breathed.

A knot welled in his throat. He pressed a kiss to the back of her hand. "I am here, *ma belle*."

"Your sister and Baillet . . ."

"I should have told you she was his mistress," he choked out. "I'm sorry."

Again he kissed her hand again, fighting to maintain his composure. "Please forgive me, for . . . not being forthright, about my sister, about my affections. I love you." Tears blurred her sweet face. He cupped her cheeks. "I am going to make this right. Stay strong. You are going to be fine. I'll make certain of it." He kissed her brow. "I love you, Catherine."

A small smile graced her lips as a single tear slipped out of the corner of her eye.

* * *

"Charlotte!" He smashed his fist against her locked door, her room close to Catherine's. "Open this door."

Silence.

He slammed his shoulder into the wooden barrier. It gave but did not open. "Charlotte!" With fury and fear, he slammed his shoulder into the portal once more.

It flew open.

He found Charlotte curled up like a child, her arms tightly wrapped around her legs, crouching in the corner of the room on the floor. Her eyes red and swollen, she'd been crying extensively. She made such a pathetic sight, it momentarily unbalanced Adrien.

"*Dieu*, Charlotte, what have you done?"

Large tears streamed down her face. "I—I wanted him to . . . l-love me . . . He—He doesn't love me." She sobbed, anguished. Broken.

He crouched down to her level. "I love you, Charlotte," he said, keeping his voice soft. "I am begging you to help Catherine."

She shot to her feet, startling him. "NO!"

It was then Adrien noticed a small pouch clutched in each of her hands.

"I hate her! She has his heart." Her bottom lip quivered as she inched her way to the window. If what she had in the pouches was the antidote, he feared she'd scatter the powders to the wind.

"No, Charlotte. She doesn't. She's not going to marry him. There isn't going to be a wedding. She doesn't have his heart. He left, without a care over her condition."

Her watery eyes widened slightly. "He—He did?"

"He isn't capable of loving anyone. Please . . . Charlotte . . . Please, tell me you have the antidote."

"Of course I do. The witch advised me to purchase both . . . in case the wrong person takes the poison. Sometimes these things are difficult to contain."

He didn't want a lengthy discussion. Or details of her misdeed. Time was of the essence. Still crouched he held out his hand. "Please, give me the antidote."

She moved closer to the window. His stomach tightened with terror.

"Why? So you can save her? You love her more than me."

He lowered his arm. "I am trying to save your life, can you not see that? If Catherine . . . dies . . . you'll be arrested and executed."

She froze.

With a strangled cry, she pressed one pouch-filled hand to her mouth. "I . . . d-don't want that." She cried hard, her shoulders slumped.

"Then give me the antidote, and I swear, I won't let anyone harm you. You'll return home. To Hôtel d'Aspe. You'll be with family who love you."

She shook her head. "No . . . noooo . . ." She moaned. ". . . I—I want to go to a cloister. The one *Maman* went to. She . . . She was h-happy there . . . I want to be happy, too."

He rose. "If a convent is what you desire, it will be so, on my word. But first, *ma chérie*"—he held out a hand again—"you must give me the antidote."

She stared at his open palm.

"*Please*, Charlotte. I love you. Let me help you. I don't want you placed in prison."

She gave him a quivering smile. "You do love me, don't you, Adrien?"

"Very much," he said from the heart.

Slowly, she stretched out her arm and held out a pouch to him.

He grabbed it from her grip. "What is in the other pouch?"

She handed him that one as well. "It is empty. It had the poison. If you want the antidote to work best, you need to mix it with wine."

Adrien shot out the door.

* * *

Midnight. And still Catherine writhed.

In and out of consciousness since Adrien had given her the wine-based concoction, she looked no better. He paced. He prayed. By the predawn hours, he was beside himself, fear and worry clawing at his vitals.

What if the witch who had sold Charlotte the antidote had lied? What if the concoction he'd given Catherine was merely crushed herbs that did nothing at all?

She was still now. Far too still. Trapped in a deep slumber.

One he couldn't rouse her from.

Sitting on the edge of her bed, he held her hand, the nearby candelabra illuminating her sleeping form and her lovely, peaceful face in the darkened room. Dear God, he couldn't lose her. Not his beloved Catherine. He couldn't stand the heart-shattering thought. She was his. His heart belonged to her. Her heart belonged to him.

They belonged together.

Tenderly, he caressed her hand, watching each breath she took, willing another and another from her.

The clock on the mantel over the hearth ticked. And ticked. And ticked.

He felt damned helpless. Utterly useless. Unable to awaken her from this wretched unnatural sleep.

He wanted to do something, *anything* to help her, but there was nothing more he could do. Except wait. It was maddening to simply sit there, fighting to hold on to hope, battling against the cold dread slowly slicing through him.

Odette came each hour to check on her mistress. She'd be back in the room soon and he hated it that he'd have to tell her that there was *still* no improvement.

Adrien squeezed Catherine's hand. "*Ma belle . . .* wake up. *Please* wake up." Leaning in, he pressed a kiss to her lips.

He heard a soft sigh, then felt her lips move under his. Her fingers threaded through his hair and she kissed him back.

His heart missed a beat. He sat up. "Catherine!" The dawn broke, spilling the day's first rays into the room. She was awake and her complexion had improved. She was better! She looked beautiful.

At the commotion, Odette raced into the room. Upon seeing her mistress awake and smiling, she let out a screech of joy and rushed forward, dropping herself down on the other side of the bed. She snatched up Catherine's hand and caressed it. "Madame, you are well!"

"A bit weak, but yes, I feel much better," Catherine said.

With a giant foolish grin on her face, Odette petted her hand and stared at her as though she were gazing upon a deity. "Worry not, madame, I'll make certain you regain your strength in no time—"

Adrien cleared his throat, snagging Odette's attention.

Odette's eyes widened. "Oh . . . I'm—I'm sorry." She rose and retreated to the far corner of the room.

Adrien's light green eyes returned to Catherine, the love that shone there making her heart sing.

"It felt as though you were asleep for a hundred years," he said.

"It has been a hundred years since you last gave me a morning kiss." She grinned. "I like being awakened like that. Now, then, was I delirious or did I hear you say earlier that you love me?"

He grinned back. "I did indeed and I will say it again and again. I love you. I can't live without you. I don't want to. The night of the masquerade, you woke me from a slumber and brought me to life, heart, body, and soul. I will awaken you with a kiss for the rest of our lives. Say you'll marry me."

She was beaming, her heart nearly bursting with joy. "Yes! Yes, I will marry you." She sat up and leaned in for a kiss. Just as their lips touched, Odette broke into a loud wail, startling both Catherine and Adrien out of the moment.

Odette sobbed, blew her nose in a handkerchief she'd pulled out of her bodice, then resumed her blubbering.

"Odette, there's no need to carry on. I'm going to be fine." She smiled lovingly at Adrien. "Everything is going to be better than fine."

"Madame . . ." Odette sniffled loudly. "I—I have a confession to make. I cannot carry this on my conscience anymore."

"Oh?" Catherine said. "What confession?"

"Well . . . you see . . . that—that night . . . when you asked me to add the aphrodisiac to Monsieur's wine . . ." Odette shifted nervously from one foot to another. "Well . . . I added the powder . . . but I made a *tiny* error . . . You see, it turns out I mixed up the powders I got from the apothecary . . . I gave Monsieur le Marquis something to boost his . . . digestion rather than his libido."

Catherine and Adrien locked gazes, then burst out laughing.

Adrien pulled her tightly into his arms. "It would seem, my love, that the passion between us has been real from the beginning." He gave her a soft, tender kiss that left her wanting more.

She caressed his cheek. He was hers. All hers. Forever more.

"You know, if you marry me, you run the risk of easing tensions between you and the King. Your father may not think you so reckless anymore," she gently teased.

He laughed. "I love you so very much, I'm willing to marry you—even if it pleases my father." Adrien kissed her soundly. It was a kiss full of passion. Full of love.

A kiss that held the promise of happiness ever after.

Little Red Writing

Moral of the Story of *Little Red Riding Hood*

One sees here that young children,
Especially pretty girls,
Who're bred as pure as pearls,
Should question words addressed by men.
Or they may serve one day as feast
For a wolf or other beast.
I say a wolf since not all are wild
Or are indeed the same in kind.
For some are winning and have sharp minds,
Some are loud, smooth or mild.
Others appear plain kind or unriled.
They follow young ladies wherever they go,
Right into the halls of their very own homes.
Alas, for those girls who've refused the truth:
The sweetest tongue has the sharpest tooth.

CHARLES PERRAULT
(1628–1703)

1

"Who is *he*?" Just as the question tumbled from Anne's mouth, the man in the light gray justacorps disappeared into the crowd. Again.

Her sister Henriette glanced over her shoulder. As usual, the Comtesse de Cottineau's Saturday Salon was filled to overflowing. Though their patroness had been called away due to a family emergency, she'd insisted that Anne and her sisters carry on with the popular weekly event in her absence. Aristos and literati who frequented her home had been admitted and were presently milling about.

Henriette turned back. "Who?"

Who indeed.

Anne was the last person to be taken in by a handsome face, but she couldn't stop herself from trying to locate the man with the disarming gray eyes. Smoky eyes that had locked with hers for several seconds and quickened her pulse. A stunning reaction on her part. Unprecedented, actually. Twice he'd drawn her attention out of the masses straight to him by doing nothing more than directing his smoldering gaze her way—once, even when she was engaged in a fascinating discussion about Spanish literature with the Marquis de Musis. Both times the beautiful dark-haired stranger had been at a distance in a different part of the Great Room, but she felt the heat of his regard long before she spotted him.

Maddeningly, he kept vanishing into the sea of faces.

Dragging her gaze back to Henriette, Anne noticed her sister's curious expression.

"A gentleman," Anne responded. "I've never seen him before. We should welcome him, but I seem to have lost him in the crowd." She felt foolish. Stepping into the Comtesse's shoes and acting as hostess to her elite guests was daunting. Unnerving. Her jangled nerves were likely the reason for her peculiar reaction. Statesmen, lords, and ladies were in attendance along with some of the most respected scholars, writers, and dramatists.

Social biases set aside while under the Comtesse's roof, they gathered together each week to debate and discuss language and literature, history, and philosophy.

It was thrilling. A place of enlightenment. A great honor to be in among such distinguished company. Such brilliant minds. And to be part of Madame de Cottineau's Salon—one of the city's most prestigious. Born into minor nobility, with little by way of social influence and finances, Anne and her two sisters would not have been welcome had the Comtesse not taken an interest in their humble writings and agreed to sponsor their works.

But today's Saturday Salon was different. And it wasn't simply because the Comtesse was missing. Or that Anne and her sisters, Henriette and Camille, were hostesses.

It was because of a single man. A most unsettling, mysterious gentleman.

Anne and her sisters owed much to Madame de Cottineau. Making her guests feel welcome while she was away was the least they could do for her. Yet the gentleman with the disquieting gray eyes was making the task even more challenging for Anne. She should have greeted him the moment she saw him, but the impact he'd had on her unbalanced her. She lost her nerve to approach him, when courage was never something she lacked.

Henriette's gaze swept the room. "What does he look like?"

His face appeared in her mind's eye. Anne felt her cheeks warm. Dear God, she was *blushing.* And if that wasn't embarrassing enough, she was at a complete loss for words. She was a writer, and yet she couldn't conjure a phrase to adequately describe the sheer male perfection she'd seen. Not without sounding as awestruck as she felt. Like some smitten ingénue.

"Madame de Pierpont?" The Comtesse d'Azan approached and looped arms with Henriette. "Excuse me for interrupting, but the Baron de Lenoncourt has brought up the subject of the Latin classics. Come join in the discussion. You have such an interesting take on the topic."

Henriette glanced at Anne.

"Oh, you must come, too, Mademoiselle de Vignon," Comtesse d'Azan said to Anne. "You are the only one who can keep the Baron focused on one topic at a time." Softly, she laughed.

Anne smiled at the gracious comment and was about to respond when something, or rather someone, caught her eye. Over the Comtesse's shoulder, there at the back of the room, was the mysterious man.

His eyes captured hers and held her riveted, the corner of his mouth lifting into a sensual smile. Her stomach fluttered wildly. The crowd shifted and he disappeared from her seeking sight. Anne snapped out of the spell he'd cast and tamped down her ire.

Enough was enough.

It galled her that she was behaving so foolishly. She knew better. She knew the damage an attractive man could cause a woman's mind, heart, and spirit.

"Madame, I would love to join you," Anne said, grasping her skirts. "But first, there is a matter I must attend to. Please excuse me." Anne turned into the throng and made her way toward the back corner where she'd last seen the enigmatic stranger.

A smile firmly in place, she moved through the crowd, exchanging brief pleasantries along the way, behaving as any cordial hostess should. Just as soon as she located the man with the silvery eyes, she intended to extend him every courtesy. She'd welcome him to Madame de Cottineau's home. And respond to him no differently than to any other guest present.

So why were her insides still quivering?

*　*　*

"She approaches. What do you think, Nicolas, is she the one?" Thomas, Comte de Gamory, asked near Nicolas's ear.

Nicolas de Savignac studied the woman in the blue gown as she made her way through the mass. Anne de Vignon. The middle sister. He'd overheard one of the guests point her out. Thanks to the sheer numbers in the room, he could easily hide in plain sight and observe her and her two siblings. Allowing them to see him only when he wished it.

Anne's bright red curls lightly swept her bare shoulders each time she turned her head to acknowledge one of the guests. The color of her hair was extraordinary. He was gripped by a power-ful urge to run his fingers through the fiery-colored locks.

She wasn't at all what he'd expected a spinster poetess to look like. He was expecting someone rather plain. This woman was ravishing. The extent of her allure, a surprise. As was the bolt of heat that shot through his veins and tightened his groin the moment their gazes met.

He didn't like surprises.

He was still reeling over the fact that their investigation had led him to *this* hôtel, of all places. To the home of one of his very own relatives.

Discreetly, Anne glanced here and there. It was obvious to him, if no one else, that she was hunting for him. What she didn't know was that he was the one doing the hunting. That he was relentless in his pursuits, cunning enough to earn the nickname *le Loup*—the Wolf.

And he was here to catch his prey.

"Nicolas?"

He pulled his gaze from the redheaded beauty back to Thomas. His friend was frowning. It took some getting used to, seeing him out of his Musketeer uniform and in formal attire. Or being out of uniform himself. But to walk in wearing the distinct blue tabard would have alerted everyone, especially the sisters in question, that he and Thomas were part of the King's private Guard. Newly promoted, Nicolas intended to prove to his King, his Captain, and the rest of the men that he deserved the honored position. That he could be as good a Musketeer, if not better, than his late legendary brother, David—Musketeer extraordi-naire. Nicolas had, after all, easily beaten out other highly quali-fied noblemen for one of the coveted few spots. On his own. By *his* skill. *His* abilities. Just as he expected to. Once he set his mind on attaining a goal, he was unstoppable. And nothing was going to keep him from successfully completing this mission—a mission His Majesty wanted kept most quiet and accomplished posthaste.

"Well?" Thomas asked. "What do you think? Is it her or one of her other two sisters?"

Nicolas gazed once again at his object of interest. Anne had stopped and was speaking to a group of ladies.

"I don't know." *Merde.* How he wished he did. From the information he'd gathered, Anne de Vignon was the author of two volumes of poetry. He'd read them both. He'd read all the books the three sisters had written. Each woman had a distinct writing style—dark, romantic, humorous—and yet, he still wasn't certain who wielded the poisonous pen.

Now that Anne was closer, he could better appreciate the womanly details of her form. No doubt about it, both far and near, she was comely in the extreme. Her gown, though not as costly as the others in the room, accentuated her curves in the most delectable way. With the discerning eye of a libertine, he took note of her creamy skin, the slight blush to her cheeks, and the rise and fall of her breasts, her breathing a bit too quick, belying her mask of composure.

Under the unruffled façade she was discomposed. And it was because of him.

There had definitely been a mutual attraction. He'd seen it in her eyes. If used correctly, it could be delicious advantage. He wasn't above using whatever means necessary to uncover the identity of the anonymous author who wrote under the nom de plume Gilbert Leduc.

"She is beautiful," Thomas murmured. "I don't know about

you, Nicolas, but I'd rather fuck a woman who looks like that than arrest her."

"You'll not touch her." *Dieu*, that sounded absurdly possessive.

Thomas chuckled. "So you've set your sights on Anne, *le Loup*? Poor woman. She doesn't stand a chance. Curious, why her? Why not one of the other two sisters?" He gave a nod in their general direction. Both were on the opposite side of the room, engrossed in conversation. "They're comely, too."

Indeed. All three sisters had the same beautiful fiery-colored hair. Henriette de Pierpont was the eldest and the only one to marry. Widowed four years, she was attractive in her own right. As was the youngest, Mademoiselle Camille de Vignon.

But there was something about Anne . . .

"We're here to discover which sister is the author of the pen portraits and bring her before His Majesty. As ordered. Whichever will confess to the truth is the one I'm interested in," Nicolas said. Those who were patrons of the arts and had enough coin couldn't collect unsanctioned books fast enough.

Nicolas had uncovered the underground press that was printing the illegal volumes of short stories. He and Thomas had spent weeks surreptitiously watching the Parisian publisher, observing the comings and goings at his print shop, and following messenger boys until Nicolas was finally led to the home of the Comtesse de Cottineau—and the three authors who resided there.

Everyone was talking about the anonymously written stories. Everyone had a strong opinion on what should be done about the author. The women praised the writer. The men, especially those who were the subject of ridicule in the published tales, demanded justice.

Pen portraits were nothing new. Many writers used real

people—mostly members of the upper class—as characters in their books. Names were changed, but the author always made it easy to identify the person being portrayed by the fictitious character. Characters that were always written with a flattering slant. However, the author of *these* pen portraits did just the opposite. This author maligned and mocked men. Important men. Powerful men. Mercilessly. It was out of control.

Anne stepped away from the women and continued on, getting nearer, her lovely dark eyes still searching for him. Unable to spot him.

His lips twitched as he held back his smile. *That's it. Come closer, pretty rabbit.*

It had taken some doing, but he'd managed to get the Comtesse de Cottineau out of her home, sending the old crone far away under false pretenses. He despised the woman. Had held nothing but contempt for her his entire life, and with her out of the hôtel, nothing stood between him and the three redheaded females.

He was focused. Ready.

The trap was set.

*　　*　　*

He wasn't there. At the back corner of the room, Anne turned to face the crowd. She scanned the Great Room but couldn't locate the mysterious gentleman anywhere.

"Pardon, mademoiselle."

She jumped at the sound of the male voice behind her and spun around.

Vincent, the majordomo, gave a short bow. "Your pardon. I didn't mean to startle you." Tall, thin, his hair completely white, he always had the same expressionless look upon his face. A longtime loyal servant to the Comtesse, he'd been unnerving to Anne from the time she and her sisters moved in last spring. She could never decipher his emotions or what he was thinking.

"That's all right, Vincent."

"Mademoiselle, the Comte de Gamory and the Comte de Lambelle are here."

"Oh?"

"They have requested a private moment. They're in the Mercury drawing room. Monsieur de Lambelle has asked to see your sisters as well. Mademoiselle Camille de Vignon has already excused herself and is presently there."

Anne frowned. "Vincent, we cannot all excuse ourselves and disappear. What about the Comtesse's guests? Who are these men?"

"Nicolas de Savignac, Comte de Lambelle, is related to the Comtesse, mademoiselle."

She raised her brows. Her patroness? "He is?"

"Yes, mademoiselle. He is her grandson and wishes to speak to you."

2

Anne opened the door to the Mercury drawing room and stepped inside. Her heart lurched.

The mysterious man.

He sat across from Camille with another gentleman to his left. The moment those gray eyes touched upon her, his tactile gaze sent a rush of warmth low in her belly.

Get hold of yourself, she chastised. She wasn't easily rattled, but *he* rattled her in the most shocking ways. It defied logic. He was a perfect stranger. Yet there was nothing logical about it. It was all physical.

Anne took in a fortifying breath before she approached.

He rose to his full height and moved toward her, masculine grace in motion, getting closer with each wild beat of her heart. By the time he stood before her, he wore the same half-smile on his handsome face as before.

Tilting her chin, Anne gazed up at him.

"This is my sister, Anne de Vignon," Camille said, having approached without Anne noticing. She was too busy being ridiculously mesmerized by the handsome man before her. "Anne, this is the Comte de Lambelle—Nicolas de Savignac. He is our dear Comtesse's grandson."

Dear God, *he* was the grandson?

His smile broadened. Taking her hand—one she hadn't yet offered, her arms still dangling foolishly at her sides—he pressed his warm lips against it. Tiny tingles shot up her arm and rippled down her spine.

"*Enchanté,*" he said, his voice rich and seductive.

Stop staring. Where are your manners? Say something.

"A pleasure to meet you, Monsieur le Comte," she said, sounding slightly breathless. This man was dangerous, his allure far too compelling. Her every instinct warned her to stay far away.

"Please, no titles or formality are necessary. Call me Nicolas. May I call you Anne?"

She glanced at her younger sister Camille and caught the sobering sight of her smitten expression. Camille's regard was directed at the other gentleman in the room. Clearly her sister was behaving as uncharacteristically as she was.

She prayed *she* didn't look like that.

Returning her attention to the Comtesse's grandson, she responded, "Anne would be fine." Only because she was trying to be gracious toward her patroness's kin did she cede to his request, though permitting such familiarity made her uneasy.

Pleased by her answer, Nicolas's smile grew. He gestured to the gentleman beside him—a man of similar age yet slighter build. "Allow me to introduce my cousin Thomas, Comte de Gamory."

Anne's greeting of the Comte de Gamory—or rather "Thomas," as he preferred—was much better.

"Forgive our intrusion into your get-together. I had no idea there would be so many guests present," Nicolas said, his smile slowly diminishing on his beautiful face. Then, lowering his chin, briefly he shook his head. When his gray eyes met hers once more, they looked saddened. "This is yet another example of how little I know of my own grandmother, I fear. I had no idea she had weekly Salons—a fact Camille was kind enough to relay."

Their patroness was a strong-willed woman, the center of attention at any gathering. Never afraid of voicing her opinion. But when it came to personal matters, such as family, she'd been silent. The Comtesse had never mentioned grandchildren and only once indicated she'd had any children at all. A son and a daughter. There were obvious familial strains in the Comtesse's family.

"I understand from your sister that the Comtesse isn't here." Nicolas's expression was rueful.

"Yes, that's true," Anne regretted having to say. "She's been called away. A letter arrived from her sister last week. She's gone to see her."

"We did inquire if there was anything amiss," Camille added. "But she wouldn't say one way or the other."

Nicolas looked at his cousin and, with a sigh, placed a hand on the man's shoulder. "How very disappointing. We've missed her. I had so hoped to surprise her."

Thomas nodded, looking not quite as aggrieved. "Indeed, cousin. I know how much you have wanted to make amends with your grandmother."

"*His* grandmother?" Anne asked. "Is she not yours as well?"

Thomas's eyes widened and all that escaped his lips was, "*Ah* . . . well—"

"No," Nicolas interjected. "Thomas is my cousin from my

father's side. My late mother was the Comtesse's daughter. Thomas is as dear to me as a brother. In fact, I lost my brother not long ago. It was then that I decided I needed to make changes in my life. One of which is trying to forge a relationship with a grandmother who has been all but a stranger to me."

"Yes, yes. That's true," Thomas concurred with a nod.

Nicolas de Savignac had had his share of unfortunate losses. The notion tugged at Anne's heart. "I see. My condolences, Monsieur de—"

"Nicolas, please," he amended.

"*Nicolas* . . . my condolences for the loss of your brother. And to you, too, Thomas—for the loss of your cousin."

"My condolences, as well—to both of you," Camille said, her brown eyes mirroring the sympathy in her tone.

"Thank you, my ladies. We appreciate your kindness." Nicolas looked at his cousin. "Don't we, Thomas?"

"Hmm? Oh. Yes. Indeed, we do."

"I'm equally sorry to hear of your estrangement with your grandmother," Anne said. "We have been living with her for a year and find her to be a most delightful, spirited lady who has a great passion for the arts."

"That, too, is something I was unaware of, Anne," Nicolas said.

She liked the way he said her name. She liked it too much. Why, when he uttered it, did it have such a heated effect?

"Camille tells us that you are writers. I had no idea my grandmother had such lovely, fascinating ladies living in her home." Nicolas's sensual half-smile returned.

Thomas offered a smile as well. "Yes. Having you ladies here, of all places, was definitely a . . . surprise."

"A good surprise, I hope," Camille remarked shamelessly,

ignoring the look of disapproval Anne discreetly flashed her. These men were of rank, and—albeit estranged—nonetheless relations of their patroness. Two very strong reasons not to flirt—no matter how innocently done. Camille knew better. She knew to be cautious around men in the noble class. Knew what some of them were capable of.

"A most delightful surprise, Camille," Nicolas assured.

Anne had to admit, the man's manners were polished and he was charming in the extreme. Not to mention that his proximity had every nerve ending in her body humming with awareness.

More reasons to keep a distance.

"Our other sister, Henriette, is a writer as well," Camille said, her approval of Nicolas's response evident by her jubilant expression. "She has penned some wonderful stories."

Anne glanced at the door. "Henriette must be caught up in conversation. We really must return to the Comtesse's guests. Her Salon means a great deal to her, so much so that she didn't want to cancel it in her absence. My apologies for Henriette—"

Nicolas raised a hand. "No need to apologize. Thomas and I arrived quite unexpectedly."

"Please, join us," Camille said. "We'll introduce you to your grandmother's friends."

"That is very gracious of you, Camille," Nicolas said. "In fact, I wish to learn as much as I can about my grandmother, but our trip from Maillard was a lengthy one. We're terribly exhausted. I hope you understand if we decline?"

Anne was more than a tad relieved, needing space between her and the far-too-attractive Nicolas de Savignac. "Of course. I'll ask Vincent to show you to your rooms, where you can rest and refresh yourselves." The faster she could leave the room, the sooner her pulse could return to normal.

"Will you be staying awhile?" Anne disliked the hopeful tone in Camille's voice and immediately worried about the answer.

"Having come all this way," Nicolas responded, "I don't wish to leave without seeing my grandmother. I've heard her sister is a robust woman in both health and form. I have a feeling the Comtesse will return soon enough. Until then, Thomas and I will be staying, and I shall anxiously await her arrival." He smiled.

Anne's stomach dropped.

He could be here *weeks*. Oh, this was bad. Very bad. Especially since she found the notion as appealing as it was horrifying.

His light-colored eyes moved to Anne as he said, "There will be plenty of time to get to know each other."

*   *   *

Nicolas listened to the retreating footsteps of the two Vignon sisters from behind the drawing room's closed doors. Only when he could no longer hear the sound of heels clicking against marble did he grin, saunter over to a chair, and drop into it.

"Nicolas," Thomas said, dragging a chair over to him and sitting down. "You are in the wrong profession, my friend. You should take to the stage. That was quite a performance you gave."

Still smiling, Nicolas propped his boots on a nearby settee, unconcerned for the damask upholstery, and linked his fingers behind his head. "It worked, didn't it? We have their sympathy. Moreover, we have unfettered access to the hôtel and the lovely authors who live in it."

"Well, I am not the actor you are. If you are going to surprise me—such as making me your 'cousin'—please give me forewarning."

In a good mood, Nicolas simply chuckled. "Do not fret,

Thomas. You did fine. And we will do more than fine with this mission. A handful of days, perhaps even less, and I'll know which sister is Gilbert Leduc, make my arrest, and impress the King."

It was Thomas's turn to smile. "You have hardly been in the Guard for long. You're not hunting for a promotion already, are you, *le Loup?*"

"Of course." It had taken some finagling, but he'd convinced his Captain, Tristan de Tiersonnier, to select him for the mission. How was he to catch the eye of the King if he didn't do things that made him stand out? "I intend one day to be Captain of His Majesty's private Guard—the King's most trusted protector. Keeping your eye toward promotion is the only way to excel."

"Captain?" Thomas laughed. "You do aim high. Not even your brother achieved that."

That decimated his jovial spirits. Any references that remotely suggested he wasn't as good as his brother had that effect. "I am not like David." He was better than David. He was a better fencer. A better loser when bested by his brother. A more gracious winner when Nicolas did the besting—and never, not ever, did he gloat. Pitting his sons against each other all their lives, their father encouraged constant competition between them, fueling their lifelong rivalry. And even though David and their father were both dead, Nicolas still wouldn't—couldn't—stop until he'd proved to himself and his superiors that he was in no way a lesser version of his older sibling.

"How do you plan on discovering which sister is Gilbert Leduc?"

Pulling his feet off the settee and placing them back onto the floor, Nicolas leaned toward his friend, his smile returning. "Anne is going to tell me."

"You think you can get her to talk?"

"I'm certain of it." The air between them practically sizzled and crackled with hot carnal awareness. He'd never admit to Thomas just how strongly her allure was playing havoc with his libido, but she had him stiff as a spike the entire time they'd spoken, hungry for the taste of her mouth and her tantalizing nipples that were so obviously hard and pressing against the bodice of her gown.

"What makes you so certain?" Thomas asked. "Because she is—if the look in her eyes was any indication—attracted to you?"

"Precisely."

"And how are you going to attain the information from her? By fucking the answer out of her?"

Nicolas sat back in his chair. "Now you see the added appeal to this mission."

Thomas laughed and shook his head. "It doesn't bother you that you'd be bedding the lady one moment, then possibly—if she turns out to be Leduc—arresting her the next?"

"Thomas, a conscience is in direct conflict with ambition. You would do well to remember that. As for the lady, if she is the author—Gilbert Leduc—then she has broken the law by using an illegal press and writing unsanctioned, not to mention defamatory, literature. If Leduc turns out to be one of her sisters, I've no doubt she's assisting in some capacity in her sibling's criminal endeavors. Either way, she is guilty. I have no qualms about doing my duty, and neither should you. If the lady offers up some decadent delights before all is said and done," Nicolas shrugged, "I'll not refuse her." No man would. Not a woman as beautiful as Anne de Vignon.

He'd seen lustful interest in the eyes of many of the men at the Salon. Did she have a lover among them? The possibility that he'd have competition didn't worry him. He'd have Anne, his instincts telling him that beneath her cool, proper layers, he'd find passion. Fire. A woman sure to offer a man untold carnal bliss.

"And what about your grandmother? She is mixed up in all this," Thomas said. "As their patroness, her funding has made it possible for these women to write and publish sanctioned—and one of them, unsanctioned—literature. This 'Gilbert Leduc' matter will backlash on her."

"My grandmother is a willful, uncompromising woman who is devoid of compassion." Nicolas couldn't keep the caustic tone from dripping off his words. "I have no doubt she's played a very important role in this smear campaign. Should the King decide to punish her, she has no one to blame but herself." He had no sympathy where the old woman was concerned. Though he'd not expected to discover his own grandmother involved in this sordid mess, he wasn't going to let that deter him in any way. Absurd as it was, the only thing that was truly bothering him was that he'd been correct in his assumption: his grandmother hadn't spoken of him, or likely his mother, either. That fact was evident by the looks on Anne's and Camille's faces. It was obvious they never knew he existed. Though the Comtesse's silence helped with his plan, he disliked that the notion had any sting at all. After all these years, he shouldn't care a whit that the heartless hag had disowned his mother—turning her back on her own daughter—and never had any interest in her grandsons, treating them all as if they were dead.

"I've read Gilbert Leduc's writings," Nicolas said, shoving the past aside. "I believe the author we seek is a woman scorned. Someone whose anger has spilled over onto the male gender at large. A man or men—past or present—have inspired her to write telltale stories that humiliate men and besmirch their reputations."

"So you think the author is using these pen portraits as a method of revenge?" Thomas asked.

"I do."

"Perhaps she simply does it for funds? With the wild popularity of the anthologies, surely it's been a lucrative venture for her?"

"Indeed, Thomas. The money is likely a motivating factor. But I think the underlying reason why she does this is much more personal. Madame Henriette de Pierpont was once married. Let's learn as much as we can about her marriage, and in particular, her deceased husband's treatment of her." Nicolas rose, suddenly feeling fatigued, intent on seeking out the old servant and retiring to his room. "Camille de Vignon seems to have an interest in you, Thomas. Speak to her. See what you can learn. I'll focus on Anne," he said as his friend rose from his chair. "I'll be with her every minute of the day."

And each night—if all went according to his plan.

This was going to be easy.

* * *

"I don't like this. Not one bit," Henriette whispered.

Anne walked between Henriette and Camille as they made their way to the *Salle de Buffet*. This was their first evening meal with Nicolas and Thomas, and Anne was as enthralled over the prospect as Henriette. Being in the same room with her patroness's grandson for an entire meal—knowing the stirring effect he had on her—had her on edge. She hadn't been able to forget the raw desire she'd seen in Nicolas's eyes before parting in the drawing room. Its seductive lure had incited a craving she couldn't vanquish.

"Really, Henriette, you are making much out of nothing." Camille's statement arrested Henriette's steps.

"Much out of nothing?" Henriette's eyes were wide with disbelief. "Dear sister, do the words"—she lowered her voice a notch—"'Gilbert Leduc' mean anything to you?"

Camille frowned. "Of course they do. They mean as much to me as they do to you, Anne, our dear Comtesse—not to mention all the women who have entrusted their stories to *him*."

"Then perhaps you can explain to me how we are to interview the very skittish Madame de Montbel and Madame de Boutette for Gilbert Leduc's next stories with these gentlemen here? You know the next volume must be brought to press in three weeks or Bruno won't print it. The more popular the books become, the more risk there is for those involved."

Camille frowned. "I'm quite aware of the deadline and the risks. What I don't understand is why you are fretting over the presence of Savignac and Gamory."

Henriette's mouth fell agape. She turned to Anne. "Will you please explain it to her?"

"Camille . . ." Anne strove for a more reasonable tone than Henriette's, though her sisters' bickering was grating on her patience. Like Henriette, she didn't relish having anyone whom she didn't know staying at the hôtel when one of Gilbert Leduc's volumes was in the works.

Especially a man as inflaming as Nicolas de Savignac.

"Leduc's identity must be protected at all costs," Anne said. "Especially since behind his pen are a number of women who have provided scathing secrets for Leduc's stories. There would be disastrous consequences for them if they were exposed."

"And the consequences for Leduc would be even worse," Henriette added for good measure.

"But these gentlemen are part of the Comtesse's family. Nicolas de Savignac is her very own grandson," Camille countered. "Surely that makes him trustworthy enough to—"

"To what? To tell him of Leduc?" Henriette sputtered. *"Are you mad?"*

Camille jabbed her fists into her waist. "I assure you I have complete command of my faculties. Henriette, you are—"

"Enough," Anne demanded. Usually the one to settle her siblings' arguments, she was not in the mood for this tonight. "Camille,"—she turned to her younger sister—"Madame de Cottineau is estranged from her grandson, and we don't know her reasons for it. Until she returns and we speak to her, we'll not reveal a thing to Savignac or Gamory. We'll not put anyone in jeopardy."

Henriette crossed her arms. "I don't trust Savignac."

"You haven't even met him yet," Camille said.

Anne had, and she didn't trust him either, or more particularly, herself around him, the physical calamity he inspired a serious detriment. And something she intended to get under control. Lest it got out of control. "We won't allow this situation to turn into a problem."

With resolve, Anne stalked toward the dining hall once more. Her sisters quickly fell into step. There was no other option, really. Leduc wrote the sorts of stories that needed to be written. Had to be told.

And would be published. On time.

After a few silent moments, Henriette conceded. "You're right, of course, Anne. Among the three of us, we can entertain our two guests until Madame de Cottineau returns—and keep them from stumbling onto our secret. Isn't that right, Camille?"

"Yes, of course."

"Good. Then there is nothing left to argue about and nothing to be concerned over," Anne said with more confidence than she felt. Why was she riddled with niggling doubts? What was the threat, really? "I doubt either gentleman has ever even heard of Leduc." Nicolas and Thomas came from the country, preferring to live at their country estates over Paris, as some nobles did. Leduc's popularity was for the most part contained inside the city. "And even if they know of him and his books, even if they see a few women come and go from the Comtesse's home over the next few days, they'd never conclude Leduc is under this roof." Anne glanced at each sister. "Right?"

"Right," they responded in chorus.

The tension in Anne's body eased the more she thought of the situation. Her biggest challenge in all this was to keep her distance from her patroness's enigmatic grandson. And how difficult could that be? With her sisters sharing the duties as hostess, she could limit her time in Nicolas's company—until she'd mastered her maddening reactions to him.

Anne's next book would go to press on time without their houseguests ever knowing that the notoriously famous author—who had tongues wagging in every Salon in the city—was right under their noses. Her books of poetry had never been as popular as her Gilbert Leduc volumes.

But she didn't write under the name "Gilbert Leduc" for the notoriety.

What motivated her pen was the women behind the stories—and their personal experiences that hit close to home and heart.

Before she knew it, Madame de Cottineau would return, deal with her grandson as she saw fit, and be delighted to find that Anne had published a new volume to titillate Leduc's fans.

She exchanged knowing smiles with her sisters. By the look in their eyes, she knew they were in accord; Leduc was a secret they wouldn't reveal.

Not to anyone outside their trusted circle.

There were many who'd tried to learn who was behind Leduc's pen. None had succeeded. No one ever would.

Keeping their secret from two men who weren't even interested in Leduc wasn't going to be difficult.

In fact, this was going to be easy.

3

Laughter rippled through the *Salle de Buffet*. The women were starting to relax. Nicolas was pleased as he chuckled along with his dining companions at the latest witty exchange.

Sweeping his gaze down the long elegant table, he glanced at each of the three sisters. Then at Thomas. Seated at opposite ends of the table, their gazes met and Nicolas could tell by his friend's expression that they were in agreement: the night was going well. Even the rather icy Henriette was beginning to offer a smile and the occasional laugh.

In short, Nicolas was making great progress; he was lowering the ladies' guards a charming comment at a time.

His eyes were drawn back to Anne. Repeatedly during the meal he'd caught himself watching her. Practically gawking at her. The candles on the silver torchères lined around the room cast an orange light, making the shade of her coppery curls bedazzling.

Making her skin look warm and so enticing.

He was dying to trail his fingers along the contour of her scooped neckline over the gentle swell of her breasts. He was dying to do far more than that with the enchanting poetess. Fantasies of her naked in his bed, wet with wanting, ran rampant in his mind.

Nicolas shifted in his chair, his stiff prick straining uncomfortably inside his breeches. *Merde.* She was seated to his right, dressed in a simple gown—hadn't done more than offer polite conversation—and she was driving him to distraction.

Anne brought a spoonful of soup to her lips.

By God, his yearning to possess that lush mouth mounted by the moment.

"Do tell us, Nicolas," Henriette's voice cut through his thoughts. "What has driven such a wedge between you and your grandmother? Why the estrangement?"

"Henriette!" Camille chastised.

Anne simply met his gaze and held it. By the look in her beautiful dark eyes, he could tell she was curious about the answer.

He decided to offer an honest one. "My mother married my father—a man my grandmother didn't care for. She disowned her when she learned of their secret marriage ceremony."

There was silence for a moment as the women absorbed his response.

"Why would the Comtesse object to your father as a husband for her daughter?" Anne asked softly. He liked her voice. He couldn't help but wonder at the sultry sounds she made in the throes of passion, what she'd sound like when she came. Or what the tight clasp of her wet sex around his thrusting cock would feel like . . .

She was staring at him. Waiting. Nicolas shot a glance at the others at the table. They all sported similar expectant expressions on their faces.

He cleared his throat. "Because my father was an ass, and he remained that way until his last breath." By the expression on her lovely face, it was obvious he'd surprised her with his bluntness. *Merde.* That could have been put a little more gently.

If he didn't fuck her soon, he was going to lose his mind.

"He—He didn't treat your mother well?" Camille voiced the question that was likely on everyone's mind.

"No, Camille, he did not." And despite her reservations, his coldhearted grandmother had never once inquired about her daughter's well-being—from the day she married until her death two years ago.

Camille lowered her head.

"Husbands seldom do—treat their wives well, that is," Anne said. "Your mother was not alone in that regard."

"Oh?" This was a direction he definitely wanted to go. Thanks to the forward Vignon sisters, they were making it easy for him. "And why do you say that?"

"Because it's the truth," Henriette interjected.

He dragged his eyes away from Anne. "Is it your truth, madame?"

She cocked a brow at him.

"Forgive me, but since we're being candid with each other, I thought you wouldn't mind my inquiring."

Henriette set down her spoon. "I do mind—not about you asking questions, for we have nothing to hide here. But about discussing the subject of my late husband. He had a lot in common with your father, you see. He, too, was an ass."

Nicolas briefly glanced at Thomas.

Henriette rose. "If you will excuse me, I shall return to my chambers now. Good night."

Nicolas and Thomas were on their feet immediately. Henriette stalked out of the room.

Camille was the next to rise. "I should make certain she's all right."

With his eyes, Nicolas motioned Thomas to follow Camille out.

"Camille," Thomas called out, halting her steps. "Please, allow me to escort you." He offered his arm. Together they walked out of the *Salle de Buffet*.

Nicolas turned his attention to Anne. She was standing and he knew she was about to offer her excuses to leave.

"I have ruined the evening. I'm sorry. I didn't mean to cause distress." This was *not* how he'd intended the evening to end. Distracted by Anne, he'd blurted out his question to Henriette when he should have taken care to ascertain the answer.

"Henriette is fine. She's still sensitive about the late Baron and doesn't like to be questioned about him."

"I gather theirs was not a marriage filled with wedded bliss?"

She shook her head. "No, hardly that. Like your mother, my sister fell in love—and suffered for it."

He walked around the table and stopped before her. A light floral scent emanated from her beautiful hair, tantalizing his senses. "You sound as though you don't care for love."

From the moment he drew close, her cheeks took on a pretty blush, and Nicolas noted the rapid beating of her pulse along the side of her slender neck. Telltale signs of his heated effect on her.

These were exactly the reactions he wanted from her.

She glanced at the door and then at his mouth. Her desire was evident, but so was her unease at being alone with him. His greedy cock twitched. *Easy now.* If he moved too quickly, she'd bolt from the room. He'd already made mistakes tonight. He wouldn't make another. This mission was too important to him.

The matter required finesse. Patience. For the first time ever, he struggled with both—thanks to the bewitching writer with the flame-colored hair.

"No, I don't believe in love," she stated firmly. He was disappointed in her answer, and he had no idea why he should be. He wasn't much of a believer in the fickle emotion either, but he'd read her works. They were filled with romantic sentiment. Romantic sentiment she'd clearly lost. Was it her sister's disagreeable marriage that had jaded her? Or Anne's own personal experience?

"But I'm told you write poetry. Love poems, to be precise."

"I do . . . rather . . . I did . . . two volumes of love poems . . . a while ago." Anne mentally cringed. She sounded like a babbling fool.

He was standing so close—too close—trapping her between the table and his tall sculpted form. From the moment she'd walked into the room and saw him standing in the dining hall with Thomas, her blood had warmed. Now it raced through her veins white-hot.

If he'd step back, she could think. As it was, it took every effort just to keep her breathing even, so that she didn't humiliate herself by panting in heat. How in heaven's name did she end up alone with him? This wasn't supposed to happen. Her sisters were not supposed to abandon her in his company, but then, they had no idea how he incited her senses.

"What do you write now?" he asked, his voice low. It

reverberated inside her, making the dull ache between her legs grow fiercer. The very ache that had started from the moment he'd escorted her to her chair and then sat so near. She resented the way he was affecting her—worse, that she couldn't curb her responses to him. He was a nobleman. She didn't trust his kind, preferring poets and dramatists. She knew what the upper class were capable of, and yet, he'd still managed to sweep into the Comtesse's home, and awaken Anne's long-dormant body with no effort at all.

"I . . . I'm working on . . . volumes . . . various ones." Another imbecilic response.

He tilted his head slightly to one side. "Volumes of what?"

"They are stories of intrigue and adventure." She didn't lie well when the most disarming pair of gray eyes was on her. Well, actually it wasn't a complete lie. Gilbert Leduc's stories did have intrigue, and getting the volumes published was an adventurous venture, to say the least.

A slight smile teased his lips. "Adventure?" He dipped his head, bringing his most kissable mouth closer to hers. "*Excitement.*" His warm breath caressed her lips. "That appeals to you, does it?"

Not this kind of excitement. *This* kind of excitement could only lead to trouble and heartache. And at the moment, she'd rather not be quite as *excited* as she felt.

Uncharacteristic thoughts of what that mouth would feel like against her skin were rushing through her mind.

"I should go." Now. Quickly. Before she did something foolish.

He didn't move. Instead, his light gray eyes held her gaze, then moved to her mouth, and for a moment she thought he might . . . would he . . . *kiss her?*

Her heart pounded. She held her breath. Waiting. Anticipating. Frozen with expectation until he took a step back.

"Good night, Anne."

Anne let out a breath and tamped down her disappointment. "Yes. Good night." Her limbs shaky, she stepped around him and proceeded toward the door.

"Wait." He caught her hand, surprising her.

Nicolas stepped closer and gently brushed a lock of her hair from her cheek. The light caress sent a rush of liquid heat from her core. What was it about this man that made her react this way? She was shamelessly vulnerable to him in a way she'd never been with any man.

Not even Jules.

"Anne, I hope I can count on your help," he said softly.

"Help?"

"With my grandmother. You know her better than I do. I want to learn everything I can about her. I need your help to do that. I want to understand her mind. Her heart. If you don't help me, I fear I'll fail in my attempt to forge a relationship with her. My mother went to her grave never having reconciled with the Comtesse. She isn't getting any younger. This may be my only opportunity to form a bond between us."

Anne forced a polite smile, her insides in a frenzy. "My sisters and I will do what we can, but I can't promise results."

"I doubt Henriette will want to have much to do with me after tonight, and Camille seems far more interested in spending time with Thomas. You're the only one who can help me. Please, say you will." His expression was beseeching.

If her thoughts hadn't been so heated, she might have chosen her next words carefully. Instead, she said, "Well . . . I suppose—"

"Excellent." Nicolas pressed his warm lips against her hand, lingering a second or two longer than necessary before he kissed it. A hot tremor shivered through her. "You can begin enlightening me on everything I should know about the Comtesse tomorrow." He flashed her a bedeviling smile, then turned on his heel and left the room.

Oh, God . . .

4

Nicolas clenched his jaw. Thomas stood near the hearth—one hand on the mantel and the other clutching his side—laughing, the irritating sound reverberating in Nicolas's chambers.

"Let me see if I have this right . . ." Thomas said, fighting back a snicker. "You manage to get the comely Anne de Vignon alone, and though there is mutual physical attraction between you, and you could tell she wanted—*hungered*," he emphasized theatrically, "for a kiss, you denied her, and purposely left her wanting more."

Nicolas crossed his arms and sat back in his chair. "There is nothing wrong with that approach," he responded tightly over Thomas's new bout of laughter.

Thomas sobered up enough to say, "But wait, that's not all. Then, you, *le Loup*—a man with a reputation for being irresistible to the finer sex and having uncanny shrewdness in all situations—cleverly cornered her into helping you forge a relationship with your grandmother, which would, of course, give you an excuse to be in her company . . ." Thomas was laughing again, unable to continue.

Nicolas uncrossed his arms and rose. "What is wrong with that? It was a solid tactic to take."

Sobering, yet still chuckling, Thomas walked over to the small side table. "Yes, and for the first time since I've known you, my friend, *le Loup* miscalculated. While you were convinced she would be spending endless hours acquainting you with facts about the Comtesse—giving you information about Leduc—and offering up promiscuous pleasures, your 'solid' tactic got you this instead." He swiped up the note.

Dear Nicolas, I know how much you want to get to know your grandmother. I have thought of how best to help you with the Comtesse and what I could offer that would aid you in that regard. After much consideration, I believe I know just what you require. Sincerely, Anne

Thomas gestured toward the open trunk that accompanied the note. "Stacks of old dusty books." Thomas pulled one out, held it up, and wiggled his brows. "All your grandmother's favorites." He laughed. "Not nearly as good as a tumble and a confession, but you might discover that you and your grandmother have some common literary preferences." Thomas roared.

Nicolas approached Thomas and snatched the note from his hand. "I'm glad you find this amusing. Perhaps you've forgotten that we are doing all this on behalf of the King." He stalked to the window and stared down at the courtyard below, clutching the note in his fist.

He'd thought he had her eating out of the palm of his hand.

It had taken enormous will not to kiss her when she'd looked at him so expectantly last eve. He'd left the room burning for her, certain that he'd be rewarded for his efforts with her company today. Not to mention her heightened ardor.

Instead he got a trunk full of books.

He cared not what his grandmother read, nor to learn any more about her. What he already knew was more than enough. He needed to spend time with Anne. Alone. He needed to sate the desire he had for her. Clearly, it was beginning to cloud his judgment. She was occupying his waking thoughts and, last night, his erotic dreams.

As soon as he'd received the books and the note, he'd gone to find Anne. Even went so far as to go to her chambers, but was stopped by the somber servant, Vincent, who informed him that the Comtesse never allowed anyone to disturb the sisters when they were sequestered in their rooms writing.

"Oh, come now, Nicolas. Allow me to enjoy your misstep. You make so few." Thomas pulled another book from the trunk. "Are you going to read any of these?"

"Put the damned books down. What success have you had?" he snapped. "Have you obtained any information from Camille?"

Thomas tossed the books back in the trunk. "As a matter of fact, I have. She told me about Henriette's late husband, the penniless Baron de Pierpont, who squandered what little money they had on drinking, cards, and debauchery. A *'cruel man, especially when into his cups,'* she'd said. And when Henriette miscarried the one and only time she was with child, the Baron refused to return home and sent her a scathing note telling her she couldn't do anything right. Not even give him an heir. I think Henriette is Gilbert Leduc. She's definitely still bitter about her husband."

"We need proof," Nicolas said. "Something undeniable and damning." Since Anne was indisposed, he was going to use his time to search the hôtel for evidence.

He wasn't finished with the pretty poetess. She wanted him. Felt the carnal heat between them, whether she wished to admit it or not. She was playing a cat and mouse game.

Well, he never backed away from a challenge. Nor would he botch this crucial mission—his very first for the King.

She couldn't hide in her chambers forever.

When she came out, he'd be waiting.

*　*　*

Madame de Montbel blew her nose loudly into her lace handkerchief.

"What he's done is cruel, I tell you," she cried. Tears dampened her rounded cheeks, her face mostly crease-free, despite her advancing years. "His misdeeds must be exposed as only Monsieur Leduc's stories can do—God bless the man."

Seated at her desk in her antechamber, Anne dipped her quill into the crystal inkwell, ready to take notes. "Yes, of course. He'll do his best," she said, compassion in her tone.

She always did her best for the women who came looking for some measure of satisfaction, their woes ranging from moderate to severe.

The men in their lives, the root cause.

As master of the household, a man had absolute authority. His actions were above reproach. Uncontestable. It mattered little to him or his male peers if those very actions caused a woman humiliation. Hardship. Heartbreak. Expected to endure it, a woman was without recourse of any kind.

Until Gilbert Leduc came along.

Born of Anne's imagination for just this purpose, Leduc offered women an opportunity to tell their stories. And exact some revenge.

Each and every story was laced with a healthy dose of scandalous yet factual detail, putting the scrutiny on the men in her tales.

The titillating tidbits were what made Anne's stories—*Gilbert Leduc's stories*—wildly popular. And what incensed the men. The angrier they got, the more it pleased the women she wrote for. These men deserved the public scrutiny, and at times, the ridicule. Not to mention the frustration of not knowing who Leduc was or where he got his information from.

It gave Anne great pride to know that the precautions she'd put in place had successfully kept anyone from learning Leduc's identity. The information that made its way into the stories was carefully chosen, so that it never gave away the woman offering up the details.

Madame de Montbel wiped her tears and leaned closer. "Have you ever met Gilbert Leduc?"

"No, madame. He's very strict about maintaining his anonymity. We simply take notes for him. The notes are dropped off in various secret locations around the city—and the locations always change. I have no idea who the man is." That was the usual answer she gave.

Together with the Comtesse, Anne chose the women Leduc wrote about; her patroness knew who could be trusted to come to her home and provide details for Gilbert Leduc's stories. And despite the cautious selection, none was told Gilbert Leduc and Anne were one and the same.

"Of course. He must be careful not to be exposed. I understand," Madame de Montbel said. "Now, where was I? Ah, yes, my son-in-law, the Duc de Terrasson, asked for a lettre de cachet to be drawn up against my dear daughter two months ago, forcing her into confinement at a cloister. She isn't free to leave. Nor is she allowed visitors. Including me and her own children! He forbids it. Her imprisonment there could be indefinite." She sobbed then blew her nose again.

Sadly, Anne had heard stories like these before. Men could have orders drawn up against an "unmanageable" wife or other female members of their family, and have them confined to a prison or convent, or in some cases, even exiled. Without trial. Sometimes with little or no provocation. It was an abuse of their power.

"What is his reason for having her cloistered?" Anne asked. Not that he really needed one.

"He doesn't approve of his wife having friends. In particular, Madame de Santerre."

Anne wasn't surprised.

Madame de Santerre was an educated, intelligent woman and a darling of the more prestigious Salons. A young widow, she was independent and witty, with a sharp mind and an impressive knowledge of literature.

"He said that Madame de Santerre wasn't fit company, that she was too high-spirited for his 'feebleminded, impressionable' wife. That's what he called *my* Eléonore," she scoffed, disgusted.

What nonsense. More like, the man was afraid his wife might develop opinions of her own, like Madame de Santerre. Or perhaps he was simply looking for an excuse and wanted the Duchesse out of the way.

Keeping her comments to herself, Anne diligently recorded Madame de Montbel's statements. Dipping her quill back into the inkwell, she said, "Go on."

"When he caught Eléonore with books given to her by Madame de Santerre, he had her tossed into the cloister. He felt she'd been corrupted and needed to spend some time in religious devotion '*to reflect on her behavior*,' he'd said. He, on the other hand, immediately moved his favorite paramour into the hôtel— under the same roof as my grandchildren—and carries on openly, making no attempt to be discreet at all. Can you believe that?"

She could indeed. Men thought nothing of the hypocrisy of it all. A man could easily see a woman's actions as corrupt but never recognize his own wrongdoings.

Madame de Montbel shook her head and dried more tears, clearly heartbroken. Anne wanted to offer consolatory words, but what could she say to diminish the woman's misery?

Setting a blue velvet purse down on the desk, Madame de Montbel said, "This is compensation for Monsieur Leduc's trouble."

Anne pushed the purse back. "He accepts no payment from those who provide him with stories, madame. Your satisfaction with the work is compensation enough for him."

"Then please provide him with a note expressing my thanks and stress to him that I want him to show, through his pen portrait and story, just what kind of scoundrel the Duc is. He's to spare him no mercy." No longer did Madame de Montbel weep. Her expression was hard, her eyes now narrowed.

"Of course," Anne assured.

"And now to address that aspect of the story that Leduc's readers love—that scandalous morsel they all devour." For the first time since Madame had been escorted to Anne's private apartments, she formed a smile, a bit of joy entering her eyes.

"There is something I have learned about the Duc that I'm certain he wouldn't want others to know. He dares to question my daughter's character. Well, I have a bit of information to expose that will have everyone questioning his."

Uncertain what she was about to hear, Anne waited, quill inked and ready. There was nothing anyone could do to have Eléonore de Terrasson freed. Or reunited with her children. Gilbert Leduc was not about to right a wrong here, but he was going to make sure that the Duc's callous actions didn't go unpunished.

* * *

Nicolas ran his fingertips along the top shelving in the library, his arm stretched high. Methodically moving around the perimeter of the room, row by row, he glided his fingers over the smooth wood, until he'd checked them all.

No key.

He glanced across the room, frustrated.

The locked desk near the windows glared back at him. He'd already searched his grandmother's chambers. There, too, he'd located a writing desk. Also locked.

He'd looked under the furniture and in every nook and cranny where a key could be hidden in his grandmother's rooms, and had stopped the search only when it was clear the key wasn't in her private apartments.

And—*merde*—he wasn't having any more success in the library than he'd had upstairs.

With Henriette, Anne, and Camille in their respective rooms, their private apartments couldn't be searched. Nicolas had hoped instead that a search of the Comtesse's desks would yield the evidence needed to prove Henriette was Gilbert Leduc.

Nicolas raked a hand through his hair. One master key could

very well open both desks. If hidden in the library, it was possible the key was between the pages of one of the thousands of books lining the floor-to-ceiling shelves.

How was he ever going to locate something so small in such a vast collection of volumes? He didn't want to resort to trying to pick the lock, but would if he didn't find the key. Soon.

One of the volumes near the door caught his eye. Nicolas pulled it off the shelf. A slight smile tugged at the corner of his mouth as he gazed at the title. He'd read this book.

A book of poetry written by an alluring woman with the most magnificent red hair.

Anne de Vignon.

A hot rush streaked through him. He was anxious to see her, and wondered how much longer she'd be sequestered in her rooms.

This time there'd be no holding back. This time he was going to give her what she'd been begging for with her eyes last night.

Nicolas opened the book and thumbed through it. He'd actually enjoyed Anne's poems. Her romantic verses at times were even moving. He found himself—to his astonishment—lost in its pages.

He could only imagine the amusement Thomas would derive from *that*.

Nicolas turned back to the first page, where it indicated that the book had been printed in Paris and—more important—that it had passed the Royal Censor and had received permission to be published.

The book was completely legal.

Unlike Gilbert Leduc's books.

Nicolas had to give Henriette credit. She'd cleverly twisted the law to her benefit. Leduc's books claimed to be printed by a foreign publisher—which made them legal for purchase in France.

Foreign books didn't need royal consent the way domestic books did.

But the claim was false. The volumes weren't being printed out of the country by a foreign publisher. They were *not* foreign at all. Acting on a suspicion he'd had from the beginning, Nicolas had tracked down the press printing Leduc's books—located right in Paris.

In short, it wasn't just the sensational subject matter that made the books a problem. The entire illegal operation—from author to printer—would have to be brought to the attention of the King.

Nicolas heard fast footsteps approaching the room. He jerked his head up, froze, and listened.

Anne swept into the library and stalked straight to the desk. Instinctively, Nicolas slipped behind the nearby door. There was a brown ledger in her hand.

Setting the ledger on the desk, Anne pulled at the gold chain around her neck. A locket slid out of her bodice. She opened it, took out a key, and unlocked one of the desk drawers. Putting the ledger inside the desk, she relocked it, placing the key back in the locket.

Transfixed, Nicolas watched as the gold pendant slid down her smooth skin into her bodice once more.

Now there's a hiding place worth exploring.

Nestled between her soft breasts was the very item he needed. The very item he intended to get his hands on. He was about to have the key and the beautiful author. *Dieu*, he liked this mission more and more with each passing day.

Nicolas stepped out from behind the door, hiding his smile.

Anne looked up and started. "Nicolas . . ." she breathed. The breathless way she'd uttered his name made his heart hammer and his sac tighten.

Clearly, she hadn't expected to see him. It confirmed for him—just as he'd surmised—that she'd sent the trunk of books to his chambers for reasons other than to better acquaint him with his grandmother. She was trying to keep him busy—a clever parry on her part. She was attempting to elude him. Moreover, she was trying to avoid the sexual lure between them.

There was no way he was going to let her.

Nicolas stopped before the desk. His cock was already stiffened and eager. "I've startled you."

"No . . . well, yes. I thought . . ." She was adorably flustered. She wasn't a giddy woman. She was educated, intelligent, and always poised, and he loved that he could fluster her. However, that she caused him to make missteps was something he didn't find quite as appealing.

"Rather . . . I didn't see you there." She bit her lip.

Oh, how he was going feast on that pretty mouth. In fact, on her entire sweet, edible form until he got his fill.

Before she left this room again, she was going to express, not avoid, her desire for him.

"Was that your intrigue and adventure story you placed in the desk?" Nicolas kept his tone light, feigning mild interest.

"No. It was simply an accounting ledger. Henriette often helps your grandmother with accounting matters. I was placing it there for her."

"I see." He would see—the ledger and the rest of the contents of the desk. Later. After he had the key. And the woman before him. "It was very kind of you to send the trunk of books. Thank you," he said.

She formed a smile, donning a cordial mask. One he wanted stripped away. Her writings had given him a glimpse of the real Anne de Vignon. Definitely passionate. He wanted to see more. Know more.

Sample some of that very passion firsthand.

"You're welcome. I hope you enjoy them as much as the Comtesse. You may discover you have more in common with her than you think."

Jésus-Christ, he hoped not. "Perhaps so. But I noticed that some books were missing. Ones I'm sure she loves."

Her delicate brows drew together. "Oh?"

He held up the book still in his hand. "Like this one."

Anne pulled her gaze away from his handsome face to the brown leather volume. Her book of poems.

"This is yours, isn't it?" he asked.

"Yes."

In his dark blue justacorps and breeches, he looked so good. So tall and strong. So potently male. Was it possible that he looked even more beautiful today?

"Why didn't you add this to the trunk? Surely the Comtesse loves your work," he said. "I doubt she'd be your patroness otherwise."

Her two volumes of poetry had been written when she was a different person. With whimsical ideas of love. Before Jules had disillusioned and disenchanted her.

Both she and Henriette had had the misfortune of knowing love and its stinging effect.

"I didn't think you'd be interested in reading a book of love poems."

Something glinted in his eyes. "You're right. I'm not interested in reading a book of love poems." He sauntered around the desk. She watched his approach, heat flaring in her belly. He stopped beside her, his body all but touching hers, and handed her the book. "I'd like you to read it to me."

5

Anne forced her gaze down to the book in her hands. It was a futile attempt to divert her attention and collect her wits. Maddeningly, she didn't have to look at Nicolas to know he was there, every fiber of her being acutely aware of him.

And, God help her, what he was doing to her . . .

Her pulse raced. Her breasts felt achy, and her sex was slick. She was a mortifying mess. What irony—for a woman who wrote the stories she did. Who tried to embolden women and discourage this very sort of vulnerability.

With his exceptional looks and charismatic comportment, Nicolas was just the kind of man who could sweep a woman off her feet, into his bed. And shatter her heart.

She'd already been down that road.

She'd never venture there again.

And yet, as he stood close to her, all the warnings, all her good reasoning were being drowned by the powerful urges clamoring in her body. He tempted her. Sorely.

She wasn't naïve. She knew he was trying to seduce her. From the moment they met, all the signs were there. It was in his every look, every well-timed touch and well-practiced tone. Other men had attempted to stir her desire with similar tactics, but none had invoked her interest. Until Nicolas.

She had no idea why this man called to her on such a carnal level. Especially since she'd been so dead inside for so long.

Nicolas moved behind her. She felt his unmistakable erection against her bottom. Briefly, she closed her eyes. The light pulsing between her legs had just turned into a hungry throb.

His arms slid forward, brushing along the sides of her waist. He opened the book in her hands, flipped a few pages, then murmured against her ear, "Read this one."

He removed his arms but the sensations remained in the wake of his touch.

Anne scanned her verses, quickly realizing he'd selected one of the most provocative, amorously suggestive poems in the book. She'd forgotten just how fervid the ardor in her words was. How ardent she once was. There was emotional and physical yearning in every line.

She felt a twinge of sadness as she realized how much she'd changed, resenting that she was revisiting old wounds—thanks to Nicolas. Her intuition told her he'd read some of her work and selected this very evocative poem intentionally. A purposeful strike at her pathetic weakened state. He might be a master of seduction, but she would not be played.

But you want this . . . She shoved the thought away, trying to mute her base needs.

Anne shut the book, tossed it onto the desk, and spun around to face him. It was time to put an end to this. She'd tried being polite. She'd tried keeping a distance. She'd even tried diverting his attention to keep him otherwise occupied by sending him his grandmother's books. All to no avail.

He might be her patroness's grandson but he was overstepping his bounds and she was going to rein him in.

"I know what you're trying to do." Her tone was firm, accusatory, yet her ire hadn't diminished her fever.

His face was unreadable, giving nothing away. "Oh? What am I trying to do?"

Jamming her fists into her hips, she rose up onto the balls of her feet so that she was closer to eye level when she responded, "Bed me!"

One dark brow rose, then his lips twitched as he held back a smile. He leaned in so that his mouth was mere inches from hers. "I know what you're trying to do, Anne. Avoid me." His warm breath made her lips tingle. "You're afraid."

She dropped back down onto her heels. "Afraid? Of you? You jest."

"No, not of me. Of you. You want me and it frightens you. Admit it."

She gave a mirthless laugh. "Good Lord, you are conceited."

A slow, knee-weakening smile spread across his mouth. "No. Just observant. Your body betrays you," he said with far too much smugness.

She hated it that he was right. Her body was betraying her. This tormenting need and the moisture between her legs were the last things she wanted.

No, the last thing you want is for him to "know" that you desire him.

"If it's bed sport you seek, I suggest you look elsewhere. I am not looking for a lover." Her body railed at her words.

"Why not? Do you already have one?"

"That's none of your concern."

"I'll take that as a *no*." He shook his head. "I'm amazed."

"At what?"

"That such a beautiful woman has a cold, empty bed, and no one to fulfill her carnal yearnings"—her sex contracted, a fresh wave of arousal flooding through her—"especially when it is obvious that she's so naturally drawn to sexual pleasures. I've read some of your work, Anne," he said. "Those poems were written by a woman of passion."

"I told you, I wrote those poems a long time ago. I'm not the same woman."

"Yes, you are. Now that the mask of propriety has dropped, the real Anne de Vignon finally appears. Spirited and fiery—just as your writing suggests. At last I get to see the real you."

"And why do you care to *see the real me*?" No one had ever expressed such an interest. Certainly no man. And only after Jules had left had she finally seen that he didn't care to know her either. "Why would it matter to you who I am?"

He brushed a curl behind her ear. "I find you as intriguing as you are desirable."

"Really," she responded blandly, though her fever spiked at his touch. "Please spare me your flowery words." She'd heard enough of them from Jules to last three lifetimes. "You are wasting your efforts."

Anne turned to leave. He caught her wrist. She snapped her head around, ready to deliver up some hot words, when he stunned her into silence by pressing her palm to the bulge in his breeches. "You make me hard every time you walk into the room.

I'm willing to admit how much I want you," he said, his voice low, intoxicating. Anne fought back the powerful urge to tighten her fingers around him. Even through his breeches she could tell he was thick and lusciously large, bringing to sharp focus the void between her thighs aching to be filled, and that a lonely bed was waiting for her upstairs. "I'm not wasting my efforts as long as the desire is mutual. Your nipples are hard, Anne, and begging for attention. Your pulse is racing and you're wet for me, aren't you?"

Wet? She'd soaked her *caleçons.*

He grazed her palm up his length and squeezed her hand hard against him. She lost her breath.

"Why not give in to the sexual pull between us?" he asked, releasing his hold of her hand. "It's going to happen eventually."

Her body burned for him . . . Could she really do this? "You're my patroness's grandson." She knew she was grasping for reasons. Dear God, she was still grasping his erection.

She released him.

In a quick fluid motion he picked her up and set her bottom down on the desk. She gasped and grabbed his shoulders. His hips were now suddenly wedged between her thighs. "That is no deterrence. She has nothing to do with this. She doesn't own your body. You do. You're a grown woman, Anne. It's your decision to make. It's just sex. Some shared physical pleasures."

He was right. Love was one thing. Physical pleasure quite another. Unfortunately, she hadn't been any more successful with sex than she'd been with love.

Nicolas could tell she wanted to surrender to him. She wanted to give in to the demands of her body. He was so close . . .

Her procrastination was killing him.

Slipping his hands around her, he gripped her soft derrière and pulled her closer, pressing her against his cock. A small sound escaped out of her throat the instant he'd come in contact with her sensitized clit. There were too many damn clothes between them. "Are you a virgin, Anne?" He could tell that her sexual experience was rather limited, but how limited, he didn't know. "It's all right if you are. I'll leave you intact until you say otherwise," he assured her. "There are still decadent delights we can enjoy." He brushed his lips against hers. "Say yes, and we'll begin right now."

The tip of his cock was wet with pre-come, his body screaming for release.

Her hands slid down from his shoulders and fisted his justacorps at his chest, still indecisive.

He ran his tongue along the seam of her mouth and lightly bit her bottom lip. "Say it, and I'll make it worth your while." Rolling his hips, he rubbed his length along her sex. This time she moaned, a long sultry sound. *Oh, yes. That's it.* Mentally, he willed her to acquiesce. It took everything he had not to push her onto her back, shove her skirts up, and thrust into her. "Say yes . . . Do it . . . and we can indulge in some mutual gratification," he added. *Seigneur Dieu*, he was practically begging.

He'd never begged anyone for anything.

She pulled back slightly. "Mutual gratification?" She was breathless and flushed. "That's . . ." She swallowed. "That's what men say, but . . . in truth . . . in the boudoir they take their pleasure. Then they take their leave."

Merde. What was Henriette filling her head with? "Not all men are the same. Some of us enjoy giving pleasure as well as receiving it. There's nothing sweeter than a woman's release." Those spine-melting ripples along his thrusting prick when a woman came were exquisite, and something he'd never forgo. "It is a heady rush—empowering—to have someone desperate for you. Desperate for what you can give."

His words hit their mark. He saw curiosity spark in her eyes. She was intrigued. Clearly, she liked the idea of feeling empowered. It occurred to him just then, *She doesn't want to feel vulnerable.*

It was a barrier for her—one he intended to knock down.

To that end, Nicolas yanked her up against him harder and said, "You've got me desperate for you. For what you can give—yourself." *Dieu*, it was no lie. "So desperate, in fact, that I've got to have your mouth, right now."

He crushed her lips, unsure whether she was going to protest. His kiss was hard and hungry, wanting to be inside her more than he wanted his next breath. She parted her lips and pressed her soft form against him. His arousal spiked, hurling him into a feral state, like none he'd known before. Voracious, he drove his tongue into her mouth. She tasted so good. He needed more.

His practiced fingers pulled at the ties on her bodice, impatiently separating it and yanking down her clothing until at last he uncovered her breasts.

Nicolas broke the kiss, his breaths harsh and rapid. He devoured the vision before him. Her breasts weren't large or small, but perfect. His mouth watered.

The gold locket dangled between the soft, tempting mounds. It was suddenly an annoying distraction. He didn't want to think about the key inside. Or his mission. Right now, all he wanted to concentrate on was satiating his lust for this bewitching woman, and showing her just how good sex could be between them, knowing instinctively from the first moment their gazes had met that any amorous encounter between them was sure to be hot and intense.

Nicolas pulled the locket off. She made a small sound in protest. "Shhhh. It's all right," he soothed. "It's in the way."

Pressing his palm against the nape of her neck, he pulled her forward and kissed her again, slow and deep, dropping the locket with a *clunk* onto the desk, so that she knew it was nearby.

She returned his kiss, her hands still clutching the lapels of his knee-length coat. He cupped her breast and grazed his thumb over one hardened nipple. She shivered.

Nicolas pinched, then lightly pulled on the pretty pink tip. Her head tipped back with a soft cry, her glorious red hair spilling over her shoulders.

Good God, she was so sensuous.

Hot urgency thundered through him. His sac was so full of come, he could barely stand it. "Anne . . ." His voice was gruff with desire.

She opened her eyes, her gaze deliciously heated.

"You want more, don't you?" He rolled her nipple between his fingers. She whimpered.

Nicolas rolled the pebbled tip a little harder and was instantly rewarded with a stronger mew. "You like that, and you want more," he repeated.

She trembled. "Yes . . ."

He pushed her onto her back and pinned her wrists against the desk. She stared up at him, her sweet breasts rising and falling with each rapid breath. "Good, because I'm going to give you more."

He lowered his head and sucked her nipple into his hungry mouth.

Anne arched off the desk with a strangled cry, lost to the wet heat drawing on the sensitive tip, each luscious pull making her writhe and her sex leak. She'd never known such keen sensations, such engulfing need.

She'd never known a man like Nicolas de Savignac. There were many reasons she shouldn't be doing what she was doing, but with each greedy suck of his mouth, her reasons eluded her and she couldn't think of one. For once, she didn't want to think. She wanted to feel. Anne closed her eyes . . . This felt sublime.

He turned to her other breast, lavishing upon it the same wicked torment—teasing licks, hard sucks, and light bites. He had her squirming, moaning, starved for more.

He was giving, not taking. Yet in giving, he was getting something in return—the pleasure of her pleasure. This was all so new. She'd never heard any man refer to sex the way he did. This was the kind of passion she'd imagined when she wrote those poems years ago. This was the kind of passion she had envisioned experiencing one day. This was the kind of passion she'd convinced herself she'd never know.

With a growl, he tore his mouth off her. Her eyes flew open.

Releasing her wrists, he yanked her skirts up, layer by layer, his handsome face etched with heated determination. Her heart pounded away the moments until she felt him untie her drawers and pull them off with a fierce tug.

Nicolas tossed them carelessly onto the chair behind him, bent her knees, and pressed them back toward her, opening her wet sex to his view. She was so far gone, she wasn't in the least bit embarrassed.

His light gray eyes rose and met her gaze. The corner of his mouth lifted in a smile. "You look delicious. Good enough to eat." Her insides danced. "Have you ever had a man pleasure you with his mouth?" he asked.

She'd never had a man pleasure her. Period. Her carnal experience was limited to her encounters with Jules. They'd left her disappointed and dissatisfied.

She was the only one who'd ever brought her to orgasm. What Nicolas was doing to her was already more pleasure than she'd ever given herself.

Somehow, Anne summoned her voice. "No."

"Then it's time one did." There was such wicked promise in his eyes, her heart missed a beat. She tensed, bracing herself for the thrill of his touch.

He tightened his grip on her knees. "Relax. All you have to do is to enjoy it."

She nodded. "Good. Fine. Hurry." She was dying. She doubted she would have objected to anything he wanted at the moment.

Amusement flickered in his eyes for an instant before they darkened with desire once more. "I'm going to savor you." He lowered his head between her legs.

The first stroke of his tongue tore a cry from her throat. He stopped; his hand flew off her knee and covered her mouth. "You have to be quiet," he said, tossing a quick glance at the door.

She nodded again, quivering from the inside out.

Gripping both her knees firmly once more, Nicolas lowered his hot mouth onto her needy flesh and groaned. She bit her lip and swallowed down her wail of pleasure.

His skillful tongue licked her along her dewy folds, stimulating every overwrought nerve ending along the way. He varied between soft licks and stronger strokes. She sobbed for more. Nothing in her life had ever felt this good. Her orgasm was building, fast and fierce.

His masterful sucks on her swollen bud sent her rushing to the precipice, but he stopped her from toppling into ecstasy every time by pulling away and lightly blowing cool air against her hot nub, holding her enthralled. Driving her wild.

"Nicolas," she said, his name a plea.

He thrust his tongue inside her. She jerked. He then began sucking her juices with famished zeal, besieging her body with deep suctioning sensations. She squeezed her eyes shut, each pull of his mouth edging her closer and closer to the release she was frantic for.

He pulled back.

Her eyes flew open, dazed and desperate. She was on the brink!

"You taste so good," he said and licked her essence off his lips. "You're going to come for me, aren't you?"

"Yes!" exploded from her lips. "*Please*, don't stop."

He laughed. Releasing one of her knees, Nicolas slid two fingers inside her. She moaned at his possession.

His clever fingers glided in and out of her soaked sex. She was lost in the rhythmic plunge and drag of his fingers making her inner muscles clench and release, pushing her once more toward a shattering climax.

"That's it, Anne. I'm not going to stop. You're going to come for me, *now*."

He swooped in and sucked her clitoris into his mouth with such stunning force, she lurched with a strangled scream.

Ecstasy burst inside her. Anne stiffened and convulsed, her orgasm rocking her body, as spasms rippled through her core, along his thrusting fingers. Nicolas grunted sharply, his mouth still firmly latched onto her, unrelenting. Digging her nails into her knees, Anne rode out the muscle-melting sensations, the shuddering contractions, until the final one ebbed.

Boneless and shaky, she felt him lower her legs and let them dangle over the edge of the desk. Her gown was bunched at her waist, her lower body still exposed.

Nicolas swiped his mouth with the back of his hand, his eyes ablaze with his physical need. "We're not done," he assured her, his voice rough with desire. Already his hands were on the ties of his breeches and he started to open them.

She didn't want to be done.

Anne rose onto her elbows and was about to tell him how much she wanted to feel him inside her, and that she wanted to bring him to a voluptuous climax, just as he'd brought her, when she saw him freeze. His chin jerked up, his attention directed at the door.

It was then she heard it. *Footsteps.*

They were getting louder, closer.

Her stomach dropped. She sat up, twisted around, and gasped. The door was ajar and had never been fully closed, much less locked.

Nicolas swore, each word a low snarl, laced with frustration and fury at the impending interruption. He raked both hands through his dark hair and let out a sharp breath. "We'll have to finish this later." He cupped her cheeks and gave her a quick, hard kiss. "I may just kill whoever is about to walk through that door." He pulled her skirts down over her legs. "Dress. Quickly." He refastened his breeches.

Her heart pounded as her fumbling fingers went to work on her bodice.

Nicolas picked up books that had been knocked off the desk during their carnal encounter, straightening the area around them. She hadn't realized they'd made such a mess.

The footsteps continued to approach at a strong and steady pace.

Finishing with her bodice, Anne smoothed her hair, then her

skirts, then checked her bodice again, making certain everything was secure.

Nicolas pulled her *caleçons* off the chair and stuffed them into the sleeve of his justacorps. He winked at her.

She felt her cheeks warm. "How do I look?" she asked.

He stepped closer. In her ear he whispered, "Like a woman who thoroughly enjoyed some sinful pleasures." She heard the smile in his voice.

Heat crept down from her face to her chest. He stepped back.

"Don't forget this." He held out his hand. Dangling from his finger was her gold locket.

"Thank you." She quickly slipped it on and tucked the pendant into her bodice.

Nicolas dropped down onto the settee, opened one of the books he'd picked up, and was thumbing through it casually when Henriette pushed the door open and swept into the room.

She stopped, glanced at Nicolas, and cocked a brow at Anne. Anne managed the semblance of a smile.

"A wonderful poem, Anne," Nicolas said. "I enjoyed it very much." He flipped more pages. "Ah, and this one, 'One Spring Night'—absolutely lovely."

Henriette cleared her throat.

Nicolas twisted around. "Oh, Henriette . . ." He smiled and rose, looking as innocent as a babe. "Good day."

"Good day, Nicolas." Henriette walked over to the desk.

Anne didn't miss that Nicolas held the book strategically before him, covering his tented breeches. Nicolas met her gaze. His smoldering look weakened her knees. Outwardly, he put on a cool and polished performance. But on the inside, he burned for her.

Henriette pulled her locket out of her bodice and removed the key inside. "I see you are reading Anne's poetry," she said as she unlocked the desk drawer.

"Yes, and enjoying it very much. Knowing how much I want to get to know my grandmother, Anne graciously gave me a number of the Comtesse's favorite books. I'm looking forward to reading yours, too, Henriette."

"Really? Do tell me what you think of them." Her sister pulled the ledger out of the desk, then relocked it.

"Of course. I anticipate being enthralled." Nicolas gave a slight bow.

Dear God, the man was flawless and unflappable. Anne admired him for it, and yet, it was disquieting.

"Are you going to work here, Henriette?" she asked. "I was about to leave—"

"No, I'll take this to my rooms. If you are through, I'd like you to join me." Henriette walked toward the doors. "Until this evening, Nicolas."

"Until this evening, Henriette," he concurred, his tone and expression genial.

Henriette stopped at the doors. "Aren't you coming?" she asked Anne.

"I'll be along shortly." Anne waited until her sister left the library and her steps had receded before she approached Nicolas. "You are too good." Her tone was light but her words were weighted.

A grin formed on his face. "Oh? And what specifically am I 'too good' at?"

He was hunting for a compliment, the cheeky devil. But then again, a man with his sexual skills had a certain right to be smug.

"Your carnal skills notwithstanding, I was referring to your comportment. In fact, your comportment always."

He lifted a brow. "What about my comportment?"

"It is always polished. You give nothing away."

"I'm afraid I don't understand. Did you want me to give away what we did on the desk your sister was just using?"

"No, of course not. It's just . . ." She shook her head. "Forget it. It's nothing."

Nicolas frowned. He tossed the book down onto the settee and cradled her cheek in his palm. "What is it? Tell me."

She looked up into his face. "I've noted that men who are too polished, are too often . . . deceitful." She moved in closer. "I want you to be honest with me, Nicolas. Always."

"What just happened between us was honest. My desire for you is genuine. My desire to spend more such blissful moments with you is sincere."

Anne smiled. "I know. I enjoyed what we did. Very much." She grasped hold of his lapels, rose onto the balls of her feet, and brushed her mouth along the side of his neck, stopping at his pulse to draw lightly on his skin. It instantly quickened beneath her lips. He groaned, his reactions to her an inebriating rush.

She craved his surrender. To turn the tables and have him completely undone for *her*. The notion was thrilling. It *was* empowering. And too tempting to walk away from, despite the niggling warnings in her head.

She couldn't wait to decimate his defenses. To peel back the layers and discover the real Nicolas. And she intended to do it, one caress and kiss at a time.

"Tonight, it is my turn to pleasure you," she murmured in his ear. "I want you inside me."

6

The moment Anne left, Nicolas slumped against the bookshelves and scrubbed a hand over his face.

Merde. His unsated body was in torment. Agony, actually, thanks to her heated words, her soft, hot mouth.

She'd unbalanced him in the worst way.

His every impulse was to race after her, take her to her rooms, and finish what they'd started. But he wouldn't do it no matter how powerful the urge. Not until he'd collected himself and was back in control.

Lifting his hand, he opened his palm. A shiny gold key stared back at him, taken from the locket just before he'd handed it back to her.

It was a victory, but it felt like an empty one. He had the key. But not the woman. And he wanted her too damned much. Her taste was still on his tongue. She tasted sweeter than any female he'd ever had. Sampling her had only stoked the fire. Having to wait several hours before he could be with her was torture in the extreme.

Nicolas clenched the key tightly. At a full cock stand, his muscles taut, he shoved himself off the bookshelves and began to pace.

She was insightful. A little too intuitive. And as ludicrous as it was, her comment about deceitful men actually bothered him. Nicolas silenced the foreign emotion that was gnawing at him. He was *not* deceitful. He was on a mission. There was a difference. He had a duty—and he was *not* going to feel guilty about it. If physical intimacies brought him closer to the truth, all the better. Especially when those ardent encounters were as fine as the one he'd just had.

There'd be no deviation from his initial plan. Anne was going to unwittingly aid him in solving the mystery of Leduc and gain him recognition in the Guard. Being a Musketeer was everything to him. Commanding the Musketeers was his long-held dream.

So why don't you check the desk? You've got the key.

Nicolas stopped dead in his tracks and dragged his gaze to it. Ebony and with gold inlay, it was an ornate piece of furniture.

And where you brought a beautiful author to a shattering release.

Thanks to their decadent diversion, now he knew for certain she wasn't a virgin. She'd had another lover, possibly more than one—though she wasn't overly experienced.

Who were they? How did they treat her?

The comment she'd made about men taking their pleasure and then their leave was also eating at him. He'd initially thought Henriette had put the notion in her head.

But now, he wasn't so certain . . .

Nicolas pulled out her *caleçons* from his jacket. Her scent swirled around him; his prick throbbed. He shoved the garment back in his justacorps.

So she'd made a comment or two about men being selfish. So what? Just because she'd made such statements, and just because she'd had some amorous experience, didn't prove she was Leduc.

Henriette was Leduc.

There is only one way to be certain . . .

His attention was drawn back to the desk. With a muttered oath, he marched over to it and sat down. Unlocking the first drawer, he began his search, trying to ignore the trepidation he felt.

His heart rate settled into slow, hard thuds as he sifted through the content of each drawer, reading every letter and note he found. His grandmother's letters. Mostly from old friends. Meaningless to him.

Nicolas closed the third drawer and opened the final one. A yellow satin box was all it contained. Frowning, he pulled it out and untied the matching ribbon around the box and pulled off the lid.

More letters.

Only these were different. These ensnared him. These were addressed to his mother.

Nicolas flipped through them. At least twenty letters, all written by a grandmother he'd never known to a mother who'd regretted her marriage—yet was never forgiven for her impetuous act.

Scanning each letter, he was astonished to read remorse in the old woman's words. Cold anger slowly seeped through his body and congealed in his blood. Damn her. Why bother writing letters she never intended to send? *Merde.* What was the point? Was this some twisted way of purging her conscience? Having never sent the letters out clearly showed the Comtesse had chosen her pride over her daughter.

Now that his mother was gone, it was too late. The Comtesse would never have the opportunity to express her regrets.

Nicolas tossed the letters back in the box, disgusted. Yet at the same time he was . . . *relieved*. There was nothing damning Anne.

There is nothing that proves Henriette is Leduc either.

Now that he had the master key, he could search for proof—in the Comtesse's private rooms as well as Henriette's chambers.

Dismayed that he was feeling reluctant at hunting for evidence, he steeled his resolve, retied the yellow ribbon around the box, and locked it in the desk once again.

The key firmly clenched in hand, Nicolas stalked from the room with purposeful strides.

He had a job to do. He'd get it done.

And in the meantime, none would be the wiser.

* * *

Anne slammed her book of poetry shut. "I've decided to take a lover," she blurted out.

Camille gasped.

Sitting behind the desk, her quill frozen in hand, Henriette's mouth fell agape.

With a squeal, Camille jumped out of her chair and clapped her hands, the book on her lap falling to the floor. She rushed over and dropped down beside Anne on the settee.

"Who is it?" she asked with breathless anticipation. "It's Nicolas, isn't it? His eyes devour you whenever he looks at you." A giggle bubbled out of her.

Her younger sister's giddiness made Anne smile. "Yes, as a matter of fact, it is."

Slowly Henriette set the quill down, rose from the desk in Anne's private apartments, and walked around it, staring at Anne as if she just sprouted a horn out of the middle of her forehead, her expression a mixture of shock and horror. "Have you lost your mind?"

"No."

Camille let out another squeal of jubilation. "I think it's wonderful!"

Henriette glared at Camille, the same incredulous expression etched on her face. "Pray tell, what is wonderful about Anne and the Comtesse's grandson?"

"Well, Henriette," Camille began, "unless you're completely blind, you may have noticed he's incredibly handsome." Turning to Anne, she beamed once more. "And he's interested in our sister!"

Henriette rolled her eyes. "Good Lord." She approached and sat down in a nearby chair. The latest chapter of Gilbert Leduc's story that she'd been editing now lay forgotten on the desk. "He has beguiled you." Henriette shook her head. "I knew I didn't trust him."

"He has *not* beguiled her. Anne knows what she is doing," Camille defended. "Go ahead, Anne. Tell Henriette she's wrong."

"Perhaps I wish to be beguiled," Anne stated.

Henriette's eyes widened. "But he's only looking for a tumble."

"As am I." Anne's answer set Camille into a fit of laughter.

"You see! I told you, Anne knows what she's doing," Camille countered, then leaned into Anne. "Has Nicolas said or done anything to initiate a physical involvement? I must say, I've been having rather shameless thoughts about Thomas and wondering if he would—"

Henriette threw up her hands. "Am I the only one who has any good sense left? Anne, you are talking about the Comtesse's very own grandson. What will she say?"

"The Comtesse is no prude," Anne said.

"I think the Comtesse will not mind at all. She adores Anne, and she'll adore her grandson, once she gets to know him. He's very charming." Camille patted Anne's hand. "However, I do think you should still be discreet."

"Anne, I think this is a mistake." Worry creased Henriette's brow. "Though it pains me to mention it, you and I have hardly had good luck in selecting men. I married out of love . . . and look how disastrously that turned out. And then there's your involvement with Jules d'Orsay. He took your innocence and your heart before he left and married the Baron de Grimaud's daughter— who, he'd conveniently neglected to mention, was his betrothed all along."

Anne leaned forward and squeezed her older sibling's hand. "Henriette, this is not about love. That is not what I am looking for." She'd found a man who stirred her. Excited her. She wanted more of the same. More of the wild abandon she'd experienced with Nicolas earlier.

He was nothing like Jules.

The sumptuous memory of what had happened in the library with Nicolas flooded her mind. Hot need unfurled in her belly, sending waves of heat shimmering over her nerve endings. Her body tightened and ached for more.

Anne picked her book of love poems off her lap and held it

up. "Do you see this, Henriette? Today, for the first time in a very long while, I reread my poetry." It had been jarring and revealing. "I realized just how withdrawn I've become. I used to want passion. After Jules, I wanted *nothing*. No passion of any kind—involving either the heart or the body. And this is how I have remained. Embracing nothing. It's empty."

She'd *gladly* turn her back on love, but in no way did she want to withhold herself from the glorious passion she'd discovered in Nicolas's arms.

With one wickedly delicious act, he'd showed her that she wasn't as dead inside as she thought. Moreover, he'd made her see the physical act of love in a whole new light. It wasn't simply an act where the man took and the woman gave. At least not with him.

Henriette frowned. "Your life is not empty. You are Gilbert Leduc. You are doing something with your writing. You are giving women a chance to speak through his stories."

"Yes, and I must confess that there are times during the interviews I feel like screaming, '*Is there not one decent man anywhere in the realm worthy of a woman's heart or body?*'" Anne let out a sharp breath and placed her book back down on her lap.

"What are you saying?" Henriette asked. "You can't be thinking of quitting—of no longer writing Leduc's stories. We couldn't earn enough to feed ourselves from our writing before. And you know how the Comtesse feels about the stories."

"What I am saying is that we live in the most powerful nation in all of Christendom. A nation of twenty million people, half of which are men and none of which seem to have any appeal," Anne said.

Her sisters fell silent.

"Well, I have found one who appeals to me," she continued.

"One can indulge in physical intimacies, share some bliss, without involving the heart. Men do it all the time. Why can't I?"

Her sisters looked at her with a mixture of emotions. The predominant one—concern.

Anne rose and helped Henriette up out of her chair. Guiding her back to the desk, she said, "Everything is fine and is going to remain that way. For me and for Leduc. His stories will continue to delight his avid readership. Now get back to editing so this story can be published."

She would never stop writing Leduc's stories. She believed in them. The Comtesse believed in them, and the people clamored for them.

She'd never allow anything to interfere with them. Not even a heavenly affair with a beautiful man. The deadline approached. The volume had to be sent to the printer soon.

She had a job to do. She'd get it done.

And no one would be the wiser.

* * *

Nicolas pressed the key into Thomas's palm. "Take this. It's the master key to the desks in the hôtel."

The afternoon had trickled by. At last it was evening. Only a few more hours before he'd be with Anne. *"I want you inside me."* Each time her provocative words spiraled through his system, his cock swelled and his fever for her spiked.

Thomas's eyes widened. "Where did you get it?"

"Anne." His response was purposely short and tight.

Thomas grinned. "I take it the lady's unaware you have her key?"

"That's correct."

Still grinning. "Care to share some details?"

"Absolutely. You have a stomach ailment," Nicolas said, grabbing the justacorps Thomas was about to put on and tossing it onto a nearby chair in Thomas's rooms. "You're in great discomfort and are unable to go to supper."

"I am?"

"Yes, and I will offer your regrets to the ladies."

"Why can't I go to supper?"

"Because you're going to be searching Henriette's and Camille's private desks in their chambers. During the day and at night, a search is quite impossible. They are almost always in their rooms. The only time one can be conducted is while they're together in the *Salle de Buffet* for supper. I've already searched both of the Comtesse's desks. Neither desk yielded any evidence of any kind. I found nothing that proved or remotely hinted at the identity of the author of the pen portraits."

Thomas held out the key. "Since you've been conducting such thorough searches, why don't you look through the desks and I'll go to supper."

"Because I'm in charge of this mission, and therefore, you're the one with the stomach ailment." Nicolas didn't mention that *he* was experiencing an annoying stomach ailment. It was driving him mad, but each time he thought of the proof he might uncover in the end, his entrails tightened.

"Ah. Yes. I see your point." Thomas's arm dropped to his side. Disappointment was evident in his eyes and Nicolas suspected it had something to do with Camille. "Do you want me to search Anne's desk, too?"

"No!" Nicolas mentally cringed at how strongly that came out.

Thomas lifted a brow.

Nicolas cleared his throat. "I'll take care of Anne's desk and her rooms. Search her sisters' rooms, desks, everything. Keep the key. I'll get it from you in the morning." If Thomas found evidence implicating one of the other two, he wouldn't have to search in Anne's private domain. "Make certain you leave nothing unturned."

7

Nicolas's heart rate doubled as he approached Anne's door.

Supper had been long and drawn out. Being forced to make witty commentary and polite conversation, with Anne so near, had been maddening.

Her cheeks slightly flushed, her breaths slightly quickened, she'd looked achingly beautiful. And—God help him—aroused by his presence at the table. He'd been impatient for the ordeal to be over, so that he could join her in her rooms. Each time her eyes met his, a bolt of heat shot through him. Starved for her, he'd barely touched his food. He couldn't get the image out of his mind of her on the desk in the library, her sweet body half exposed, her glistening pink sex slick with desire, looking every bit like every man's fantasy.

Because Anne and her sisters had been in their rooms all afternoon and he couldn't search Henriette's chambers as he'd wished to, he'd had to find other ways to fill the long hours before he'd be with Anne. Caring nothing about the books in the trunk—his grandmother's favorites—he was drawn to Anne's volume of poems.

He'd reread them.

He shouldn't have done it.

Her words had affected him more strongly this time. This time he found them even more moving than before. Because this time he knew the woman behind the words. Her smile. Her voice. Her taste. Intimately.

Her heart was on those pages. But her heart had changed. She didn't believe in love anymore. It was absurd that the notion continued to bother him but he couldn't shake it. A heart that had had such depth had closed itself off. It was a shame.

Worse, rereading her work, knowing now that she'd had some intimate experience with men, had stirred up suspicions he'd spent most of the day trying to mute. He refused to believe Anne was Leduc without definitive proof.

Entertaining thoughts of his mission only aggravated that annoying emotion in his gut that wouldn't go away. He had absolutely nothing to feel guilty about. He was not the guilty party here, and yet he was left wrestling with that very emotion that clashed with—even threatened—his lustful longing for her.

Nicolas reached Anne's door.

In short, he'd been in turmoil when he'd walked into the *Salle de Buffet* for supper, and he was in turmoil now.

He took a deep breath and let it out slowly.

On the other side of this door is an alluring woman no man would refuse to bed. She's waiting for you, warm and willing. Knock on the bloody door!

He rapped on the door lightly.

It flew open and he was yanked inside. The door slammed

shut. Shoved hard, his back slammed against it. He grunted. It took a moment for his eyes to adjust to the dimmer light in the room.

Anne stood before him, hair down in long fiery-colored curls, wearing nothing but her chemise, her palms pressing against his chest.

He feasted on the sight of her. He had to remember to breathe. *Jésus-Christ*, she looked incredible.

Anne frowned. "What took you so long?"

He swallowed before he could summon his voice. "I—"

Rising onto the balls of her feet, she crushed her warm mouth against his, thrust her tongue between his lips, and he forgot what he was going to say. Her taste was inebriating.

She stroked his tongue with zealous swirls, kissing him with magnificent intensity. He hauled her up against him, his cock pulsing between them, and trailed his hands down her back, returning her kiss with equal ardor. Skimming his fingers up under her short chemise, he was stunned to find his hands on her pert—and very bare—derrière. *Dieu,* she wasn't wearing any *caleçons.*

Anne pulled away abruptly.

Nicolas reached out to drag her back, but she shook her head.

"Take this off." She was already pulling off his justacorps, her breaths as rapid and rough as his own.

Nicolas shrugged the knee-length jacket off his shoulders. Before the garment even hit the floor, her hands were tugging at the fastenings on his breeches, trying to open them.

He loved it when a woman got straight to the point.

Her fingers fumbled. He brushed them aside and opened his breeches in haste.

She pulled his shirttails out. He pulled his shirt off and discarded it.

Anne froze, her gaze slowly moving over his chest, down to his aching cock now straining out of his breeches.

"You are more beautiful than any man has the right to be," she breathed.

Before he could respond to her endearing comment, her soft fingers wrapped around his erection and slowly pumped his prick. His words were lost in his groan. He closed his eyes and leaned heavily against the door, basking in the sensations radiating along his cock.

Her other hand slipped inside his open breeches and cradled his sac, gently caressing. "I want to pleasure you, Nicolas."

Oh, she was going to pleasure him, all right. Satiate him fully. He'd see to it. Then finally, *finally* this lust that had invaded his mind and was torturing his body would dissipate. He'd have it under control and be able to think clearly once more.

Suddenly, her hands were gone. His eyes flew open, dazed, his body rioting for more. He found her kneeling before him, the candlelight in the room giving her bright beautiful hair a bedazzling glow.

She grasped the base of his shaft and licked her lips.

Essence oozed from the tip of his eager cock as thoughts of feeding his length into her mouth burned in his mind.

Nicolas delved his fingers into her hair. This was not what he'd intended when he first walked in. Thanks to her parting words in the library, all he'd thought of the rest of the day was being inside her juicy core, riding her hard. But the famished look in her eyes and the lure of that hot wet mouth were . . . irresistible.

He brought his prick closer to her moist lips. "Are you hungry for my cock, Anne?"

Anne squeezed her knees together, trying to find relief from the throbbing ache between her legs. Yes, she was hungry for it!

She was ravenous for him. Seeing how aroused she made him had her on fire and filled her with an exhilarating sense of power. She wanted him in her mouth. She wanted him filling her sex with that thick, glorious part of his male anatomy.

Undaunted by his size and her limited experience, she said firmly, "Yes. Tonight, it's all mine to pleasure." She should have been shocked by her words, her brazen behavior, but wasn't. It thrilled her to see his eyes darken and feel his shaft twitch in her hand.

He brought out a side of her she never knew existed. She had no idea how he drew it out of her—so effortlessly, when no one else ever had—but was grateful for the remarkable revelation.

"We're not stopping at tonight," he wickedly promised. "We're going to have at each other until we're sated."

His words sent a hot shiver through her body. Briefly, she wondered how long it would take to satisfy the hunger she had for this man.

"Tell me if this pleases you." She swirled her tongue around the engorged tip of his shaft. He grunted sharply. Hiding her smile, she moistened her lips, then closed them over the crest of his sex. His breath hissed out through clenched teeth, his reaction causing her nipples to tighten and her core to cream. The sudden surge of desire made her light-headed.

"Take more," he growled.

His feral state was an aphrodisiac. She slid him farther into the wet heat of her mouth, drew him out, then plunged him back in deeper still, growing more and more emboldened and sure of her actions. His hips jerked.

He swore softly. His control snapped. Rearing back, he pushed back in, her mouth widening to accommodate him. He began to thrust. She matched his rhythm, her tongue caressing the underside of his penis with each rhythmic stroke as she sucked and sucked and sucked on him. The taste of his surrender was sweet. A moan, a sound of pure pleasure, escaped her throat and drew a hearty groan from him.

Anne slid her hands inside his breeches to grip his buttocks, his muscles tightening under her fingers. She held on to him, listening to his ragged breaths, keeping to the pace he desired.

He slowed his movements.

"Anne . . . I'm going to come . . . hard . . . in your mouth. If you don't want that, you've got to stop *now*." He stopped thrusting, his body straining with effort.

Her heart pounding, she responded by tightening her hold and drawing him in and out of her mouth, hard and fast, refusing to stop. He stiffened, his head falling back against the door. A guttural sound erupted out of him as spurt after spurt of come shot into her mouth and down her throat. She drank him in, digging her nails into him, wanting all he had, taking everything he gave, until his fingers loosened in her hair, his body relaxed, and she'd taken his last drop.

Slouched against the door, his breaths were short and shallow, his muscled chest rising and falling rapidly.

Drawing his sex from her mouth, Anne rose on shaky limbs, reeling, licking a small drop of his essence from her bottom lip. His eyes were closed, and on his handsome face was the undeniable look of rapture.

She'd done that to him. Joy filled every empty chamber in her heart. Making him desperate for her had been, as he'd said, a "heady rush."

He opened his eyes, his usual knee-weakening half-smile forming on his lips the moment he met her gaze.

Nicolas pulled her to him. He was amazed at the transformation

in her and delighted in it. No longer hiding behind a façade—
the cool erudite author—she'd embraced the passion that was so
much a part of her.

And dear God, there was such perfect passion between them.

She laced her arms around his neck, a grin on her face despite
the fervid need he saw in her eyes.

"You liked that," she stated, looking adorably pleased with
herself.

That was an understatement. He couldn't recall the last time
he'd come that hard. At least now, the edge had been taken off
his lust.

"Really? What makes you think so?" he teased, unable to
keep the mirth from his tone.

She snuggled closer, her soft bottom giving a sweet little wig-
gle. "I suppose it's just a guess," she teased back.

He chuckled. She felt so good in his arms.

She caressed his cheek, her smile fading. "Thank you,
Nicolas."

He furrowed his brow. "For what?"

"For showing me that there is more to physical intimacies
between men and women than I ever knew. In fact, I never would
have believed it had I not enjoyed it firsthand. What we've done
today is a first for me. I'd heard of such acts, but never experienced them. I'm glad I shared them with you."

Her words were touching, and he cautioned himself against
having any more tender emotions where she was concerned.

"You're a natural in the carnal arts, *chère*." It was a neutral
comment and one he believed with his heart to be true.

He should take advantage of her amenable mood and draw
information out of her. But he didn't want to ask questions
related to Leduc. Or her past lovers. Not now. He nuzzled her

neck, enjoying the way her silky hair felt against his face. He didn't want to spoil the moment and found himself wishing that there wasn't anything more complicated between them than their desire for each other. "There is still more to experience," he murmured. "Show me where the bed is."

He felt her shiver of excitement before she stepped back and took his hand. The chemise hid little from his view. Her nipples were pebbled and her shapely thighs were bare, looking satiny smooth. His semihard cock thickened.

He couldn't wait to nestle between those soft thighs, feel them wrapped around him.

They entered her bedchamber of soft pinks and light greens. She climbed onto the bed and was sitting on her heels in the middle, waiting for him, looking so lush.

At the foot of the bed, Nicolas began discarding the remainder of his clothing. Her lovely eyes moved over him, stopping on his cock. He loved the way she looked at him, with such hot need. *How will she look at you when she learns what you've been up to?* He abruptly arrested the errant thought.

Her delicate brows rose slightly. "You're already . . . uh . . ." Her voice trailed off. She was unbalanced and endearingly flustered again; her nervous excitement, tangible. Accustomed to women with a more casual attitude toward carnal encounters, he found her refreshingly different.

She is different. You'll likely be arresting one of her sisters soon. How often have you done that to a woman you've bedded? Nicolas cursed the mental distractions. That was later. The future was in the future. This was now. And at this moment, all he wanted was to be inside her.

"I've been hard for you for two days. One orgasm isn't going to be enough—even an orgasm by such a talented mouth." Nicolas tossed the last of his apparel onto the floor. "Come here," he ordered, sinking his knees on the bed.

Her nipples were driving him mad. They strained for him against the soft material of her chemise, and he was going to give them all the carnal attention those luscious peaks deserved.

She moved close. He slipped her chemise off. Her arms were just about to circle his neck when he caught her wrists and held her arms apart.

He let his eyes drink her in, taking in every appealing curve of her body and the pretty auburn curls covering her sex, already moist from her juices.

He met her gaze, and realized she was watching him closely for his reaction. He wanted her to have no doubts as to what he thought. "You're breathtaking."

She looked a little embarrassed but mostly pleased by his comment. "So are you."

Dieu, she was sweet—and disquieting. His thoughts were far too jumbled and soft for his liking, and he decided to blame them on his yet unsatisfied appetite for the ravishing poetess.

She pressed her warm mouth to his and kissed him. Nicolas released her wrists and pulled her tightly against him, squeezing his cock between them. He groaned.

Finally he was going to bed her and end his obsession to have her.

Suddenly, she pushed away, taking him by surprise. His eyes snapped open.

"I have something I need to tell you about myself." Her hand was against his chest, staving him off. He didn't like the earnest expression on her face. "I want to be honest with you."

No! Honesty was bad—and given the timing, the last thing he

wanted. Whatever she was about to say, his instincts told him he didn't want to hear it.

Nicolas clasped her wrist and gently removed her hand from his chest. Slipping his other hand onto her nape, he pulled her closer, bringing her mouth to his. "Later. Not now," he murmured against her lips. "No confessions during sex. Just mutual pleasure."

"I am not a virgin," she blurted out.

He jerked his head up. *Merde.*

"I'm not sure if you've guessed it or not, but I wanted to tell you just the same."

"Fine. Good. It doesn't matter." But the voice inside him screamed otherwise, more suspicions rushing through his mind. He crushed his mouth to hers, desperate to drown them out with a fresh wave of lust.

She cupped his face between her soft hands and pulled away again, her breathing as quickened as his own. "There's been only one other man, and he never bestowed the pleasure you have. I wanted you to know the truth."

She was back to kissing him, trailing hot, wet kisses along his neck. Nicolas closed his eyes. And even though his prick was as stiff as wood and his body achingly aroused once more, his mind balked. *Merde. Not now!* He wanted carnal gratification. Not details about the man she'd been with. Not thoughts about what he'd have to do if she turned out to be Leduc. Or how she'd react if instead he had to bring one of her beloved sisters before the King.

And especially—*most especially*—not the guilt over his lies.

He wanted to lose himself in the sweet sensations of her mouth, her touch. He took her hand and brought it to his cock. Her fingers immediately curled around him and gave a little squeeze. The sound of bliss escaped his lips. But as hot pleasure rippled through him, his mind refused to quiet, growing more insistent. Getting louder. And louder.

The next thing he knew, he was staring at her surprised expression; his hands were on her shoulders—and to his astonishment—he was holding her at arm's length.

Merde, he'd just pushed her away.

"I need a moment," he tossed out, climbed off the bed, marched into the antechamber, and closed the doors.

8

In the antechamber, fire crackled in the hearth, the sound mingling with Nicolas's ragged breaths. He curled his fingers. Choking on his frustration and rage, he wanted to smash his fist against the wall. *What the hell are you doing? What is the matter with you? She's so damned desirable. She is hungry for it. This is no time for a crisis of conscience!*

He couldn't believe he was with a beautiful woman. Naked. Painfully hard. And was actually hesitating to bed her.

Something caught the corner of his eye. The fire from the hearth cast an orange light into the two rooms that stemmed from the one he was in. In one of those rooms, he could clearly see a small writing desk. With several drawers. Some books were on it. As was a crystal inkwell.

"Nicolas?" Anne's voice grabbed his attention. She stood at the door, and to his disappointment, she'd placed her chemise back on. "Is everything all right?"

No. Never, not ever in his life had he become discomposed—and certainly never with a woman. He was highly disciplined. Trained in combat. Skilled in weapons. And when he wasn't plotting his next ambitious promotion, he was participating in his favorite pastime—recreational sex.

He liked women. Loved a good tumble.

He didn't think he could be unraveled—by her or anyone. It horrified him that she had.

Anne approached and, by her expectant expression, was awaiting his response.

"I . . . uh . . ." *Dieu*, he was actually *flustered*. He gnashed his teeth.

Something flickered in her eyes. "Say no more. I know what you're after."

He tensed. "You do?"

"Yes. It's rather obvious." The knowing look in her eyes made him uneasy.

"It is?" It couldn't be. How could she possibly know a thing about his mission?

"Of course. It's why you came in here." She stepped between him and the rectangular wooden table in the middle of the room. "I know what you're looking for."

His eyes narrowed. "And what is it I'm looking for?" He'd be damned if he confessed a thing.

She lifted her brows. "You want me to say it?"

He curled his fingers under her chin. "Say it."

"The door you're looking for is over my shoulder—the *Salle de Bain*. You'll find the chamber pot in there, next to the tub."

Nicolas froze and blinked. Then he tossed his head back and roared with laughter at the sheer ridiculousness of the situation.

"You think I need to . . ." He shook his head, unable to finish the sentence, laughter erupting from him again.

Perplexed, she frowned.

It took several moments before he could finally sober up. This was not his typical sexual encounter. It was high time to put an end to his imbecilic behavior.

He picked her up and placed her bottom down on the table behind her. Her eyes widened. Nicolas cradled her face between his palms. "I came in here because you overwhelm me."

Her eyes softened. "You overwhelm me, too." She smiled. "And I rather like it. I want to be overwhelmed some more."

He liked her answer. Actually, there was a lot about her he liked.

"Good. Because I'm going to take you—*slowly*." Nicolas pulled off her chemise and dropped it onto the table. "Would you like that, Anne? Would you like to be fucked slowly?"

Her breathing had begun to escalate.

"Yes."

Nicolas reached behind her and slid her derrière closer to the edge of the table. "Show me how wet you are for me." He took a step back.

She paused, and he got the sense she was wrestling with inhibition.

"Do it," he prompted softly.

Slowly, she parted her thighs.

"That's good, Anne. Lean back."

His heart raced as he watched her place her palms down on the table behind her, her hips now perfectly angled for his viewing pleasure.

Her sex glistened with her juices. Unable to resist, he scored his finger from her moist opening up to her clit, stopping to press on the sensitive nub with enough pressure to make her gasp in delight.

"I'm going to take you right now." His cock jerked.

"Nicolas . . ." Her thighs trembled. "There's a bed—"

"Next time." He hadn't intended to have her on a hard surface again, but he'd finally quieted his brain. He wasn't going to do anything to disturb the delicious desire flowing through him or jeopardize this moment. "It will be just as good. I promise."

He'd make her forget any discomfort she felt.

Taking his prick in hand, he guided it to her slick entrance. Her head fell back with a soft moan. A tremor of expectation quivered through her and radiated up his cock. He shuddered. Oh, how she turned him inside out. It felt as though he'd waited forever for this. For her. He had to have her or die.

Gripping her hips, he pressed into her, watching as the crest of his cock sank into her wet heat. He was thick and full and she was wonderfully snug. He pushed, sinking deeper, her cream coating his cock. Taking his time, he stretched her slowly, savoring the shuddering sensations as she enveloped him, gloving him an inch at a time. She whimpered and lowered herself onto her back, trembling.

A bead of sweat formed on his forehead. He continued his steady progress, bearing down on her, unrelenting. "You're going to take all of me, aren't you, Anne? You want it all, don't you?"

"Yes," she panted, lolling her head to one side. "Yes . . ."

Nicolas butted against the entrance of her womb and groaned. At his possession, she made the most sensuous sound. He loved that. He loved everything about sex, not just the climax but all things preceding it. Especially the initial penetration, that first thrust—fast or slow—that buried him inside. And being inside

Anne, feeling the hot clasp of her tight sex clenched around him, the light quivering of her inner muscles along his length, was more heaven than any man deserved.

She was primed. He knew it wouldn't take much to send her over the edge.

Leaning forward, he grasped the edge of the table and slipped an arm under her waist, arching her body to him. He latched onto her breast and suckled hard. She cried out, her fingers tangling in his hair. The tip instantly distended in his mouth.

Laving and lightly biting her nipple, he pumped his cock in her, giving her short, shallow thrusts that kept her enthralled, but also kept her from coming. She mewed in protest and strained toward him, trying to draw in him deeper. Her efforts were futile. He wouldn't acquiesce. He continued, his measured strokes unbroken.

"Nicolas . . . please . . ." She wrapped her legs around him, still desperately squirming and arching.

Releasing her nipple from the confines of his mouth, he flicked it with his tongue. "Please what? Please, make me come, Nicolas? Please, fuck me harder?" Turning to her other nipple, he lightly raked his teeth across it.

She gasped. "Yes, to all that. *Right. Now!*"

Nicolas lifted his head, softly chuckling. "You're being very demanding for a woman who's at my mercy," he teased and gave her a deep thrust before returning to his shorter strokes.

She made a frustrated sound. "Nicolas, if you make me wait any longer, I swear, I'll—I'll . . . make you pay."

"Mmmm, now that sounds delicious." He suckled her breast gently with just the right amount of finesse to snatch her breath away. "How will you make me pay?" He drew her hardened nipple back into his mouth.

"I'm a writer . . . I have . . . *ahhhh* vivid imagination . . . I'll . . . think of something."

With his cock dipped in glory, and this passionate woman pleading for more, Nicolas ceded. He slipped his arm out from under her, straightened, and grasped her hips again. Suddenly, he didn't want to make her wait. He wanted to give her all the pleasure she craved and more. To make this an unforgettable experience for her.

Tilting her hips, he plunged, driving the full length of his cock inside her. Her cry of pleasure resonated in the room.

Briefly, he closed his eyes, unable to move or breathe as a wave of hot pleasure crested over him.

Tightening his grasp, he plunged again, and began giving her deep, solid thrusts. "How does that feel?" By the sultry sounds she made, by the way she flexed her legs and squeezed them around him, he knew she liked the depth and angle of his thrusts, but he wanted to hear her say it. "Tell me, *chère*."

A light sheen of perspiration glistened on her flushed skin. Her eyes were closed, her sweet breasts jiggling with the force of each downstroke.

"So. Good," she said, each word rushing out on a pant.

She clenched around his thrusting prick, tearing a growl from his throat. Oh, it was definitely good. In fact, the best. He reveled in the stunning sensations washing through him. He could never tire of this. Never tire of her.

She was his. His sensual soul mate.

His perfect match.

Nicolas released her hips. "Come here," he said hoarsely, and grasping her wrists, he pulled her up, dragged her closer, and drove his cock into her with such intensity it made them both gasp. Fisting her hair with his one hand, the other splayed against her lower back, he rode her with fast, powerful plunges, holding nothing back. He thrust his tongue into her mouth, wanting to possess every part of her. To his delight, she returned his voracious kiss, feeding his desire.

He felt her arms slide around him, her heels dig into his backside. She held on, her lush form enveloping him completely. Breaking the kiss, she moved her hot, hungry mouth along his jaw, toward his ear.

The pressure in his sac was exquisite torture, his body raging for release.

"Nicolas, I think I'm going to . . . I'm truly . . . actually going to . . . to . . ."

"Do it. Let yourself go. You're on the edge. Your sweet cunt is quivering around me." Still ramming her, he pushed up against her clit, and then again, adding jolting sensations without breaking his rhythm. "Come!"

She lurched sharply in his arms. Throwing her hips forward and her head back, she screamed, her orgasm wracking her body. Nicolas tightened his hold and clenched his teeth, glorious spasms suddenly assailing his plunging cock, her sweet sheath sucking at his shaft, pulling and pulsing around him in magnificent waves. Each knee-weakening contraction squeezed him so fiercely it made his prick throb. He battled back his release, refusing to let go, determined to enjoy her orgasm—the voluptuous sensations coursing along his cock—before he indulged in his own.

He pumped his hips as the spasms faded, but then she jerked and gave him an unexpected firm clench that sent him over the edge. Hot come rushed down his cock.

He reared just in time. Semen shot from him with stunning

force. Burying his face in her soft hair, he shuddered and groaned, come purging from his prick in draining spurts, euphoria flooding his body.

Dieu, he didn't want this to end, and he knew he was referring to more than just the sex act.

Finally spent, his legs shaking, his breathing as erratic as hers, Nicolas lifted his head and met her gaze.

A smile shone on her beautiful face.

"I've never felt anything like that," she whispered.

Neither had he. Softly, he kissed her mouth, sounds of contentment emanating from them both. This was unlike any sexual encounter he'd ever had. It was more than just a sating of his body. The fulfillment he felt went as deep as his heart and soul.

He needed more of this. More of her.

He'd found the perfect bliss.

*   *   *

"What do you mean, *nothing*?" Nicolas asked Thomas, incredulous.

"I mean, *nothing*."

"You checked every drawer in Henriette's desk?"

"Yes."

"And all over her rooms?"

"Yes! I checked everywhere," Thomas snapped, looking uncharacteristically haggard this morning. "There was *nothing*." He slammed the key down on the table in Nicolas's rooms and marched away.

Nicolas had hoped all the evidence he needed would be in Henriette's private quarters. Damn it, where was she hiding her notes, her drafts?

What if it's not Henriette at all? His stomach clenched. It would be difficult enough to arrest one of Anne's sisters. But to have to arrest Anne. Beautiful Anne. His Anne. Images of last night, of her, of her in his arms, filled his mind and made him ache.

He glanced up at Thomas and caught him raking a hand through his hair as he paced near the windows.

"What is it, Thomas?"

Stopping in his tracks, Thomas exhaled sharply and turned to look out the window.

Nicolas approached. Something was amiss. "Thomas?" He placed a hand on his friend's shoulder. His body stiff, his jaw tight, Thomas met his gaze.

"You found something in Camille's rooms, didn't you?" Nicolas asked.

Thomas returned his attention to the window, staring blankly at the courtyard below. For a moment, Nicolas thought he wasn't going to respond, but then, ever so slightly, he nodded. "I haven't been able to sleep all night."

Nicolas's heart raced. "What did you find?"

Keeping his eyes straight ahead, Thomas responded, "Camille came to my rooms after supper. I'd just finished invading her privacy, reading the contents of her desk, looking for possible evidence to arrest her, and she was worried about me. Concerned for my welfare. Do you know what that made me feel like?"

Nicolas had a very strong idea.

Thomas turned to him, his expression rueful. "I kissed her, Nicolas. I shouldn't have, but I couldn't help myself. I'm not like you, my friend. You can kiss a woman, even bed her, and remain detached. You don't let anything distract you or get in the way of doing His Majesty's bidding. I can't do that. I can't act. Nor be indifferent. I'm a failure as a Musketeer."

Nicolas was failing, too. Failing to accomplish his objectives. Failing to break the libidinous hold Anne had on him, and worst of all, failing to keep the soft sentiment she inspired at bay. The more he'd had her last night, the more he wanted her. Everything she did, everything she said stirred his desire and tender feelings he couldn't quell.

He had not remained detached.

Nor had he used last night's situation to his advantage as he'd intended—to gain information. He'd never questioned her once the entire night. Hadn't wanted to.

"Nicolas, I found Camille's old journal." Thomas's voice was quiet. "Many of the entries were filled with venom directed toward her late brother-in-law, the Baron de Pierpont, for his treatment of Henriette, and toward a gentleman named Jules d'Orsay."

"Who is Jules d'Orsay?"

"The third son of the Comte de Galard. Apparently, he charmed Anne, made promises he never intended to keep, claimed her maidenhead, and then married another."

Nicolas chest tightened.

Jules d'Orsay. The man she'd mentioned last night.

Not only had d'Orsay denied her carnal pleasure in bed, but he'd deceived her. Used her. *Jésus-Christ*, no wonder she had such a lowly opinion of men.

And yet, she set aside her biases to be with you.

Nicolas felt like a scoundrel of the lowest order. And though he reminded himself that he was on a mission for his King, it did nothing to combat the self-condemnation welling inside him.

He was using her. And it bothered him when it shouldn't. When it couldn't.

When there was the chance she was the one he might have to arrest.

"I didn't think sweet Camille had it in her to loathe so deeply. I have a terrible feeling that Leduc is Camille." Thomas shook his head. "This is not just a mission anymore. I'm fond of her. I like all three of them. *Seigneur Dieu*, I even like Henriette. How can we do this? How can we arrest any of them? How can I arrest Camille?" Thomas hung his head.

"We have a duty to uphold." He'd forced each word off his tongue. He was fond of Camille, too. Nicolas had no idea how he'd arrest Camille either. But he knew he could manage it. In fact, he knew he could manage to do just about anything, except arrest Anne.

"We need something more conclusive than some old journal entries," Nicolas was constrained to add. "It isn't enough proof."

"I didn't find anything else. What about Anne? Have you searched her rooms and desk?"

His body turned rigid. "No. You had the key, remember?"

Thomas walked over to the table, picked up the key, and returning with it, placed it on his palm. "Well, you have it back. Now there is nothing to stop you from examining the contents of her desk."

Nicolas looked at the small gold key.

Burdened with what he had to do, it felt heavy in his hand.

It burned his palm.

9

"I've been cast aside!" Madame de Boutette sniffled, wiping her tears with a lace handkerchief. "I've been completely and utterly replaced by that whore, Pauline Pradeau. She's bewitched him, I tell you."

Anne fought back a second yawn. For the last few glorious nights, Nicolas had given her little rest—and more bliss than any heart could hold.

"I have been with him for years," Madame de Boutette continued, her tone getting increasingly angrier. "I was his favorite mistress. Now he favors another. After I've endured all of his disgusting habits, and amorous encounters of the blandest sort! Do you have any idea how dull and distasteful it is to bed the Marquis de Ranvier?"

"No, madame. I don't." Anne dipped her quill in the inkwell and wrote, *"Ranvier has disgusting habits. Is dull and distasteful to bed."*

"Well, then allow me to tell you that I've had to moan and carry on as if . . ."

Madame's words drifted away as images of Nicolas and memories of her moaning and carryings-on in his arms ran through her mind and quickened her pulse. Every reaction he drew from her was real and sublime. She loved how insatiable he was around her. How wonderful it felt to be so desired.

How wonderful it was just to be with him.

During their short time together she'd transformed. For the better. Her heart and soul felt light, and she had Nicolas to thank. What was just as incredible, she'd begun to do something she'd completely abandoned and had lost all desire for after Jules; she'd started writing poetry again!

She'd forgotten how much pleasure it brought her. Wanting his reaction, last eve she'd worked up the courage to show Nicolas her new poems. Poems she hadn't even told her sisters about.

By his expression, his eyes, and his words, he adored them; his praise of her work filled her with as much joy as his kisses and touch. Everything was so perfect between them, except . . . something was bothering him. If only she knew what.

He denied it. Hid it. In fact, he hid it quite well. Yet she was attuned to it. She sensed it. Saw fleeting flashes of it in his eyes. And she didn't believe it had to do with his grandmother.

"He rarely bathes. It's like bedding a barnyard animal. And his rounded belly keeps getting in the way," Madame finished with a huff.

Anne sighed and put down her quill. "Madame, may I be frank?"

The woman who was only a few years older than Anne raised her brows. "Well . . . I suppose . . ."

"If the Marquis de Ranvier is so unappealing, why bemoan the end of the affair?"

"Well, because I love him! And he loves another. He's tossed me aside like a pair of old shoes."

"Love? You've described your *love* as a barnyard animal."

"That's because he smells like one."

"And his touch is unpleasant to you, correct?"

"Well, yes." Madame de Boutette smoothed her skirts. "It is."

"Madame, with all due respect, it's rather clear that it is your pride that's wounded, not your heart."

The woman's mouth fell agape.

Undaunted, Anne continued, "If you loved Ranvier, you wouldn't be repelled. In fact, you'd find him highly appealing. You'd crave to be with him. As much as possible. The thought of him would make you happy, not sick. You'd want his touch. Enjoy his company, and cherish it."

Anne knew her speech was about more than the Marquis de Ranvier. It was about her feelings for Nicolas. She was in love with him. How could she not be?

Why shouldn't she allow herself to be?

She'd denied herself happiness long enough. Why shouldn't she take another chance on love? Love was worth the risk. As was Nicolas.

After what she'd been through with Jules, after witnessing Henriette's suffering, after hearing countless stories of other women's heartbreaks, Anne had become convinced that there wasn't an honorable man left in the realm.

But she'd had a change of heart. And she had Nicolas to thank for that as well.

With love inside her heart, there was no more room for the

bitterness she'd harbored there. For the first time, the thought of
writing a Gilbert Leduc tale—the particular kind of tale Madame
de Boutette wanted her to write—left a sour taste in her mouth.

Anne rose. "Madame, go home, and find yourself someone
worthy of your love. Do not despair over the loss of a man who
causes you such distress. Consider yourself fortunate to be rid
of him." It was the attitude she should have taken long ago with
Jules. She'd been a colossal fool to allow Jules to make her miserable long after his departure. It was clear to her now that by
clinging to her heartbreak, she'd actually held on to Jules, making
him a part of her life when he didn't deserve to be.

Madame de Boutette stood up, looking aghast. "But—But
what about my story? Monsieur Leduc?"

"Monsieur Leduc is quite fatigued." Anne ushered the woman
to the main door of her apartments, knowing Vincent would
show her out.

"He is?"

"He's long overdue for a respite."

"Really?"

"Yes, and I can't say when or if he'll be ready to write again."
At least not stories for embittered hearts. She wouldn't do it. She'd
talk to her sisters and the Comtesse. Leduc was going to be much
more selective. If Leduc's stories were to continue, they'd have to
be fewer and only in instances where a woman found herself in
truly dire circumstances—like poor Eléonore, Duchesse de Terrasson, who was still unjustly confined to a convent.

The moment Madame de Boutette left, Anne moved toward
her desk. She wanted to seek out Nicolas, perhaps spend the day
with him, but couldn't. Leduc's book was due at the printer's
soon and she needed to finish Eléonore's story.

Sitting down at her desk, Anne pulled out the draft of her

work in progress and dipped her quill in the inkwell. When the Comtesse returned, Anne intended to talk to her about her grandson, and then tell Nicolas everything about Leduc.

She wanted no secrets between them.

She felt a smile tug at her lips. Nicolas would likely praise her for her stories as he had her poetry. He'd be completely understanding and utterly supportive of her efforts.

*   *   *

Nicolas was smiling as his eyes tracked Anne in the crowded Salon. Another of his grandmother's Saturday Salons was under way. This one was just as crowded as the last.

He knew he should be mingling with his grandmother's friends. He was, after all, supposed to be interested in learning about the Comtesse and getting to know the people in her life. But he had no desire to make polite conversation. He was content to simply watch Anne as she moved from guest to guest, charming them all.

As with last week, Nicolas noted how the men looked at her. Their interest keen. Many made no attempt to hide their desire. But as they watched her, gaped at her, her attention, when she was not engaged in conversation, was directed at *him.*

Repeatedly, she'd turn, seek him out in the crowd, and smile when she met his gaze.

It sent a jolt of joy to his heart each time.

"Nicolas." He heard Thomas's voice.

Nicolas pulled his attention from Anne and found his friend standing beside him. "Where have you been?" he asked. Thomas had been missing all day. He'd learned from Vincent that he'd left the hôtel.

"I need to speak to you. Privately," Thomas said.

Nicolas didn't like the look on Thomas's face.

He led Thomas out of the Grand Salon, across the vestibule, and into the servants' stairwell. It was dark and quiet once he'd closed the door.

"What is it?" Nicolas hated the uneasy feeling building inside him.

Thomas rubbed the back of his neck. "I couldn't take it anymore, Nicolas. All this deceit with Camille is getting to me. I left to clear my head. Before I knew it, I found myself at the Arsenal. Tiersonnier was there. He demanded to know about the mission."

Nicolas tensed. "What did you tell him?"

"That you had things well in hand, but . . . that didn't satisfy him. He pressed for more information. He wants this matter done."

"Go on," Nicolas prompted, seeing there was more that Thomas wasn't saying.

Thomas looked away. That wasn't a good sign. Nicolas's stomach tightened.

"He demanded details," Thomas said, not meeting his gaze.

"And?"

"And I told him . . . where you were. Who—Who we suspected was Leduc."

Nicolas grabbed his lapels and shoved him against the wall. "You did *what*?"

Thomas's eyes widened. "We have sworn an oath. Did you want me to lie to the commander of the Guard?"

Yes! Nicolas took a long deep breath and let it out slowly. By force of will, he uncurled his hands and released his friend. "No."

"You've had the key for days, Nicolas. Have you searched Anne's desk yet?"

"I have not had the key for days," he responded sharply. "I told you the other day that she noticed the key was missing. I had to toss it onto the floor in the library, so she'd think she lost it there. The library was the last place she'd seen it."

"That was two days ago. The key is back in her locket. You're fucking her, for God's sake."

"So?"

"So, surely during the time you've spent in her rooms, you've had an opportunity or two to take the key and have a glance at the desk?"

Nicolas's eyes narrowed. "I have not had the opportunity." *Liar.* He was avoiding the desk. Avoiding the search.

"This mission cannot continue indefinitely."

"I will get to the desk, when I can. Until then—"

"You have one more day," Thomas blurted out.

"What do you mean, *one more day?*"

"Tiersonnier said if you don't make your arrest by then, he'll send Musketeers here to search for the evidence and to bring in Leduc."

The look of horror must have been on his face. Thomas's gaze shot down to his feet. "I'm sorry." His voice was a whisper. Or maybe it simply sounded faint with the blood roaring in his ears.

Thomas reached into his justacorps and pulled out a gold key. "I managed to get this from Camille." He handed the key to Nicolas. "Anne, Camille, and Henriette are busy with the guests. I'll make sure no one goes upstairs. This is an ideal time to search Anne's rooms and desk."

Nicolas's heart plummeted. He knew Thomas was right.

He couldn't avoid the task any longer.

He had to learn once and for all what was in Anne's desk.

* * *

Nicolas leaned against the doorway in Anne's antechamber looking at the desk he had to search.

Anne's rooms were quiet and still. The air, without her there, was thick and hard to breathe. This was the last thing he wanted to do, his every instinct screaming, *"Don't look!"*

Nicolas glanced back at the bed in the bedchamber. For the first time in his life, he wasn't simply having sex with a woman. There was emotion involved. He was making love. And he'd found the intimate encounters and the time he spent with her far more pleasurable and gratifying than he could have ever imagined.

He didn't want what he had with Anne to be over. But he knew, as he stood holding the key in his fist, that their time together was running out.

There wasn't a thing he could do about it.

It sickened him to know that soon her warm looks, her soft words, her kisses would vanish. In their place, he'd have her disdain. It didn't matter who Leduc was. No matter whom he arrested, she'd feel betrayed. Deceived. Despise him for his numerous lies.

Thomas was right. Nicolas hadn't been doing his duty. He'd procrastinated simply to delay the inevitable.

He'd done the unimaginable; he'd allowed feelings to be fostered for a beautiful red-haired poetess who was like no woman he'd ever known.

And a suspect.

He was under the King's command. If he didn't do this, it would be done just the same.

Pushing himself toward the desk, Nicolas approached it with

dread. Slowly, he sat down, took a deep breath before he inserted the key, and unlocked the first drawer.

Jésus-Christ, the best he could hope for in this dismal situation was that the author wasn't Anne.

Sliding open the drawer, he then pulled out the contents: a small stack of parchments. Upon close scrutiny, he realized they were poems. New poetry. Despite the trepidation he felt, a small smile pulled at the corners of his mouth. She'd been so joyful about her new poems. He'd been moved and honored that she'd wanted to show them to him.

She had a gift for writing poetry, and they were as lovely as she was.

He checked the next drawer, and the next, growing ever more hopeful with each one that yielded no evidence of Leduc.

Turning the key in the lock of the final drawer, Nicolas opened it and found parchments and a ledger. He pulled them out. The words "Eléonore, Duchesse de Terrasson" were across the top of the first parchment.

He scrutinized the writings on the loose parchments, and then the contents of the ledger, his heart sinking lower and lower. Each page that condemned her consumed him with grief and tore him apart.

He closed the ledger.

Closed the drawer.

Closed his eyes, and hung his head.

*   *   *

Anne grinned the moment she spotted Nicolas in her rooms. "There you are!"

Seated near the hearth in her antechamber staring at the fire, he looked up at her and smiled. But his smile didn't reach his eyes. His light gray eyes were rueful.

Her grin had completely dissolved by the time she reached him. "Nicolas, is everything all right?"

He pulled her onto his lap and drew her close, his sad smile still on his lips. "It is tonight." Lightly, he ran his knuckles along her cheek.

She wasn't sure what he meant. She wrapped her arms around his broad shoulders. "Something is bothering you and has been for some time. Tell me what it is. Perhaps I can help."

He shook his head. "No. In the morning . . . We'll talk in the morning. This night belongs to us. I want nothing to interfere with it. Or spoil it."

What could spoil it? she wanted to ask, but he threaded his fingers through her hair and pulled her forward. Their mouths met and her thoughts scattered. An intoxicating rush of arousal and emotion flooded her body. Her nerve endings sparked to life. Parting her lips for him, she welcomed his tongue into her mouth, stroking it, caressing it, loving his taste, his scent, the sounds of his escalating breaths. She loved his every heated reaction to her.

She loved him.

"Tonight you are all mine," he murmured and kissed her harder, with enough intensity to make her head spin.

Vaguely, she felt him lift her in his arms. He deposited her onto the bed with infinite care, then straightened. His hands moved to the fastenings on his breeches. Sitting up, she watched him undress, transfixed. Expectant.

Nicolas yanked off his shirt. His sculpted chest, his strong body were mesmerizing to behold, and protruding from his open breeches was his sizable sex, the sight of which made her both hungry and weak.

As soon as he was naked, she rose to her knees, her heart giving a small flutter of joy. He knelt on the bed in front of her, cradled her face between his palms, and gave her a long, languid kiss. It was only when he pulled away that she realized he'd released her cheeks and had opened her bodice. Anne quickly helped as he pulled and tugged, tossing off article after article until she, too, was naked.

He moved his gaze over her, slowly, in a way he never had before. He took his time to take her in, as if he was trying to commit her to memory.

"How will I ever stop wanting you?" he whispered, seemingly more to himself than to her.

"You don't have to stop." She smiled. "In fact, I'd prefer it if you didn't."

"Ah, Anne, I'd love that." He caressed the outside curve of her breast, then cupping her, grazed his thumb over her hardened nipple. She jolted at the lush sensation. "I'd love this to go on forever." His thumb continued its delicious torment. Her sex moistened and contracted.

"I have no objections to something more indefinite."

"I pray you'll always feel that way." He threaded the fingers of his free hand in her hair. "I never expected to find a woman like you here."

He lowered her onto her back and covered her with his hard body, the delectable press of his muscled form sending hot tingles through her.

Resting on his elbows, he said in all earnest, "This passion, desire, the . . . emotions between us . . . are all real. I don't want you ever to doubt that, no matter what happens. I want you to remember how good it is between us. Promise me you'll always remember how you feel right now. How incredible it feels when we're together." He brushed his lips over hers. "Promise me, Anne."

"Nicolas, what are you trying to say?" She couldn't quell the unease that was beginning to permeate her.

"I want you to promise you'll remember this night—all the nights we've shared—and how perfect they were. Promise me."

She stared up into his beseeching eyes, unsure of what to make of him tonight.

He dipped his head and kissed the sensitive spot beneath her ear. *"Promise,* Anne." Lightly, he bit her earlobe, his knees spreading her thighs wide apart. She shivered.

"I promise. I won't forget."

"Not ever." He stroked his thick, solid shaft along her folds, her body bathing him with her juices.

"Never."

"I need to have you." He dipped his head lower still and gave her shoulder a tiny bite. She moaned and surged against him, the sensation of his cock gliding over her sensitive nub and needy flesh sending frissons of pleasure streaking to her core.

"I need you right now," he said.

He'd planted the head of his shaft firmly against her opening and pushed inside. Thank God, he didn't make her wait. Her body opened and gave way to his insistent possession. The steady pressure as he slowly filled her was glorious.

With a flex of his hips, he butted hard against her womb. She gasped. He had her deliciously pinned to the bed. Her sex squeezed around him.

"You feel so good," he groaned, giving her slow, solid thrusts, increasing her fever. "So warm . . . silky . . . tight. *Dieu,* so tight.

Let me feel it, Anne. Let me feel those delicious little clenches around my cock. Bear down on me, *chère*."

She tightened and released her inner muscles, reveling in the way he growled and groaned, lost to his desire for her, his cock driving into her faster and faster.

He swore. "I'm having you again"—he thrust—"and again. All night."

"Yes . . ." she panted out.

She loved him with her body, her hands, her mouth, kissing, tasting, lost to the friction, the frenzy of their lovemaking. She relished the feelings he'd awakened in her, feelings that swirled around her heart. She relished him, without words, just actions, caressing him, milking him. Knowing she was barreling toward a powerful release.

He captured her nipple between his finger and thumb and lightly pulled then pinched. A shock of pleasure shot through her. She came with a scream, uncontrollable shudders rolling though her body.

He roared her name, his thrusts unrelenting. Just as the spasms inside her faded, he jerked his length out and crushed her to him. Grinding his cock between their bodies, he let out a primitive growl, hot semen pouring onto her stomach as a tremor and then another jolted him. She held him tightly until at last he relaxed, their breathing slowly returning to normal. Caressing his back, she felt sated and languorous, basking in a wonderful sense of peace in the quiet afterglow.

He lifted his head. His tender smile moved her to one as well.

"Do you have any idea what you do to me?" he asked.

"I think I have some idea."

He chuckled. She loved the sound of his soft laugh.

Nicolas snagged his discarded shirt, rolled onto his back, and after wiping them both clean, tossed it to the floor.

Lying on his back, he rolled her on top of him, her breasts pressing on his chest. He tucked a lock of her hair behind her ear. "You are extraordinary" was the last thing he said before he kissed her.

Anne lost track of time, unsure how long they lay naked, simply kissing, each kiss stirring her heart and reawakening her desire.

I love you . . . The words were on the tip of her tongue. Words she never thought she'd utter to any man ever again.

Tomorrow. She'd tell him tomorrow. He wanted to talk. And she decided she, too, had something to say.

10

Nicolas woke up in an empty bed. A sharp stab of disappointment cut into his heart. He wanted to wake up with Anne by his side. He wanted to squeeze out a final few tender moments before everything imploded on him. But Anne was probably with her sisters, writing.

Writing under the name "Gilbert Leduc."

Closing his eyes, he felt grief stricken and cold. But not cold enough to numb or in any way lessen the suffocating misery inside him.

There was no getting out of what he had to do today.

What could he say to her? How on earth was he going to do this? He had no idea what the King would do with Anne once he brought her in.

A week ago, being in the King's Guard was everything to him. He never thought there would ever come a day when he hated being a Musketeer. But he hated it now. He loathed it. With all of his being and every piece of his breaking heart.

Nicolas forced himself out of bed. His thoughts awhirl and his agony steadily rising, he went through the motions of washing and dressing. By the time he'd left Anne's rooms and reached the bottom of the grand stairwell, the pain inside him was excruciating. He'd rather face his own arrest than arrest her.

If only it were an option.

Looking for Thomas—praying he'd say something to Nicolas that would make this easier—he crossed the vestibule and froze when he heard Anne's voice.

"I don't believe it!" he heard her say. She was in the library.

A woman responded, "I'm afraid it's true." Her voice was unfamiliar.

Unable to turn back, constrained to push forward, Nicolas moved his leaden legs and approached the room he'd find his Anne in.

Stopping just inside the threshold, he was met with a jarring sight. Anne stood with her back to the windows, her eyes glistening with tears.

The moment her gaze met his, he lost his breath. *She knew.* It was etched on her expression and in the silent condemnation in her eyes.

He had no idea how she knew. But she did. *Dieu*, she did.

His eyes darted to his left. Henriette was seated on the settee with her arm around Camille. While Camille quietly wept, Henriette glowered at him with open contempt.

"Well, who do we have here?" A woman's voice snared his attention.

Nicolas's gaze shot to the right. There in the corner of the room stood a thin older woman. A lady, as her clothing indicated. His instincts told him this was the Comtesse de Cottineau.

His grandmother.

Anne approached him slowly, her breaths quick and shallow, her expression incredulous.

She stopped before him and stared at him as though he were a complete stranger, as if she were seeing him for the first time. As if he'd never been her lover. Had never held her in his arms. Had never loved her through the night.

"You're . . ." She paused and took a deep breath before she began again. "Are you a *Musketeer*?" That last word was laced with a mixture of distress and disbelief.

He wanted to lie. He wanted to take her in his arms and hold her until the pain inside him subsided. But he couldn't do either.

He swallowed. "Yes."

Her beautiful mouth fell slightly agape. "Why—Why didn't you tell me?"

Nicolas clasped his hands before him to keep from reaching out and pulling her to him. He knew it was the very last thing she wanted at the moment. "Because I was—*am*—on a mission for His Majesty."

"*A mission?*" Her voice escalated. "What sort of mission are you on?" Her tone and demeanor told him she knew the answer—or at least suspected it. He glanced at the Comtesse.

Her expression hardened, and she had a knowing look in her gray eyes. He realized she'd been the one to tell Anne these details about him, but how did she know?

"Answer her," the Comtesse demanded. Nicolas would have done nothing, *absolutely nothing* the old woman asked of him, for he owed her nothing more than his disdain, but the request was for Anne. And for Anne, he'd do anything.

"I'm to determine who Gilbert Leduc is and bring him before the King," he said softly.

"So your coming here had nothing to do with getting to know your grandmother," Anne stated. It wasn't a question.

"No." He answered just the same. He owed her the whole truth.

"And you spent the entire time lying and scheming," Anne accused. He could tell she was fighting back her tears, trying to maintain the semblance of composure. He knew this was going to be bad, but in the thick of it, it was far worse than he'd imagined.

Nicolas lowered his eyes, because it was too painful to see her pain. "I have a duty to the King." He found himself despising those words more and more each time he uttered them.

"A duty?" She laughed, without mirth. "I see. And was it part of your duty to bed me?"

His gaze shot up to hers. Her eyes were narrow and she trembled with outrage.

"Anne, perhaps we can have this conversation in private."

"Why? My sisters and the Comtesse know what a fool I've been. What is there to hide? I must congratulate you. Your skill at duplicity is excellent. I actually believed you were different from other men. In truth, you are by far the most contemptible of the lot."

The lump welling in his throat rendered him momentarily speechless.

"You did not answer my question," Anne pressed sharply. "Was it part of your duty to bed me? Did the King request it of you?"

Dieu. "No. Of course not."

"So you decided to indulge in some carnal diversions while you worked on your 'mission.' Is that it?"

He hated the disgust in her tone, especially since she was speaking of their lovemaking. "What began as casual copulation became something . . . special. In the end it was not mere bed sport."

"Oh, please," she scoffed. "Spare me more lies. What we did meant nothing to a man like you."

"That's not true. It meant—means a great deal to me. You mean a great deal to me."

She gave another hollow laugh. "Oh, of course. I mean so much to you that you have been conspiring and plotting against me, my sisters, and my patroness, stooping to trickery at every turn. Pray tell, when were you going to tell me the truth?"

"Today."

"And why today? What makes today so special?"

He didn't want to say it, but he didn't have a choice. He forced the words from his mouth. "I have to . . . make an arrest today."

Camille let out an audible sob and buried her face in Henriette's shoulder.

Anne didn't flinch. Stock-still, she said, "Well, it looks as though you are going to disappoint the King. Gilbert Leduc is not here. You're mistaken."

"That's right," Henriette concurred. "You are sadly mistaken."

"He is here," Nicolas gently countered Henriette. "He's in this room." He dragged his gaze back to Anne. "You are Leduc."

To her credit, she didn't crack or crumble before him. "You have no proof."

This was only becoming more and more torturous. "The proof is in your room, Anne. In your desk drawer. Your latest story about the Duchesse de Terrasson is ready to be sent to the illegal press for printing."

She blanched. "You got hold of the desk key?"

"On a couple of occasions, yes."

"Dear God . . ." She jerked back, her hand covering her heart. He saw the dawning on her cherished face. "You took it from me in the library, didn't you?" Her bravado cracked, as did her voice. "After what happened in that room, after the intimacy we shared there, you *stole* the key from me?"

Unable to speak, he simply nodded.

She stepped forward and cracked her palm against his cheek. "You are vile!"

Nicolas briefly closed his eyes. He'd never allowed anyone to strike him, but with self-recrimination slicing through him, he'd made no attempt to raise his hands and ward her off, even though he'd seen the blow coming. The sting from her slap was barely noticeable in comparison to the consuming anguish wracking him.

"Henriette, go upstairs and burn everything incriminating in Anne's desk," the Comtesse ordered.

Henriette and Camille rose together.

"I'll help her," Camille said.

Nicolas shook his head. "Burning the contents of her desk won't make a difference. If I don't bring Leduc to the King today, Musketeers will be here to arrest you all. They are aware that Leduc is among you. You will be interrogated until there is a confession. If the King feels it's warranted, torture can be used, even on a woman."

They looked at him with dread and fright.

What they didn't realize was that those very same emotions were among the many goring his heart.

"I'm sorry," he said. Those words weren't enough and didn't

begin to express how he felt. There was so much more he wanted to say—to Anne. He wanted a private moment to talk.

Would she even give him the chance?

"If the King wants Leduc, then that is what we shall give him," the Comtesse announced. "I will tell him I'm Leduc."

Surprised gasps pierced the silence. But no one was more surprised than he. His cold-hearted grandmother, a woman who'd been indifferent toward her own daughter, was willing to take the blame here and spare Anne?

Hope soared inside him. The Comtesse was hardly guiltless in the Leduc matter. This was good. No, this was an excellent solution.

"No, madame, I cannot let you do that," Anne said.

"Nonsense." The Comtesse approached and placed her arm around Anne. "I am your patroness. I encouraged—*strongly encouraged*—you to write these stories. I am not blameless here. And when the King sees me—an old woman—I doubt he'll have the stomach to do much to me."

"I'll say it was me." Henriette spoke up.

"What? No!" Anne shook her head, dismayed.

"Anne." Henriette approached her. "I'm the one who is constantly reminding you how dire our finances are."

"Yes, and I have been a burden, too," Camille said. "Henriette and I have both made it impossible for you to quit, Anne."

"I didn't wish to quit," Anne said. "I still don't intend to quit. I will be the one who appears before the King as Leduc. I will explain to him what I have done and why." Her jaw was set.

Nicolas's heart constricted. "And what will you say? That you have been besmirching the reputation of prominent men because you once suffered a broken heart? Do you think the King—who happens to be a man and prominent—will understand? Let the Comtesse take your place. It is the best option."

Pain seeped back into Anne's eyes. "You know the details of what happened with Jules, too?"

Nicolas approached and stopped before her. "He never deserved your affections."

Tears in her eyes, she squared her shoulders, took in a ragged breath and let it out. In a cold voice she said, "You need to make an arrest today. I will get my things. You will arrest me and only me." She stalked from the room, her sisters on her heels.

Her words knifed into him. He had to reason with her. *Jésus-Christ*, he had to tell her how he felt about her. And that he refused to let anything happen to her.

Nicolas turned to leave.

"Just a moment," the Comtesse de Cottineau said, stepping in front of him. "I'd like a word with you."

"I have more pressing matters to attend to. So if you'll kindly step out of—"

"You searched my desks, I presume," she injected.

"Yes. *So?*"

She nodded. "Then I suppose you read the contents of the yellow box in that desk over there." She gestured toward the ebony and gold desk near the windows.

"You wrote some letters to your daughter. You didn't send them. What of it?"

"There are facts about what happened between your mother and me that I'm certain you're not aware of."

"And I'm not interested in learning about them either."

She sighed. "You despise me, Nicolas. I suppose if I were you, I'd despise me, too. You must have been quite gleeful when you learned I was mixed up with this Leduc matter. Not only could you bring in the elusive Leduc, but you could legitimately sweep me up in the mess, too."

Though prolonging his conversation with his grandmother was the last thing he wanted to do, he couldn't help but ask, "How did you know I was on this mission?"

"I didn't. Not for certain. I knew you'd been appointed to the King's private Guard. When I arrived this morning and was told you were here and that you wanted to forge a relationship with me, I didn't believe it. Given the controversy Leduc's stories have stirred and that you are a Musketeer, it seemed the only logical explanation for your presence was that you were looking for Leduc. I knew you were brighter than most. Other men have tried to locate Leduc and never came close."

He was about to respond when she raised her hand to silence him. "You sent me on a fool's errand, and for that alone, I should be furious with you, not to mention the other things you've done here in the name of your 'mission.' But I'm not angry with you— for two reasons. The first reason is—"

"As I said, I have more pressing—"

"Because you're in love with Anne."

That froze the words on his tongue. *Merde.* Where the hell was she going with this?

"You are suffering, as much as Anne is. I can see the anguish in your eyes. What you have to do is difficult. I'll not condemn you for your actions, for I can see that you are efficiently condemning yourself. I'm sorry you are both in this predicament."

He hadn't expected this—the soft sadness in her gray eyes, the compassion in her tone. This was not the woman he envisioned his grandmother to be.

She gave him a sad smile. "You have my Joséphine's eyes, you know." To his surprise, she touched his cheek. "You look like her. I'm glad. I feared you'd turn out to be like your father."

"No, I am not like my father." His late brother David was.

Her smile turned brighter, seemingly pleased by his answer. "The second reason I'm not angry with you, Nicolas, is because I don't want to make the same mistake with you that I made with your mother. I learned a terrible lesson: words said in anger can cause irreparable damage. I said things to your mother in anger I should never have said. Things I have regretted ever since. I was furious with her for running off and marrying your father. I knew it was a terrible match. And your father loathed me for my low opinion of him. Within a few months of their marriage, I began writing letters to Joséphine, letters of apology, hoping to make amends. I never heard back from her. She ignored them. Ignored me. Never bothered to tell me of the births of her sons. But still I wrote and wrote, hoping that she'd break her silence and forgive me. I was informed of her death by your father. In his letter he also advised me that he'd been intercepting my letters. He returned each and every one to me in the yellow box. Your mother never saw any of them. She went to her grave thinking I hated her." Tears welled in her eyes and quietly slipped down her cheeks.

He was speechless. Every fiber in Nicolas's being told him that what the Comtesse said was true. All of it. His father was just the sort of man who'd do such a thing. Of that he had no doubt.

"What your father did broke my heart, and I'm certain he often broke Joséphine's heart. Though I could not communicate with her, I made certain I was kept abreast of the goings-on in her home. Coin placed in the correct palms will garner much information. I was well aware of his heavy-handed ways, that he kept her isolated in the country, away from me and friends. I knew of your brother's death and of your recent appointment to the Guard." She shook her head. "It is because of your father and men like him that I encouraged Anne to write the kind of stories Leduc writes."

His brows shot up. "My father helped inspire these stories?"

"I'd say your father and Jules d'Orsay were the inspiration, yes. Anne suggested the idea of Leduc and I fully endorsed it. I helped by supplying her with trustworthy women to offer similar tales of woe for Leduc to write about."

The lump in his throat was huge.

"You don't believe me?" she asked quietly.

Nicolas had to clear his throat before he could speak. "I believe you, madame. I know what kind of man my father was and how unhappy he made my mother."

"Well, I must confess that for the first time ever, I find myself unable to utterly despise the man." The Comtesse took his hand. "He sired you. Now that I have you near, I'll not lose you. You are my family. You are all I have left of Joséphine. I hope we can have the relationship I have always prayed for." Fresh tears were in her eyes.

Nicolas's head was spinning. Emotions were inundating him. There was so much to absorb with this newfound information about his grandmother. Feeling discomposed, he held his tongue. But he didn't pull away. Instead, Nicolas squeezed her hand, then covered it with his other.

She smiled through her tears. "Now then, Nicolas, you have some important matters you must attend to—or as you called them, 'pressing matters.' First, you must convince your beloved that you are not the contemptible man she accuses you of being. Next, you'll have to keep her out of prison."

Dieu, why didn't she ask him to part the Red Sea?

*   *   *

Anne waited with her sisters near the carriage to be escorted to Versailles. The day had grayed, and by the angry look of the dark clouds, there was a threat of rain. The gloom inside her was mirrored by the skies. In a few hours she'd be before the King and face the consequences. She was afraid. Terrified. She wouldn't lie about her role as Gilbert Leduc. However, when it came to the women who'd offered their stories to Leduc, she was prepared to do whatever it took to protect their identities.

A gasp from Camille yanked her from her thoughts. The Comtesse and two men wearing the distinct uniform of the King's private Guard were descending the stairs in front of the Comtesse's home. Thomas and Nicolas. It was the first time she'd ever seen them in uniform. Her heart pounded as she took in Nicolas's blue tabard with its silver cross, blue breeches, and black boots. His baldric rested on his right shoulder and crossed over his chest to his left hip.

With his powerful form, his confident stride, and his fierce expression, he looked intimidating. Dangerous to cross. There was no doubt about it—Nicolas made the perfect King's protector.

The sight of him made her ache. She turned away.

Strong fingers curled around her arm. She was yanked sideways. Suddenly, she was stumbling along behind Nicolas as he dragged her back inside the hôtel. The door slammed shut and he pushed her up against it.

Her mouth fell open, stunned by his actions. She was just about to offer up a few choice words when he crushed his mouth against hers, giving her a hot open-mouth kiss. A mindless rush of desire surged over her. Her knees practically buckled.

She fisted the front of his uniform. *What are you doing? Push him away!* But shamelessly her mouth was still latched to his, and she was trembling.

Abruptly, he pulled away. His strong hands clasped her cheeks, his breathing as quick as hers. "I love you."

Her heart lost a beat.

He released her and pressed his palms against the door on either side of her head. "I love you, Anne. So much. A maddening amount! I came here to do the King's bidding. I didn't care about you, your sisters, or the Comtesse. You're correct there. I wanted to impress the King. I wanted a promotion. All I ever wanted was to rank highly in the Guard. But you, you have a way of affecting me." He shoved himself off the door. "I have no understanding how you manage it. But you do!"

He placed his hands on his hips and let out a sharp breath. "I love you and I know you love me. I could tell you wanted to tell me last night. And—*Dieu*—I wanted to hear it." He stepped closer to her and pulled her into his arms. "I wanted you from the moment I saw you. And yes, I set out to have sex with you. Heated, intensely pleasurable—meaningless—sex. You weren't supposed to matter to me. I wasn't supposed to fall in love with the woman I had to arrest. I'd been walking around for days thinking up excuses not to search your desk for evidence."

He pressed his cheek to her hair. "I don't care about the promotion, or the Guard. If they put you in prison, I'll do whatever it takes to see you freed, including bribing the prison guards and fleeing the country with you. They can take away anything they want, as long as they don't take you from me."

Anne was shaking harder by the time she raised her arms and wrapped them around his neck. Closing her eyes, she buried her face at the base of his throat, inhaling his scent and taking in his warmth. Relishing the strength of his arms as they practically held her up.

Tenderly, he stroked her hair. "Anne, please say something."

She raised her head and gazed up into his beautiful eyes. "You weren't supposed to matter to me either. But . . . I love you." The words came out in a joyful rush, unrestrained. Straight from the heart.

She'd finally found the love and passion she'd always dreamed about.

In a few hours, her world could collapse.

* * *

Nicolas's expression was tightly guarded as they waited in the Mars drawing room at Versailles. With Anne, her sisters, and the Comtesse already gripped with fear, he refused to add to their distress by showing any outward signs of the terror he felt.

The occasional sniffle or soft sob from Camille broke the silence, as did the laughter and music that drifted in from the gardens. Thomas tried consoling Camille as best he could, without success.

The King was in the gardens, as usual. Preferring the outdoors, Louis spent most of his day outside surrounded by courtiers and musicians who followed him around the expansive lawns covered with massive flowerbeds and fountains, bushes and orange trees.

The wait was maddening. How much longer before Louis finally pulled himself away and entered the State Rooms? They'd already waited for what seemed an eternity.

He glanced at Anne. She stood by his side, quiet and brave. He was amazed and proud of her courage. Most would have collapsed under the weight of worry and fright. She shed no tears the way Camille did, nor did she wring her hands as Henriette was doing.

Needing to touch Anne, every once in a while Nicolas reached out and squeezed her hand reassuringly, uncertain if he was trying to reassure her or himself. He would have held her the entire time but the Captain of the Guard, Tristan de Tiersonnier, entered and exited the room frequently.

Nicolas wrestled with the possibilities and probabilities of what the King might do, his restless mind making his heart race. The Mars drawing room offered little by way of diversions. Its walls were a plain red and the ornately painted ceiling depicted various scenes that he didn't want to look at. Especially the one directly overhead. It was Claude Audran's *Mars in a Chariot Drawn by Wolves*. *Le Loup* was a nickname he'd never minded, but rather liked.

Now he disliked it immensely.

A wolf was a predator. He'd come to realize he wasn't that cold. He'd been well on the road to becoming just like his father and brother, and he was grateful that he'd veered off that path, for that path had led him to Anne. To love. And even more surprising, to a grandmother he actually wanted to know more about.

The Comtesse took Anne's other hand. "Anne, I'm too old for this. This wait is taking years off my life. We'll assure the King that Leduc is through. He'll not write again."

Anne glanced at the older woman and then at Nicolas.

"She's right, *chérie*. Leduc is done," he said. "He has to be. Even if the King is in a generous mood, he'll not permit you to keep breaking the law."

Anne gazed straight ahead and then softly ceded. "I know.

But who will speak for those women in distress? Leduc was their only voice."

"We'll think of another way to aid women," his grandmother offered. "But it will be legal. Something that won't perturb the King."

The door burst open, causing Anne to jump and Nicolas's heart to lurch. The King and his Captain, Tiersonnier, marched in.

Immediately, Nicolas and Thomas bowed as the women curtsied low.

Louis sighed. "Which one is the author?" he asked Tiersonnier.

Nicolas didn't like the annoyance in the King's tone. His mood wasn't particularly genial today. His fear spiked.

Anne stepped forward. "I am, Sire."

His insides knotted. Nicolas wanted to yank her back and shout, "No! There's been a mistake."

Louis cocked a brow, then tilted his head to one side. His gaze moved over Anne, a slow assessment that made Nicolas's nostrils flare and his fists clench. At close to fifty years of age, his King was a notorious womanizer, and the leer he'd directed at Anne gave him great unease.

"Come with me," Louis said, spinning on his heel and stalking from the room. Anne fell into step behind the King.

Nicolas stepped forward, but Tiersonnier pushed his hand against Nicolas's chest. "Not you. Just her. Everyone else waits here." Tiersonnier fell in behind Anne.

The doors closed.

Nicolas's heart sank. His ire rose. There were State Rooms on either side of the Mars drawing room. It didn't escape his notice that the King was headed in the direction of his private apartments—*where his bedchamber was located.*

Camille wept openly now, accepting Thomas's shoulder as her sobbing worsened.

Nicolas's mind was besieged with unwanted thoughts far worse than before. Was he supposed to just wait here while the King took Anne and . . . He couldn't finish the thought.

Teeth clenched, he marched to the window and looked down at the north gardens, but all he saw were the images flashing in his brain of Anne in the King's bed. He slammed his fist against the wall.

"Nicolas." His grandmother placed her hand on his shoulder. "I know what you're thinking but you mustn't torture yourself so. Anne is an intelligent woman. She's been propositioned by powerful men before. She knows how to be tactful, yet to the point."

"She's never had to refuse a King."

"I believe in her, Nicolas, and so should you," she countered.

"I do believe in her. But I know Louis's vice-ridden ways," he said tightly. It took every ounce of will he possessed not to race down to the State apartments after Anne.

The doors swung open, ensnaring Nicolas's attention.

Tiersonnier stood at the threshold. "Follow me." He turned and left.

The Captain of the Guard led them through more State Rooms, down the stairwell, and eventually to the doors leading out to the gardens.

"Are the King and Mademoiselle de Vignon outside?" Nicolas asked.

"No," was all Tiersonnier offered.

Nicolas wasn't about to relent. "Will the mademoiselle be escorted to the gardens to where her family is waiting?" He needed answers. He was about ready to jump out of his skin.

"If that is what His Majesty chooses." Tiersonnier was a large, imposing man, only a few years older than Nicolas and beyond irritating.

"Do you have any idea how long her family will have to wait out in the gardens before His Majesty 'chooses'?"

Eyes narrowed, Tiersonnier stepped in close, a gesture meant to intimidate, knowing he had a deterring effect on the men in the Guard. But Nicolas was neither deterred nor intimidated. He glared back, wanting nothing more than to deliver his fist against the man's arrogant jaw.

"Savignac, you'd do well to remember not to question your superiors. You'll wait in the gardens as ordered by the King until you are told otherwise."

"Of course, Captain," Thomas said, yanking Nicolas away and shoving him out the door.

Outside in the gardens, the noise from the throng abraded Nicolas's jangled nerves. He tried to maintain his composure, but he couldn't stop thinking, as his eyes scanned the windows on the upper floor—where the King's private apartments were located. Anne was alone up there, with their lascivious monarch.

Was the King striking a bargain with her? Her freedom for a fuck? Worse still, what if Louis asked her to be his next mistress? Versailles would become her gilded prison. And until the King lost interest, she'd be lost to Nicolas.

"Forget about it, Nicolas," Thomas murmured in his ear. "You can't go back in there."

"Anne," Camille gasped.

Nicolas snapped his head around, searching the crowd, his heart suddenly pounding in his throat. He caught sight of her brilliant red hair as she maneuvered through the throng.

She was alone. Her expression was unreadable.

Forcing his legs to eat up the distance between them, he grabbed her by the shoulders the moment he reached her. "What happened?"

Her sisters, Thomas, and the Comtesse grouped around her, insulating her from the scores of people around them.

"It seems that the King is about as fond of the male aristocracy as Leduc is," Anne said, sotto voce.

"What do you mean?" Henriette asked.

"He told me that he *enjoyed* the stories."

Camille placed her hand on Anne's arm. "Enjoyed? He really said that?"

Anne nodded. "He has a great dislike for many of the men I depicted in the pen portraits and found the volumes amusing. He confided that since the Fronde, he hasn't had much regard for the men in the upper class."

The Comtesse let out a laugh. "*Ah*, the Fronde, of course! Louis was still a boy, not yet old enough to rule, when his cousin and many noblemen rose up against him, almost dethroning him. It happened before any of you were born. It was a horrible uprising against the Crown. In fact, he and his mother had to flee Paris in the middle of the night and live in exile until the country could be brought back to order."

"Well, he's not forgotten the ordeal, I can assure you," Anne said. "It has colored the way he looks at men of power."

"What does this mean?" Nicolas asked. "Are you free to go?"

A beautiful, radiant smile formed on her lips. "Yes. But I am forbidden to write any more stories by Leduc. He gave me praise and a warning."

Nicolas let out a whoop of joy and pulled her into his arms. He didn't care who was watching. He just wanted to hold her, the tension and fear draining from his body.

Then a thought struck him.

He pulled her away. "Excuse us," he told the others, clasped her hand, and strode off, stopping several feet away from their group and the crowd. Holding her by the shoulders, he asked, "Did the King try to . . . Did he . . . proposition you?"

She lifted a brow. "Oh. Yes. He did." Her tone was flippant.

"And?"

A smile twitched on her lips. "I'm not going to be the next royal mistress, Nicolas—if I get a better offer, that is." Mischief twinkled in her eyes. She was clearly enjoying herself at his expense.

He pulled her to him and dipped his head, her smile contagious. "You're being very naughty, Anne," he murmured in her ear, his cock swelling between them. "Perhaps I'll take you home and tie you to my bed and keep you bound for my pleasure. That way there can be no other man."

"Perhaps the only offer I'll accept is having you tied to my bed, bound for my pleasure."

He laughed. "I like it when you're saucy." He kissed her, enjoying the wet, silky warmth of her mouth. "Anne de Vignon, you are mine. I love you."

Her cheeks were a pretty pink, a small sign that she was already heated from their short exchange. "I love you, too. With all my heart. And I'm going to help those women somehow, Nicolas."

He brushed an errant red curl off her cheek. "I know you are, and I fully support it, as long as you stay away from the King."

She placed her hands on his chest. "I'm also going to write a lot more poetry."

He grinned. "The world will be enriched by them."

Anne's smile grew and she slipped her arms around his waist. "And what are your plans for the future, sir?"

He lowered his head and brushed his lips lightly over the sensitive spot under her ear, enjoying her gasp. "I intend to marry one very beautiful redheaded poetess and spend the rest of my days cherishing her."

Bewitching in Boots

Moral of the Story of *Puss in Boots*

If a man has quick success
In winning such a fair princess,
By turning on the charm,
Then regard his manners, looks, and dress,
That inspired her deepest tenderness,
For they can't do one any harm.

CHARLES PERRAULT
(1628–1703)

1

"Do you *really* think your plan will work?" Claire swiped a curl from her damp forehead. The summer breeze stealing its way into their moving carriage was a mixed blessing. It offered some relief from the heat, but brought with it wafts of dust.

This wasn't the most comfortable trip Elisabeth de Roussel had ever taken, but it was the most important—to her. "For the third time, yes." Her voice was calm, belying the disquiet she felt. Her nerves jangled; she didn't need her sister to keep repeating the same question.

"You're going to seduce Tristan de Tiersonnier, a man who makes other men quake with fear and women tremble with desire. And you're going to do it, dressed like *that*?"

"That is the plan." Elisabeth glanced over at her maid, Agathe, and caught her rolling her eyes. Elisabeth fully expected the older woman to voice her dissent over the plan, but instead Agathe was uncharacteristically quiet, and stared out the window, lips pursed.

Claire leaned in. "Elisabeth, you are dressed like a *man*. A shirt, breeches, black boots—those are men's clothes. Well, perhaps not *those* black boots. No man would wear something so snug around his calves."

"I'm quite aware of how I'm dressed, dear sister." Her younger sibling didn't need to know what an utter mess Elisabeth was inside, nor was she going to admit that having her prized sword at her hip gave her confidence and helped bolster courage. And courage was what she'd need to execute her plan.

Especially when the plan centered on the only man who intimidated her. The imposing, sinfully beautiful former commander of the King's private Guard—the Musketeers—Tristan de Tiersonnier, Comte de Saint-Marcel.

One look from his intense blue eyes and she was undone—when no man shook her, not even her father, the King. By doing nothing more than walking into a room, Tristan commanded her attention and ignited her senses—reducing her into some gawking, unsophisticated ingénue. With his confident manner, his tall and powerful body, he exuded authority. And—God help her—such potent sensuality. He made her ache. Heart and body.

He burned in her blood.

Sadly, nothing had lessened her fever for Tristan. Not marriage to another man. Not the lovers she'd taken since the Duc's death. Not time nor distance.

"I'm all for being a part of one of your schemes, Elisabeth," Claire said. "In fact, I'd never refuse. They're far too much fun. But this one is rather involved."

That was an understatement. Claire had no idea just how involved her plan was or what Elisabeth truly hoped to accomplish during this sojourn, but she couldn't explain any of it to her sister. Claire always looked up to her. As much as she adored

Claire, Elisabeth couldn't reveal to her, or anyone, just how vulnerable she was to Tristan.

It was a weakness. She never showed her weaknesses. One didn't survive at court by being transparent—ever.

And Elisabeth had survived plenty of attempts to diminish her, both at court and in the eyes of the King. Her late mother had taught her well. She'd been a fine example of how strength and a cunning mind benefited a woman. She hadn't kept the King's interest longer than any of his other mistresses without knowing a thing or two about how to be clever in a man's world. Elisabeth had adopted her mother's finesse and fortitude and had risen among the brood sired by His Majesty to become the favorite royal daughter. And she used her favored position to protect Claire—who went mostly unnoticed and unprotected by their father—from the constant courtly intrigue.

"Hrrmph. Seems like a lot of trouble to go to just to bed a man," Agathe mumbled. "We could have stayed home. There are plenty of men at Versailles to choose from."

"There are indeed," Elisabeth said. Her period of mourning over, during the last year she'd had her choice of lovers. Had the freedom to pick and choose whom she wanted. She'd enjoyed the freedom that came with widowhood.

But her freedom was running out.

If she was going to do something about Tristan, it had to be now.

"The men at court bore me," Elisabeth added, affecting her usual tone. One that was purposely blasé. One that gave the world the impression she was indifferent. "The timing is perfect. Veronique is no longer Tristan's mistress. This is the most opportune time."

Claire crinkled her nose. "Veronique . . ." she muttered with disdain. A disdain shared by Elisabeth for their unscrupulous half-sister, the court filled with too many just like her.

"Opportune?" Agathe snorted. "Perhaps Madame has forgotten that the man was dismissed from his position as Captain of the Guard—and the reason why?"

"I haven't forgotten, Agathe," Elisabeth said, "and it is not a permanent situation. Tristan is strong and skilled. Sooner or later His Majesty will reinstate him." She'd see to it. It was part of her plan, important for many reasons, including thwarting Veronique's ambitions. Three months ago, Tristan had been injured in the line of duty. For two and a half months he'd convalesced at the palace until the King, acting on the advice of the royal physicians who felt he'd never completely heal, had replaced him as commander of the Guard.

"So how do you plan on seducing him?" Claire asked, her eyes twinkling with mischief.

Elisabeth smiled. "Now where would be the fun in telling you that? You'll just have to wait and see." She had no idea how she was going to go about seducing Tristan. Her mother had taught her how to entice men, what they liked in and out of the boudoir. But Tristan was not like any man she'd ever known. He wasn't the sort of man who could be led around by the nose. He wouldn't be easily lured.

Claire frowned. "I will still get to help, yes?"

"Of course. That's why I brought you along." Elisabeth glanced at Agathe. "I'm going to need both of you to help."

Her old and faithful servant looked about as thrilled over the prospect as she'd be at developing a body rash.

"Excellent." Claire beamed. "I do so admire your bravery, Elisabeth. Normally women wait to be approached by Tristan de Tiersonnier. You're the only woman I know who is willing to approach him. He's a little too serious, a little too intense for me. I've always found him to be rather unnerving."

So did she. For entirely different reasons: the unbreakable pull he had on her and the need she had for him that was far too keen. *If all goes well, you might have him tonight* . . . Her nerve endings quivered with life, the notion as thrilling as it was terrifying. It took all she possessed not to abort her plan and race back to Versailles. But she couldn't. Wouldn't. It was time to take control and sate the tormenting desire she had for this man—who'd barely noticed her and had only spoken to her out of duty.

Well, today he'd notice her.

Acting on the signs she'd read in her father, on the subtle comments he'd made, Elisabeth knew he'd select a new husband for her soon. She'd be trapped in another marriage filled with lonely nights fantasizing about Tristan. More lonely years spent starved for his touch, his taste.

She wouldn't go through that again.

If she was going to be forced to marry once more, then her husband may as well be Tristan. A husband of her choosing. If she failed to seduce him into the idea of marriage, then at the very least she wouldn't fail to seduce him into her bed for a week of unbridled sex. It was unwise, utterly foolhardy, for a woman to crave a man as intensely as she craved Tristan. To be as spellbound as she was by him. Her mother had taught her better than that. One way or another, husband or lover, he'd bed her and she'd at last satisfy this hunger, snap this fascination, and purge him from her heart, body, and soul.

She'd never find any contentment in her life—know any peace—if she didn't break the power Tristan had over her.

"I find Tiersonnier appealing," Elisabeth remarked. "And as for his 'intensity,' I think that could be put to good use in the boudoir."

Claire giggled. "Too true, sister."

Agathe pursed her lips firmer together.

Elisabeth's plan was simple. Before she could marry Tristan, she had to convince both the King and Tristan that the irresistible ex-Musketeer was her perfect match.

There were only two problems with her plan. One, the King saw Tristan as infirm and not fit to marry her. And two, Tristan wasn't going be easy to seduce into her bed, much less into marriage.

He hated her.

The carriage stopped. Her entourage of Musketeers and a second carriage filled with their trunks and necessities halted as well.

Elisabeth alighted from the carriage with the help of one of the King's Guardsmen. Her stomach dropped at the sight before her.

"Good Lord, Elisabeth, is that Tiersonnier's château?" her sister asked, stopping by her side.

Agathe simply shook her head in dismay.

Standing in the courtyard, overgrown with weeds, was an old two-story country mansion, its stone masonry crumbling in many spots. The once proud mythical statues adorning its roof-tops were blackened with dirt and age.

Elisabeth took a deep breath and let it out slowly. "It's in some need of repair."

Agathe snorted. "That is putting it mildly."

This isn't a setback. She wasn't going to be discouraged by the state of the abode or, more important, what it suggested about the finances of the lord of this château and how that diminished her already slim chances of being with Tristan beyond the week. She'd come this far. She'd forge ahead.

She'd simply add to the plan. What was one more obstacle in her path? After all, she was already attempting the impossible. In addition to convincing the King that Tristan was capable of commanding His Majesty's Guard once more, and making Tristan want her, clearly she'd have to convince her father that Tristan was richer than he was.

She was wearing her lucky boots. Good thing.

She was going to need all the luck she could get.

* * *

"Is this what you do all day? Sit in the library?" Gabriel de Tiersonnier asked with a smile as he strolled into the room.

Seated on the settée, his leg propped up, Tristan stared out at the gardens. Without glancing at his brother, he responded dryly, "No. Sometimes I sit in the salon." His tone was caustic. Embittered.

He wanted to be left alone and tried to ignore his brother and his good mood. It was as infuriating as the unrelenting dull ache in Tristan's leg. An incessant reminder of his debilitated state. All these weeks and no bloody sign of improvement. He still walked with a cane. He still couldn't make peace with his crippled limb. He hadn't wanted to believe the royal physicians' prognosis. Now he was beginning to lose hope of a complete recovery. And his frustration and fury over it mounted daily.

Still smiling, Gabriel shook his head and sat down in a nearby chair, making himself comfortable.

Merde. His brother meant to stay.

"Really, Tristan, this sedate existence of yours is as exciting as living among celibate monks."

"You should know. You were one of them, until they tossed you out last week." Gabriel had returned two days ago, shattering Tristan's solitude, and he resented it.

He resented just about everything nowadays. He resented how far he'd fallen. He'd had it all: command of the most prestigious, most elite corps in the realm, the ear of the King and his esteem, magnificent apartments at Versailles, and a number of women to bed whenever he chose, including his favorite, Veronique. But his favorite turned out to be a conniving little opportunist, who was quick to leave. The moment he was replaced as Captain of the Musketeers, she was bedding his successor.

What did he have left when all the dust had settled? A lame leg. A broken-down château he cared nothing about. And worse, staid, empty years stretched out before him—a life so contrary to his active existence. He'd fought in countless campaigns for his country during his distinguished military career. He'd risen through the ranks to eventually head the King's private Guard, and had conducted covert operations and quashed conspiracies while in charge of the safety and protection of the royal family.

Gabriel chuckled good-naturedly. "I was not a monk, and well you know it. I was in the seminary. I hadn't taken any vows yet. Our dear departed father felt he needed to have one son in the service of God. I told him it was a mistake to send me."

"I suppose 'our dear departed father' overestimated your restraint. Here you thought celibacy was a mere suggestion and not a requirement for a man studying to become a member of the Holy Church."

"Exactly." Gabriel grinned. "Glad you see my point."

"Yes, and who knew they'd take it so seriously when they caught you with two women at the same time—twice."

Gabriel laughed. "Ah, now Tristan, those women were well

worth being expelled from the seminary. Who needs to wait to die to go to paradise when a man can sample those four lovelies right here on earth?"

"Tristan." His uncle Richard de Tiersonnier entered the room, his brow furrowed. "Are you expecting a Duc?"

"A Duc?" he repeated. "Of course not, why?" No one from court had visited him since his departure from the royal palace. He'd been well forgotten in mere weeks—after years of loyal service to the King and his family.

"There is a six-horse carriage among the entourage outside."

Tristan was baffled. Entourage? A six-horse carriage was definitely a Duc. What Duc? Why was he here?

Grabbing his cane, he struggled to his feet, refusing help from Gabriel, and made his way to the courtyard to greet his notable visitor, his uncle and brother falling in behind him.

Tristan arrested his steps outside the main entrance of his château. Two carriages, one with six white horses, and thirty of his former men each on horseback filled his courtyard.

But if that wasn't enough, by far the most astonishing sight was the King's favorite daughter, Elisabeth, Duchesse de Roussel. Flanked by her maid and her sister, she stood not twenty feet away dressed in breeches, black boots, and a white shirt—male clothing custom-fitted to her form.

She looked nothing like a man.

Her breeches accentuated her mouth-watering curves, black boots—like none he'd ever seen—molded to her slender calves, and then there was her shirt. The breeze fluttered the white material, teasing him with glimpses of creamy flesh above her breasts. He felt his prick harden.

Tristan clenched his teeth. *Jésus-Christ*, he hadn't had sex since his injury. He'd definitely gone too long without a good fuck if the sight of the King's most spoiled offspring, dressed in men's clothing, was stiffening his cock.

"Where is the Duc?" his uncle asked.

Gabriel stepped around Tristan. "Never mind that, Uncle. Who is that woman dressed in breeches?"

"One of His Majesty's illegitimate daughters." Tristan couldn't keep the disdain from his tone.

"I thought he legitimized all his children born to his mistresses," Richard stated.

"He did. He gave them status and arranged powerful matches for them, too," Tristan said. "This is one of the more self-indulgent among those in the royal brood."

Tightening his jaw, he made his way across the courtyard, hating it that his former men had to see him hobbling like a cripple. Whatever Elisabeth wanted, he'd refuse. Whatever game she was playing—and it was obvious she was up to no good—he wouldn't engage in it.

He was going to send her and her entourage straight back to Versailles.

2

Elisabeth's heart hammered in her chest as she watched Tristan approach. He wasn't happy to see her. No surprise there. The summer wind caressed his dark hair and pressed his shirt against his strong chest. Normally in uniform, this was the first time she'd ever seen him in plain clothing.

He looked even more dangerous and delicious.

Elisabeth felt the usual hot quickening in her belly at the sight of him.

He stopped, towering before her, and gave a short, stiff obligatory bow. "Madame, to what do I owe this honor?" The last word was particularly weighty with sarcasm.

Here we go, Elisabeth . . . She prayed he didn't notice how she trembled. Schooling her features, she lifted her chin a notch. "And a good day to you, too, Tristan." She'd never addressed him in such a familiar manner, but if she wanted a more intimate involvement, she might as well speak to him in a more intimate way.

"Yes, I am well and I had a good trip. Thank you." She kept her tone light and her gaze fixed to his, anxiety and arousal swirling through her system. Just being this close to him made her sex moisten.

His eyes narrowed slightly. "Forgive my manners." His reply was tightly dealt. "I should have inquired about your well-being and your trip. I'm glad all is well. The point of your visit is?"

The man didn't believe in mincing words, did he? He couldn't make it more obvious he wanted her gone. Posthaste. Well, she wasn't going anywhere.

"Agathe, the letter, please." She held out her hand to her maid.

Agathe pulled out a folded parchment from inside the sleeve of her dress and handed it to her.

Elisabeth held it out to Tristan. "From the King."

Taking the letter from her, Tristan broke open the seal with one hand, leaning heavily on his cane with the other, and scanned its contents. He snorted. "This asks that I help you secure a new fencing instructor."

"That's correct." Every so often the breeze blew just the right way and delighted her senses with his scent. He smelled wonderful. All male. Potent and virile, his leg injury diminishing him in no way in her eyes. She wanted to lean in and inhale deeply, and had to fight back the urge to lace her arms around him and brush her lips along his neck, his skin tempting her in the worst way. Too many nights she'd lain in bed, wondering how he'd feel against her, inside her. Her every instinct told her that any carnal encounter with this man would be like none she'd ever known. Behind the cold glares he gave her was a man who was naturally— deliciously—dominant in the boudoir. With a wicked blend of hot sensuality and sinful skills, he knew how to drive a woman wild. Stories of his sexual talents abounded at the palace.

Sadly, he didn't even need to lift a finger to affect her. She was already wild and wet for him.

"I'll be staying awhile. We all will." She gestured toward the large group she'd brought. "Now if you will show me to my rooms."

Gripped by anger, his light blue eyes shone with such bedazzling fire.

"I'll not show you anywhere, madame, except back to your carriage. I have no fencing instructor to suggest to you. Inform the King of my regrets. Kindly take your party and return to Versailles."

Where most would have stepped back when on the receiving end of one of Tristan de Tiersonnier's fierce looks and sharp tones, boldly she took a step closer to him. A delectable rush of heat flooded over her. Her nipples tightened and pressed hard against her shirt.

"I don't think so. I am staying." She forced herself to hold his regard without wavering. "You see, my father knows how much I love to fence and has always provided me with fine instructors in the past. I've learned all I can from my last instructor. Therefore, I need a new one. He has ordered you to assist me in finding one to my liking, and I've chosen the instructor I want. *You.*"

Tristan gave a harsh laugh. "*Me?* Madame, are you blind? Perhaps you missed my injured leg?" he all but growled at her.

Unfazed, she responded, "I'm aware of your injury. It won't hinder you, I'm sure. You are the best swordsman in the country. You have a lot to teach me. And you'll not disobey your King's orders."

She stepped around him. Without turning back, she walked toward the château with purposeful strides, passing the small group of servants who'd formed a line outside, her sister and maid

on her heels. She hated sounding spoiled and demanding, knowing it fed into his preconceived notions of her, but he left her no
choice. He needed persuasion. Only by throwing the King's name
and authority around could she bend his will to hers.

"Oh, this is good. This is so much better than the seminary."
Gabriel snickered. "Tristan, I don't believe I've ever seen a woman
order you about."

Tristan watched the saucy sway of Elisabeth's luscious derrière as she walked away. He held back the expletives bellowing
in his head. He was at a full cock stand—in front of a fucking
squad of his former men. In fact, the moment she'd stepped close
and he'd noticed the telltale sign of her stiffened nipples, he was
slammed with a hot wave of arousal. He was exciting her. *Merde.*
It was affecting him.

He didn't need this. He was already in torment thanks to his
leg. He didn't need his prick to add to his misery. Elisabeth de
Roussel was nothing more than a coquette—a flirt who didn't
offer up the ultimate prize. He'd seen her cock-teasing at court.
She had it down to an art. With her beauty and wit, she had men
all but panting for her. She lapped it up, purring with pleasure
over their interest and thriving on the power she wielded over
them. Countless fools had vied for her attention and were ultimately turned down.

Few had ever made it to her bed. It was a game to her. A mere
diversion.

The royal family was, by and large, self-absorbed and full of
artifice—Veronique and Elisabeth among the worst. Only Veronique never received preferential treatment from the King the way
Elisabeth did. Loyalty, honesty, and honor meant nothing to any
member of His Majesty's family. Not a sincere soul in the bunch.
He didn't miss the games at court or those who played them.

Clearly, Elisabeth was bored, looking for new diversions.

He wasn't about to become that diversion.

Tristan glanced at the men he used to command. Most were dismounting and wouldn't make eye contact with him. Their first meeting since his dismissal, the awkwardness and tension in the air was palpable. He missed leading these men. Every one of the twenty-seven hundred that made up the King's private Guard was of noble birth, impeccable character, and superior skill. If he were still in charge, he could order them to escort the Duchesse de Roussel back to the palace with a letter to the King recommending that for her own safety his daughter not travel the countryside in her outrageous attire. But he had no authority over them any longer. They had to abide by their mistress's wishes, unable to take orders from him.

"Tristan, what do you wish to do with all these men?" Richard asked.

Out of the corner of his eye he could see Gabriel smiling, thoroughly enjoying himself.

"Send them to the stables until I settle this matter."

They wouldn't be there long.

She was leaving.

* * *

She wasn't leaving, she told herself. *You are going to collect yourself and not allow him to overwhelm you. Not with his size. Not with his scratchy temperament, and most especially not with his potent allure.* It was bad enough she was having a difficult time thinking clearly with him near, her thoughts dominated by the shameless fantasies he inspired.

"Well, at least the inside of the château looks better than the outside," Agathe remarked, glancing around. Standing in the vestibule, Elisabeth gazed up at the grand staircase, caring little about the condition of Tristan's home at the moment. Not when she needed to steel her resolve so that she didn't run back to Versailles like a coward. In a few moments, Tristan would enter the château and she had to be ready for another round of wits and wills.

She was supposed to be seducing him. Have him mindless with hunger for her. She thought she'd seen heated interest in his eyes. Or was that simply wishful thinking? Her senses were so frenzied, she couldn't say for certain if she was having a warming effect on him.

Claire placed her hand on Elisabeth's shoulder. "Are you all right? You look a bit flushed."

Elisabeth forced a smile. "It's this terrible heat. I'm fine." Nothing could be further from the truth. She was in over her head and drowning fast.

Tristan entered with the same two men who'd been with him outside, both men bearing a striking resemblance to him, though one gentleman was at least twenty-five years Tristan's senior.

The second Tristan spotted her in the grand entranceway, he marched to her, his cane aiding him along.

Anytime he entered a room, his male beauty took her breath away. Now was no exception. Her breath stuck in her throat for a moment and her heart gave a flutter.

Oh, Elisabeth, you are so under his spell. She was all but ready to throw herself at him and beg him to take her just so she'd have some relief from the yearning throbbing through her core. Anything that would put an end to this attraction and affinity.

She dropped her gaze briefly and couldn't help but notice the pronounced bulge in his breeches. Dear God, he . . . desired her. It was indisputable. It was incredible.

A sudden surge of much-needed confidence welled inside her. Her insides danced.

Frowning, he halted before her.

Smiling, she looked up at him. *Oh, yes . . . This is going to happen.* He was going to be her lover. *Maybe even more . . .* her heart whispered.

"I don't know what game you are playing, nor do I wish to know," he said. "If you're looking for new forms of amusement, I suggest you seek them out at court. Not here."

"My brother has completely forgotten his manners, madame." The younger man elbowed past his older sibling. He had the same dark hair, but his eyes were not as vibrant as Tristan's. "Allow me to introduce myself. I'm Gabriel de Tiersonnier." He took her hand and pressed a kiss to it. "This is our uncle, Richard de Tiersonnier."

The older gentleman stepped forward and kissed her hand, too. "*Enchanté*, madame."

"A pleasure to meet you both." She introduced her sister. Her nerves were beginning to settle as she became surer of herself. If Tristan desired her, even a little, she had him.

Tristan simply glowered silently at her, then reluctantly murmured an apology and a greeting to Claire.

"Now then, about my lessons." Elisabeth leaped back into the subject before Tristan could begin a new tirade. She stepped close to Tristan again, this time leaving less room between their bodies than she had outside. Something flared in his eyes, something she read as hunger.

Her fever spiked.

Praying he couldn't tell just how undone she was by him, lest she lose ground, she managed to state firmly, "You'll provide a lesson every day. First thing in the morning. You see, I've challenged someone. By week's end, I expect, thanks to your instructions, to be able to best him."

He held her stare for a moment. "Whom have you challenged?" There was skepticism in his tone. He thought she was lying. Well, she was lying. Normally, she didn't give a whit what people thought of her. Would she have taken up fencing if she had? But Tristan's low opinion of her bothered her.

Had always bothered her.

"That is none of your concern. You'll be paid generously for your time and skill."

"Madame . . ." he began, his voice low and thick with ire.

"Call me Elisabeth."

"*Madame*," he repeated, this time sharply. The man was beyond stubborn. "If I cannot command the Musketeers, I most certainly am not fit to be your instructor—the King will quite agree with me." Each word was laced with bitterness. She couldn't blame him. Elisabeth had hated how quickly her father had dismissed and replaced Tristan. His years of devoted service completely ignored. That his injury had occurred during an assassin's attempt against the King, Tristan saving his life, had been seemingly inconsequential to her father. "Get back in the carriage and return to your palace. Your father—"

"Was right to send you here," Gabriel injected. "Tristan *is* the best swordsman in the realm. And of course, we wouldn't want to offend the King, now would we, Tristan?" He patted his shoulder. "You and your lovely sister are most welcome." Gabriel smiled.

Tristan dragged his gaze from her to give his brother a murderous glare.

Gabriel's brows shot up. "What? It's but a week. Only seven days. A flash of time then it's over." His brother glanced at Claire then back to Elisabeth, his smile returning. "Such a short time to spend in such charming company."

"I agree with Gabriel," Richard said. His uncle was a man of few words. This was a fine time for him to start voicing his opinion. "You are welcome to stay . . . and if you change your mind and want a different fencing instructor, you may look to me, madame. I taught Tristan everything he knows. I was once in the Musketeers myself before I retired from active service, you know."

Tristan strived for patience. His uncle and brother didn't know what kind of woman they were dealing with, although her mode of dress should have alerted them to the obvious—she was trouble. Willful. Acting as though society's mores didn't apply to her because she was the King's favorite daughter. A week with Elisabeth running about in her tight-fitted, stirring attire. Of her trying to garner the very physical reactions she'd wrought from his unruly cock.

Jésus-Christ, of her entertaining herself at his expense.

It wasn't going to happen.

Yet, if she wished to stay, he couldn't toss her out—just as she'd gleefully pointed out. He may not be in His Majesty's employ any longer, but was still obliged to his King. And he had to oblige the King's favorite daughter, because of it.

However, the key here was *if* she wished to stay.

This was his home. His domain she was under. And there were a number of highly appealing ideas flitting through his mind on how to sway her into wanting to leave and abandon the fencing lessons she was demanding.

For the first time since she'd arrived, he found himself fighting back a smile.

"Are you sure you'd be comfortable staying here for these lessons, madame?" he asked. "This isn't Versailles."

She smiled at him, though it didn't reach her large hazel eyes. "I'll manage," she said tightly. For the first time he saw a break in her façade. He'd irked her. She didn't like his comment that suggested she was pampered. Odd. Why would the obvious annoy her?

"I'd like to refresh myself now. Could you order me a bath?" Elisabeth's features were schooled once again, and she was speaking as though the matter were settled. As if there were never any doubt he'd comply with her demands.

Normally he'd be vexed, but he wasn't, not while plans were taking shape in his mind. By the time he was through with her, she'd bend to *his* will. And leave, taking his former men with her.

"Of course," Tristan ceded, and caught the surprised looks on his brother's and uncle's faces. Tristan called to his majordomo standing in the vestibule. "Please escort our guests upstairs to the east wing."

"The east wing?" Gabriel said. "But, Tristan—"

"The. East. Wing." Tristan gave his brother a look of warning, silently ordering him to hold his tongue.

Once the women were upstairs, Gabriel didn't waste any time in questioning his decision. "Why did you give them rooms there? In the summer those rooms hardly get any breeze at all. They're terribly hot."

Richard shook his head. "That is exactly why he chose them, isn't it, Tristan?"

"Precisely. I want them gone. The sooner the better. I don't want to be responsible for any more of the royal brats. Especially Elisabeth de Roussel. She'll be uncomfortable and she'll leave."

It was Gabriel's turn to shake his head. "Brother, you are daft. She is beautiful, and in case you missed the way she looked at you, she's all but begging you to fuck her. How could you have missed the signs?"

"I missed nothing, Gabriel. She's not begging for anything of the sort. She's flirtatious with no intent on carrying through with an amorous encounter. It is nothing more than a coquettish act. One I've seen her play many times."

"Oh," Richard and Gabriel said in chorus, clearly disappointed.

"Are you sure, Tristan?" Clearly, Gabriel didn't want to let this go. "She certainly looked as though she'd be willing . . ."

"She's not. And even if she were, I am not fucking the King's daughter."

"Why not? You bedded Veronique."

"Veronique is not the King's favorite daughter. Elisabeth is. And she holds no appeal for me." Liar. His stiffened cock proved otherwise. Before she put him through any more discomfort, he was getting rid of her.

There were a number of ways to chase her away. If the hot rooms didn't work, he could start responding to her sexual attempts. In fact, the more he thought about it, the more appeal it held for him.

He just might teach her a lesson on the folly of arousing sexual interest with no intention of finishing what she started.

"She'll be here a day, two at most."

She wouldn't last the week.

3

Elisabeth was miserable. It was early in the morning, the sun still new in the sky. Waiting for Tristan and her first lesson, she stood in the gardens—if the weed-ridden expanse littered with poorly tended shrubs and bushes could be considered a garden. Her scabbard rested against her hip, her precious sword sheathed within.

He was late.

She was exhausted.

She hadn't slept at all last night. Tossing and turning in her bed, thoughts of Tristan, images of his aroused body warming her, added to the heat in the stifling rooms. In fact, she suspected that if she'd slept in the kitchens near the cooking fires, she'd have been more comfortable.

She was no fool. It didn't take long for her to realize he'd selected the "east wing" for a reason. To make her stay as uncomfortable as possible so that she'd pack her trunks and return to the palace. Elisabeth was willing to wager the other rooms at the opposite end of the château were much cooler.

Yesterday, she'd bathed. She'd primped. Spent the better part of the afternoon preparing for supper and had donned one of her favorite and most becoming gowns. With her pulse racing with nervous excitement, she'd made her way to the *Salle de Buffet* with Claire, only to find Richard and Gabriel there.

But no Tristan.

Gabriel had offered Tristan's apologies, claiming that his leg was troubling him. But she didn't believe it. She was troubling him. He was avoiding her.

And she hadn't traveled out to his château to be thwarted this way.

If he was avoiding her, then she was affecting him strongly. Good.

That made the time she spent with him during the fencing instruction all the more important to advancing her plan.

From the moment she'd laid eyes on him years ago, she'd been hopelessly enchanted. Other men paled in comparison. She'd tried not to look his way at the palace. She'd tried not to think of him. She'd tried to silence the errant emotions her heart had attached to him.

She'd failed.

She wouldn't fail this time. This was her final opportunity to quell this maddening infatuation.

The sooner he bedded her and diminished his hold on her, the better.

Then, if she succeeded in marrying Tristan, she'd have the civilized marriage she'd always wanted to a husband she respected and shared common interests with, like fencing—without the unsettling influence he presently had on her.

The sound of footsteps snatched her out of her thoughts. She snapped her head up and saw Tristan approaching, cane in hand, his baldric across his chest. He looked strong, despite the cane. And fierce. A formidable opponent on any battlefield, she often heard others say. He was well respected by his men. Admired by the realm. A highly decorated officer, his valor in battle was legendary.

His tan-colored breeches outlined his powerful thighs, his plain white shirt hung loosely from his broad shoulders, yet she could still detect the dips and ripples of his chiseled chest. A tiny thrill shivered down her spine when he stopped before her.

He looked so good, it hurt.

"Good morning, Tristan." She smiled.

"Let's begin." Again no mincing of words. No exchange of pleasantries. She tamped down her irritation. Would it kill him to be less abrasive?

He unsheathed his sword. "I trust you know the basics?"

She knew more than the basics. Her passion for fencing was great. As a young girl, she'd watched the Musketeers practice as often as she could sneak away. Whenever they entertained the court with demonstrations of their skills, she'd been transfixed. It had taken carefully planned, carefully worded conversations with the King over a period of months before she'd finally managed to secure her first instructor. That was years ago. Prior to her marriage. She still fenced. Still took it seriously. Practiced whenever she could.

She'd become so good at swords, she'd bested all of her instructors.

She was about to impress Tristan at last. Perhaps even garner herself a bit of praise for her skill and elevate his opinion of her.

"I'm no novice at swords." She unsheathed her blade and squeezed the hilt. She felt strong and it felt so right in her hand.

"Good. Then show me what you know. Step back and begin when you're ready."

She was smiling now as she assumed the proper stance. "*En garde.*" She lunged at him on the attack.

His arm whipped up, his blade striking hers with stunning intensity, his defensive move ripping the hilt from her hand, sending her sword spiraling in the air before it landed twenty feet away with a *thump* in the weeds.

Her mouth agape, her palm throbbing, she simply blinked at him, astounded, reeling over how easily he'd disarmed her.

Calmly, he sheathed his sword and stepped close to her, a mimic of what she'd done to him yesterday. Slipping his fingers under her chin, he tilted her head back, bringing her mouth within inches of his. For a moment, she forgot to breathe.

"Lesson one." His warm breath caressed her lips. "If you are going to engage in a sword fight, hold on to your sword."

He released her and walked away.

Her chin nearly collided with the ground in open-mouthed astonishment. Ire erupted inside her. She clamped her mouth shut and raced up to him, jumping in the way of his path, halting him in his tracks, her fists clenched at her sides.

"What was that?" she demanded.

He cocked a brow. "What was *what*?"

"That," she said, jabbing her finger in the direction of where they'd been. "Surely you don't consider what just happened there a lesson."

"You didn't specify how long these lessons had to last. I feel I've taught you something. Practice holding your sword. And speak to your father. You told me you know the basics. Your instructors have either been inadequate or you lack the ability to grasp basic concepts."

"L-Lack the ability?" she sputtered, so outraged she could barely speak. Oh, how she wanted to plant her fist against his arrogant jaw. It was the first time in her life she ever wanted to strike a man—anyone, actually. "I do not lack ability!"

"Really," he said blandly.

"Yes! *Really.* You hit my sword—" Abruptly, she arrested her words.

"Too hard?"

She cringed, embarrassed that he'd guess what she was mistakenly going to say. Her palm and her pride both hurt. She'd never come up against an opponent as large and as strong as Tristan.

"Madame, I assumed you were interested in being able to take on any opponent. Are you only going to fight *women?*" She hated the slight taunt in his tone.

"I *can* fight any opponent. I have only fought men. And I've bested them all!" She stalked away; so scorching was her fury, she wondered if her eyebrows had been singed off. She was infuriated with herself for being so easily beat, and with him for being so insufferable. She didn't care that she was showing too much emotion—knowing full well that by showing anger she was showing weakness—alerting Tristan to the fact that he had enough influence over her to affect her this strongly.

Nor did she care a whit that she was doing what others didn't dare—chastising the mighty Tristan de Tiersonnier.

He needed a dressing-down. He deserved one.

She turned and marched right back up to him again. "You—"

She poked him in the chest with her finger. "You are . . . rude! And *arrogant*."

She marched away, picked up her sword, and sheathed it with an angry stab.

Tristan was having a difficult time holding back his smile, the corners of his mouth tugging hard. Her cheeks were pink, her eyes ablaze, and her breasts rose and fell with her quickened breaths. She looked adorable and incredibly alluring in her fiery state.

She stomped back to him. Back for another round. This time Tristan had to fight even harder to keep a straight face.

"And another thing—you know nothing about me." She rose onto the balls of her feet and stuck her pretty face in his. "NOTH-ING!" She stormed off. Tristan watched her stalk away.

Now, that's not true. He knew she had the sweetest derrière he'd ever seen. In her breeches, it was perfectly defined and inspired an assortment of salacious thoughts. He wanted nothing more than to strip away her clothing, push her down on all fours, grip that luscious behind, and sink his stiff cock into her warm, wet core.

She disappeared into the château. At last he allowed himself to break into a smile. *Dieu.* The woman wasn't dull, and she had more fire in her than he'd have guessed. He'd rather direct all that fire into more carnal endeavors.

She is also highly intelligent . . . She couldn't have maintained her elevated status with her father otherwise. Too many royal siblings had tried to knock her off her privileged perch. Without success.

She was crafty. Cunning. And he'd just provoked her in the worst way.

His smile died.

* * *

Fool. Fool. Fool! Elisabeth walked across the Grand Salon, making her way to her rooms. Never in her life had she lost her temper like that. Never had she behaved in such an infantile manner.

She'd completely lost control and made a spectacle of herself in front of Tristan. She was mortified. Why did it have to matter how he perceived her? Why couldn't she be indifferent to him the way she was to every other man she'd ever known?

Why would her heart and body not relinquish their incessant longing for this impossible man? For this impossible situation.

You know why, Elisabeth. Besides his masculine beauty, his sexual allure, he was a man with honor. Something rare in her world. Something that touched her deeply. How could she not want him? Despite his personal feelings, he'd stand in front of an assassin's blade for her or anyone else he'd sworn to protect—just as he'd done for the King. That was something she didn't believe the new Captain of the Musketeers, Antoine de Balzac, would do—and that was yet another reason to see Tristan reinstated.

He was the right man to hold the esteemed position. He deserved it above all others.

"Madame?" Tristan's voice arrested her steps.

By the time she turned, he'd reached her and grabbed hold of her arm. Her in tow, with his cane and his purposeful strides, he ate up the distance to the first door on the right.

Tristan opened it, pulled her inside, and slammed the door shut.

She didn't know what to make of his actions or of him pulling off his baldric and tossing it down on the nearby settee. Stupefied, she let him pull hers off as well, without question or protest, and watched as it landed on top of his. His cane followed.

Before she could form a question, he shoved her back against the wall.

Her eyes widened.

Pressing his palm against the wall near her head, he slipped the fingers of his other hand beneath her chin. Her nerve endings sparked to life.

"Why are you here?" he asked.

"You brought me in here." Tingles rippled from his touch down to the tips of her breasts, tightening her nipples.

"I mean at my château. Why have you come here?"

"I told you, I want fencing lessons—"

"That's a lie and we both know it." He cut her off abruptly. "I want the truth. I want you to admit you're here for your amusement and that you've been purposely behaving like a coquette."

She pushed his fingers away from her chin. It was too difficult to talk when he touched her. "I'm not here for my amusement, and I have not been behaving like a coquette."

He pressed his other palm to the wall, hemming her in between both hands. "No? What do you call this outrageous outfit of yours?"

"My fencing attire. You don't expect me to fence in a gown, do you?" she countered.

"I would expect you to dress like a woman once in a while—and for God's sake, where did you get those boots?"

"What is the matter with my boots? I happen to like them. They're comfortable. As for dressing like a woman, I do. In fact, I did. At supper. You wouldn't know that because you weren't there."

He tilted his head to one side. "Disappointed, were you?"

Oh, she wasn't about to respond to that.

He continued. "Were you saddened you missed out on an

opportunity to flirt? To stand too close, and bat your pretty eyes at me?"

Again, she held her tongue and simply gazed up at him, refusing to admit to a thing. It was one thing to attempt to seduce him, quite another to confess to it.

"I am not like those men at court you toy with. If you make sexual overtures to me, you'd better be prepared to be taken and fucked—any way I choose."

Her knees almost gave way. Dear God, how she wished he would fuck her.

He grasped her hand and pressed it to the sizable bulge in his breeches. "This is what you want, what you're trying to accomplish with your teasing, isn't it? To stiffen my cock."

Her sex answered with a warm gush. Through the cloth of his breeches, he felt hard as iron, his proportions more generous in size than any man she'd ever known.

"There aren't going to be any more 'lessons,' any more games. And no more cock-teasing. If you're still here tomorrow night, Duchesse, I am going to fuck you."

Her clit gave a fierce throb, then pulsed in rhythm with her wild heart.

He grasped her wrists, raised them above her head, pinning them against the wall with one hand. Her heart lurched. She tested his hold. His grip was strong and firm. Unbreakable.

"Tristan?" she questioned, his name tumbling from her lips between rapid breaths.

The corner of his mouth rose in a half-smile. "For the first time in your life, you won't be dictating, demanding, or commanding a thing. Tied and bound for my pleasure, you'll submit and surrender your control to me. That's how I'm going to take you. That's how it's going to be."

A jolt of fear rocked her. She wanted to be with him so fiercely . . . but tied and bound? She wasn't afraid he'd harm her in any way, but . . . *surrender her control?* He couldn't possibly be serious. "You—You jest." What was even more frightening was how appealing she found his wicked words. The thought of completely acquiescing to him, not being able to hold back in any way, set her ablaze.

He cupped her breast and pinched her hardened nipple through her shirt. She jerked with a sharp gasp. "No jest. There won't be a part of your body I won't avail myself of." His thumb languidly stroked her nipple, sending delicious sensations swirling down her spine. "You'll be all mine to do with whatever I wish." He pinched her sensitized nipple again. She barely caught her cry of pleasure in time and swallowed it back down. Oh, God. He was serious.

If she wanted him to take her, it would have to be his way. If she stayed, she'd have to cede to him in the manner he described. He wasn't going to let her finesse her way around it.

Warnings against giving a man complete power over her— especially this man who wielded so much power over her already— sounded in her head.

Ever so lightly he brushed his mouth against her lips. "You'll be at my mercy, Duchesse, and you're going to come harder than you've ever come before."

*   *   *

Tristan rested his head against the back of the chair in the library the next day and swirled the brandy in his goblet.

She'd bolted.

Thirty Musketeers, two carriages, close to forty horses, and two royal daughters—gone.

He'd done it. He'd chased Elisabeth de Roussel away. So why didn't he feel any joy from his accomplishment? Not only had he rid himself of the King's most errant daughter, he'd also gotten rid of the men who'd escorted her. He'd never hidden from anyone or anything in his life, yet he found himself avoiding his former men. The last thing he wanted was for them to see him move about in his depleted state. It was more than his pride could bear.

He should be rejoicing at the sudden solitude, but instead he was gripped by the most irritating sense of disappointment.

He wanted Elisabeth. He wanted to do to her everything he'd described. Beneath her masculine clothing was a highly excitable, very feminine form, his every instinct telling him that fucking her would be one of the most intense carnal encounters he'd ever have. He'd seen the arousal in her eyes as well as the fear. She'd been torn between wanting to be possessed and wanting to run.

It had taken all that he had not to taste her and stroke her into an eager willingness, driving everything from her mind except her desire for him. He had to remind himself over and over as his cock throbbed harder than his leg that she wasn't just the daughter of the King, but the daughter whom His Majesty doted upon.

Held most dear.

And, therefore, that made her untouchable as far as he was concerned.

Besides, after Veronique, the last thing he should want was to bed another of the King's daughters. The hot rooms hadn't driven Elisabeth away, nor had the ridiculous "lesson" in fencing he'd given her.

He'd run her off with the promise of a simple sex game, and he wasn't going to waste another moment feeling regret over it.

"Good riddance, Duchesse."

Tristan tipped the goblet and let the brandy flow down his throat, hoping that the burning liquid would take the edge off the pain in his leg.

Fast, hard footsteps approached the library.

His uncle entered the room. "Tristan, are you expecting guests?"

"No."

"Well, there are a number of men here."

Tristan sat up. "Not more Musketeers?"

"No. More like workers."

"What are you taking about?"

Gabriel walked in. "He's talking about the fifty men who are here, clearing the gardens, repairing the façade of the château."

"Fifty men?" Tristan grabbed his cane and struggled to his feet. "Where did they come from?"

Gabriel and Richard exchanged looks.

"You tell him," Gabriel suggested.

"No, I'd rather you be the bearer of bad news."

Tristan didn't like where this was going. "Will someone tell me what is going on?"

Gabriel cleared his throat. "Very well. The workers are here at the behest of the Duchesse de Roussel."

"*What?*" He couldn't have heard correctly.

"There's more," Richard advised, then turned to Gabriel. "Go on, tell him."

"I'm trying to do that. But I keep getting inter—"

"Get on with it!" Tristan's ire was beginning to mount; he sensed he wasn't going to like what he was about to hear.

Gabriel gave a nod. "Since you are in such a fine mood, I can't wait to tell you the rest." His sarcasm only served to grate on

Tristan's nerves. "We were a tad mistaken when we told you the Duchesse de Roussel had left."

Tristan's stomach clenched. "*Merde.* You jest."

"No. I don't. It turns out, she took it upon herself to change rooms," Gabriel continued. "You see when we saw that the Musketeers and the trunks were gone, we assumed the Duchesse and her sister had left—permanently. We were unaware that their trunks were moved to the west wing."

"The west wing? Where my . . . *our* rooms are?"

Gabriel sauntered over to him and placed a hand on Tristan's shoulder. "Precisely."

Tristan tightened his jaw. "Where is the Duchesse now?"

His brother shrugged. "Who knows? She's out and about with her entourage. In the meantime, we are having some lovely repairs done to our château." He smiled.

By the looks on his uncle's and brother's faces, they were pleased.

Tristan was ready to strangle the King's favorite child. The woman was beyond intrusive. She knew no boundaries.

The sound of horses' hooves striking the cobblestones in the courtyard grabbed his attention. He rushed out of the library and down the tapestry-lined hall.

The moment Tristan entered the vestibule, he froze. So did his breathing.

Standing on the opposite side of the grand entrance, talking to her sister and her maid, Elisabeth was in a yellow gown embellished with golden bows. Her tantalizing form was outlined so enticingly, his mouth went dry.

As though she felt his gaze, she turned and smiled when she saw him. Immediately, she approached. Her dark hair adorned with small golden bows was perfectly coiffed, long silky curls he wanted to touch. His hungry gaze devoured her, moving down to her décolletage, enjoying the sweet little bounce of her breasts with each step she took.

Her bedazzling smile was still on her lovely face when she reached him. She looked like an angel.

She folded her hands before her. "Good day, gentlemen."

He peeled his eyes off her and looked beside him. *Dieu*, he'd been so transfixed, he hadn't even realized his brother and uncle flanked him.

They exchanged pleasantries, while Tristan, for the first time in his life, was speechless.

"I hope you don't mind that I left for a bit of an outing," she said to him. "I purchased something for you in the town." She motioned to her maid and sister.

The moment the maid handed Elisabeth the wooden box she carried, Claire gave a giggle then quickly looked down, covering her mouth with her fingertips.

Elisabeth handed him the box and opened the lid for him. Filling the box were numerous silk scarves.

"They're for later," Elisabeth said.

His gaze shot up to hers. She was smiling still and with a wink, sauntered away, heading toward the staircase that led to the west wing. Another giggle erupted from Claire before she quickly fell in step with her sister and servant.

Jésus-Christ. The scarves were for binding—her. He hadn't scared her away. She'd called his bluff.

She meant to *stay*.

Gabriel sifted his hand through the scarves and frowned. "These are for women. *Merde*, brother, she dresses like a man. If you're going to start dressing like a woman, I don't wish to know about it."

Tristan gnashed his teeth. The noise outside, from the workers, the newly returned Musketeers, and their horses, all merged into a nerve-grating clamor invading the inner sanctum of his home. The hammering outside was keeping time with the throbbing in his cock. Once again he was stiff as steel. Once again his château was overrun.

All because of the most ungovernable woman he'd ever met.

Tristan slammed the box shut, tucked it under his arm, and limped toward the staircase.

Most unwise to give a man who wishes to strangle an unruly woman the very means by which to do it.

4

"Do you think Tristan will be here soon?" Claire asked while seated comfortably in Elisabeth's newly acquired rooms. The private apartments on the west side of the château were not only cooler, but better furnished and far more pleasant.

"I predict within the next few minutes." Elisabeth voice sounded calm, giving no indication of just how discomposed she was. She stood near the windows, too nervous to sit, her stomach in knots. She'd just made a bold move downstairs. The boldest in her life.

The next step was up to Tristan.

He was angry at her—for reasons she fully expected him to voice when he entered her rooms—but he was also undeniably interested in following through with his vow. She'd seen arousal flare in his eyes when he saw the contents of the wooden box.

Her very entrails quaked with anticipation. An amorous encounter was at hand. With tall, strong, beautiful Tristan de

Tiersonnier. The notion made her feel warm, weak, and a bit apprehensive—especially when she thought about how he was going to take her.

She'd never done anything like this in her life.

Claire burst into a giggle. Elisabeth jumped a little. Claire's spontaneous fits of joviality hadn't ceased since Elisabeth purchased the scarves and told her of their intended purpose.

"Did you see the look on Tristan's face when you handed him the box of scarves? I can't believe you're going to let him do something so wicked," Claire said.

Neither could she. His provocative promise consumed her every waking thought and had teased and tantalized her all last night. She'd vacillated, and in the end, she decided she'd come too far to quit now. She was so very close to having him. It was what she'd come there for.

It was the only way to douse the fire.

The door to her antechamber swung open.

Tristan entered, a scowl on his handsome face, the wooden box under his arm. He dropped the box onto the marble-top table in the room with a clunk.

A fresh wave of nervous excitement crested over her. "A knock before entering a lady's apartments is customary, is it not, Tristan?" Elisabeth said.

His nostrils flared. "I'll do as I bloody well please. This is my château. A concept you don't seem to grasp." He spoke in a low snarl, slowly advancing upon her, his purpose to intimidate, no doubt. She rooted her feet to the floor to keep from bolting from the room. "You don't change rooms without asking my permission. You don't order my staff to move your trunks. And you certainly do not hire men to alter my château! Do you understand?" he barked, stopping before her.

Clearly, he was quite livid. Perhaps the workers were too much to add to the mix today.

"Yes, Tristan. Of course." Her mother had taught her that the best way to counter a man's ire was with soft tones. Agreeable words. If she had anything at stake, a woman only stood to lose, to suffer, if she didn't promptly calm the storm.

Elisabeth had something at stake. He wouldn't take her when he was this angry.

Yet unlike her dealings with other men, she didn't want to simply voice empty words just to appease him. For the first time ever, Elisabeth found herself wanting to offer a man an explanation. It actually mattered to her that she made him understand.

"Claire." Her sister had shot to her feet the moment Tristan had barged into the room. Warily, Claire watched the exchange between Elisabeth and Tristan. "Why don't you go back to your rooms. I shall speak to you later," Elisabeth said.

Claire glanced at Tristan and then back at her. "Ar-Are you certain?"

"Quite certain," she assured her with a smile.

Reluctantly, her sister murmured a "good day" and left Elisabeth's apartments.

Elisabeth tried to ignore the wild fluttering in her stomach. She was, for the first time, alone with Tristan in her chambers. She folded her hands before her. Just being this close to him made her quiver. "Now then, I seem to have angered you. That wasn't my intent. The men were hired as a gesture of thanks."

"*Thanks?*" he snorted. "For what?"

"For two reasons: first, for my personal gratitude for your years of loyal service to the King and our family."

She saw the surprise in his eyes. An expression she couldn't name crossed his face, his features softening slightly. Her words had come from her heart. His effect on her was so strong, she had to be careful not to go any further. Not to offer up any more emotional revelations.

"The second reason for the workers was in thanks for the fencing lessons. On the day we arrived, I sent one of the men to you with a sizable purse as payment—though at the time I didn't know your lessons would be quite so brief. In any event, you wouldn't accept payment. That night I had two of the Musketeers ride back to Versailles with the order to return with gardeners and workers. What I did was meant as a gift. I had hoped you'd be pleased. Obviously, I misjudged your reaction." All right, perhaps that wasn't the *whole* truth. She'd hoped to fix up the château lest the King see it in its current state. It would help cast a more favorable light on Tristan as a potential husband. "The men will cease immediately, if that's what you wish. As to the changing of the rooms, you and I both know you purposely placed me in rooms that were uncomfortable. You want me gone. Clearly, I've earned your disdain."

He remained silent. His expression was guarded.

Elisabeth pressed on, her heart pounding. "It is because you think I'm spoiled. His Majesty's favorite daughter, privileged and self-indulgent. Oh, and yes, let us not forget a *coquette*. That accurately sums it up, doesn't it?"

He took a deep breath and let it out slowly. "Actually, it does, madame." The man believed in being honest—even when that honesty had bite. Still, it made him a better man than others she knew. She didn't know any other honest men.

"Tell me, Tristan, how many men have you seen around me at court?"

"Many," he said without hesitation.

"And of those men, how many have you seen me turn away?"

"Almost all."

"And did it ever occur to you that I may have had good reason to reject them?"

"Really," he said dryly. "What reason would you have?"

"Because I know they wanted to bed me simply to get close to the King."

He cocked a brow.

"The King's favorite daughter has great appeal to those driven by ambition, Tristan. You've been at court. You've seen the maneuvering. The backstabbing. Too many of the men have no qualms about using a woman to get to the King. I refuse to be used that way." She never left herself open to it. By maintaining an emotional distance, a level of detachment, she was able to keep a proper prospective and see the scheming. She never fell for false words of affection and devotion. Her mother had taught her that a woman had to be strong, stay strong, and never—not ever—allow herself to be vulnerable in matters of the heart. It clouded a woman's judgment. Should Tristan become her husband, she still had to distance herself emotionally. Even as his wife, she couldn't permit herself to continue to feel the things she felt for him.

It laid her bare. And a woman could never do that.

Too many women had made the mistake of allowing tender sentiment to go unchecked for their husbands or lovers—to their detriment. At times, to their ruin.

With Tristan, she'd already broken too many of the rules she lived by.

"I'm selective, Tristan. Not coquettish. There is a difference. Besides my husband, I've only been with two men." She'd never admit she'd given herself to Selle and Leymont with the hopes of quashing her yearning for Tristan.

Unfortunately, it hadn't worked.

He gave a nod. "The Marquis de Leymont and the Duc de Selle."

He'd noticed? He'd watched her that closely? *Of course he had. It was his duty. He was responsible for the welfare of the royal family.* He was supposed to know who was in the inner circle.

Elisabeth looked down at her hands and immediately squelched her disappointment.

"Everyone thinks that being the favorite daughter of the King is an enviable position to be in." She looked up at him. "It has its serious flaws. The King gave his favorite daughter to his friend, the Duc de Roussel, as a gesture of his esteem for the man. It didn't matter that the Duc was twenty-five years my senior. That he had no interest in having another wife, or any more children. The Duc accepted his "gift." Shortly after our marriage, Roussel shipped me to his country château. I lived in that dilapidated, drafty abode for three years—until the Duc's death—so I am not as pampered as you think."

He studied her quietly for a moment. "This is the first time I've ever heard you be in any way candid. It's a pleasant surprise."

It was true. It was the first time she'd been candid with anyone. As wrong as she knew it was, it felt good to open herself up a little to him.

He reached out, grasped her arm, and pulled her to him. She collided against his hard body. A jolt of sensations shot through her distended nipples the moment they came in contact with his chest. She barely caught her moan in time.

He snaked his arm around her waist, his enormous shaft

pressing insistently against her belly. "Why have you come to me? I want the truth."

"I want lessons from the finest swordsman in the land," she said honestly, having always been in awe of his skill.

He removed his arm from around her waist and placed his hand at the nape of her neck. "Why else?"

Gazing up into his beautiful blue eyes, she silently begged him to kiss her, needing it with jarring desperation, the bud between her legs pulsating wildly, each hungry throb a torment. *Say it, Elisabeth. It's just three words. Tell him the truth here, or this won't happen.*

"I . . . want you." She'd never said that to any man and meant it.

"You're truly going to let me have you?"

"Yes."

"I warn you, Duchesse, once we begin, I'm not going to stop, so if you're having any qualms . . ."

She shook her head. "No qualms. I won't stop you."

The most sensual smile lifted the corner of his perfect mouth. "Excellent. Then you're mine." He lowered his head.

She held her breath and braced herself for the thrill of his lips. He didn't disappoint. At the first touch of his mouth, he sent a hot rush streaming through her body, leaving her toes tingling. He tasted better than any man had a right to. Better than she'd dreamed. His tongue pushed past her quivering lips and possessed her mouth with a hot thrust. Her sex tightened in response and in anticipation of his possession yet to come, of his cock in her core.

His hand held her head securely, and he angled it slightly, confidently commanding her senses the way only a master of the carnal arts could. She gripped his strong shoulders and held on in the maelstrom of sensations radiating out from the feel of his body pressed so sumptuously against hers, and his heated, hungry kiss.

His mouth was gone.

She snapped her eyes open, bereft, dazed. Ravenous.

He was watching her. "I like the way you taste." His voice was darkly sensual. Removing his hand from the nape of her neck, he lightly trailed the pads of his fingers over the tops of her breasts. Her breathing hitched. "How wet are you for me?"

She had to swallow first. "Very."

"Good. I can't wait to taste you everywhere, especially your sweet sex." She didn't know how much more of this her body could take. She was ready to shatter into orgasm on the spot.

"Are you ready to be bound and taken?" he asked. Her knees weakened.

Oh, God. He was so sinfully delicious. This was beyond any fantasy she'd had of him. Far more carnal than she'd ever imagined. Her sex wept.

Dipping his head, he said in her ear, "Tell me you want it. Tell me you want to be bound and taken."

Out of her mouth—the mouth of a woman who was always tightly guarded—tumbled, "Yes! I want it."

He pulled back and gazed down at her. She could tell by the smile in his eyes that her answer pleased him. "Tell me what it's doing to you to know I'm about to tie you with the scarves you so graciously provided and feed your cunt my cock."

She shivered and fisted his shirt. "I . . . can't." She didn't know how to put voice to it. This man was too overpowering for her senses. He always had her off balance. He was pushing her beyond her limits.

Tristan carefully gauged her reactions. She trembled, her

breathing quick, and her skin was flushed from her cheeks to the tops of her breasts. *Dieu*, she was so responsive—with so little effort, he could undo her.

He liked that.

What he didn't like was the nervousness he detected. He didn't want her to be nervous or tense.

"Have you ever played sex games before, Elisabeth? Have you ever had a man bind your wrists and legs apart?"

"No," she said softly.

This was going to be a first for her. The thought quickened his heart.

"I want you to relax and enjoy the experience. I won't do anything you don't wish me to do. You have my word."

Her large hazel eyes held his firmly. "I know. I trust you," she said without hesitation. That this beautiful, strong, feisty woman was bestowing such trust in him by allowing him to bind her moved him. Layers were being peeled away, and he was seeing sides of Elisabeth he'd never seen before.

Sides of her he liked. Very much.

She stepped away from him, retrieved the wooden box with the scarves, and handed it to him. "Take me."

Sweeter words were never spoken from sweeter lips. He'd heard those very words from other women, but when she said them, it rocked him, his thick cock jerking hard and hungrily.

"Sweet Elisabeth, I am going to take you in ways you've never been taken before. And you're going to enjoy every one of them." He gestured toward the bedchamber. "After you, my lady."

Entering the bedchamber with Elisabeth, Tristan spilled the contents of the box on the bed and tossed the box and his cane aside. It occurred to him that for the first time since his injury, his leg was hardly bothering him.

Impatient, he turned to Elisabeth, hauled her up against him, and claimed her mouth. She moaned softly and immediately laced her arms around his neck, her body molding so perfectly to his. She felt wonderful in his arms. His tongue invaded her mouth, plundering the soft recesses, enjoying the way she returned his kisses with equal ardor. There were so many reasons he should stop. So many reasons not to take her. But as he stripped away her clothing, revealing her soft skin a little more with each article he removed, those reasons fell away with her attire. He couldn't come up with an argument strong enough to make him push her away. Not when he wanted her this much. Not when his sac was so heavy and so tight. Not when his prick pounded in rhythm with his wild heart.

Her eager hands opened his breeches. Tristan yanked his shirt off, tossed it away, and sat down on the edge of the bed.

Standing before him in her knee-length chemise and *caleçons*, Elisabeth's gaze was riveted to his erect cock boldly protruding from his breeches. She bit her lip, her confidence faltering briefly. He hid his smile.

"We're going to be the perfect fit," he assured her. He knew he was big, but he also knew how to use every inch of his length and girth to pleasure a woman.

He removed the last articles of clothing from her body, then paused to admire the beauty before him. Lush curves, lovely breasts with the pinkest, most mouthwatering nipples he'd ever seen. At mouth level to him, they were erect and begging to be touched, sucked.

"You are beautiful," he murmured and pulled her closer. Her hands gripped his shoulders and he felt her tense, bracing for his touch. She thought he was going to go straight to the sensitive tips that were pebbled and straining for him. Instead, he ran his hands slowly, teasingly around the contours of her perfect tits, purposely avoiding the taut peaks. Her fingers dug into his arms. She closed her eyes and arched to him—her silent demand for more. Watching for her reaction, he lightly brushed his fingertips across her nipples. She gave a soft cry and shuddered.

He smiled.

Grasping her hips, Tristan leaned in and kissed around each nipple, building her excitement, her anticipation for when he finally suckled her.

She jerked and tried to press her nipple to his mouth.

Tristan pulled away, smiling. "No, you don't, *chérie*. I'll get there when I get there."

"I . . . can't take any more."

Despite the urgency thundering inside him, he was intent on savoring her. "Yes, you can." He licked the underside of her breast. She made a strangled sound.

Tristan turned her around, her pert bottom now facing him. "Give me your wrists."

Shaking, Elisabeth put her hands behind her back for him. "Do it. *Hurry*." She'd never been so lost to sexual abandon. Never had she been on fire like this. Gripped by carnal cravings, her nervousness had disappeared.

Grabbing one of the scarves off the bed, he brought her wrists together, bound them, then spun her back around. His hot mouth immediately latched onto her breast, sucking her nipple in. She cried out, her knees all but buckling beneath her. She might have fallen to the floor had he not had an arm around her waist, holding her strongly. He sucked her other nipple and moved back to the first, his teeth and hot tongue creating sensations that reverberated in her sheath, her feminine muscles tightening and releasing of their own accord.

He was most definitely not hurrying.

Clearly, he was intent on torturing her with his inflaming mouth in the most exquisite way.

Securely in his hold, her wrists bound behind her back, she couldn't do anything other than drown in the pleasure flooding her body. Her head fell back and she squeezed her eyes shut, rapid breaths dragging in and out of her lungs.

His tongue gave her nipple a last flick.

"On your belly, Elisabeth." He rose, thankfully keeping a strong hold on her waist; she wasn't certain her legs would support her weight. "Keep your feet on the floor." He moved her to the edge of the bed, bent her forward, and lowered her torso down onto the bed.

The coolness of the counterpane against the overheated skin on her breasts and her belly made her gasp. Looking over her shoulder, she saw him strip away the remainder of his clothing, her eyes drinking in his perfect physique, all muscular and sinewy, and his impressive cock. Arousal quavered in her belly. He moved behind her and skimmed his hands down her arms to her bound wrists.

"Are your arms all right?" he asked, setting his palms on her bare bottom. She wiggled, her skin feeling extrasensitive. Unable to summon her voice, she simply nodded. Tristan caressed her derrière. "You've been driving me mad in those breeches of yours. They show off this fine part of your anatomy. I couldn't resist having you this way."

Dear God, couldn't he just get on with it?

"Spread your legs for me," he ordered.

At last! Quickly, she complied, widening her stance. The cool air against her wet private flesh made her shiver.

He lowered himself down onto his knee, her sex open for

his viewing. A smooth scarf was suddenly around one ankle, his hands quickly binding it to the bedpost, repeating the same action with her other ankle, securing her legs apart.

His strong masculine hands skimmed up her legs. "*Dieu*, you're the most arousing sight I've ever seen." He cupped her slick sex with a warm palm. She gasped and lurched but couldn't move far. "So wet for me." Tristan rubbed her lightly, a gentle stroking of his hand over her sensitive flesh, not enough to make her come, just enough to keep her keen. Hungry. Tormented.

He leaned a little closer. "You look delicious and ready for any way I want to claim your pretty sex." His warm breath tickled against her bottom. She felt him part her folds, and then came the slow swipe of his tongue. She jerked and whimpered, the bud between her legs aching for his attention. He licked around it, and she suspected he was avoiding her clit on purpose, knowing she was wavering on the edge of a stunning release. Bound as she was, she was unable to press hard against his mouth the way she longed to. She was at the mercy of his mouth, his every wicked lick over her erogenous flesh.

He slid his hot tongue inside her. She curled her toes, the sound of pleasure bursting from her lips.

"The sweetest cream," he groaned. "I could make you come with my mouth, but I'm going to do it with my cock instead." She heard him stand.

Before she could rejoice, his fingers slid inside her. She didn't know how many fingers, but knew he was using enough to create a delicious pressure, his skillful hand lightly pumping her, making her moan.

"You're so tight. How do you want it, Elisabeth? Slow and deep? Hard and fast?"

She tightened around his fingers, desperate and so out of

control. So out of character. On unfamiliar ground. "I want it this minute. Right now!" No man had ever touched her the way he did.

He chuckled, leaned over her, and kissed her shoulder. "I see you've found your voice," he said in her ear and then straightened, pulled his fingers out of her, and gripped her hips.

"How's this?" He butted the head of his shaft at the slit of her sex. A sound shot up her throat, a mixture of a moan and a sob of joy. Tristan pressed forward, his cock stretching her as he fed it to her one slow inch at a time. She couldn't hold back the sultry sounds she made. He was so large. This moment monumental. A fantasy come true. A dream brought to life.

And she was afraid.

It was suddenly too much. He was too much for her. The moment too intense. Would she be the same afterward—after she completely abandoned herself to him?

He swore. "Relax," he growled. "Don't tense. Take me in."

You want this. You ache for him! You've got to have him. Taking a deep breath, she released the tension in her body. He felt it immediately and drove his cock into her deeper than any man had ever been.

Elisabeth cried out, so completely filled and possessed.

"Oh, yes," he groaned, filling her again and again, driving away any sense of emptiness. Quickly, he picked up the pace and she reveled in it. "You feel *incredible*."

He rode her, hard and fast, his grip on her hips tight, his sizable sex creating exquisite sensations, the likes of which she'd never known.

Her helpless body took every fierce thrust, rejoicing in each one as he plunged and dragged his shaft.

Elisabeth dug her nails into her palms, unable to control the contractions quivering through her sheath. She sagged heavily on the bed. Her legs were shaking so badly, they were no longer capable of holding any of her weight. Yet she arched, lifting her bottom high, straining toward him to take him in as deeply as she could.

Her release was imminent. She buried her face in the counterpane, not wanting to let go. Not wanting this perfect pleasure to end.

His powerful thrusts were gloriously unrelenting, driving her closer to the edge. "Come for me. I can feel how close you are, clenching and pulsing around me."

She was. She couldn't stop it. She couldn't stop the orgasm thundering down on her.

A large, hot wave slammed into her, vaulting her into ecstasy. She screamed into the mattress, rapture flooding her body. He drove in harder, ramming her repeatedly as Elisabeth basked in the sublime sensations, her sex wildly pulsating around him with each spasm of her slick walls.

Tristan suddenly reared. His palms came down hard on the mattress near her shoulders and he gave a long, deep groan, his warm semen shooting onto her back.

Elisabeth pressed her cheek against the counterpane and briefly closed her eyes, the contractions of vaginal muscles ebbing, her heart and breathing slowly returning to normal.

Tristan lightly bit her shoulder. She flinched, turned her head, and found herself gazing into his sensual blue eyes. He was smiling, looking so beautiful, it made her stomach flutter. He kissed the spot on her shoulder where he'd bitten her, then straightened, untied her hands and ankles, and wiped her clean with a scarf.

Elisabeth didn't move. Her muscles were so lax, she didn't think she could. Tristan picked her up as if she weighed nothing at all and deposited her in the middle of the bed. Stretching out beside her, he propped himself onto his elbow and began to knead one of her wrists.

"Are you all right? Are your arms sore?"

She'd never felt better. She'd never felt this kind of bliss in her life. "I'm fine."

His smile broadened. "That was very good." Closer to incredible, she wanted to say. In fact, it was beautiful and intense, just like the man beside her. "There is definitely a delicious carnal connection between us."

She couldn't argue with that. The fire between them burned white-hot.

He tilted her chin up and gave her a long, inebriating kiss. "Now that we've taken the edge off, I can fuck you slowly the rest of the night . . . and into the morning."

Into the morning? He meant to stay the night? *No, you should ask him to leave once you're done.* She never allowed men to stay after sex. Neither Selle nor Leymont was permitted to remain. And as for her late husband, he'd thankfully left promptly after their brief one-time copulation. Having consummated the marriage, he departed for his hôtel in Paris and never touched her again.

The thought of spending the night with Tristan had her body vibrating with renewed hunger. It was astounding that he could inflame her so quickly, so easily, after such a strong orgasm, with just his words. That alone was a good enough reason to refuse and put a bit of distance between them.

But instead, she told herself it was a better idea to stay with him through the night. She told herself that this was part of her plan; she was, after all, trying to have her fill of this man.

Then she wrapped her arms around him, snuggled close to his hard body, and gazed into his stirring eyes.

"I'd love that, Tristan."

She told herself she had the situation well in hand.

5

His cock was in heaven. As Tristan drifted out of sleep and into consciousness, the glorious sensations swamping his shaft became stronger, the wet heat enveloping it—keener, and the soft sucking noises in the quiet room—louder.

He opened his eyes, looked down his body, and was met with the erotic sight of Elisabeth drawing on his hard prick, her head lowering and rising in a steady, sublime rhythm. He closed his eyes briefly and smiled.

Is there a better way to greet the morning than waking up to a beautiful woman sucking you off?

Last night had been delicious. Today was starting out just as fine.

She gently cupped his sac, and he groaned. She looked up, his cock popping out of her mouth when she met his gaze.

Her smile was radiant, her cheeks slightly flushed. "Good morning." She sat back on her heels, yet still held on to the base of his shaft. Rays from the morning sun shone into the room, allowing him the pleasure of seeing her lovely naked form in the bright light of the day.

"Good morning, Elisabeth." Images of her bound by silk scarves, wet and eager, filled his mind. Memories he'd never forget. Last eve wasn't the first time he'd engaged in that kind of sex play, but with Elisabeth, it had been different. She was different from any woman he'd had.

She was different from the woman he'd believed her to be.

And she made him feel different than he'd been feeling the last three months.

Since his injury, he'd felt depleted and diminished. It didn't escape his notice that not once since her arrival had Elisabeth treated him as anything but whole. Not like a man with an infirmity. She'd treated him simply as a man—fully capable. And had even demanded fencing lessons. Lessons he intended to provide her with—proper lessons this time.

"I hope you don't mind," she said, leisurely stroking his cock from base to tip in her warm fist, his greedy prick luxuriating in the pleasure radiating along its length. "But I noticed this particular part of your anatomy—of impressive proportions, I might add—was awake and looking for attention."

She drew another smile from him. She was the only one who'd made him smile since his injury. "I don't mind at all," he said. "By all means, help yourself."

Mischief twinkled in her eyes. "Thank you, sir. I must admit I find you rather delicious."

He chuckled, but his laugh was choked off by a gasp the moment she lowered her head and gave the tip of his cock a lush lick.

Elisabeth plunged him deep into her mouth. He closed his eyes and hissed out the air from his lungs. Intent on delving his fingers into her soft dark hair and guiding her movements, he reached for her, only to have his hands stopped short.

He snapped open his eyes and looked up. *What in the world . . . ?* His wrists were bound with silk scarves to the outside posts of the bed.

He shot a look at Elisabeth.

She drew him from her mouth. "It's just a sex game. I thought I'd return the favor."

He was a leader. Dominant by nature—in and out of the boudoir. "I don't get tied up."

She tilted her head to one side. "Really?" She was doing a poor job of hiding her smile. "I'd say, by the looks of things, you do. Now just relax and enjoy the experience." *Merde.* Those were the very words he'd said to her last night.

"Elisabeth." There was a distinct command in his voice, a sharpness to his tone that always arrested anyone's actions.

Except the woman kneeling between his legs.

Lowering her head, she plunged him back into her hot, moist mouth, tearing a groan from his throat, and immediately resumed her rhythmic sucks.

He glanced at one of the posts he was tied to and tested the binding by giving it a yank. To his surprise, the knot gave. As he tried the other knot securing his other arm, it gave, too.

Tristan glanced back at the spirited woman pleasuring him, completely unaware that he could, with moderate effort, free himself.

She pulled his prick from her mouth, and licked her lips. His rock-hard cock pulsed, famished for more. "You know, I don't know what I find more delectable—your taste or having the mighty Tristan de Tiersonnier tied to my bed, at my mercy."

He hid his amusement. She wanted to play games.

Oh, he'd play. His way.

Looking adorably smug, she crawled up his body, her sweet face stopping inches from his. "I can do whatever I want to you," she teased. Her palms were pressed into the mattress on either side of his chest, her knees on either side of his hips. He detected the faint scent of her arousal. She was wet; her little sex play was exciting her.

He looked down and took a moment to admire her pretty breasts. Her nipples were hard, looking like two tempting berries he just had to taste.

"Put one of your nipples in my mouth." To toy with her, he purposely worded the phrase as a command.

A slight frown pulled her delicate brows together. She was clearly dismayed over his lack of submissiveness. "You are in no position to dictate—"

"The left one. I'll start with that."

"I don't think you understand. You're tied up . . ."

Angling his head, he bent his knees, the tops of his thighs bumping her soft bottom, sending her body forward—one tasty teat landing in his ready mouth.

He sucked. She gasped sharply. Tristan snapped the knots binding his wrists, wrapped his arms around her to hold her still, and drove his cock up into her warm, dewy sheath. She gave a cry. He groaned. The quick movement had sent a jolt of pain down his leg, but it was a small price to pay in comparison to the pleasure of being back inside her hot, tight cavern. He'd had her most of last night, yet he wanted her again with untamed intensity.

"I hope you don't mind," he said. "But I noticed there were parts of your anatomy that were awake and looking for attention." Tristan bit and laved her nipple while giving her long, luscious strokes with his shaft, building her slowly and steadily into a frenzy. She shivered, seductive sounds escaping her with each soft pant. He couldn't believe he'd ever thought this woman was a tease. She was sensual, passionate, a woman who enjoyed sex as much as he did. Yet she was more than just a good tumble.

She rocked her hips, trying to dictate the pace, to quicken the tempo, unable to contain the urge. He easily thwarted her efforts, his tight embrace holding her still as he drove in deep with deliberate thrusts. She made a sound at the back of her throat, and slumped slightly against him, her body completely yielding to his possession; all attempts at control had slipped away from her.

Her surrender drove him wild, made him fuck her harder. Faster. Arching to him, she mewed loudly.

He loved fucking her.

He loved having this alluring, willful, fiery woman completely abandon herself to him.

Though bedding the King's most cherished daughter wasn't the wisest thing he'd ever done, he couldn't seem to muster any regret.

Releasing her wet, distended nipple from his mouth, he lightly pinched and rolled it as he turned to her other breast and suckled its sensitive tip.

His name rushed past her lips on a ragged breath. She tightened her juicy walls around his thrusting cock, bathing it with a fresh gush of warm cream. It inflamed him further. His heart hammered. His sac was so tight and full, he could barely hold on to the load of come.

A light sheen of perspiration coated their bodies. Tristan released her nipples and rolled her onto her back, the force of each solid plunge of his prick driving her into the mattress. He claimed her soft mouth in a ravenous kiss, shoving his tongue past her lips. Her arms encircled him, an endearing embrace, and she shuddered.

She was beginning to come. He could tell by the sweet sting of her nails on his back, the pulling of her cunt, and the tensing and arching of her body. He braced himself. Tearing her mouth from his, she threw her head back and screamed in orgasm. Her sex contracted around his cock.

Tristan gripped the sheets in a white-knuckle hold, thrusting, knowing he was about to go over the edge any moment. On the next fierce pull of her sex, he reared, jerking out his cock in the nick of time, sending hot blasts of come onto her belly. He threw his head back and bellowed out his pleasure until the last draining drops.

On all fours, he hung his head, trying to catch his breath, not caring a whit that his leg was punishing him for this position. He looked down at Elisabeth. Her skin was flushed. The nipples he'd feasted on were still hard, but her features were soft, a warm smile adorning her lips. She looked sated. Beautiful.

Jésus-Christ, he could easily get used to this if he wasn't careful.

Theirs was a brief, temporary arrangement. Elisabeth wasn't Veronique. He couldn't keep her as his mistress, and it was certain the King's thoughts had turned to marrying her off again. He'd heard His Majesty's comments with his own ears. Her next husband was sure to be someone notable, of significant standing. Like the late Duc de Roussel.

She reached out and caressed his cheek. Rising up on her elbows, she kissed him, a soft, sensuous meeting of the mouths. "I love what you do to me," she said with touching sincerity.

The problem was, he loved doing it to her—a little too much.

*   *   *

"Elisabeth, did you hear me?"

Claire's voice broke through Elisabeth's thoughts. She dragged her gaze from the window to her sister. Sitting in Elisabeth's apartments, wearing a green brocade gown, her younger sibling was frowning.

"I'm sorry, Claire. What did you say?"

"You said you've devised a plan for tomorrow. What is it?"

"Ah, yes, tomorrow's plan." Elisabeth turned toward the window again, easily locating Tristan among the many men below. Three days of the most indescribable bliss she'd spent with that man. Fencing and making love with Tristan de Tiersonnier. Could there be anything finer? Unable to hold back her smile, Elisabeth watched as he spoke to a group of the King's Guard. Their respect and regard for him were evident on their faces and in their stance even from her second-floor vantage point. There was no doubt about it, Tristan was still the Captain in their hearts. If she had anything to do with it, he was going to be their Captain in truth once more.

"Tomorrow is the day of the King's monthly hunt," Elisabeth said, turning away from the window. "In attendance will be the usual courtiers—who'll be vying for the King's attention—and their wives." Disdain crept into Elisabeth's voice. Having been around powerful men all her life, she should have been accustomed by now to the way they used women. Yet, it still bothered her to see women serve as pawns for social promotion. It happened in so many ways—through marriages, the swapping of mistresses, and in His Majesty's case, well, she couldn't count the number of times she'd seen men subtly and not so subtly offer up their wives to the King just to gain his favor—as dispassionately as one would offer a ride on a horse.

It didn't help that her father had a roving eye and had been known on occasion to express his interest in another man's wife—*sans* the offer. Her own mother had been a married woman when she became his royal mistress.

"Yes, yes. I know all that," Claire said. "What I don't understand is why you want to leave here to attend? You don't like the hunts. You don't care for those who attend them—and I thought your point for being here was to enjoy Tristan. Why leave before the week's end?"

"Because we are going to get Tristan reinstated as Captain of the King's Musketeers."

Claire's brows shot up. "We are? Why?"

"Because I quite enjoy him and wish him to be back at the palace—where I can continue to enjoy him." How she wished that was all there was to it. How she wished there wasn't any emotional longing involved. But her feelings for Tristan had only deepened.

Last night, lying in Tristan's arms as he slept, she'd decided the King's hunt offered an opportunity she couldn't pass up. One whereby Tristan could impress her father. With her affections now stronger, her desire for him keener than ever before, she couldn't simply finish her week with Tristan and let it end there. She decided to cut the time short, gamble, and possibly gain something more permanent.

Thus, the need to escalate her plan.

Claire cocked her head to one side. "Is that the only reason? You're going to have Balzac removed just to have easier access to your lover?" There was something in Claire's eyes that gave

Elisabeth unease. A certain knowing look—as though she was seeing inside her heart. Impossible. She hadn't become that transparent about her feelings for Tristan, had she?

Dismissing the notion as absurd, Elisabeth continued, "No. As a matter of fact, there is another reason. Antoine de Balzac is no better than the rest of the men at court, and well you know it, Claire. He shouldn't be the Captain of the Musketeers if he is corruptible, which I believe he is. And what's equally worrisome is that he and Veronique are now lovers."

Not exactly the primary motivation driving her plan, but it was all she was ready to admit to and far easier to voice than her undying love for Tristan.

Claire frowned and gave a nod. "Veronique only welcomes Balzac into her bed because of his esteemed position. As the commander of the Guard, he is close to the King. She wants to get close to the King through Balzac. She wants to replace you in His Majesty's affections, become his favorite daughter, and reap the benefits that come with it."

Unfortunately, that was true.

Elisabeth had better apartments, better treatment from the courtiers, more influence than her lesser siblings. Veronique wanted to take that from her.

"We cannot let Veronique succeed in her schemes," Elisabeth said. It was all about survival. Those who didn't have the favor of the King were treated poorly and had a miserable existence at the palace.

Elisabeth had Claire to think about. To protect. Even when she was married to the Duc, Elisabeth had protected Claire and had kept her sister with her at the Duc's château, away from the glittering, corrupt court of Versailles.

If Veronique ever managed to win favor and any kind of

influence with the King, she'd cause undue misery to Elisabeth and Claire, simply because she could. Simply to exercise her power. A power Elisabeth had, but never abused in her privileged position.

Born months apart, Veronique and Elisabeth had always been rivals. Elisabeth's mother had replaced Veronique's mother, Diane, as the King's favorite mistress. Diane had spent the rest of her days trying to gain preferential treatment for her daughter she couldn't get for herself.

Since her mother's recent death, Veronique had not relented in her ambition to advance her status at court. It motivated her every action. Her every move.

Veronique was using the unwitting Balzac in her plot—positioning and angling, trying to get close enough to the King to affect his choice, to influence the King in selecting a powerful husband for her. Elisabeth didn't care who Veronique married, though she suspected Veronique had someone high ranking in mind. If Elisabeth hoped to secure a better match for herself this time around—and a good match for Claire—she couldn't lose her standing.

Once Claire had a good husband, she'd be safe. Elisabeth could then breathe a sigh of relief. Elisabeth's betrothal to the Duc had been a surprise. She hadn't known her father had been in talks with the man or she would have delicately swayed the King away from Roussel.

This time she knew the King was looking for husbands for his unwed daughters.

This time she was doing something about it.

Elisabeth turned toward the window again and spotted Tristan once more. Her insides danced. She was beyond besotted with him.

Being wedded to Tristan would be heavenly.

Claire walked up behind her and wrapped her arms around Elisabeth's waist. Resting her chin on Elisabeth's shoulder, she said, "Why don't you tell him you love him?"

Her heart gave a hard thud. Elisabeth twisted around to face her sister. *"Pardon?"*

Claire dropped her arms to her sides and sighed. "Don't bother to deny it, Elisabeth. You're in love with Tristan de Tiersonnier. That is why we are here, isn't it? You want to wed him. That's the reason for the workers and gardeners. That is why you want Tristan reinstated—though I am not saying the other reasons aren't valid as well. You are trying to convince the King that Tristan is a suitable husband for you."

Elisabeth was gripped by fear. "How—How did you—"

"Know? I've caught you looking at him, not just here, but at Versailles when he was Captain, too. It is the briefest of looks—in a way you don't look at any other man. Don't worry, Elisabeth. Tristan can't tell. No one can—except me. I'm your sister and I know you best of all. I'm the only one who sees it."

Elisabeth's heart pounded. "You'll swear to me, you'll not tell a soul. Do you hear me?"

"Of course I swear. I've known for some time and I've never breathed a word. I don't understand why you don't tell him of your affections. He seems to have grown quite fond of you. I don't think he'd find the notion of marrying you disagreeable. Discuss it with him, then with the King."

Lord, how naïve Claire was. Perhaps she'd sheltered her too much. "It isn't done that way. Nor is it that simple. You cannot embark upon any course of action without first reducing the chances of failure. Even if Tristan were agreeable, the King likely won't be. Walking up to His Majesty to request Tristan as my husband could and likely would be met with a resounding no. Then what? Once the King makes a decision, he'll not change it. The matter must be carefully handled, steps taken that are well thought out."

"Fine. Perhaps being more prudent with the King is a good idea, but why not tell Tristan how you feel?"

Elisabeth was aghast. "Are you mad? Claire, it is bad enough that I have done the unthinkable—fallen in love—when I know better. When I have seen the devastation that particular emotion causes women. We live at the whims of men. You know that. A woman under the influence of love who makes the mistake of declaring her affections pays the ultimate price. You know what happened to our mother when she professed her love to the King. Soon after, he became disenchanted and sent her away to the Convent of the Sacred Heart. This after she'd maintained his interest for *years*."

Claire lowered her gaze to the floor, looking doleful. The subject of their mother was difficult. Claire had been young and devastated when their mother had been sent away. Elisabeth had consoled her sister as best she could, despite her own broken heart.

Placing her hands on her sister's shoulders, Elisabeth sighed. She didn't want to distress Claire by bringing the subject up, but God help her, she had to be made to understand. "You mustn't ever wear your emotions on your sleeve." She squeezed Claire's shoulders. "You must remain guarded—with your thoughts and emotions. Never give anything away. Unless you wish to suffer. Unless you wish to lose the man you love."

Elisabeth had come to Tristan with the hope of ultimately purging him from her blood. It was now clear, it would take much longer than a week to accomplish.

It would take several lifetimes.

She hadn't wanted to love him so deeply, but she did. With all her heart. She always had.

She didn't want to lose him, and so she was forging ahead with her plan.

"I'm sorry, Elisabeth. You're right, of course." Her sister's eyes were large and sad.

Elisabeth hugged her. "You'll help me tomorrow, then?" She purposely changed the subject, not wanting to distress Claire further.

Claire pulled back, a small smile on her lips. "Yes. Whatever you need, I'll do."

"Good. We're going to show the King that Tristan is as capable as he always was to command the Guard."

Until today, Tristan had been avoiding his former men. Elisabeth could make no sense of it until Gabriel had confided that it was a matter of pride. She couldn't believe Tristan actually thought he'd been diminished by his injury. That he'd truly believe the King's foolish physicians and their ridiculous notions about his being unfit.

Or that Tristan would take to heart the King's misconceptions.

It only made Elisabeth want to see Tristan's reinstatement all the more.

There was only one man fit to command the King's elite corps, standing head and shoulders above any other candidate, and that was Tristan de Tiersonnier, Comte de Saint-Marcel.

The door opened. She pulled away from her sister and turned toward her visitor.

Tristan had walked into the room, filling it with his commanding presence.

Her heart swelled with joy.

Even with his cane, he still moved with a certain masculine grace that made her pulse quicken.

"Forgive me, I thought you were alone, Elisabeth." His rich, sensual voice was like a warm caress down her spine. She loved how he spoke her name. There was such sinful promise to it. It swamped her senses and made her feel dangerously reckless and out of control. As much as that unnerved her, it also had a certain astonishing allure. At the moment, she could barely keep from throwing herself against his chiseled form and claiming his mouth.

"I was just leaving," Claire said after exchanging pleasantries with Tristan, and left the room.

A half-smile on his lips, he approached. Her insides danced with excitement. He stopped before her and slipped his fingers under her chin. "Have I kissed you good morning?" he asked.

She couldn't hold back her smile. "Yes." He'd done a lot more to her than kiss her that morning.

"Good. Because it's afternoon." Then his lips were against hers, his tongue possessing her mouth, and her arms by their own volition drew around him. She moaned.

She could make him a good wife. He would make her an excellent husband.

She'd failed to convince him to keep the workers and gardeners she'd sent, but she couldn't fail in any part of her plan tomorrow.

This hunt was too important.

So much hinged on its success. Briefly, she wondered if she should wear her lucky boots. Then Tristan's hand caressed the curve of her breast and her thoughts turned as heated as her body.

6

Claire peered into the streaming river at the water's edge. "Have I told you how much I don't like this idea?"

The sun was high in the sky. Standing in the glen, Elisabeth could hear the voices and laughter coming from the King and his party as they drifted down into the narrow valley. The hunt had ended an hour ago. Elisabeth and her entourage had arrived just in time for the feasting and gaiety that were afoot.

Tristan was up there. It had taken well-placed words and kisses to convince him to join the escort that would take her to the picnic after the hunt—not that she minded the kissing. Or the amorous encounter that ensued. Only when she lay weak from the second intense orgasm in a row did he advise her—with the most devilish smile—that he'd had every intention of seeing her personally delivered to the hunt all along.

How could any woman be angry at a man who was so wickedly charming and had just melted her with his carnal talents?

"Yes, Claire, I believe you've mentioned it more than a dozen times."

"Why do I have to be the one who falls into the river? Why can't it be you?"

"Because I'll look like a drowned rat. Not an enticing way for Tristan to see me."

Claire clamped her mouth shut, and frowning, glanced back at the river streaming past. "You think it's cold?"

"I'm sure it's not."

Claire shook her head. "This is definitely not going to be as much fun as the time we hemmed nasty Cecile de Brun's gown up an inch each night to make her think she was growing at an alarming rate after she relentlessly teased me about being short."

Elisabeth patted her sister's shoulder. "No time to reminisce about our girlhood pranks. You're a strong swimmer, Claire. You're going to be fine. I promise you, you won't be in the water long. Now then, Agathe is up there on the top of the glen to your left. Do you see her by the large walnut tree?"

"Yes," Claire said, spotting Elisabeth's trusted servant. Agathe stood well apart from the King's party. In point of fact, she was the only person in sight. The others were far from the edge of the glen.

"I will give Agathe the signal, then she will signal to you. When you see her nod, you jump in and start screaming. Tristan will be along shortly to save you."

"Fine," Claire said tightly. "Make certain he gets here quickly. I'm only doing this because I know you would do it for me."

"You know I'd do anything for you." Elisabeth's words rose from her heart.

"I hope this works, Elisabeth."

So did she.

* * *

"The sex must be excellent." Gabriel smiled as he stood beside Tristan looking out at the royal gathering before him.

Tristan muted his irritation and kept silent. He could clearly hear the mischief in his brother's tone. Without glancing Gabriel's way, Tristan kept his gaze fixed on the crowd of men and women clustered in a giant group around the King, mostly praising His Majesty's abilities in the successful hunt.

Gabriel chuckled. "You heard me well, but I'll repeat myself nonetheless. I said, the sex must be quite good. You told me you wanted nothing to do with these people ever again and here you are, at the King's hunt—because of a woman."

Not just any woman. A very unique woman. For a very long time Tristan had wanted never to see Versailles again. Now he wasn't so sure. There was someone at Versailles that he wanted to see a lot more of.

Elisabeth.

"She's the King's darling. I felt it necessary to escort her." Not to mention Tristan wanted to prolong his time with her. But he wasn't going to tell his brother that. He'd never hear the end of Gabriel's ribbing. Especially if he knew Tristan's interest in Elisabeth went beyond the physical.

Upon arriving with her entourage, she'd promptly brought him before the King. It pleased Tristan that His Majesty was glad to see him. Had seemed delightfully surprised, actually. Clearly, the King had expected Tristan to be far less mobile and agile. Tristan had exchanged pleasantries with him, then moved to the outer perimeter of the gathering, where he presently stood. A habit for a man whose job it was to keep a watchful eye from a distance, making certain he and his men maintained a safe radius around the King and his family at all times.

What dismayed him was that his replacement, Balzac, was mixing in with the group, parading about, usually at Veronique's side, when he should be maintaining a professional decorum. Just as disturbing were the sidelong glances and discreet smiles Veronique was giving Tristan. He knew what she was after. What message she was conveying. That he could fuck her if he wanted to, and she was doing this while Balzac panted at her side.

He couldn't believe that woman had ever held any kind of appeal.

"Sir."

Tristan glanced at the man addressing him. One of his former lieutenants, Valesque.

"It is good to see you, Commander," Valesque said.

"Not 'Commander,'" Tristan corrected.

"Of course. Forgive me. An old habit, I'm afraid. I hope you don't mind, but I wanted to tell you that the men and I are delighted to see you again."

Tristan glanced past Valesque's shoulder. Every Musketeer he could see, all standing well apart from the King's party, had their eyes on him. He looked at them one by one, as each gave a deep nod—an expression of respect.

"Lieutenant, tell your men to keep their eyes focused on the royal gathering," Tristan said. The men had a job to do and Tristan didn't want to be a distraction.

"Of course, Comm . . . er . . . sir. Sadly, that is an order that should be coming from Balzac, but I'm afraid he doesn't take matters seriously enough."

That was painfully obvious.

Valesque gave Tristan a short bow. "Good day, sir."

"Good day."

Valesque turned to leave.

"Lieutenant Valesque," Tristan called out.

The man turned back around.

"Please tell the men I'm delighted to see them also."

Valesque smiled. "Yes, sir. And, sir, when the men learned the Duchesse was in need of an escort to your château, well, suffice to say, it caused quite a commotion among the Musketeers. Every man wanted to be in the entourage that would escort Madame la Duchesse to your abode." Valesque gave him a bow and walked away.

Tristan felt his chest tighten. He was touched. And grateful to one very spirited, beautiful favorite royal daughter.

Had she not come to his home, bold as could be, he'd likely still be in his château, feeling sorry for himself. She'd brought him back to life after he'd slipped into a dark hole. He'd enjoyed his time with her immensely. Not just in his bed. But her company in general.

He even delighted in providing her with lessons in fencing.

A smile tugged at the corners of his mouth as he remembered their second lesson. Determined not to drop her sword again, she'd shown up in the gardens, one of her silk scarves binding the blade to her hand. With determination etched on her lovely features—her goal, he knew, was to best him—she made improvements by leaps and bounds.

He loved her spiritedness—both in and out of bed.

Tristan scanned the crowd, looking for Elisabeth. She'd been with the King not long ago. Now she was nowhere to be found. The cooking fires were well in the distance surrounded by cooks hard at work preparing the meal. But he doubted Elisabeth would be there.

"Where are Elisabeth and Claire?" Gabriel, who'd been uncharacteristically silent, voiced the very question running through Tristan's mind.

Where could they be?

Moving his gaze from face to face in the distant throng, he suddenly spotted her emerging from the crowd. Smiling, she approached, looking far more alluring than any woman should. She made his heart race.

She stopped in front of him. "Are you enjoying yourselves, gentlemen?"

Since they'd become lovers, whenever she greeted him, she touched him. Though he understood why she couldn't at the moment, he hated it nonetheless that her hands were folded before her and not on him.

"I'm enjoying myself immensely," Gabriel answered with his usual smile.

"And what about you, Tristan? Are you enjoying yourself?"

He couldn't stop himself from luxuriating in the vision she made. In her pale gown, she looked ravishing. The décolletage accentuated her lovely breasts ever so deliciously. He was starved for the taste of her sweet nipples. Though he'd had her that morning, he wanted nothing more than to take her into the nearby forest and have her again. "I'd say the gathering has suddenly much improved now that you're here." Her presence would improve any gathering, regardless of how arduous it was.

"Why, thank you, Tristan." She blushed slightly, her eyes telling him his compliment pleased her. "I don't suppose either of you have seen my sister?"

Tristan frowned. "She wasn't with you?"

"No. I don't know where she is." Elisabeth tugged at her ear.

Tristan looked the crowd over again. "I don't see her."

"I wonder where she could be?" Gabriel said, scanning about, trying to spot her.

"I don't know. I'm a bit concerned. I haven't seen her for a while." Elisabeth tugged her ear again.

"Is there something wrong with your ear?" Tristan asked.

She dropped her arm down to her side. "No."

A scream ripped through the air. Tristan turned in the direction of the startling sound. More screams. They were coming from the glen.

Half running, half limping, he tore toward the edge. The moment he saw Claire flailing in the river below, his blood chilled. Vaguely, he heard Elisabeth's cry.

Without a thought, he ran down the hill as best he could, jarring pains stabbing through his leg along the way. Somehow he managed to reach the river's edge before anyone else. Somehow he'd made it without falling.

Tristan tossed down his cane, threw off his justacorps, and dove into the river after Claire. She was screaming and thrashing when he caught her around the waist. "Calm down, Claire. It's all right. I have you." She quieted the moment he turned her onto her back. Swimming toward the shore, where Elisabeth and a number of Musketeers were waiting, Tristan pulled Claire to safety.

Arms reached out and dragged Claire out of the water. Two of the men lay Claire carefully down onto the grass, while two others pulled Tristan onto the shore. Elisabeth immediately dropped to her knees and wept against her sister's cheek.

Tristan rose and accepted his cane from one of the Musketeers.

Raking a hand through his wet hair, he glanced up to the top of the glen. The King and the rest of the gathering stood in a line, witness to what had transpired.

The crowd burst into applause.

His Majesty locked gazes with Tristan and gave him a simple nod of thanks.

Just then Balzac came racing down to the shore line.

Elisabeth shot to her feet. "Where were you!" she shouted at him.

Balzac, two years Tristan's senior, stopped short. He glanced up at the audience on the top of the glen, then back at Elisabeth.

"My sister could have drowned!" she continued. "Are you or are you not ultimately responsible for the safety and well-being of the royal family?"

Balzac looked gray, clearly embarrassed by the very public dressing-down. "Y-Yes, madame, I am."

"And yet it was left to the Comte de Saint-Marcel"—she gestured at Tristan—"to rescue my sister because you were nowhere to be found."

Balzac tossed a nervous glance at the King. "Madame, perhaps one should examine what your sister was doing in the river in the first place."

Tristan mentally cringed. That was an imbecilic mistake. Balzac's comment suggested Claire was to blame for ending up in the river. One didn't blame members of the King's family for anything—whether they were at fault or not.

Elisabeth placed her hands on her waist and jutted out her chin. "I'll tell you what she was doing. She was *drowning* in it—while you, sir, were enjoying the fresh summer air." She turned toward two Musketeers. "Please take my sister to my carriage." As Claire was being helped away, Elisabeth turned to Tristan.

"Thank you for saving Claire."

Tristan noted that Elisabeth didn't have any tears in her eyes. Nor did her eyes look red from crying—even though she'd been sobbing against her sister. She spun on her heels, grabbed her skirts, and marched up the hill to the top of the glen, straight for her father, glimpses of black boots appearing and disappearing as her skirts swayed.

Jésus-Christ, she was wearing her boots beneath her gown.

Tristan couldn't shake the feeling in his gut. One that suggested all was not as it appeared.

*　*　*

"Go ahead and say it . . . I was brilliant." Claire giggled as she lay in the middle of her large bed. Back in Versailles, in Claire's private apartments, Elisabeth sat on the edge of the bed, holding her sister's hand.

"You were brilliant." Elisabeth smiled warmly at her. "I am forever grateful."

"Well, it was worth it. I think it worked. Did you see Balzac when you yelled at him? I think he may have soiled his breeches." Claire burst into a fit of giggles, her laughter contagious. She added as soon as she was sober enough to speak, "Veronique's face was precious. She was scowling, furious over the spectacle made of her lover."

"He has no business holding such an esteemed position as Captain of the King's private Guard. He is incompetent. I told the King as much."

Claire sat up, her eyes wide. "And? What did the King say? Is he going to dismiss him?"

Elisabeth sighed. "I don't know. I know he was impressed by Tristan. It is heartening that he insisted Tristan return to the palace with the rest of us. At this point, I will remain guardedly optimistic."

Her father had allowed her only a few private words after the river incident. The King was a difficult man to read. She had no idea what he was thinking. Or what he wished to do.

Moreover, she had the added problem of Veronique. Elisabeth hadn't missed the sultry looks she'd cast Tristan today. Veronique would shamelessly welcome both Balzac and Tristan into her bed. One of them was sure to be Captain of the Musketeers, and she wanted to make certain that man was her lover. She'd aggressively chase Tristan if she needed to.

There was a knock at the door.

Agathe entered with a member of the King's Guard. "Madame, this gentleman wishes to speak to you."

The Musketeer stepped into the room and bowed. "Madame, mademoiselle," he greeted. "The King has summoned both of you. He wishes to see you straightaway."

Elisabeth rose. Her stomach clenched. Claire was being summoned, too? A cold sense of foreboding sank its teeth into her. She didn't like the sound of this. She couldn't quell her unease.

*   *   *

With a smile fixed to her face and a strong and steady stride, Elisabeth entered the Hall of Mirrors and made her way to the opposite end. Though she'd lectured Claire en route about walking with confidence, Claire scurried along beside her looking every bit like a frightened mouse. At the end of the long corridor, His Majesty, Veronique, and Tristan awaited them. Seeing Veronique looking spiteful was no surprise. But seeing Tristan standing to the King's left beside her half-sister unbalanced Elisabeth.

Feeding her trepidation was the fact that the Hall of Mirrors was empty, and the doors that led to the gardens, closed. The Hall of Mirrors was always filled with courtiers and Musketeers. That the King wanted a private audience unsettled her further.

By the time Elisabeth reached the end of the long hall, her anxiety had swelled considerably, leaving her legs feeling wobbly.

She and Claire stopped before the King and curtsied low.

"Your Majesty," Elisabeth said, thankful that her voice hadn't quavered. Standing before his solid silver throne, several carpeted steps above her, her father looked every bit the monarch of the most powerful nation in all of Christendom, his tall red-heeled shoes lending to his grandeur.

Elisabeth could see Tristan from the corner of her eye. His expression was tight and unreadable.

"Go ahead and admit the truth." Veronique stepped toward Elisabeth.

Elisabeth turned to Veronique. "The truth?" she responded coolly, though the pounding of her heart was so hard and fierce now, she worried the others could hear it.

"Yes. Tell the King that today's 'drowning' was contrived, meant to fool His Majesty."

Claire shifted her weight next to her, her nervousness tangible. Yet Elisabeth gave no indication of her agitation and dragged her gaze away from Veronique and to her father. Dear God, Veronique was making yet another attempt to ruin her before the King.

"Your Majesty," Elisabeth began. "I have no idea of what she speaks."

"Your Majesty," Veronique injected.

The King silenced her by raising a hand. "Elisabeth, Veronique is under the impression that you are scheming, trying to have Balzac removed as Captain of the Musketeers."

Elisabeth gave a mirthless laugh. "I don't need to scheme, Sire. Balzac does a poor enough job to have himself removed as Captain of the Guard."

"Claire," the King called out, making Claire jump. "Tell me how you ended up in the river."

To Claire's credit, she lifted her chin and met the King's gaze. "I . . . I was refreshing myself when I slipped and fell in."

"She's lying," Veronique accused. "She'd say anything, do anything, to protect Elisabeth, Sire. I saw how Tristan de Tiersonnier looked at Elisabeth today. You sent her to him to obtain an instructor for fencing—a ridiculous pastime for a woman, I might add." Veronique tossed Elisabeth a hateful look. "I believe while she was there, they became lovers. It's obvious that Elisabeth is plotting, trying to ensure that her lover holds the esteemed position as the commander of the Musketeers."

"That's amusing coming from a woman who beds Balzac," Elisabeth drawled.

Veronique opened her mouth, clearly intent on venting her outrage, but the King intervened. "Enough!" He turned to Tristan. "Tristan, you have never lied to me. I want the truth from your lips. Are you Elisabeth's lover?"

Elisabeth could scarcely breathe. She couldn't look at Tristan, afraid her strong emotions for him would somehow be detected.

"Yes, Your Majesty."

Elisabeth's stomach plummeted.

"I see." The King's response was tight.

Terror gripped her. The last thing she wanted was for Tristan to be punished in any way. She wouldn't allow him or her sister to pay for her mistakes and miscalculations. This was all her doing. The entire muddled mess. Her schemes had always helped her and Claire. Elisabeth had become a master at them, successfully countering the constant jostling and plotting that were so a part of court life.

And she was good at it. It was all she knew. All she knew how to do.

There was only one thing she could do to protect Tristan and Claire and keep Veronique from succeeding with her plan to discredit and diminish her before the King—and that was to sacrifice her own plan.

What choice did she have? Forcing the words from her lips was the most difficult thing she'd ever had to do.

"Your Majesty," Elisabeth said, despite the lump in her throat, "I attended Tristan de Tiersonnier's château with two intentions. The first was to obtain lessons in fencing from the best swordsman in the realm. The second was to bed him. I find him appealing and I seduced him." She tilted her head to one side. "Surely this doesn't surprise you, Sire? After all, such appetites are in our blood. In our very nature, Your Majesty. And the opposite sex simply cannot resist our charms. No?" Tristan stiffened, but he held his tongue.

The King studied her for a moment, then his lips twitched and he tossed his head back in laughter. "Ah, dear Elisabeth. There are times I believe you should have been born a male." He stepped down, chuckling, and offered his arm. She took it, and somehow maintained her smile, though her heart was fragmenting into a million shards.

"You are correct, daughter," her father said to her, leading her out toward the gardens. "It is in our nature to crave and enjoy decadent delights."

"But—But what about—" Veronique began.

"That will be all on the subject, Veronique," their father tossed over his shoulder, not bothering to glance Veronique's way.

Elisabeth couldn't look at Tristan. Keeping her eyes straight ahead, she let the King lead her outside into a throng of waiting courtiers, her heartache keen and suffocating. She'd thwarted her half-sister and managed to retain the King's favor. Claire would be all right. As would Tristan. She'd managed to quell any ire the King may have had toward him as well.

But it had cost her dearly. She'd lost Tristan. He was an honorable man, honest and true—qualities she loved about him. He favored those qualities in others. She knew he despised those who deceived and schemed. She'd just confirmed in his heart and mind—with her own words—that she was a liar. A conniver. That his original perception of her was right—she was nothing more than a schemer, spoiled and looking for diversions.

Worse, for all her bravado, she was a coward. A woman who didn't have the courage to speak the truth, let down her guard, and expose her true emotions to the man she loved to mend matters between them.

7

Elisabeth stared out the window of her apartments the next day. Her eyes felt raw from lack of sleep and copious tears. Pacing her rooms most of the night, she'd thought of different things she could say to mend matters with Tristan. All of which were foolish. None of which professed her love. By morning she'd come to the conclusion that though she had the ability to give Tristan her body, she'd no ability to voice the words burning in her heart for him—knowing full well that if she tried to voice those three words, they'd lodge in her throat.

How was she to undo the training and ingraining she'd been subjected to her entire life? She had no idea how to wrestle down her fear of laying herself bare. Of making herself vulnerable emotionally. It was irrational, yet gripping and real.

Besides, she had no confidence at all that Tristan would even believe her if she tried to explain everything and told him how much she loved him.

By early afternoon, Elisabeth didn't have to torture herself any longer. Agathe had advised her that Tristan was gone, his rooms at Versailles vacated.

The door to her antechamber swung open and slammed shut. Tristan walked in, his cane in hand, surprising her. Looking so beautiful.

A stab of longing pierced her heart.

He stopped before her. "Let me see if I understand this correctly. You convinced your father to send you to my château for a fencing instructor, intending while you were there to get me to bed you. Is that accurate?" His tone was very matter-of-fact. She didn't know what to make of it or his presence.

She clasped her hands and looked down.

"Answer me, Elisabeth," he insisted.

"Yes," she responded softly.

"Then you decided to attend the King's hunt, when you don't like the hunts, convinced your sister she should jump into the river so I could save her, look like a hero, and reclaim my former position as Captain of the King's private Guard. Is that correct?"

Oh, God. "I . . ."

He hooked her arm with his cane and yanked her to him. She collided against him with a gasp. His strong hand clasped her arm. "I've obtained answers from your sister. I'll have answers from you, too. Now then, I'm going to ask you again: did you contrive the incident at the river yesterday just so I could be reinstated?"

Clearly, Claire had confessed. What was the point of denying it? This was going badly. Anguished, she didn't have any fight in her today. Being this close to Tristan, and knowing he wouldn't kiss her or touch her the way she longed for, was torturous.

"Yes" was all she could muster past her lips.

"You think I needed your help in returning to the Guard?"

She looked into his eyes and said firmly, "No. You are highly skilled and respected. If you wanted to return, you'd succeed. You don't need help from me." She meant that. It was no lie.

His features and voice softened. "There you are wrong."

"Pardon?" she asked, perplexed.

"After the injury, I was filled with bitterness. Anger. I was not myself at all. I might have been that way indefinitely had you not arrived and wedged yourself into my life."

Speechless, she simply blinked, surprised by his answer.

He released her arm and shook his head. "When the King dismissed me from my post as Captain of the Musketeers, I made no attempt to speak to him about his decision. I simply left, reeling from the sting of it. I should have spoken to him then. I should have told him that, injury or not, I'm still capable of commanding the Guard. Your antics yesterday inspired a conversation with him. A conversation that was long overdue. And I have you to thank for it. Who knows if or when I would have stopped brooding like a fool and talked to His Majesty." The smile formed in his eyes before one touched lightly upon his lips. "I have been reinstated as the Captain of his Guard."

Her eyes widened. "Truly? What about Balzac?"

"Veronique will be marrying Balzac and leaving the palace with him. He is being given lands to take away any sting *he* may feel from being replaced."

She smiled, overcome with joy for him. "I'm very happy for you, Tristan."

He caressed her cheek with the back of his knuckles. "You didn't look very happy when I walked in. In fact, you look like you've been crying. Tell me . . . why did you want me reinstated? Why did you want me to have you? Why have you gone to such lengths where I'm concerned?" His tone was as gentle as his touch. "We both know the answer. Speak the words. Let me hear you say them."

Her breaths slipped past her parted lips, shallow and sharp. Unable to summon the words, they remained trapped inside her.

"Elisabeth, at the risk at sounding immodest, I have had a woman or two in love with me in the past. As clever as you are, some things are impossible to hide. Especially during and after sex. Tender looks, tender touches point clearly to tender emotions."

Tears stung her eyes.

"You've spent a lifetime suppressing every emotion that would leave you exposed and susceptible. You're afraid to be open and vulnerable."

Was it written on her forehead? Just how obvious was she to this man?

He curled his fingers under her chin. "You're trembling. You can't say it, can you?"

She lowered her eyes. Part of her wanted to so badly.

He lifted her chin, capturing her gaze. "Repeat after me: *Tristan*."

He wasn't serious?

"It's just my name, Elisabeth. You've said it many times before. At times you've even screamed it as you were coming." The start of a smile pulled at the corners of his mouth.

"Let's hear it, Elisabeth. *Tristan*."

She took in a ragged breath and ceded. "Tristan."

"I."

She remained silent.

"*I*," he pressed.

"I."

"Love."

Elisabeth swallowed hard against the lump constricting her throat. "L-Love."

He smiled. "You."

A tear slipped down her cheek. "*You* . . . so very much." The words tumbled from her mouth, surprising her.

His smile turned into a grin. "Excellent. Now then, let's continue: *Tristan*—Say it."

"T-Tristan . . ."

"I want you to be my husband."

Tears flooding her eyes were making it difficult to see his cherished face. "I want you to be my husband," she said, the words flowing out of her mouth, unhindered.

"Because I can't live without you."

Quietly, she wept. "Be-Because I can't live without you."

He brushed a curl off her damp cheek. "That wasn't so difficult, was it?"

She shook her head no. "Yes."

He tossed his head back and laughed. "Elisabeth, you are one of a kind, *ma chérie*." He gave her a soft kiss. A warm quiver shimmered down her spine.

He broke the kiss, leaving her wanting more.

"Now that you've agreed to marry me," he said, "I suppose I should tell you that my conversation with His Majesty included the subject of your future husband." Dipping his head, he whispered in her ear, "You will be my wife."

Her knees almost gave out. It was all too incredible. So glorious! She stepped back, stunned. "How—How did you convince him? What did you say?"

"That I am the best man for you and he should give the man who saved his life and the life of his daughter, Princess Claire, the hand of his favorite offspring."

Oh, how she loved him!

"There is one more thing I want to hear you say." He cradled her cheek in his palm. "Tristan, I really want you to . . ."

She was beaming now. "Tristan, I really want you to . . ."

He leaned in and brushed his lips along her neck, sending shivers of delight through her. "Make love to me right now and every day for the rest of our lives."

She laughed. And cried. And reeled with happiness. "Make love to me right now . . . and every day . . . for the rest of our lives."

That devilish grin spread across his mouth. "Now there is a request I can't deny."

Then he led her to the bedchamber, her body heating up every step of the way. Once inside, they stripped away their clothing posthaste, and he tossed her onto the bed, his urgency snatching away her breath.

The press of his naked form against the length of her body was sublime. Her hungry core clenched and creamed, eager for him. He had her mouth, claiming it. Famished, she sucked his tongue into her mouth, thrilled by his groan.

His hand skimmed along her skin from her shoulder to her breast, a fiery path straight to her taut nipple. He pinched it, holding it captive between his fingers until it began to throb, a delicious pulsing sensation that radiated from her breast and echoed in her sex. She arched and writhed, delirious with need, her body on fire. He released her nipple and sucked it into his hot mouth, his wicked fingers capturing her other nipple, treating it to the same sweet torture. The sound of pleasure shot up her throat, the double pleasure almost too much to take.

"Please," she panted. "I want you now."

"I'm going to come inside you," he rasped against the pulsating tip of her breast. "Do you understand me? I'm not pulling my cock out."

All she could do was moan. The thought of him filling her with his essence made her hotter. Wetter. "Yes. Do it."

Tristan filled her sex with one solid thrust. She wrapped her legs around him. He wanted to howl with pleasure, love and lust burning inside him with equal fervor. He couldn't believe it when Claire had told him Elisabeth had loved him from afar for so long. He couldn't believe the touching lengths she'd gone to just to be with him.

And he was going to spend a lifetime returning her love. Cherishing her every day.

"*Dieu*, I love you." He pumped his hips, hitting the sweet spot on her clit with his every downstroke. "I can't get enough of you."

"I love you!" She was breathless and so wet, her cream was seeping from around his thick cock. "I love you, Tristan."

She was already on the edge, and *Jésus-Christ*, so was he.

"Come for me . . . Come with me."

Her body tensed. "Oh! I'm coming!"

Tristan gathered her tightly in his arms and rode her for all he was worth, fighting back his release, waiting for hers to hit so he could let go. He felt the tremor in her sheath, her body arch. And with her scream of rapture, he held nothing back. His come shot down his length. In shuddering waves he poured semen into her quivering cunt in hot, steady streams, driving his cock as deeply as he could with each powerful thrust. Overwhelmed by her orgasm, she moaned and whimpered, clenching all around him, her arms, her legs, her sex, sending a growl rumbling from his chest. He'd never known such stunning pleasure, such pure ecstasy, as the mind-numbing joy it was to drain himself inside her.

With her now quiet in his arms and his prick emptied, he reluctantly withdrew.

Tristan looked down at her. There was a smile in her eyes. She lifted her head off the bed, cupped his cheek, and gave him a warm kiss. He'd just come inside her, claimed her for his own, and yet she said with a lazy grin and a soft sigh, "You're mine."

Tristan couldn't hold back his own grin. He nuzzled her neck. Breathed her name. "And you are mine," he assured her.

He'd never met anyone like Elisabeth. She was the only woman he knew who could drive him wild in a pair of breeches and the most irregular boots he'd ever seen.

She made him feel like the richest man on earth. The luckiest man in the realm.

Tristan had won the heart and hand of the fair princess.

Glossary

Antechamber—The sitting room in a lord's or lady's private apartments (chambers).

Le Beau—Masculine word for *the handsome one* or *the beautiful one* (male).

Caleçons—Drawers/underwear.

Chambers—Another word for private apartments. A lord's or lady's chambers consisted of a bedroom, a sitting room, a bathroom, and a *cabinet* (office). Some chambers were bigger and more elaborate than others. Some *cabinets* were so large, they were used for private meetings.

Chère—Endearment for a woman (*cher* for a man). Meaning: *dear one.*

Chérie—Endearment for a woman (*chéri* for a man). Meaning: *darling* or *cherished one.*

Comte—Count.

Comtesse—Countess.

Dieu—God.

Duc—Duke.

Duchesse—Duchess.

Fronde, the—A civil uprising that started in 1648 and ended in 1653. Incited by power-hungry nobles, they almost dethroned their boy King. (Louis was only ten years old when it began.) Louis was forced to flee Paris in the night with his mother and live in exile for a while. He never forgot what he and his mother endured during this tense, tumultuous time. He developed a lifelong dislike and mistrust for the aristocracy. Intent on being absolute ruler, he spent his reign intimidating them.

Hôtel—A mansion located in the city. The upper class and the wealthy bourgeois (middle class) often had a mansion in Paris (hôtel) in addition to their palatial country estate (château).

Justacorps—A fitted knee-length coat, worn over a man's vest and breeches.

Lettre de Cachet—Orders/letters of confinement—without trial—signed by the King with the royal seal (*cachet*).

Ma belle—*My beauty*. Endearment for a woman.

Merde—*Shit.*

Pour l'amour de Dieu—*For the love of God.*

Salle—Room.

Salle de Bain—Bathroom. A small room located in one's private apartments/chambers in either a château or hôtel. The room usually had a fireplace, a tub, and a toilet (that looked like a chair with a chamber pot). The room was small on purpose so that the fire from the fireplace would keep the space warm while one bathed.

Salle de Buffet—Dining Room.

Seigneur Dieu—Lord God.

Turn the page for a preview of Lila DiPasqua's
next collection of Fiery Tales . . .

The Princess in His Bed

Coming November 2010 from Berkley Sensation!

"My life is over!" Louise d'Arcy exclaimed the moment after she'd yanked Aimee inside her elegant private apartments and slammed the door shut.

Aimee de Miran sighed. She'd just arrived at Versailles. Her sojourn at the palace was only ten minutes long and already she was rethinking her plan to attend court and visit with her cousin.

Dear Louise was always in the midst of chaos. It seemed now was no different.

Parched from the long carriage ride, Aimee walked over to the pitcher of water and orange slices on the ebony side table and promptly filled two crystal goblets. "Louise, darling, I'm certain your life isn't over." She held a goblet out to her cousin. "Now why don't you tell me what's wrong."

"What's wrong? Renault is what's wrong. He's cast me aside!" Wringing her hands, Louise began to pace, completely oblivious to Aimee's extended arm and the goblet of fresh water being offered.

Aimee availed herself of the refreshment instead and set the goblet down.

A lovers' spat. Nothing new.

"I see." That would be all she'd need to say for the next hour while Louise ranted. When she was done, her cousin would collapse in a chair, quite theatrically, and weep for at least twenty more minutes.

Aimee had been through this before. Many times. Louise was always having spats with her longtime lover, Renault de Sard.

Louise stopped dead in her tracks. "No, you don't see. You've no idea what has occurred. Everything is a mess. And it's over this time! Truly over!" Her hazel eyes filled with tears. "He'll not have anything more to do with me. He's said so!" She dropped her face into her palms and sobbed.

Aimee approached and put a consoling arm around her cousin. Of similar age, they'd always been close. She did adore Louise, despite her histrionics. "Louise, it will work out. You'll see. He always comes back."

"Not this time," she said without lifting her head, the words muffled by her hands.

"You say that every time."

Her cousin's head shot up. "This time it's true!"

"You say *that* every time, too."

Louise let out a sharp breath. "Aimee, he favors another! I have been replaced. He's with Diane de Millon. I'm no longer his mistress at all! I tell you, he is a horrible, horrible cad! He purposely misled me."

"Oh? Misled you how?"

"I was positively thrilled when he asked me to accompany

him to the palace for his regular official visit with the King. He'd been so cold and distant lately that I didn't think he'd permit me to attend this time. In truth, his plan was to bring me here to end our affair. He thought I wouldn't pitch a fit at the palace. And do you know what I did?"

"You pitched a fit at the palace."

"No. Well . . . yes." Louise waved her hand dismissively. "But that was in private. And that's not what I'm talking about." She began to pace and wring her hands again. "I did something. Something terrible. Something I regret."

Trepidation was mounting in Aimee. Louise had always had a flair for the dramatic, but Aimee couldn't shake the disquieting feeling tightening in her stomach. There was a certain look in Louise's eyes that made her a little anxious.

"What did you do?"

Her cousin smoothed her hands down her gown. A habit. Something Louise always did when she was nervous. Or uneasy. Or terribly guilty.

"Well, you see . . ." Louise began and smoothed her hands down her gown again. "You must understand, I was quite angry with Renault at the time, and very hurt by his cutting coldness toward me. So I . . ."

Aimee braced herself. Having no idea what she was about to hear, her instincts told her it was going to be bad. Quite bad. "You what?"

"I took something of his."

"Took?"

"All right, I stole. Is that better? There, I said it. I stole something he holds dear."

Good Lord. This was a new low, even for Louise. "What on earth did you steal?"

Louis threw up her hands. "The man has never given me any-thing, Aimee. In all these years, no lover's trinket. No jewelry at all! I felt he owed me at least that much."

Aimee struggled with her patience. "Louise . . . What. Did. You. Take?"

"His jeweled ring. One of the ones given to him by the King."

"Oh, Louise, you didn't."

"I did!" Louise flopped down onto the nearby settee, dropped her face into her palms again, and wept audibly.

Aimee shook her head, dismayed. Of all the predicaments Louise had landed herself in, this one was by far the most shock-ing. "Didn't it occur to you that Renault is the King's Lieutenant General of Police? A man who is overzealous when it comes to the duties of his post and would arrest his own mother for the most minor infraction?"

Louise looked up. "Well, not at the time, but it certainly has over the last few hours . . ." She choked on a sob. "What am I going to do? My life is over! He'll throw me in one of those hor-rible cells without batting an eye. If he's angry enough, he could have a *lettre de cachet* drawn up against me. I'll be held without trial—for who knows how long."

Aimee took in a fortifying breath and let it out slowly. She walked over to her distressed kin and placed a hand on her shoul-der. "Everything is going to be fine. We can remedy this problem. This really isn't as great a dilemma as you think it is."

Her cousin swiped away the tears on her cheek. "Oh, but it is."

"No, it isn't. You will return the ring with a sincere apology—"

"I can't."

"You're right. The man is so rigid and uncompromising, he won't understand. I have it," Aimee said as an idea occurred to her. "You'll sneak into his rooms and put the ring back, without him being the wiser."

"I can't do that either."

Aimee frowned. "What do you mean, you can't?"

"I lost the ring."

"You *what*?"

Louise rose from the settee. "Well, it's not entirely lost. I know where it is. Sort of."

"Where in the name of God is it—sort of?"

"I was in the Hall of Mirrors yesterday. It was very crowded, as ususal. I was bumped from behind, and it fell out of my hand and into the pocket of one of the courtiers."

"Do you know who?"

"I do. Adam de Vey, the Marquis de Nattes."

Aimee's heart missed a beat. "The Marquis de Nattes?" she questioned, hoping she'd heard wrong.

"Yes." Her cousin grasped Aimee's hands and squeezed them. "Aimee, I can't let Renault learn what I did. If the ring is found on the Marquis de Nattes's person, Renault would never believe he stole the ring. He has one of his own. You must help me get the ring back before Renault discovers it missing. He'll not stop until he uncovers the thief—me!"

This was only getting worse. She didn't like the direction this conversation was taking. "What exactly are you suggesting I do?"

For the first time since Aimee entered the room, her cousin smiled. "You know as well as I do the Marquis de Nattes would be receptive to any attention you would give him. Since Marc died, he looks at you 'that' way. You could easily get close enough to him to search his clothes."

Aimee's brows shot up. "Have you gone mad? You want me to

encourage that libertine just so I can dip my hands in his pockets in search of your ring?"

"Precisely. And perhaps you can search his armoire in his private apartments, too. The man does have a rather extensive wardrobe . . ."

"No. Absolutely not." Adam de Vey was the worst sort of man. The very type she detested. He was no different from her late husband: beautiful as sin, a master at seduction.

And completely faithless.

A man who believed women were interchangeable, who cared nothing of what he did to a woman's heart—only what he did with her body.

It was no wonder that the Marquis de Nattes and Aimee's late husband, Marc, Comte de Gremont, had been friends. They were of like mind and poor character. Since Marc's death on the dueling field three years ago—in a duel over his favorite paramour at the time—Aimee thankfully had had nothing more to do with her late husband's licentious friends.

Louise's bottom lip began to tremble, her eyes welling with fresh tears. "Renault will show me no mercy. He cares nothing for me at all now. If—if you don't help me . . . then I will surely be arrested, Aimee. You won't let that happen, will you? You'll help me, won't you?"

The pitiful look on her cousin's face tugged at Aimee's heart fiercely. She wanted to help her, but . . . she'd noticed the lingering looks Adam had given her since Marc's death, too. The last thing she wanted to do was to make him believe she'd be receptive to him.

"Louise . . . There's got to be another way . . ."

"There isn't! Oh, please, Aimee. I haven't anyone else who can help. I know you don't care for Adam de Vey, but think of it this way: you can do something most women cannot. You can easily flirt with Adam, yet resist him and in the end do what no female has done—rebuff him."

Now, that did have a certain appeal. Men like the Marquis de Nattes toyed with so many women, luring them with their polished manner, potent sensuality, and false affections. She would definitely love to play him. Lure him. She could flirt a little, draw close enough to locate the ring and save Louise.

She was likely one of the few women in the realm who'd resist his allure.

After being seduced by Marc on every level imaginable—heart, body, and soul—leaving herself open to the humiliation and heartbreak she'd ultimately endured, Aimee knew she'd never fall into the arms of another rake again.

"All right," tumbled from her mouth.

Louise squeaked with joy and threw her arms around Aimee. "Thank you! I knew I could count on your help."

Aimee sighed. "I don't suppose you have any idea what he was wearing when you dropped the ring?"

"I do!" Louise was smiling again. "He was wearing a blue justacorps."

"Blue? That's it?"

"I know how much the man adores fine clothing. And I did hear he had a new wardrobe delivered yesterday, but really, how many blue justacorps could he have in all?"

True. But, given the number of knee-length coats he owned, what were the chances he'd wear the same blue justacorps again anytime soon? Just how mindful was he of such things?

"Between the two of us, we'll be able to locate the ring quickly and easily," Louise said confidently.

Aimee couldn't believe she'd become embroiled in this mad

plan. Outfoxing a seasoned roué; locating and lifting a ring out from under the nose of a man who, by his very womanizing nature, was highly attuned to the opposite sex. Reading women was his forte. He knew how to detect signs of amorous interest and sexual desire. Her performance would have to be believable and flawless, despite her limited skills at being a coquette.

Success hinged on her ability to stay focused. Problem was, she hadn't been touched by a man in over three long, empty years. Though she'd never admit it to anyone, she craved a man's arms around her. The press of his hard body against hers. His body inside her. Her marriage bed had been most satisfying. Too satisfying. There had been many nights she wished her late husband had never introduced her to the pleasures of sex. That his conjugal visits had been more typical of his peers—brief, obligatory, and for the purposes of procreation only.

Awakening her to physical delights had caused her nothing but suffering, for many reasons.

But no matter how much she'd love to have a lover, she wouldn't take a man like the Marquis de Nattes to satisfy her carnal yearnings.

For Louise's sake, Aimee had to succeed. She couldn't fail. She would best Adam in this cat-and-mouse game they were about to play.

And she was going to use his libertine nature to her advantage.

*   *   *

Adam de Vey, Marquis de Nattes, surveyed the various justacorps— fitted knee-length coats of various fabrics and colors. He'd had a second armoire placed in his private apartments to hold his recently delivered new clothes.

Doors to both armoires were open wide as he decided on

his attire for the afternoon. The news of Aimee's arrival made his selection a little more important, made his heart beat faster and his blood course hotter just knowing she was in the same building.

Close by.

Adam couldn't believe his luck. Just when he'd reached his breaking point. Just when he'd been racking his brain, trying to orchestrate an opportunity to spend time under the same roof with the dark-haired beauty, she fortuitously showed up at the palace. He'd had no idea when he'd been summoned by the King for an official meeting that she'd be in attendance at Versailles as well.

It was a good sign. A great sign. Somehow the stars had aligned and he was getting what he'd been wishing for for years: access to Aimee. She wouldn't be able to leave anytime soon, either. The King took personal offense to brief visits at the palace.

Her stay would have to be no less than half a month. Plenty of time for him to do something that he should have done long ago.

Bed her.

It was going to be a challenge—his very first when it came to seducing a woman.

Dressed in black breeches and a white linen shirt, he watched as his loyal servant pulled out yet another justacorps, this one gold-colored, and brought it to him.

Adam touched the silk sleeve. "Not this one, Laurent," he said. Too bold.

The man, ten years his senior, returned the gold overcoat to the armoire.

"Really, Adam, I don't understand your interest in all these clothes." Reclining in a plush chair, his fingers laced behind his head, his friend Robert, Comte de Senville, smiled.

"I like the finer things in life. Fine clothes. A fine château. Fine women." Aimee de Miran was by far the finest he'd ever laid eyes on.

"How is this, my lord?" Laurent held before him a red justacorps.

Also bold. "I don't think so."

He was looking for something more understated. With a quiet elegance. Just like Aimee.

"All this trouble for a tumble. Don't think I don't know you're planning on seducing Aimee de Miran. And it's about time, I say." Chuckling, Robert crossed his arms over his chest and shook his head. "Six years . . . *Dieu*!"

Adam placed his hands on his hips, cursing the night he'd gotten drunk last month and let it slip to Robert about his longtime fascination with their dead friend's wife.

Ignoring Robert's irksome remarks was easier than ignoring his own hardened cock—his body's natural reaction to the mere thought of the Comtesse de Gremont.

The moment he'd met her, during her betrothal to Marc, she'd incited his libido. He'd spent a ridiculous amount of time famished for this woman.

Merde. He could make no sense of this incessant, unbreakable pull to her. His desire for her plagued him. Haunted him. The longer it went on, the more it tormented him.

The stronger it got.

So she was beautiful, elegant, graceful, and intelligent. There were others who shared those qualities. So Marc had boasted that his wife was passionate and sensual and highly receptive to his husbandly rights—a woman who saw her marriage bed as a joy rather than a duty. So what? There were other women who enjoyed sex.

He'd fucked scores of them.

Nothing he did got golden-eyed Aimee de Miran out of his head. Out of his system. Not time, or women. He was tired of wanting her—and worse, comparing other women to her. It drove him to distraction.

Jésus-Christ. He couldn't recall the last time he'd bedded a woman when Aimee hadn't intruded into his mind, where he didn't fantasize that it was her he was buried inside.

For the last six years, Adam had kept his distance from Marc's beautiful wife for two reasons. First and foremost, Aimee was in love with her husband, and he never poached where real feelings were involved. Second, Marc was a friend—one who was completely undeserving of his wife's affections. Marc knew full well he'd stirred her heart. He'd laughed about it and found it 'adorable,' and without discretion of any kind, bedded every woman who crossed his path.

"What about the blue, my lord?"

Adam scrutinized the blue-gray justacorps held out before him.

It was of the finest cloth, yet not boastful. And a fine cut, too. "Perfect."

"I think the lady will be most impressed, my lord." Laurent smiled as he handed Adam the matching vest—his usual statement whenever he sensed Adam had a new conquest in mind.

Adam slipped on his vest. "Do you now, Laurent?"

"I think you overestimate your charms." Adam could hear the humor in Robert's tone.

He glanced at Robert. "I think you should leave the lady to me and concern yourself with the King, and whether or not he'll approve of our drawings and ideas." Adam slipped the justacorps on with Laurent's assistance.

A member of the Royal Academy of Sciences, he was recognized for his engineering expertise. Over the years, Adam had worked on a number of projects for the Crown—the fortification of strongholds in case of attack. Now, with the country at peace, at least for the time being, Louis had turned his attention to his prized palace. Versailles. Unhappy with the water pressure of his fountains, His Majesty had asked Adam to offer a solution to rectify the deficiency the original engineers had produced.

Robert stood and walked over to him grinning. "It's far more fun watching Adam de Vey fail for the first time with a woman." He placed his hand on Adam's shoulder. "In all seriousness, the lady doesn't much care for either of us. Marc broke her heart. She sees us as being no different from her late husband."

That much he knew.

But Adam wasn't looking for her love. Or to replace Marc in her heart, if he was still there. He was looking for a few hours of shared carnal pleasure. He simply wanted to—no, had to—put an end to this inexplicable mental and physical torment. There was only one way to kill the longing—and that was to have Aimee every which way he could to sate his lust for her.

Success hinged on his ability to stay focused. Patient. Problem was, just as Robert stated, she disliked him.

"I'll succeed," Adam said.

Robert lifted a dark brow. "You're that confident?"

"I am."

A slight smile lifted the corner of Robert's mouth. "Oh, I can't wait to see this. I predict she'll run the other way each time you draw near."

A realistic prediction.

For his sanity's sake, he had to succeed. He couldn't fail. He would best her in this cat-and-mouse game they were about to play. Beautiful, passionate Aimee hadn't had a lover since her Marc's death. He'd left his wife at their country château while he'd carried on with his favorite mistress in the city, and hadn't been anywhere near her for months prior to his fatal duel. In short, she hadn't been touched in a very long time.

And she was ripe for the taking.

Adam was going to use her passionate nature to his advantage.